PASTICHE

A CHARMS OF ALBION BOOK

CELIA LAKE

ABOUT PASTICHE

Can a chivalrous lord and his clear-sighted wife find love together?

As a child, Richard dreamed of knighthood and gallant deeds. As a grown man, he is committed to doing his best as an officer of the Guard, as a Lord of the land, and as a father. Living up to his oaths is easy. Being a good husband is much more of a challenge.

Alysoun has done everything expected of a woman in her position. She has married well and had two clever, healthy children. That's not enough. Richard is kind, but increasingly distant. Alysoun herself has pain and fatigue magic can't fix. In truth, she is isolated and more than a little bored.

When Alysoun visits a new museum exhibit, she sees something odd in one of the stained glass pieces. Investigating could bring her closer to Richard or at least give them something to talk about. But it might threaten his position or even his life.

Join Richard and Alysoun in 1906 as they explore a

mystery, take on new oaths, and discover each other after years of marriage.

Pastiche is set in the Edwardian era of Albion, the magical community of England, Wales, and Scotland. It is a stand-alone novel of an arranged marriage turning into a true love match.

ONE

1ST JUNE 1899 NEAR STROUD, GLOUCESTERSHIRE

Alysoun was ready, as ready as she would ever be. Her gown was perfect, exactly the right shade of sapphire blue to complement her complexion and dark hair. It fell in long draping folds to the floor, covering her slippers. The gem-crusted girdle was settled low around her hips with the wedding clasp that only her husband-to-be would be able to undo. And over her head and shoulders, there was the saffron-dyed palla, ready to be drawn down from her hair for the ceremony itself.

In a minute, they would go downstairs, and her father would present her to her husband's family, to their assembled family and allies. She had a few moments for reverie, however, and she intended to take them, the last moments before the flow of her life changed to run in a new channel. She wanted to fix in her mind these last few minutes in her childhood room, with her dolls and her childhood stories. Even a few of the romances she'd loved of dashing knights and beautiful maidens.

It wasn't going to be like those stories, she knew that. This was an arranged marriage, for all she thought their courtship had been pleasing to both of them. They had not had time yet in private to discuss their hopes for after the wedding, beyond the obligations she knew the nuptial agreements discussed. She hoped, though, that there would be more than simple kindness, something between them beyond the expected children and social commitments.

This marriage was everything she had been raised to expect, and everything she had been told to want. And she had done well, she knew that. Richard Edgarton came from a fine family, one that had been prominent in Albion for centuries. Magic ran strong in their blood, and deep as well. Her mother had been in raptures about how well their lines and tendencies in magic might combine, what that might mean for the expected children.

And he was likely to inherit the title in not too long. His father was here today, but Richard had been a very late son, born of a second wife, when his father was past sixty. Now, his father was slowing down. There had been more than one health scare that had brought the Healers flocking. She knew he was downstairs now, her mother had told her, but carefully tended, with a wheeled basket chair, an attending nurse, and others seeing to his every need.

Lord Edgarton had already ceded the family home, Veritas, to his son as part of the marriage settlement. The elder generation had retired to a luxurious townhome in Trellech, in the middle of the aristocratic quarter. There, they were close to their friends, and to the clubs, concerts, and social gatherings they both preferred.

Alysoun would do her duty. To be honest, it was likely to be a much more pleasant duty than for most of her friends and cousins. Richard was young - only five years older than her twenty-two - and beginning to make a name for himself in the Guard. He had completed his apprenticeship most promptly, she had been told, though she had no idea what that meant in practice. Not when it came to the Guard. Perhaps he would explain it sometime.

Most importantly, he had been kind to her when they had had the approved outings during their courtship. She had been surprised when he showed an interest in her after her debut and their initial introduction. He had continued sending his card, and partnering her at dances. He had escorted her to concerts, to museums, to the theatre and the opera. In the brief times together they had had, Richard had been interested and interesting, talking about things beyond the weather, the wedding planning, or the usual small talk of their social class.

She rather expected he found the museums and the opera boring, but he had been very good-natured about it, admitting he didn't know much about either. More to the point, he had been glad to have her explain what she found interesting, and she did not think he had been feigning politeness.

When he had proposed, it had been beautifully done, albeit with a certain formal precision. That was the Guard influence, she suspected, or perhaps something more military. She knew that Richard had done some brief service in the Sudan, during the Mahdist war, though he barely spoke of it. Frankly, they still had a lot to learn about each other. He had come home after only six months because of his father's failing health.

The knock on her door startled her, but it was just her mother. "Darling, you look truly lovely. They're all ready downstairs. And your father is just so pleased and proud." Her mother was bubbling over with delight, breaking Alysoun's more thoughtful mood.

Alysoun stood, carefully, picking up the folds of her

robe carefully. The movement shook the wreath of flowers on her head, and she inhaled the fragrance, taking one last moment of peace before she knew everything would begin. Her mother fussed over the arrangement of the palla, but then nodded, and led the way downstairs.

The wedding itself turned into a blur. She had practised each piece so often, not just in the past few months, but all her life. She knew there were stories of her playing at being wed as young as five. She thought it only practical. She knew that it was her role, as the only daughter of the dwindling line of her direct family, to marry well to improve her younger brother's possible connections.

First came the swarm of attendants, more distant cousins on her side and others from Richard's family. It was an excuse to gather the extended family, a chance for aunts and uncles to play their own status games. Despite that, the joyous congratulations from the cousins were contagious. By the time she entered the great hall, the place she'd known and loved and played in for so many years, she was smiling naturally, beaming at everyone she saw.

Her own particular friends, Isabella and Emmeline, had married well before her. They were both at home, expecting children in the next few months. Both were far enough away that a trip by land was awkward and uncomfortable. And no one wanted to risk the portals, just in case something happened to the unborn child.

Richard was waiting for her, and from there, it was like being swung into a dance whose steps she had known for so long she didn't remember learning them. She drew back the palla, so he could see her face clearly. The light fabric fell around her shoulders and framed her face, highlighting the delicate complex braids sewn and pinned atop her head.

She inhaled, smelling the flowers and the sharp bite of the mint and bay leaf as well.

Richard nodded at her. She was terrified something had gone wrong, but then he smiled broadly, and, on the side no one could see but the celebrant, winked once at her. It made her smile, and he took her hand and squeezed it.

There was the ceremony of the fire and the water, and the charm that showed the will of the ancestors, of their family lines, and the gods of the families. Much to her relief, the flame appeared pure and beautiful, flicking across the top of the cup and burning for a full ten seconds before fading away. Her aunts would count that as an excellent omen, the deep blue of the flame and the duration indicating it would be a long, fruitful, and prosperous marriage.

Then there were half a dozen more specific blessings said over them, over the rings they would exchange, and over her in particular, that the marriage might be fruitful. She blushed at that, and a sidelong glance up at Richard's face didn't help. He was standing there, stoic and handsome, just patient and unreadable.

When it came time for the kiss, that was the most memorable part of the ceremony. He bent to her, the first time they'd touched like that, and she realised how much taller he actually was. The spark when their lips met was stunning, and she hadn't expected that at all.

A wave of warmth and goodness swept through her, like nothing she'd ever felt. She knew then this was much better than simply a good choice, there was something here that was far beyond the quotidian magic of her life. It had the magic of her romances, and the intimacy they hinted at behind closed doors. It gave her hope that this might be more than a marriage of expectation, that there might, in time, be affection, even passion. She clung to him for a moment, but then gathered herself to turn and be presented to their guests as Madam Edgarton. Then, she was permitted to slip her arm through his to be escorted into their wedding supper.

It was not until much later that night that they had any time for more than a few words with each other. Each time she thought they might have a chance, some new person came with good wishes and blessings, or someone came to clap him on the shoulder or offer a toast. She had been flattered more today than in her entire life, it seemed.

Finally, though, they were escorted to the portal, and met on the other side by the staff of Veritas, the great house. She had been there only once, during the negotiation of the wedding contracts, and it seemed even larger than she remembered. It was near enough midsummer that it was sunset, rather than dark, even though it was nine at night.

It was not until they drew close to the doors that he spoke again. "This must be very strange to you."

She nodded, but said, "I know you'll make it easier." It came out without her thinking it through, and she worried it would seem strange to him. Instead, he smiled again, warmly.

"Tomorrow, I can show you the house and the estate. And your rooms - they're clean, of course, but we thought you'd prefer to decorate them yourself. Mother made sure there were some pleasant things in there until you decide what you'd like."

That made her blink, but she nodded. "My rooms." The echo made her sound foolish.

"Oh, I won't trouble you at night. Not other than the necessary." He said it as if he were certain that was what should happen, as if he were pleased to have anticipated her preferences so smoothly.

She almost stopped dead, but made herself keep walking. "If that's how you would prefer." Her voice was quiet, but her mind was roiling. "We haven't had much chance to talk about any of that."

"No, our parents were - well. So set on everything being proper. It is all right, though, you needn't worry I'll be demanding, that way. I know women, that it's sometimes difficult. I'll do my best to be good to you." There was an earnest note in his voice, something she heard, but didn't know how to make sense of.

He led her up the stairs, and she didn't speak again until he was showing her down the hallway, the main family hallway. "These are my rooms, now. They were my father's. I'm almost done redecorating them." He didn't offer to show her. "Private study, dressing room, bathing room, bedroom." And then further down the hall, "These are yours. The bedrooms adjoin, through a little passage, but as I said, I won't bother you."

"Tonight, though..." Now she really did sound nervous.

"Oh, tonight, yes." He sounded pleased. "You're not scared of it? I mean. My cousin was terrified."

She didn't know what she felt, precisely, but she tried to find words for it. "I'm nervous, but one of my aunts explained what to expect. And she said that women could enjoy things. Bedding. She did." It made her blush, and she looked away. Her mother's attempts had been pragmatic, and had not sounded appealing at all.

He stopped, reaching to cup her cheek. "I will do my best. You tell me what you like, and I'll do my best." There was something very earnest in him, that made him sound five years younger rather than five years older. "I want you to be happy. It's a big old house, and my work keeps me quite busy. But I want you to be happy. Better that way."

With that, he turned, and opened up the door, showing a brilliantly lit room, all sparkling chandeliers and bright whites. It felt quite sterile, uncomfortably so, and it made her head hurt for a moment.

But that could be dealt with later. Now was for coaxing him into the bedroom, and undoing her girdle, and seeing what married life was like.

TWO

4TH MARCH 1900, VERITAS IN KENT

That had all gone as well as she could have hoped, even if it had all happened a week earlier than expected. Now she had been cleaned up by the midwife and a small army of healer's assistants. Then her lady's maid had fussed over her and chivvied her into a clean and freshly made bed. Her son was in her arms, though, and that made it all worthwhile.

The nursemaid had made a gesture at taking him away, tucking him in the nursery, but Alysoun was having none of that. She might have to put up with them fussing, and doing to her as much as for her, but she was insistent on keeping her son by her as much as possible. She hadn't been entirely sure what she'd feel when he was a real person, outside of her, but so far, what she felt was mostly awe.

Oh, of course, there was also satisfaction. She had fulfilled the most significant clause in her marriage contract, and very promptly. It was March, less than a year after her marriage, and here was a proper heir, healthy and strong. And that was all the more important, since Richard had inherited the title last December, after his father's final decline. She wished he'd survived long enough to meet his grandson, but at least he'd known there was going to be another generation, carrying on the obligations and the titles.

Richard, though, had been quite absent throughout most of her pregnancy. Some of it was simple logistics. She had read some of the healer literature, and she thought the fears about portal use in pregnant women were rather exaggerated. There was nothing for it, though, with a potential heir, but to allow herself to be safely contained and minimise all possible risks. Perhaps especially the risks of gossip and scandal, as it would hardly do for Richard to have to answer for a reckless wife.

Of course, if you read some of the literature, anything a woman did might cause dangers to the unborn child. Eating too little, eating too much, eating meat, not eating meat, wearing certain clothing or colours, not wearing those colours. The discussions of benefic magic and charms one might wear were even worse. She had been funnelled inexorably into a confined life, staying at Veritas. She hadn't seen anyone outside the household and two or three friends since the former Lord Edgarton's funeral.

Nobody had explicitly said that enduring the tedium of late pregnancy was done without the presence of one's husband. It didn't seem the sort of thing people actually thought to mention. On the other hand, it was hardly surprising or something she could raise an objection to, particularly not when he had such important things to be doing. His work with the Guard, that mattered to far more people. At least she hoped it did, he rarely talked about it.

Oh, Richard had been very kind, she couldn't deny that.

He'd arranged for catalogues of books to be sent, and not blinked at how many she wanted to order. Decorators had come out, to make sure her rooms were furnished with every comfort. Where it had been a stark and sterile white, now there were the colours of a summer garden pond, all deep blues and glowing greens, with brushes of other colours like blooming flowers in a broad sunny meadow.

Richard had even encouraged her to add to the estate's collection of art and antiquities, though she was being far more choosy there. No one really needed more portraits of horses, hounds, or decorative ruins than they already had, at least without some connection to the beast or place depicted. However, she had started wondering whether adding something to complement the stained glass in the library or the dining room might be worth doing, some fixture or decorative object that would pick up the light the same way.

Now, once they had the naming, she could at least accompany Richard sometimes, and return to the concerts and performances in Trellech. That was something they'd both enjoyed, in the weeks before she'd known she was expecting, and she had resented having to cut it off. He was gone so often. The logical part of her - mind, not the part currently loudest - knew he had reason.

She was sure he was working, too. Some women had husbands who strayed, who found mistress after mistress, displaying them with no concern about what their wives or mothers or sisters thought. Some men drank, or squandered futures in gambling or the more legal speculation on property, mining rights, or magical materia. Some had other distasteful habits, abuse or manipulation, she'd heard whispers about that.

No, her isolation was not at all to her liking, but it was done in kindness. And she had obligations, as a Lady of the land, now, to set an example to others. More than that, it was her duty to not worry the people around her by doing things they disapproved of.

But there were challenges. Her mother-in-law was not here at all. She suspected the dowager Edgarton had found childbirth utterly awful, and she refused to be anywhere near it. She was still in Trellech, though in a form of deep mourning, only seeing her closest three dozen friends or so. Alysoun tried to have sympathy, even if it seemed the Dowager Lady Edgarton hadn't particularly been in love with her late husband. But hearing about the women coming and going, their literary readings and gatherings, made Alysoun yearn even more for her own few friends. She wanted to just curl up with Emmeline and talk books, or wander through a museum with Isabella.

Alysoun's own mother had come early in her labour, but taken to her bed with a sick headache before things even got properly started. She couldn't blame her mother for her headaches, but they always came at rather inconvenient times. It had spared her a certain amount of unnecessary fussing, but it had also left her alone when there should have been family around her.

Well, alone except for the staff, who were many, but who were not at all the same sort of thing as her friends or her mother or even her cousins. They saw her in the most intimate of ways, but even with Miss Newcomb, her lady's maid, she could not talk at all freely. The staff themsleves made such faces if she said something out of place.

There was a knock on the bedroom door that startled everyone - except the baby, thankfully. The healer's assistant went to open the door, speaking to someone on the other side. Then she closed it gently, and came back over to the bed, bobbing in a curtsey. "Pardon, my lady, his lordship asks if he might visit for a few minutes if agreeable to you." That sounded exactly like what Richard had said, really.

Alysoun smiled. "Please. And if you'd give us as much privacy as can be arranged?" He might not be terribly loquacious with her, but he would be far less so with three different women of varying ages hovering, as well as his wife.

The woman bobbed again, and went to get the door, retreating to Alysoun's dressing room with the nursemaid as soon as she closed the door. Richard came to about ten feet from the bed, then stopped awkwardly. She thought he'd had Guard business this morning. He'd been wearing his uniform when she saw him going to the portal from her window, but now he was in country clothes.

The tweed suited him well, really, and the dark emerald vest he had under the jacket brought out his clear green eyes. That made her glance down at her son, whose eyes were that uncertain baby colour, but she rather hoped he'd take after his father that way, not her own muddier hazel.

"Alysoun." That was a good start, at least, her name and not her title. "I hope, I mean, they told me it went well?"

She nodded. "Would you like to hold your son?"

He shook his head immediately, but after a moment, he gestured. "May I come closer?"

"Oh, please do." She did not care to have this conversation with him halfway across the room, so she had to shout. Among other reasons, that hurt right now. Also, it was undignified. There was nowhere for him to sit, they'd cleared away the chairs and stools from earlier, but after a moment, he gingerly perched on the side of the broad bed, and glanced at their son again, then kept looking.

That was proper, and reassuring. She let him look for as long as he liked, and it was only when he glanced up at her that she asked, "Settled on a name, then?"

They had chosen half a dozen they thought might suit, but he had been quite uncertain about picking one until he could actually see the baby himself. He nodded, and said. "I don't think he's an Alfred, no. And we'd already decided we weren't choosing Icarus, no matter how much Grandmama argued for it."

"No, we weren't. Entirely tempting fate." It got her a flash of a smile from him. His grandmother terrified him, she rather thought. Alysoun, from the privileged position of producing an heir so promptly, had a bit more leeway, if she cared to spend it that way. And for naming, she did. The poor wee thing would have to live with whatever they saddled him with.

"Gabriel Anthony, do you think?"

That had been her preference of the options from the start. Gabriel had a good rolling sound, it went well with the surname, and if and when he inherited the title, it went well with that, too. Though she very much hoped that would be decades away, thank you. She was fond of her husband, all things considered, even if she so rarely saw him. And Anthony, that was for his father, who had been an Antonius. "I like that very much. Hello, Gabriel Anthony." She beamed down at her son, who wriggled very slightly in her arms.

"I wrote to Mother, and she said she'll comewhen you're ready for visitors. She thought a day or two? Perhaps at the end of the week?" His mother really did not care for birthing rooms, then.

"That is entirely fine, of course. If you could ask Mrs Bascom to make up her rooms, and air them out?" That was the housekeeper.

"I think I can manage that. You've been doing a great deal of hard work. Oh, and I did manage to catch Isabella." Her best friend. "She promises to come tomorrow, if little Alexandra's sniffle isn't actually a cold. And if it is a cold, she'll write and come as soon as she can."

"Thank you, dear." She meant it. Many husbands would have forgotten, she'd heard enough stories. Or considered the visits of other women to be beneath his attention.

"And when I was in Trellech, oh, the meeting went well. Much shorter than expected." He hadn't actually explained what meeting it was, but that was good. "I had a chance to stop in the bookshop. I've several new books for you, I'll send someone up, I forgot them on the study desk. That novel you were hoping for, and a new history of Trellech I thought you might rather like, the first chapter was very good."

That was even more considerate. "The history had quite a good review in, oh, I can't remember now. Thank you, dear. Most kind."

He ducked his chin, standing again, a little hurriedly. "I shouldn't tire you out. I'll come see you tomorrow, shall I, and send the books up right away. And you let me know if you need anything, or if any of the staff turn out not to suit. I don't want you to worry about anything, other than recovering."

She wanted him to stay longer, but she couldn't deny she was exhausted, so she merely nodded. There would be other days for talking. She very much hoped. "Tomorrow. Please do."

Richard smiled, bent to kiss her forehead, and then he was going, out the door before she could gather her thoughts and say anything. The nursemaid swooped in, tucking the baby tidily into the crib beside her bed, and dimmed the lights, with a "You rest now, my lady."

THREE

18TH FEBRUARY 1903, VERITAS

"Afternoon, dear." Richard had had a long day already. He'd been called out before dawn that morning, with a problem for his particular unit of the Guard. He couldn't tell if they were getting the difficult problems to keep them out of the way, or because they made headway on them more often than not. Either way, it made him glad he had a separate bedroom. Alysoun had not been sleeping well since the new baby, and he didn't wish to disturb her more than necessary.

His mother had made it abundantly clear, near any time he'd been around, that men could be quite overbearing and demanding without being at all specific about how he might avoid being so. His father had been no help at all, other than as a model of how to live a life among men, going from club to private gathering to club to house party when he wasn't at home in his own library.

It made it hard to know what to do. Richard could tell Alysoun sometimes got frustrated, for all she was very careful not to show it to him. He could at least avoid making things worse, expecting her to rearrange whatever her plans for her time were because he showed up unexpectedly.

At least he'd made it home for tea, and a chance to see the children before they were bustled off to bed. Sometimes he missed even that. More often than he liked, frankly, between the Guard, and the duties elsewhere in the area, and consultations at the Ministry and his clubs about various projects and charitable events. Which reminded him, there were several invitation cards Alysoun hadn't replied to, and they really should give some indication.

He knocked on her day room door, and heard a quiet "Come in."

His wife was stretched out on the sofa, with a long blanket draped over her, though she was sitting up. She didn't precisely look ill, but she didn't look well, either. She had a pallor to her that troubled him, and he was struck by how quiet and motionless the room seemed. "Still not feeling well, dear?"

Alysoun shook her head. "They took Charlotte up to the nursery already, but I think Gabriel is hoping you'd be back. You could take your tea up there?"

Richard glanced up toward the nursery rooms. "I don't want to disrupt their routine, but I'll go up and say hello." He hesitated. "Would you like me to take tea with you?"

For just a moment, her eyes lit up, and she nodded. "Please. Give me, oh, fifteen minutes? We could take tea in the parlour, downstairs? Do you need to go out again?"

He nodded. "There's a meeting tonight, the charitable ball for the library roof repairs, I really should be at it."

"To make sure they don't make short-sighted decisions, quite. It's dangerous enough doing the repairs, no sense doing them more often than needed."

"Exactly. If you were there, you'd set them all to rights

immediately, I know. I shall have to do my best imitation." He made sure his voice was brisk and cheerful. He knew she would do better if she were able to be there, she had a way of arranging things sensibly. Whatever she touched seemed better. Except Alysoun herself, somehow.

Alysoun flushed, and looked away for a moment, and Richard felt suddenly awkward. These moments happened more and more, and he wasn't sure what to do with them. "Let me go see the children, and I'll meet you downstairs."

"Excellent." Mind, she didn't move until after he left the room. He didn't know what was wrong with her, and the healers she'd seen so far hadn't been much help. They'd made arrangements for her to see the senior healers, the ones who didn't make house calls except in the direst emergencies. That would happen once she could travel enough with the baby to go to Trellech.

The healers they'd seen had at least assured them both that the difficulties were pain and fatigue, but nothing that would cause long-term damage at the moment. He would have to trust that, much as it bothered him. It wasn't a problem he was used to solving, it didn't get better when she rested, or when she tried different foods or exercise. It must be far more frustrating for her, but he just wanted to make things better and could see no plausible solution.

The nursery was, in contrast, all bustling energy. Gabriel was tottering around while the nursemaid focused on getting his sister ready for bed, and that at least meant Richard could be some slight use. The nursemaids usually were entirely on top of things. Frankly, he was often terrified he'd put a foot wrong and be scolded for exciting the children or promising them something they'd been forbidden.

Today, though, it was all smiles and laughter. As soon as

Gabriel saw his father, he came rushing over, and Richard swung him up, balancing him on his hip. "Just here to say hello, Nanny." Nanny Wain was bustling out of the night nursery when she heard a new voice, but she nodded. She'd been here for a year, and knew their routines well. Unlike the nursery maid, who'd only been here a month or so, and much of that disrupted by baby Charlotte's arrival.

"If you have a few minutes, your Lordship?" Nanny gestured to the reading chair.

Richard considered. "Time for a short book, yes." Gabriel bounced a little in his arms, and he brought him over to the little reading nook, in the window looking out over the gardens. It was a lovely view, even in this rather muddy stage of later winter.

Richard managed to settle without being too awkward, and Nanny Wain handed him a book once he had Gabriel more or less settled. It was one he remembered from his own childhood, a selection of tales about magical creatures. No dragons, not yet, but there was one here about a hare chasing the moon.

Reading it went well enough, and when it was done, Nanny had sorted out the tea tray, and was ready to encourage Gabriel through the proper steps of the evening.

"I'll get out of your way, Nanny," he said, promptly. "I hope to be up for a bit longer tomorrow, events willing." He appreciated a routine, and he knew he didn't want to interrupt theirs. And besides, he was still sure Nanny thought he was up in the nursery far more often than most fathers were.

"Of course, your lordship. A pleasure, as always. Give your papa a kiss goodnight, Gabriel, like a good boy." That got him a peck on the cheek, before Gabriel wriggled down and went to cling to Nanny's skirt as Richard got up.

He nodded to the nursemaid, not wanting to get anywhere near the changing Charlotte apparently required. "Good night, all."

By the time he'd washed up and retreated downstairs, it had been a good twenty minutes. Alysoun had clearly only just arrived downstairs herself. She was wearing a loose tea gown, in a shade of twilight blue that flattered her, but without, he suspected, any corseting. His mother would have commented on it, where Alysoun could hear, and not kindly. Richard saw no reason she should need to be laced into something he could barely unlace her from with a map and a good stout pair of scissors in case of error. Especially not when she was in so much pain.

Fortunately, his mother had come for a bare week's visit after the birth. Then she had retreated to her townhouse in Trellech, and from there on to her usual late winter tour of sunnier and warmer climes. And Alysoun's mother's visit had been brief, overlapping enough that they had kept each other busy. There was no need to worry either of them with Alysoun's health. Alysoun was quite capable of telling her mother what she wished, and Richard's mother, well, it was better not to upset the expectations.

His mother had been very clear, all along, that he had duties, and that he should spend his time and energy on them. That she herself had no need of his attention, and that his future wife would likely prefer to be left to her own pleasures. Richard felt there was something he was missing in the equation. His training as a Guard had taught him to pay attention to the small cues, but it kept failing him when it came to his wife. He could not tell if she wanted him to spend more time with her, or if she considered him an irritation and interruption. She could simply be saying what she thought he wanted to hear.

He took his place at the informal table, across from his wife, and smiled at her. "I read a story to Gabriel. And Nanny seemed to have things well in hand." She was a cousin of Alysoun's own nanny, apparently, and this was her third household, with the other sets of children having graduated to governesses and tutoring houses. Talking about the children was a safe topic, he'd learned that quickly.

"I'm sure he liked that. He was asking about you earlier, when she brought him down before their walk."

"A bit brisk out there. You didn't go out?" It was hard to keep the worry out of his voice. He'd hoped she'd at least been able to enjoy the terrace and the sunshine.

Alysoun shook her head. "I couldn't get warm today as it was, even with the warming charms on the blanket. Thank you for that, dear, it does help."

He tilted his head. "Just not as much as you'd like."

She nodded. "I, yes. I'm sorry it's such a bother." He felt sure she was apologising for her illness, she kept doing that, and he wasn't sure what the apology was meant to do.

"They did say you might improve." He tried to be hopeful about it, but if anything the past week was worse. More pain, in her muscles, more headache, more poor sleep.

"Perhaps." She sounded unconvinced, and he really couldn't blame her. "How was your day? I thought I heard you, early this morning."

He immediately said, "I'll have someone check the sound charms, I really didn't want to disturb you, darling."

She waved her hand. "It was, I was awake anyway. If you see the light on, you could poke your head in?"

There was something tentative in the last part of that, and he immediately frowned. "I don't want to - I might wake you." It was the instinctive response, but surely, with her sleep as bad as it was, she couldn't want him to risk waking her at five or six in the morning.

Alysoun deflated, that was the only way he could describe it. "And you're out tonight. Tomorrow?" He'd definitely handled that wrong, but he wasn't sure how to fix it.

"Not tomorrow unless something comes up with the Guard."

"Like this morning?" She didn't pry about his work, but he found himself wanting to say a little more.

"Like this morning. We keep getting sent on the odd calls. The ones that are a bit queer."

"Oh?" She was picking at her food a bit, but she was eating, that was encouraging.

"This morning's was someone who thought she was seeing ghosts. Shapes outside the window, that sort of thing. And she stormed into the local Guard at something like three in the morning."

"Did you figure out what it was?"

"Oh, there's a man, a veteran, discharged nearby. Near as we can tell, he got a head injury in South Africa, and the keep-away enchantments don't work well on him. He didn't mean any harm, he was just trying to figure out why there was a house that everyone seemed to be ignoring."

"At three in the morning?"

Richard thought she sounded honestly curious, and so he ventured a bit more detail. "Well, mostly he was aiming at the hayloft, I gather. He - he was in pretty bad shape, poor man. He'd been walking for days, no money, sure he couldn't trust his eyes, because sometimes he'd see a house, and sometimes he wouldn't." He had a lot of sympathy for the man, honestly, it must have been terrifying. He was glad there'd been a Guard in the village who could call in more help, so they could figure out how best to sort things out.

Alysoun tilted her head, and nodded. "That must be terrifying. What did you do?"

"I went and collected him, and he's going to the chaps in London who can figure out what will work for him. At least there, he'll get himself in less trouble. It sounded like they were going to see if they could help him find something stationary well away from our places. Make sure he's connected to some of the housing and work options for veterans in need and all that. There's a whole office in London that does that sort of thing."

"Huh." She frowned, before asking directly, "What kind of services are there? I admit I've never thought much about the details."

"Well, there are chaps who can help with finding work. And our fellows will see that that's somewhere away from the magical spaces, the best they can. Of course, people can and do travel, so they also circulate the particulars, in case he stumbles in somewhere again. There aren't too many like that, though, it's manageable."

She considered that, thinking through it. "Is that a lot of your work, then?"

Richard shrugged. "Sometimes. It varies, depending on what's needed." It was part of why his mother disapproved of his going into the Guard. It would have been one thing if he were investigating matters of significance. Richard, though, felt strongly about doing his part, he always had.

"A third are something like that, some puzzle or problem that needs a solution. Things where no one's done anything criminal, just needs a hand. About a third of the work is actual crimes, sorting out evidence, figuring out who's involved. The rest is a mix, helping out when there's a flood or fire or some other danger. Boxton and his lot got called out for a possible wolf, the other day, or a dangerous dog."

She nodded, chewing on her lip, an unguarded moment. "And you have people who do all of that?" He realised he really hadn't explained much about the structure of his work to her. Most people either knew it or made it clear they found it tremendously tedious.

"I'm based in Trellech, like most of our specialists, but we go wherever we're needed, whoever's skills are the right thing. For something like this man, it would often just be the local Guard sorting it out, making sure someone gets the help they need, or a chance to make a new start somewhere the history doesn't keep snarling them. This was different because the man isn't magical. They thought I'd be young enough not to intimidate him too much, but enough authority he'd respond to it."

And Richard was quite good at the necessary memory cantrips, the ones that would discourage the poor man from saying things that would make matters more difficult all round. He didn't spell that part out.

Alysoun smiled at that. "Kinder than a lot of people would be." She paused, looking at him, then added, "Thank you for telling me about it. Your work." She seemed to be about to say something more, then she grimaced. "Sorry, my dear. I should go rest again. And not keep you."

He stood, and when her maid stepped forward from the back corner of the room, he immediately said, "Let me walk you upstairs, and then I'll go off."

The walk upstairs was slow. She was clearly in more pain again, unwilling to take large steps and leaning on his arm more heavily than she had a day or two ago. By the time they got to her rooms, she was breathing more shallowly. He kissed her forehead. "Tomorrow, my dear."

Then he backed carefully out of the room and left her to the ministrations of her maid. He was sure she wouldn't want him seeing her at her worst, or interfering in the care she needed. His mother had made it quite clear men weren't good for that.

FOUR

27TH JUNE, VERITAS

By the time Richard got home, he was about done in. There had been an earthquake that morning. It had rattled buildings well past Trellech, and all the Guard had been called in to check on the various magical holdings throughout southern Wales. He'd drawn a particularly hilly bit of land, which had meant hard riding.

He'd also had two of the more impatient Guard apprentices with him, who were inclined to assume things were all right if they looked all right. That was not the kind of diligence he wanted or expected. They weren't hot-headed, that sort never lasted far past taking their early oaths as apprentices, but they were too hasty in a way he didn't care for.

Worst of all, he'd been riding one of the horses borrowed from the nearest Guard. His mount had been a rather stocky Welsh cob with a hard mouth and a jarring trot, not at all comfortable to ride at length over less than familiar countryside. But he wouldn't say a word about it. He knew there were half a dozen senior officers looking for an excuse to relegate him to purely ceremonial duties. They'd be glad to use the slightest complaint as proof that he had earned his rank so far through his title, not through his skills.

So he had taken a breath and done his best to ride with the jostling, not against it. And he'd kept the two apprentices close by until he could turn them back over to their apprentice master at the end of the day. They, at least, would have an uncomfortable wait for the baths in the apprentice barracks, and he could retreat to a proper bathing room.

Once he was through the portal, he headed straight for the front door, nodding at the butler with an "I'll be bathing." There was a noise behind him, and he ignored it, going straight up to his rooms to peel out of his clothing. He'd beaten his valet up there, and so instead he left his clothing over the clothing rack. The boots were a state, but there was no helping that, they'd had to go through mud as well as over rock.

Pulling a robe around him, feet in slippers, he made his way down the back staircase to the bathing room. As far as he knew, it had been there for two millennia, in the midst of the oldest part of the house. He didn't see or hear anyone, but he could see the steam from the caldarium coming through the archway that led there. That was easy to do at least, the great furnace under the house ran on ancient but well-behaved magics, with the heat radiating out from beneath this room.

Richard took a few moments to rinse himself clean, in water more tepid than he liked. Perhaps someone had been through recently - it took a bit for the sluicing barrel to warm up again. Shrugging, he turned to the caldarium. Then he took a deep breath of the warm air, the steam thick today, before making his way by long practised memory to ease himself into the tub.

His feet were in the water when he heard the voice. "In the corner, dear."

He managed not to lose his balance in making sure not to jostle her. And, he hoped, behaving with some last remnant of dignity. He ended up sliding onto the bench seat under the water with more of a thump than his spine or shoulders wanted. "Alysoun? How long have you been in here?"

"Oh, an hour or so, rotating." Her voice was relaxed, even, far less tense than he'd heard her for a while. "It feels good."

He nodded, then realised she could likely see him no better than he could see her, just a faint darker shape behind the steam. "Bad day, then?"

"Not the best. Long day for you?" Her voice was cautious, like she wasn't sure what he'd say. And granted, they'd not been naked together, since Charlotte was tiny. He'd not wanted to impose on her, especially after the healers had made it clear they should not consider another child. He knew he'd hurt her when they had tried any particular intimacy and he had no desire to do that. He couldn't heal her, but he could at least avoid doing her more harm.

Granted, neither of them had turned out to be particularly body shy. He certainly wasn't, he'd changed around other people since he'd gone to school. They'd certainly had plenty of dinners and outings clothed, talking at night once they were in their night things. But anything more physical had disappeared due to her unpredictable but persistent pain.

"Oh, you'd not have felt it here. There was an earthquake in Wales this morning, they called us all out to help make sure everyone was all right. Long day on horseback, checking a dozen remote houses and two hamlets, tucked away."

"An earthquake? How queer." She was thinking about something, but he couldn't begin to tell what. "People must have been badly hurt."

"Oddly, no. Some chimneys came down, things fell off shelves and broke, but nothing worse, it looks like."

"A miracle, then." Alysoun's voice was thoughtful, behind the steam. There was a long pause, and when Richard was about to say something, he heard her again. "What's the countryside like there?"

"Oh, lots of sheep. We were a bit northwest of Cardiff, there are dense woods, quite rocky territory. The horse they lent me was - well. Not what I'm used to."

"Terribly jarred, were you? Pity you couldn't have taken one of ours." Alysoun's mare, Silk, was a true lady's palfrey, with some of the smoothest gaits Richard had come across. He'd brought her home after hunting for a good three months, through every horse fair he could get to with his stableman. The look on her face when she'd tried Silk out had been amazing and worth every minute and every coin.

He'd loved the challenge of finding something that would give her back at least some of what she'd lost. A year later, he'd bought up Silk's half-brother for himself. Damask was taller but just as nicely gaited, and responsive and flex-ible as the wind.

"Terribly bounced around," he agreed, and let himself sink into the hot water with a sigh. "How are the children?"

"I told them you'd been called away. Charlotte picked some flowers for you."

"Not the front garden, I hope?" That had been last fortnight, and had had their head gardener nearly in tears. Poor man. And then he was caught by something, a vague memory. "What were those, do you remember?"

There was a long pause from the other side of the bath. It gave him time to wonder what she was thinking of this conversation, but she seemed to be encouraging it. Him. "Nothing dangerous to her, of course, we don't plant that where they can get to. One of the orchids."

"There was something today." He was thinking out loud. He'd found that was helpful sometimes, though usually he ended up talking to Simons, his aide, who put up with it.

Alysoun shifted in the water, moving a bit closer to him. "Something while you were out? Not about the earthquake?"

"No. One of the outlying houses, near the edge of Afan Forest. There was something queer there, like the man was hiding something."

The water picked up small waves again, and after a moment, he could hear a voice from the entrance to the baths. "My lady?"

"Later, Wallis, please. His lordship and I are talking. I'll ring when I need you." Alysoun's voice was crystal clear, and while polite, the sort of command voice he wished he could provide as an example to his female Guards.

"Of course, my lady." The footsteps retreated.

Alysoun sighed. "They'll be talking about it in the servants' hall, I'm sure."

"Us?" He blinked several times. "Why?"

"We're not often entirely private, dear." She sounded decidedly amused now.

Richard frowned, then said, more plaintively than he meant to. "They gossip about us?" He hadn't, in all honesty, thought much about the servants at Veritas. They did things, generally very well, but often entirely invisible to him. It shouldn't be a surprise that they talked about Alysoun, or Richard himself, but he hadn't considered it at all, somehow. It made him wonder what else she took for granted that he was missing entirely.

"We do live out in rural Kent, darling. There is not a great deal of notable gossip. And you are quite dashing in your Guard uniform, and heroic." Her voice was a little fuzzy with amusement. Or at least he thought it was amusement.

"Is that what they think? Not much heroism today." Then he couldn't help asking, "What do you think?"

There was a long pause that grew increasingly uncomfortable. Finally, she said, "You are a good man, Richard. A diligent and attentive one. You have always been kind to me, and gentle. And thoughtful. My mare, the books you bring home. Not, not the traditional gifts, but ones that mean a great deal to me. They talk about that, too." Then she stopped, a bit abruptly, as if there was more there she wasn't willing to say.

He didn't let it linger, he had no desire to press if she were uncomfortable. Instead, he said, "You'd asked about today."

"Yes." She sounded relieved. "An outlying farm. What is the land like around there? No, wait. How did you get called out, first, how does that work? Who did you go with? Tell me all the details." There was a sudden eagerness in her voice, something he'd not heard from her for a long time.

It made him blink at her, not that she could see it, but he

wanted to respond to it, to feed it, as best he could. "The earthquake happened, and they sent someone through the portal, to bring us word. They didn't know much, the point was to get us out so we could find out what the damage was."

"What if the portal hadn't worked? I mean, I suppose they could be damaged in an earthquake, possibly?"

"They can, in which case they'd send someone on horseback or by train or boat. All the Guards out in villages have maps and lists of the fastest way to get somewhere. The practice is to send three people in different directions, until they can get through. There's a stipend that goes with it, so there are usually plenty of responsible folks willing to go."

That made Alysoun hum, softly. "Interesting. Having it be a known thing, that has to help. So someone comes to Trellech, and you all get called out."

Richard grinned, leaning back, liking this a great deal. "There's a bell, you've heard that. They rang out the change pattern for the alert, we formed up in the courtyard, and divided up into groups. Usually an officer, and two or three Guards, and whoever else might be helpful. Sometimes that's the Penelopes, to untangle magics on the other end. This time, we had a few illusion specialists, in case we needed to hide something magical that had been exposed, and a few healers, used to more rural countryside."

"So, again, a set way to do things."

"Set, and flexible enough to adapt. We mostly work in those small groups, three to six or so. Small enough not to attract too much notice and to work independently."

"You go through the portal, and then you get assigned to specific areas?" Alysoun shifted a bit, he could feel the ripples in the water, as if she were stretching. "What's the area like?"

"Steep hills down to a river valley, and as you might guess by the name, a rather dense forest. The cottage was up near the rim."

"And what kind of trees?" Her voice was still curious.

"A mix - the trails were quite dark, with the foliage."

She nodded. "So, the cottage."

"Not a big place at all. One large room downstairs, a steep stair, and a room upstairs, I suspect. We didn't see that part. Thatched roof. There's apparently a particular thatching tradition there, that's getting lost, one of my men told me."

"What was curious, then?" She clearly felt - and Richard agreed - that there was nothing too unusual here.

"There was a clear area, behind the house. And there were, pardon, thinking through it." He hadn't been able to name it at the time. Then he asked, "When you've gone to the village here, what are the cottages like?"

"They vary." Her voice was patient. "Depending on the family. How they're doing, who's working, and at what."

"But you would expect people making do. Repairing things."

"Oh, certainly. It's part of what we think about when packaging things up. Wallis and I took the salves and herbs down last week, and we wrapped things up in squares of fabric that could be reused. Tins that could be cleaned out and used for storage."

Richard spoke slowly, considering each word. "There was new furniture in the cottage. A chair, two of them, not darkened with use. New curtains. Nothing unusual, exactly. Not like a smuggler's cottage. But not quite the norm."

Alysoun considered that. "Is it something you should investigate?"

He shrugged slightly. "Without anything specific to point to, I don't have much right. I can report it to the local Guard."

"Even if it's smuggling?"

He wriggled his hand, forgetting she couldn't see it. "It depends on the smuggling. We'll prosecute smuggling, if we find it while investigating something else, but if it's people avoiding taxes, that's for the Ministry to sort out, not us to be suspecting everyone. We only step in if there's harm to people or protected animals or places or what have you."

There was a long pause, as she considered that. "You hear stories, sometimes. About people going and investigating something on their own. That always struck me as dangerous."

"It's bad practice, and more or less against the Guard Oath. We're supposed to report our concerns, anything that isn't immediate or urgent, so the proper steps can be taken. There's documentation, so that people aren't using the Guard for their own whim or benefit."

"And the oath?" Her voice was quieter now, and she sounded almost wistful. "You took it before I ever met you."

"Took two, one for my apprenticeship, one when I became a Guard with all the responsibilities thereof." He considered. "It's based on some of the chivalric oaths. I have a copy of the full text with annotations, in my study, if you'd like?"

"Please." Again, there was that note of pleasure in her voice. "I looked in our library, last year, and I read that history, the one by Bowfield, but it didn't talk much about the oath. If that's not, I mean, I know sometimes oaths are private."

"It would be a poor sort of oath for the Guard to take if no one knew what we'd committed to." Richard had to smile at the idea. "Roughly speaking, it's a commitment not to king or country or even Council, but to magic and those who bear it. And a commitment to protect those without magic."

He paused, gathering his thoughts, because the other part of it always felt far more personalto him. "The rest is about behaving like a knight should, near enough, to be men and women who strive to be good and honourable, to use the least force, restraint, or compulsion possible, magical or otherwise. Not using our positions for personal advantage, being fair to all we deal with as a Guard, regardless of their station or status."

Alysoun was quiet again, for rather longer this time, before she said, "Quite different from your oaths as Lord, then."

"As Lord, I am not required to be a good man. I could be cruel or kind, foolish or clever, a wastrel or a careful provider, so long as I showed up to tend the lands under my hand. It's a much more spacious oath, really, if you do the necessary offerings and wardings and other magics, or make sure they're done."

"Huh." Alysoun was thinking, he could tell that, but he had no idea what direction her thoughts had gone in. Finally, she spoke again. "So your suspicion about the cottage, you report them to someone, and they decide what to do about it? Since there isn't an obvious crime or problem or immediate danger?"

"That's the rule. That's reported both to the local Guard station and to the Hall in Trellech. But they won't follow up for a bit, I'm sure. We're stretched thinner than anyone likes to admit. And I don't have much to report. One of them could have come into a bit of money, maybe an inheritance, just enough to replace a few things and put a bit aside."

"Report it, then. Just so people can keep an eye out."

"You are a great deal more optimistic than I am, darling. But here, you've been soaking for ages. May I help you out, and get Wallis to help you change?"

The steam had finally begun to clear enough he could see her, her hair coiled back loosely, hanging damply, but he thought she looked beautiful. "If it's not a bother. You wanted to soak, though."

"Oh, I'll do that once you're settled. And then supper? Can Mrs Glenwilliam put it back an hour or so?"

"I wasn't sure when you'd be home or if you'd be hungry, so yes, it will hold. I'll let her know."

He beamed. "Grand." Then it was pushing himself up to stand. It gave her rather a view of his naked body, but his robe was on the other side of the room. She didn't seem to object, anyway, not like his mother did, looking away even from male statues at times. Holding out his arm, he held steady while she levered herself slowly out, though moving more easily than usual. The heat clearly was a help, then.

Then he escorted her to the small dressing room to the side of the baths, helping her on with her robe and then his, before ringing the bell. Wallis appeared so quickly he suspected she had been lurking outside the door. The bells were enchanted to signal watches the senior house staff carried on them at all times, but even so, that was remarkably efficient.

"Wallis." Alysoun's voice was pleased. "His lordship will be joining us for supper. If you'd run down once I'm upstairs and let Mrs Glenwilliam know, and Lewis." His valet.

"Of course, my lady. I've your rooms nice and warm as you prefer. Your lordship." She bobbed once, and then waited for Alysoun to precede her to the stairs and up to their private rooms.

FIVE

3RD JULY, VERITAS

It had been a better week, finally. She often felt better once the year turned into summer, but it had been a long, cold, and often damp spring and summer so far. In short, it was entirely too full of the kind of weather that sent her to soak in hot water for much of the day, even though she hated how little she got done. She couldn't even read, though Wallis could be persuaded to read aloud some of the time, when she didn't need to see to other duties.

Finally, though, the weather had broken, and Alysoun had felt well enough to go to Trellech for a new exhibit she'd been looking forward to. She had plans for supper with Richard, and then she would decide if she were staying in town for a few days or going back to Kent. Town was decidedly more interesting, but it lacked the Roman baths she had come to rely on at Veritas. On the other hand, it felt like she'd been stuck there for months, between the weather and assorted minor childhood illnesses.

And this exhibition, it was a particular treat. A new advance in charm work had meant the curators could safely transport stained glass from three dozen private collections and bring it together in one place. There were tours arranged, of course, for visits to permanent pieces. They'd be hosting one of those at Veritas late next month. In August, the countryside was in its glory, and it was before the hops pickers swarmed.

If her health held, she hoped to attend a few of the other tours. The pieces at Veritas were apparently quite notable, and Richard was very proud of them, but she knew he enjoyed visits elsewhere. And he'd charm everyone he met along the way. She did enjoy watching him do that, there was something of a dance about it.

He'd been solicitous, since their time in the bath, taking care to tell her a little more about his day. Nothing so expansive, but a few sentences here and there. He had no particular need to charm her, but he was doing it anyway. She couldn't bear to ask him to stop, much as it hurt to see him talk to her, and then turn away from her, whenever they might have a little more privacy. He did not hate her, he did not ignore her, but she was more and more certain he thought her too fragile to lean on, or be with for long.

For now, though, it was the museum, with Wallis walking beside her, until she met up with Isabella for the morning. The unspoken part, of course, was that no one - not Alysoun herself, or Wallis, or Richard - entirely trusted her not to fall or need help without warning. She wanted to go by herself, leave Wallis to her own errands, but she deferred to their worry, at least when there was a longer walk involved. She wanted to rage against it, but that wouldn't help. Sometimes she used a cane, but that tended to cause even more comment and fuss than having someone with her.

At least she'd have a change of company. It was rare she got a chance to spend much time with Isabella. They both had young children and that had limited travel one way or both for far too long. But now her own children were settling into the steady growing up they needed to do, and Isabella didn't intend to try for another for a year or two. She had come out to Kent a few times, but it was a treat to be somewhere else. Isabella, too, never fussed over her, just asked what she needed and made sure it happened.

Alysoun had a suspicion that it was easier to do that if you were used to running a large house. The lady of the manor, whatever her formal title, didn't do everything herself. But she had to be able to make adjustments if a particular servant left or some calamity happened out of season.

She'd started thinking of her illness, whatever it was, as a manor house with unpredictable leaks and shudders and dry rot in the bones of the building. Once she'd realised that, she'd found herself more patient with the fact nothing worked quite right. The problem was, though, that there was no way she could see to patch the leaks or shore up the upper stories. The heated baths were a palliative, but it was rather more like painting over cracks in the plaster instead of mending them than she liked.

Those musings brought her up to the museum, and she paid for Wallis's ticket, so her maid would be able to come find her when needed. Of course, being a Lady of the land didn't hurt. Half the staff recognised her by sight - there weren't so many women with that title as all that - and assured her it was no problem.

Isabella showed up precisely fifteen minutes late, like always. You could set a clock by her, as long as you didn't need it to match any other clock. "Alysoun! There you are, so sorry, the little ones wouldn't let go when I was on the way out the door, you know what it's like." Then her friend was looking her up and down, her dark curls bobbing. "You're looking much better than last time."

"Feeling it, too. It's been a rough few months."

"And you're in town for a few days?"

"I hope, yes. Richard said there's a new restaurant I'll like. Well, not terribly new now, but he says they'll just have settled into the service better."

"The Mountain, then?"

Alysoun nodded, then levered herself up. "We should go have our look, yes?" They walked along, arm in arm, amiably, down the long marble hallway of the ground floor, into the atrium. She stopped, startled, when they entered the space, which was glowing with different colours of light. It was rather like walking into a rainbow, only the colours came from all sides.

Isabella grinned. "Worth leaving the house for, isn't it?"

There were different pieces of stained glass everywhere, well protected in the atrium, but with charm lights illuminating the space in a warm glow, like the sun in the mid-afternoon. Not glaring, but ever-present. Each piece stood so that the viewer could walk around it, see the impression from inside the house and outside. Or, Alysoun supposed, wherever it was hung. Some of these were in fact from temples and churches, not private homes.

In the kaleidoscope of colours, it was difficult to figure out where to begin. In the end they followed the guidance of the exhibit guide, which had them begin sensibly with the oldest pieces. There were ancient works, two Egyptian, three Roman, all various sorts of containers, lit to demonstrate the range of colours available. Along with them were other items like a beautiful faience scarab with brilliant red coral beads, to show other colours valued in the culture.

They both lingered there, perhaps longer than either of

them meant to. "I do find the old pieces have an elegance," Isabella said. "You can see it in the Roman portions of Veritas, I'm sure."

Alysoun nodded. "This colour, the green, that's rather like some of the mosaics in the baths." Then her eye caught one of the other displays, early mediaeval pieces, set in windows. She drifted that way. "This one, oh, you'll like the designs."

Isabella peered at it, then circled it, to look at it from the other side. Alysoun stayed where she was, saving her steps for other pieces she was more interested in. This one was from a Christian church, apparently, a depiction of a biblical story, David and Goliath, picked out on the two long halves of the window.

The next one was the Queen of Sheba, complete with the mythical depiction of her goose-foot, meeting with King Solomon for the first time. This one, she circled, taking in the piece as a whole, then leaning in to read about the reconstruction. This had come from a church in Trellech, and had been removed and thoroughly restored.

She noticed the docent bustling in, with a "Pardon, Madam Lofton?" That was Isabella. "There is a message for you, rather urgent, I'm afraid." She held out the note, which must have come from Isabella's home, by the seal on it.

Isabella broke it open, and then grimaced. "Alysoun, I'm so sorry, but I need to get home. Marcus has had a bad tumble, and Nanny and the Healer want to consult about treatment."

"Oh, no. Do, please, go as quickly as you can. And let me know if we can help. Even taking the others for a few days. I'm sure Nanny Wain would rise to the occasion."

Isabella came over and kissed her cheek. "I don't think it will come to that, but you're so generous, darling. I'll write as soon as I know what happened. I don't want to spoil our outing, but..."

Alysoun shook her head. "I'll be quite fine, I promise. And I've supper with Richard to look forward to. Go on, go."

Isabella nodded, and the docent escorted her out, leaving Alysoun alone in the exhibit for the moment, except for one of the formally attired museum guards. She shook her head, glanced at the small watch she kept inside her reticule, and then decided she would take her time rather than call Wallis back.

She progressed steadily through the mediaeval pieces, but slowed down once she reached the art created within the magical community after the Pact. There was a particular flourishing in the 1500s and 1600s, especially during the Civil War.

Those with great magical homes didn't have to fear attack - they were already hidden and well-protected - so there had been quite a fashion for more delicate forms of art. There were beautiful details of colour, using a particular charm technique to layer pigments. It was not refined yet, but she found the overlaid colours fascinating, looking at them from every direction and reading every word of the description. She found herself taking note of the way it was done so that she might see how it developed in more recent pieces.

From there, she kept going. The restoration process was intriguing, but she was tired enough not to linger there. She suspected that the catalogue of the show would have more. She could always come back another day, when she'd read more and could properly appreciate the work. That brought her up to more modern approaches, and those artists within the magical community who had been influenced by the Pre-Raphaelites.

Something about one of those pieces struck her as odd, and she couldn't quite figure out what. It wasn't the colour, exactly. Instead it was something about the quality of the light through the glass, as if it was coming through differently than other pieces by the same artist. Was it a quirk of the glass in that one piece? She leaned in, making note of the name, one Augustine Reynard, almost certainly a pseudonym of some kind. Not an artist she knew, and quite recent. The dates she could see were from the middle of the last century.

By that time, her feet ached, and her hip, and her hand. She was glad to retreat to the small café. When Wallis returned to meet her, she insisted on a few minutes to acquire the catalogue of the exhibit, and two other books on stained glass they had on sale. Then she gave Wallis her head and let her fuss and arrange a carriage to take her back to the townhouse.

SIX

4TH JULY IN TRELLECH, WALES

"Are you up for staying in town a few more days?"

Richard honestly wasn't sure what the answer would be, but he hoped she'd say yes. He had come into her dressing room, where she sat on a comfortable bench in front of the dressing table while Miss Wallis did her hair. He was never sure why that took so long, but the end result was quite attractive. And most appropriate, which was a consideration for the immediate future.

"I think so? I'd not mind another chance to go to the museum, actually." Alysoun's voice was steady, not pained, which was a decent indication. He knew the travel was harder on her than either of them like. That was true even with all the not inconsiderable comforts he could and did provide, from the smoothest carriages to the most up to date cushioning and warming charms.

"We didn't get much chance to talk about it yesterday, I'm sorry. Donaldson came over at the worst moment. He has no sense of tact." He'd ended up having to draw the man away to the smoking room to avoid him discussing a rather upsetting case the Guard was currently investigating, about unexplained injuries to a young boy of eight. Not his command, mind, but he knew the captain in charge well, and Donaldson had wanted all the gossip.

"I know you have duties, dear. And less than pleasant obligations. No sense irritating people unnecessarily." She almost turned over her shoulder, only stopping when there was a quickly repressed murmur from Wallis.

Richard stood up, wandering over to her desk. "So, how was the exhibit? Should I try and make time for it? Probably not with you, I'm afraid, at least not this week. My diary's packed."

"Oh, yes. And they have some excellent pieces that date from the 900s, contemporary to ours at Veritas. You'd be interested in the commentary." She clearly was tracking where he was in the room, because she added, "The books on the desk are both related, and I got the catalogue as well."

He nodded, flicking through the pages of the last. "What did you think, then, of how they put the exhibit together?" This was at least a safe topic, without anything that might be a worry.

"It is a lovely historical overview. And such a treat to see things all in one place. There were a few pieces that puzzled me, though, which is why I'd like to go back. Some of the more recent ones. Mmm. Flip to Augustine Reynard. Near the back, there's a bookmark."

"That sounds distinctly like a chosen name, doesn't it?"

He could hear her laugh before she said more, with a "That's the first thing I thought. But, oh, the images don't really capture it, but there's something quite queer about the light, the way the light responds. I don't have any of the proper vocabulary for it, that's part of why I got the books."

"Your own particular puzzle, then?" he suggested. She had that note in her voice again, lit up like the glass. "If it intrigues you, then why not. It's a pleasant place to spend the day. And perhaps Isabella can come out again next week."

"I hope so. Isabella said the arm's healing well, but it was a difficult break, and the little ones are all insisting on clinging to her skirts at every possible moment."

"That would make it difficult to get through the portal and to the museum." He had to smile at the image. "Well." Then he stopped, unsure of how to discuss the thing he needed to.

Wallis finished with Alysoun's hair, and stood back. "My lady?"

Alysoun glanced at the clock on the dressing table. "Thank you, Wallis. We'll be down for the carriage, I'll rest until then."

Richard waited until Wallis had withdrawn. "How long do we have?"

"Twenty minutes or so. You have something you're nervous about." Her voice was considering, but not at all yielding.

He grimaced. "I can never hide anything from you. How do you do that?"

Alysoun turned to face him, sitting sideways on the bench now. "Practise. Tell, then, you know it's better once you have."

"They offered me the magistrate's seal this afternoon."

She blinked. "They did?" She seemed unsure what to say. "You weren't expecting it yet, were you?"

"No, I wasn't. They usually wait longer after the Heir inherits. Especially when they're as young as I was. Am. It's only been three years. Three and a half." He ran his hand through his hair, wondering if she'd understand without him having to explain.

"Come sit, please?" Of course, she wouldn't want to get up. He made his way to the other half of the bench as she moved over, each of them turning to talk, trying not to be distracted by the mirror.

"I can't turn it down." It came out of his mouth before he could stop it. He was simultaneously frustrated and relieved that she was the only person that happened with, where things slipped out he should keep contained.

There was a long silence, the sort that grew increasingly uncomfortable for him. Finally, she said, "There's a reason you feel you ought." It wasn't quite a question.

"I'm terribly young. They usually ask people in their sixties. Fifties, at least." It was the thought that dogged his days. He was young to be a Captain, young to be a Lord, young to be a magistrate. He was barely thirty-four. A fair number of men his age were barely married, they were still sowing wild oats, or doing scandalous things with chorus dancers. He'd never done any of that. Even if he hadn't much wanted to, he wondered what it would be like not to have to be responsible. Or to have a way to share it better.

Alysoun took his hand in hers, and he let her, suddenly wanting something warm and reassuring. "They're asking you early. That suggests they think you're ready. Or ready enough."

"You'd think." He was decidedly less certain.

"Why do you think they're asking you?" He hated how she pressed but he needed it. It was why, even with the difficulties she'd had, he hadn't turned away from her. Some men would, he knew. Many, probably. He'd certainly had many a frustrated night, when he'd wondered if he shouldn't at least find a mistress. But in the end no one had struck him as interesting enough and sufficiently able to keep things private at the same time. He had no desire to embarrass his wife, and he didn't want to thread the needle of his oaths, either.

"They're short on reliable magistrates. There are half a dozen who can't travel, another three who are elderly enough that even service here in Trellech is a strain. And they're two short in south-east England, in particular. One place is open in Kent, which is the excuse for asking me, and they're one short in East Sussex as well."

"The excuse?"

"If they don't ask me now, and ask someone else fairly young and hearty, it might be a decade before it opens up again. Political manoeuvring, I'm quite sure."

"Should I listen at the party, then? When you men abandon us for smoking and port and whatever else it is you do?"

"If you wouldn't mind." He was relieved she'd offered.

She nodded, absent-mindedly, as if she'd gotten caught by some other thought. He waited. Rushing never made sense if the person you were talking to was at all intelligent. It was one of the things he'd learned first in his apprenticeship.

As if she could read his mind, she asked, "What did Captain Torham say?" He had lunch with his apprentice master at least once a fortnight. Richard respected his advice and still treasured every bit of praise, at the same time he didn't want to be a bother. In this case, of course Richard had talked to him immediately after getting the offer. Alysoun at least didn't sound offended.

"We haven't had time to discuss it fully, he agrees there's something going on below the surface. But he thought I should take it."

That made her laugh. "And you're asking me?"

"Well, among other things, it will mean regular hostessing for you. There's a monthly gathering, it rotates among the circuit. And I know you don't care for Rogers."

She made a rather glorious face of dismay. "He is awful, and he has grabby hands with the staff. And - isn't Ralham in that set, too? Something about him makes me uneasy."

"We can hire imposing footmen, if that will help. One or two more wouldn't go amiss, you thought."

"Why are such difficult and rather awful men magistrates? Shouldn't they be upstanding types?"

"That is the hope." Richard tried to figure out how to put this. "But the magistrate's seal, the commitments. It's about being a channel for the Silence oaths, the ritual obligations, the things that aren't about the person specifically, just them having strong enough magic."

"Which is a more limiting factor than ethics, I suppose."

He snorted. "Alas, yes. Mind, several of that set are quite fascinating. I know you like the Dowager Lady Witham."

"Marietta, yes. I'd love a chance to see more of her." Alysoun's relationship with that intimidating woman was far different than his. As far as Richard could tell, Alysoun considered her a fairy godmother, who swept in and changed everything around her with a seeming effortlessness that Alysoun very much aspired to.

She had been a magistrate for decades, quite senior among them now. She often coordinated their needs with the Guard. Richard found her exceedingly precise and with resolutely high standards, something he appreciated but felt like he never lived up to.

Then he added, "It probably will mean a secretary for

me, someone who can be sworn to the Silence for confidential materials."

Alysoun pursed her lips, considering. "Secretary. That means an office and suitable housing, let me think about where would be best. Hosting, what, twice a year?"

"Probably more often. Three times, maybe four. Several of them are older widows or bachelors, without space to host a larger group."

"And space we have in spades. I see what you mean." She was still thinking through something. "I've been thinking Mrs Glenwilliam might be wanting something easier, nearer her family. What would you think about moving her here to Trellech, and hiring someone new for Veritas?"

He hadn't thought of any such thing, but he could see, dimly, why Alysoun brought it up. He generally left the management of the house to her, she was brought up to it and quite adept. He remembered an occasional comment here or there about Mrs Glenwilliam missing seeing her sisters and nieces and nephews, most of whom were in Trellech. Many houses wouldn't take such things into account, but there was no reason they couldn't.

"If you think she'd be interested, make the offer, and see what she says. I trust you to sort it out."

That made her smile, and she leaned to kiss his cheek. "Thank you for not meddling, dear. Much appreciated."

He nodded. "So I should tell them yes?" He still didn't know how he felt about the offer, but he couldn't put it into words. Alysoun was willing to take on the additional obligations, at least he'd managed to sort that much out.

"You should." Then she glanced at the clock. "And we should go down to the carriage."

The party was more or less what Alysoun had expected. Her dress was fabulous, of course, a sweep of twilight-blue silk and chiffon, decorated with small seed pearls. As usual, she could not decide if she appreciated the steady support of the corset or resented it for restricting her and making her ache. The shoes, though, she was clear on. Gorgeous, but painful.

The dinner itself had gone smoothly. As one of the higher ranked but younger women there, she had been partnered through the meal by a cousin of Richard's mother. He was not a lord of the land, but respected and with a suitably pompous role in the Ministry. Despite that, he unbent nicely with a glass of wine, and he spent most of the meal telling amusing stories of house parties.

They were something she rarely went to. Being away from home and the things that eased her pain and discomfort was complicated to arrange, and she never knew if any particular weekend would be worse than usual. At least if they were hosting, she could slip down to the baths, or curl up in her own bed. And she could easily change out a pair of gloves for one with warming charms, or perhaps discreetly send for a masseur.

After the meal came to a close, the women made their way to the drawing room, leaving the men to their drinks and smoking. Alysoun wasn't sure at all why Richard had accepted this invitation. He'd not explained. He often didn't, just trusting that she'd spot something useful. Sometimes, she knew the appearances were to defuse gossip about her ill health, or bolster him in some piece of social manoeuvring.

In this case, most of the guests were a bit older than she was. More to the point, many of them were people she didn't know well, half a step down from the circle they saw most often socially. There had been one other titled couple there, and a dowager lady, in her seventies at least, holding court at the end of the table. She had departed after the meal, or at least she was nowhere to be seen now.

Half were in their later thirties or forties, with children away at school in many cases. She settled on a chair, appreciating the way it supported her more comfortably. She accepted a cup of coffee from the servant who brought it around, and listened to the conversation flow around her.

There had clearly been some scandal she'd missed, the way people were talking around two or three topics. They weren't mentioning names, and she couldn't quite figure out the antecedents. She let it wash over her, filling her memory, so she could ask Richard later. Or more likely Willis, who among her other duties kept up with the gossip columns, so she could inform Alysoun of the necessary details.

She was sufficiently lost in thought that she didn't realise someone was addressing her until at least the second try. "Lady Edgarton?"

It was the eldest daughter of the family, perhaps a decade older than Alysoun, here with her husband, and one of the ones talking about Schola gossip. Dido, her name was.

"Yes, I do beg pardon, I was enjoying listening to you all talk."

"I do hope you've had a pleasant evening so far? Such a rare joy to have you here, and Lord Edgarton is charming, of course."

Alysoun inclined her head. "You're most kind."

"You married quite young, I understand?"

"I was twenty-two. We'd delayed briefly, actually, so Richard could finish his apprenticeship."

"He saw service in the Sudan, didn't he?" Dido was leaning forward, as if seeking something out like a terrier. It did not suit her.

"He did, but it's not something he cares to discuss. Your husband did as well, didn't he?"

"Oh, yes. He discusses it regularly, morning, noon, and night. We were quite careful you weren't seated with him, he'd bore you to pieces." Then Dido nodded. "You really are quite fortunate. Lord Edgarton was quite a catch, I understand."

Alysoun nodded. "It was an arranged match, of course." Not everyone did that, but the explanation made it clear to people. "But we have grown quite fond. And of course, we've two healthy children, now." Certainly, she was quite fond of Richard, even if she were less sure what he actually thought of her.

"That must be a joy for you. And there's a family estate?"

"Veritas, out in Kent, is the main family property. It's been in Richard's family since, goodness, the Romans."

"You're both First Families, of course." That had an air

of deference to it. Their hosts were Second and Third, respectively. It explained Dido's name - the Second Families were fond of drawing attention to their non-Roman antecedents.

"We have that privilege, yes." Alysoun went a little tight-lipped at that. "And your family?"

"Oh, Second Family. Third on Maman's side." She glanced across her room to her mother. "The house has been in her family since the 18th century."

The Terror, Alysoun rather suspected, given the choice of language there. Some families clung to the traumatic moments of their history more than others and wanted to make a point about it. "And your husband?"

"An arranged match, like yours. Only, well. I wouldn't say we're fond."

One of the other women snorted, and said, "You live in rooms at opposite ends of the house. That's not terribly fond, no."

Dido nodded slightly. "My husband is very fond of his drinks and his cigars, and spending his time at his club - he's at the Arthur, most of the time."

Alysoun nodded. "So much of men's life does seem to revolve around their clubs. Richard spends quite a lot of time at the Tower." The club for the Guard officers, beyond their set-aside places within the Guard precinct itself.

"And you were both Fox house at Schola - you must spend time in the Den?"

Alysoun nods. "When I'm in town, yes. With the little ones, that hasn't been so often the past few years." It was a way to pass off the number of days she'd had to retreat to her rooms at Veritas, barely coming out even to bathe and see the children.

"Do you care for it?"

"You weren't Fox, I assume?" Alysoun settled back. This was a much easier conversational tack.

"No, alas. Maman was very disappointed. You make connections to the best families in Fox. Horse, can you imagine? I really didn't fit in there, and I don't care for the club now. All people earnestly wanting to do good in the world. Very virtuous, I'm sure, and I'm glad someone is doing it, but I don't see why that should be me."

Alysoun could see why such a person might have been steered somewhere other than Fox, but she asked, now intrigued, "How do you fill your time, then? Do you have any particular projects?"

Dido waved a hand, languidly. "Oh, the usual social obligations. I'm chairwoman of the membership committee for the Albion Inheritance. We were rather hoping to encourage you to apply, actually."

Ah, that was the reason for the invitation, unless someone were baiting Richard for something as well. They probably were, unsubtle as that was. Alysoun inclined her head. "I spend most of my time at Veritas, overseeing things there. With Richard so busy, he entrusts the care of the estate to me. We have an excellent steward, of course, he's been there twenty years, but there are times that won't serve."

Which was true enough, she realised as she said it. Richard wanted to know the estate was being handled well. He certainly did his part of it unstintingly, from the seasonal rituals to spending hours going over the estate books. But Alysoun was the one who handled the regular expenses. And she was the one who met several times a week with the steward about all the little issues that arose, and who kept an ear out for what things around the estate and among their tenants needed his attention.

"A large estate?"

"Ancient, and yes, quite extensive, in terms of land. We have a number of tenant farmers near Veritas, of course, and there's a small village - our kind, of course." She wouldn't mention the other, non-magical village nearby there, no one would. They had a different relationship to it, but she thought it was better for everyone when they had what they needed as well. Clear water and a bit of help when there was a bad harvest or a fire. She could be lady of the manor without them knowing about magic i

"That's just the kind of thing the Albion Inheritance encourages. Proper attention to the old estates and customs. Some people want to modernise dreadfully, and I think that's such a pity."

Alysoun wasn't nearly as convinced as Dido thought she was, but she inclined her head. "I'm flattered, of course, but I don't think my commitments would permit adding something else." Especially something requiring regular travel by portal to Trellech, uncomfortable chairs, tediously tasteless food, and a lot more clothing fittings to have suffi-cient new dresses to be seen in.

Being a semi-invalid was not particularly enjoyable, but it did mean she had less of that particular kind of social tedium to deal with than she might. If she picked up a new cause at all, it would be something for the Healing Temple garden parties or gala ball, honestly. The people were more interesting, and even if they were total bores who had no other topic than their work, their work was at least meaningful.

Dido nodded, and then leaned forward again. "I heard a little gossip today, that your husband might be offered a new honour?"

Alysoun was suddenly tremendously grateful that

Richard had managed to tell her before they left. She just raised an eyebrow, as her governess had trained her. Then she set her cup and saucer gently down on the table beside her, where it was immediately swept away by one of the staff.

After a long enough silence to be clearly taking her time, she replied, "Richard is quite serious about his duties and obligations of course, as is only proper. And our family is well established, the estate in good order. If he were honoured with additional responsibilities, of course, I would be delighted to support him."

That did what it needed to, and Dido nodded once, and said, "Do keep us in mind, as well? We can't just allow our husbands to run everything, we women, now, can we?"

Alysoun nodded once, and then she turned the conversation to other topics. There was an upcoming concert she hoped to attend and expected she wouldn't.

EIGHT

6TH JULY, TRELLECH

"Simons, I have a list for you."

Richard's aide appeared a moment later from the clerk's room on the other side of the doorway. He was a year younger than Richard, dark hair slicked back, wearing the clerk's uniform of dark jacket and trousers, the badge of the Guard, and a striped cravat.

"Captain?" There was a slight precise click of his heels, everything snapping into place.

"An order of flowers, to be taken out to Veritas, with this card attached, and a matching one for the townhouse, both to Wallis's attention. This card to go on the one for the townhouse, this one to Veritas. They're labelled." He'd written them earlier that morning, before three different minor crises had ambushed him. "And pick up a box from Olden's on the upper Trivium way for me on the way back."

"The jeweller, Captain?"

"Yes. I have supper with my wife this evening, and I am not to be disturbed while I'm there. I can be found before seven or after half-nine at the townhouse."

There was a nod, then Simons said cautiously. "Not to be disturbed?"

"It is our anniversary dinner, I've arranged a private room. No less than the last six suppers we've had out, someone has interrupted. Seven seems entirely too much, under the circumstances. Alysoun is tolerant, but there are limits."

Simons was not yet married. The run-of-the-mill Guards weren't encouraged to marry until they'd made it a few more steps up the ladder. But he nodded. "Jeweller, flowers, and keeping everyone from figuring out where you are for two and a half hours." It was entirely within his capabilities.

Richard smiled. "At least two and a half, but yes. I trust you'll get it done."

Simons puffed up a little with the implied praise. "Yes, Captain. I'll get right on this." He turned around, almost bumping into a larger figure who had come up to the doorway.

"Got a minute, Richard?"

"Captain Torham, of course. Come in, close the door. Tea?" His mentor looked quite well. His hair was a grizzled red-roan, but he looked as if he'd been outside more than he managed some months. And he had quite the look of muscle under his tunic, as always.

"No, thank you. And I gather your Simons has a number of tasks to be getting on with."

"My anniversary dinner, some weeks deferred." he agreed. "We couldn't make the original plans, so..." He shrugged. It had been a bad day for Alysoun. But he'd also completely forgotten about having any evening commitments until nearly seven when he finally made it back to his office after a long day.

By the time he made it home, at eight, Alysoun had long since gone to bed, her door firmly closed. Richard had had to settle for a rather pathetic meal on his own before coming back to the office for a late night. It meant he wanted to do things properly this time.

She had been pleasant about it the next day, but he had felt the distance between them increase. None of this self-recrimination, though, was helping him in the moment.

Captain Torham shook his head. He didn't venture his advice on Richard's personal life, for all they talked about all manner of other topics given the chance, but Richard had no idea how to ask whether that was deliberate, or why. "I keep telling you not to make me your example there. I'm married to the job, but there's no reason everyone should be."

It was a long-running joke. Richard half-suspected that the Captain had some paramour tucked away. Someone he never spoke about. Whoever it was was certainly tolerant of the fact he was in the Guard precinct dawn to past sunset every working day and for eighteen or twenty hour stretches at times. Always willing to fill in when they were short-handed.

Richard certainly wasn't going to ask. Even though they were technically of equal rank in the Guard now, he couldn't even bring himself not to call Captain Torham by his forename, rather than his title or 'sir'. Realising with a start the silence had dragged on, he said, "Doing my best, sir. Is now a good time for that chat we were trying to arrange?"

"I thought so, if you can spare twenty minutes or so. I've got to be out in the training grounds in half an hour." He waved a hand. "Young bucks needing the rules and safety precautions trained into them."

"I can be brief. You did train me."

It earned him a broad approving grin, the praise that he still clung to, needed, even though he wasn't supposed to. "Go on, then."

Richard took a breath, the trick he'd learned in his first days of apprenticeship. It had been drilled into him ruthlessly not by Captain Torham but by the senior apprentices under his watch. Then he gathered his thoughts, and said, "The question of the magistrate's seal. I discussed it with Alysoun, of course, given the additional obligations for hosting. She was quite willing, and had several thoughts about rearranging some household duties. I mentioned to her that I would likely need a proper personal secretary to see to things."

Captain Torham nodded. "You don't have enough hours in the day to manage it all yourself, and there are some risks to mingling the paperwork. Best to keep it quite simple. Magistrate queries go to your personal secretary at Veritas, Guard duties come here."

Richard hadn't even considered that part of it, not in so many words, and he barely managed to suppress a flinch at how tenuous his ability to keep all the pieces in play was. "I've not had time to see about finding someone. Not even to find an agency."

"Have you considered asking your wife to review possibilities, and arrange interviews with two or three and see if they suit?" The question was quite mild, but it almost made Richard flinch again. He hadn't talked to his mentor about Alysoun's health, beyond saying she was somewhat delicate at times. The idea of asking her to take something else on bothered him.

Torham continued, "She doesn't need to interview them, but she could write up the advertisement, review letters of application as they came in, and refer the best to you. You'll get quite a few who are entirely unsuitable."

Richard swallowed, trying to hide how he felt. Torham had made a few suggestions of that kind before, here and there. Richard always took them, but silently, without discussing them afterwards. Or at least, not in more detail than a passing comment that made it clear he'd applied the advice. He wasn't sure how to talk about it more, his father had been no kind of exemplar, and his mother was worse.

He grimaced and finally figured out what to say in reply, he hoped before Torham noticed him woolgathering. "More than a few, I suspect. Even with careful wording," he agreed. "I'll, I'll ask her, and see what she says."

"Good. Now, do you have concerns about anything else?" The tone was brisk but amiable, full of the kind of confidence that Richard would pick up the important information and run with it without needing prompting. At least Torham was no longer directly nudging him about personal matters.

Richard had concerns about everything else, honestly, but saying that wouldn't do. "Largely what I mentioned, that I'm quite young for it, and people will assume it's a sinecure, earned by my blood or my title, not what skill I have. Same as the rest of it." He knew his former master would catch all the resonances. They had talked often enough about whether Richard had actually earned his rank in the Guard or just been handed it.

Torham leaned back, the wooden chair creaking slightly. "We've not enough time to have that old argument over again," he pointed out. "You know what I'll say, argue with yourself about it."

Richard snorted. He did know how it would go. And how Torham would win, not least because he was actually right, and they both knew it. The man could read him so skillfully it was impossible to come up with a proper counter. "Still. The magistrate's seal is more of that. And there's already discord about it. And I know it's complex, being Guard and magistrate both, though some people are."

"The grumbling comes from people who don't put in half the work you do. You're not showy, you just get it done. Oh, you're plenty charming when it's actually necessary, but you refuse to do it when it's just flash." He tapped the edge of the desk. "Heard you'd been out riding the Afan Forest, after the quake."

Richard nodded. "There was something odd there, I reported that much. No one's asked me about it."

"That's because your report ran right into Smedley." Who was both rather possessive about certain kinds of reports, and a slow reader.

"So it should make it off his desk round about September?" Richard's voice turned dry.

"About then, aye. You think about how you might get around that. Might do you a bit of good. Having a case that's doing something because of what you spotted."

Richard nodded, thinking through his current cases. Most of them were necessary, routine, but not the sort of thing that attracted any particular attention. Or required any particular specific expertise. Most cases for the Guard went to whoever was handy when something new came in, because so often it wasn't clear what was going on. There were specialist groups, of course, for murder, for certain kinds of magical compulsion or alteration, for more delicate matters.

His cases, though, were varied, and he rather enjoyed that. At the moment, that included a routine review of the warding protections at one of the banks, a minor embezzlement case, and most notably a case of some folks from one of the magical villages stealing from one of the non-magical communities nearby. That happened from time to time. The process for making things right was well-established but fiddly and time-consuming.

Captain Torham let him ponder it in silence for half a minute, then pushed himself standing. "I should get out to training. You come give me a proper fight next week. Get your aide to put it in the diary."

"I will, sir." Richard stood, out of politeness, until he was waved back into his seat.

"And Richard...."

Richard looked up.

"This is me reminding you, you should think about a proper apprentice. This magistrate business buys you, oh, three or four months after you take the oath before I start hounding you again. With some help."

There really was no escaping. Torham was rather like a rushing river, insistently carving a path before him.

"Sir." Richard was resigned. "I will take it under proper advisement." One more obligation he wasn't sure how to do properly, but Torham was insistent he take that on as well.

"See you do. And see you on the field." Then, with a smile, the older man got up, and made his way out the door.

Richard sighed, and once he was alone again, made a note to spend an hour or two drilling several times before next week.

NINE
THAT AFTERNOON

Alysoun was not at all certain that she should have risked two outings in the same day. There had been a talk at the museum that sounded particularly interesting, though, which happened to fall on the same day that Richard had rearranged their anniversary plans.

She had no idea how to tell him that it wasn't the anniversary that mattered, exactly. It was doing things with him, ideally things that weren't all about the social show. It was different when they were done up like peacocks, both of them, to show off finery and be charming, giving people an ideal to aspire to.

Alysoun was fortunate, in some ways. Her hair behaved in the approved styles. Richard was generous with her clothing allowance. The collection of family jewellery was extensive, and more often than not in surprisingly good taste. And she looked well enough in the currently fashionable dresses, even if she thought the pigeon-fronted designs a tad ridiculous.

The anniversary dinner would at least the two of them

on their own. He had promised her tonight. There would be none of the interruptions that had plagued their last half dozen outings. How it happened, she wasn't sure, but people found him and insisted on talking. No matter. Lecture first, supper later. And if she paid for it tomorrow, well, she had no commitments for a few days, and she could retreat to Veritas and soak in the baths.

The lecture had a promising start. They had laid out reasonably comfortable chairs in the small hall used for lectures and performances. Once she had dismissed Wallis to her own pursuits, she settled in to watch other people arriving. It was the sort of crowd she expected, with two-thirds of it women of the upper classes, largely the set who liked a bit of intellectual stimulation in among their other obligations.

She nodded across the room at a number of acquaintances. Her row had filled in early with people she didn't recognise, and there was only one seat left behind her. Since women of her social class tended to lunch before or after, they usually travelled in at least pairs, if not flocks.

That was no trouble. She'd brought along the exhibit catalogue, and thus had plenty to read and consider while she waited for the lecture to begin. Promptly at two, the lights dimmed once, and then the chief curator came out. He made the usual pleasantries, announcing the speaker, a historian of stained glass who had consulted on the exhibit, but who was not the primary organiser.

The talk began with the typical outline of what to expect. Half an hour here, to give context, and then time in the exhibit itself, to examine several pieces in more detail. There was the presentation of proper credentials, and the expected but somewhat tedious use of specialist jargon. Why academics had to prove themselves by overly complicating their explanations, she had no idea, but it seemed to be a most consistent pattern.

Professor Arden was perhaps in his forties. He wore the formal academic robes to which he was entitled in a way that rather suggested he clung to them as a visible sign of how others should respect him and hang on his every word. It wasn't the robes themselves, precisely, it was something in the set of the shoulders that reminded Alysoun of a number of the Guard officers she'd met at various functions with Richard. There was a hint of something challenging about it, as if he were prepared to have a fight he expected the regalia would win.

This exhibit was clearly a particular gem in his academic career. He kept leaning on it more than Alysoun thought entirely reasonable, given the way the catalogue and the chief curator had phrased things. She didn't know nearly enough about the power struggles of an academic, but she supposed they must have them. Every community of people she knew did somehow, once it was big enough.

She glanced down at the catalogue, sniffing quietly for a moment. Out of the corner of her eye she caught the woman behind her, who was about her age, suppressing a quick smile.

The woman was wearing the sort of robes that made Alysoun suspect she might be a member of the museum staff, or at least an apprentice in the field. Since they didn't wear a formal uniform, she wasn't certain. She was quite clearly not one of the set who was in search of idle entertainment with an intellectual veneer. In all fairness, Alysoun had to at least somewhat count herself in their number. She turned her attention back to the lecturer, frowning again. She kept doing that, and she did her best to school her face into something more socially appropriate.

Alysoun was also none too certain about some of the arguments Professor Arden made. She was no expert, but he seemed to be arguing for a through-line of design and implementation that several of the sources she'd read had insisted had been broken, with people having to reinvent techniques or figure out new options. Sometimes that had been because certain materials became less readily available, or because trained workers became in very short supply after the plague years. She frowned again, not entirely sure what to make of it.

When he finished the explanation, she considered whether it would at all be worth her time to follow him. But she was curious what he'd say about the actual pieces, and perhaps even more interested in the reaction of others in the crowd. Certainly, some of them seemed rather convinced by his arguments. When the rest of the audience followed him along the broad marble hallway to the atrium, she waited until most of them had gone past, and then brought up the end.

Conveniently, this meant she was toward the back once they got into the exhibit, and could find herself a comfortably padded bench rather than standing. The young woman who had been behind her in the lecture came into the exhibit just after Alysoun settled down. She found a place to stand, hands folded in front of her, to one side of Alysoun's bench.

Following along turned out to be worthwhile. The discussion began with some rather perfunctory remarks about a late mediaeval piece, a heraldic charge, chosen to show off particular features of colouration and contrast. Then there was a Renaissance piece, figurative, Prometheus bringing fire to mankind.

She found herself frowning yet again at some of the

description. She had thought this piece didn't have the stained enamelwork Professor Arden kept talking about, that it was the larger window with the nine Muses that he meant. Whatever else he was, he was imprecise and careless, and that did not encourage her to think well of either him or his ideas.

Then, however, he moved on to the pieces by Augustine Reynard, and Alysoun leaned forward slightly. Professor Arden made much of the mystery of the artist. It was unclear, apparently, if it was one man responsible, or a studio. Apparently having one man doing all the work wasn't impossible, but it was improbable. Professor Arden argued, rather energetically, his hand raised, his voice drumming out each point, for the idea of the individual genius. But he did not support his theories with actual facts, as far as Alysoun could tell.

He finished, in rather a pitiful decline, with a few mild comments on a contemporary piece, done for the Lord and Lady Delwyn some years ago. It depicted views from the manor house that the windows were intended for. They had apparently been generous patrons to the exhibit. Alysoun could see the museum staff looking away, as if they were avoiding difficult moments, given how brief the comments were. She looked around, and, yes, there were Lord and Lady Delwyn, an older couple she knew slightly. Not part of their closer circles, but she knew them by sight. Their elder son had been at Schola at the same time as Richard.

Finally, Professor Arden finished, and there were few questions. The chief curator thanked him, and encouraged everyone to stay and enjoy the exhibit, or of course the café was glad to provide refreshment. A fair number of people filtered out, and after a few minutes only Alysoun and a few resolute art enthusiasts were left in the exhibit. Alysoun got up to look at the Reynard pieces again, more closely, moving slowly.

"Pardon..." Alysoun startled at the quiet voice behind her right shoulder. It was the woman who had been sitting behind her.

She inclined her head. "Good afternoon." It came automatically, but that was no reason to be rude.

"Pardon, I saw you looking at these pieces, and I wondered if I could help with anything. I am Hebe Milton, I am a junior curator here." Her voice was even, but rather cautious.

Alysoun smiled, and let her gaze shift to check for a ring. "Miss Milton. Lady Alysoun Edgarton."

"Lady Edgarton." The other woman had very fine manners, and she didn't seem scared off by the title, as some were. "You were at the exhibit a week or so ago. May I ask what you find interesting?" There was an edge of eagerness to her voice.

"I was rather hoping for a bit more detail on more of the pieces. I read the catalogue, of course, after I was here earlier, and two of the books your bookshop recommended." She added the titles. "But I'm afraid the lecture wasn't exactly what I was hoping for." She waited a tiny moment, before commenting, casually and deliberately artless, "Please do convey that to your superiors, if you think it would be useful."

That earned her a flashing grin, before Hebe brought her face back into a more appropriate expression. "I will be glad to, Lady Edgarton. And of course, if you were to write a letter, they take those most seriously, especially from our regular patrons."

"I rather had the impression Professor Arden's actual role in the exhibit was relatively small. Was he the one who pressed for these pieces to be included? Is that a particular specialty of his?"

Alysoun got another of those flashing smiles, which she felt were quite charming, even if she probably shouldn't encourage them. "Very insightful, my lady." Hebe fell quiet, as if needing to sort out what was permissible to say. "Professor Arden did make a case, successfully, as you see, for the inclusion of the Reynard pieces. May I ask why you're interested in those in particular?"

"When I was first here, I was caught by something about the colour of the light. No, not the colour itself, but the quality of it. I'm afraid I don't have the technical vocabulary to explain it, it's rather frustrating. And reading the supplemental materials didn't answer my questions, either." Alysoun considered, then asked, "I gather Professor Arden hasn't published anything on Reynard?"

Hebe shook her head at the last question, and considered. "May I ask which pieces particularly drew your notice that way? If that wouldn't be a bother, my lady."

Alysoun shook her head. "Give me a moment, but certainly." She then shifted, taking the weight off the hip that was starting to ache. Then she moved slowly, with what she hoped looked like graceful ease, to look at the four pieces that were on display from Reynard.

"This one, the flowers, seems comparable to the other contemporary pieces. The colours, the design." She then gestured. "But this one, the heraldry, there's something in the yellow, here, that seems a bit odd. Out of keeping with the other yellows. And this one, the way it shades through the browns, the mottling is curious."

"You have an excellent eye, my lady. Do you have formal art training?"

"Oh, not more than is expected of someone who lives in

a house with rather a lot of art collected over the years. Veritas is on the tour schedule for next month, we've several fine windows."

"I'm especially hoping to attend that. The library, isn't it? And the great hall?"

Alysoun nodded. "They're very striking pieces, and complement each other, while not being directly similar. I've always rather liked the contrasts." She then turned back to the Reynard pieces. "And this one, here, isn't that opalescent white an entirely different technique?"

"We had wondered the same thing, yes, but the research available to us suggested Reynard might have been experimenting. Others were doing similar things around that time. There's a specific alchemical process."

Alysoun nodded. "Perhaps you might recommend some additional reading? And about what's known about this Reynard."

Hebe bobbed slightly. "Of course, my lady. Would you perhaps take tea in the cafe while I find some items that would suit? It will take me a few minutes."

"That will do quite well, thank you." She could scarcely follow the young woman back to whatever desk or office she might have.

TEN

THAT EVENING

The evening's plans had gone well, Richard thought.

Alysoun had looked lovely when she came out of her rooms. He didn't know much about fashion, other than that it mattered, in its minute details, to many of the people they socialised with. He was glad he could fall back on his Guard uniform most of the time, and that his other social obligations were nearly as clear about the expectations.

He appreciated that Alysoun not only navigated those crocodile infested waters with apparent ease, but chose things that he particularly liked on her. He suspected that part was a trifle harder than it looked, based on what he saw other women wearing. There were all sorts of frocks that looked rather uncomfortably tight or binding, or came with an overabundance of ruffles.

He had been delighted to escort her from the carriage to their private dining room. Their supper had been set up in a rooftop garden terrace in the centre of Trellech, a rare chance to enjoy a beautiful night and a fair bit of privacy.

Charmed curtains, so finely woven they were barely noticeable, kept out any possible insects and kept the noise from around them to a quiet murmur. The necessary intrusions of the staff had been brief and utterly professional. The wine selections had been excellent. He still felt nervous about that, as if the sommelier was judging his choices. His father had had a famous, even infamous palate, and Richard knew he did not measure up. In that way, and in rather a lot of others, he felt.

The conversation had been a touch less easy, there had been awkward pauses on both sides. Sometimes he found it easy to talk to his wife, but at other times, he looked at her, and he didn't know her at all. What she cared about. She handled the duties of being his wife, mother of his children, with great attention to the finest details, barring the limitations of her illness. But he still had remarkably little idea of her likes and dislikes, other than some of the books and music she enjoyed.

He had almost inquired about the art museum, but each time he'd thought about it, something else had come up. Now they were drawing up in the carriage to go back to the town house, and he knew there would be at least a few messages waiting for him. Suddenly, he didn't want to deal with them at all, and murmured, "May I escort you to your chambers?" It was not at all the usual sort of thing, and he quite hated to impose his presence upon her unnecessarily. But once again he was there, blurting out his impulses to her like a schoolboy.

She blinked, but then she smiled. "Of course. I'd enjoy your company a bit longer."

They climbed the stairs at her pace, which was to say rather slowly, but Richard was willing to take the time. Wallis was waiting by the door, but Alysoun said "Unfasten me, and take my hair down, if you would, and then you can go to bed, Wallis."

Wallis's eyes widened for a moment, but there was a bob, and a "Yes, my lady." Alysoun turned, letting her maid undo the fastenings, but not shrugging the dress off. Another thirty seconds, and all the essential pins had been undone, and then there were the swift movements of brushing and plaiting Alysoun's long hair into a loose braid.

"You braid it?" He blinked. Every time he'd come to her bed, her hair had been loose.

"Generally, yes. For sleeping. It keeps it from tangling." She then rolled her shoulders, and nodded. "Thank you, Wallis. I'll ring if I need anything." There was another little bob, a quick aborted move toward the dressing table to tidy up, and then the maid withdrew.

Leaving Richard alone with his wife, who was, if not actually undressed, rather more so than he'd seen her recently. The baths didn't count, there had been clouds of steam.

Alysoun watched him, her body entirely still, before she arched an eyebrow, and went over to a screened corner of the bedroom, saying over her shoulder. "Do have a seat, if you'd like. Talk to me?"

Talk. That did not suggest a subject. There was a light behind the screen, enough to show the shadow of her silhouette through the front. He had no way to ask whether she meant that or not. He had a sudden realisation that she might, in fact, have set this up, in hopes of drawing him into her bed again. But he couldn't tell if she were actually inviting him, or wishing to continue the conversation more innocently. He certainly couldn't ask, because if he got it wrong, she would never forgive him. And rightfully so, really.

Retreating through the adjoining door into his dressing room would be cowardly. And also unforgivable.

"Richard?" A reminder that he had been silent entirely too long.

He coughed. "It was delightful to have a few hours without anyone knocking to demand my attention."

"Do feel free to hide up here from the notes that have certainly arrived in your absence." Now he was certain she was teasing him deliberately, but he still couldn't figure out what she wanted.

He watched the shadowy form of her body through the screen. She had definitely removed the dress now, there was a long blurry fall of fabric that hadn't been there a few moments ago. She was moving in a way that suggested she was taking something else off, shadows of shoulders and arms moving. Then, finally, brave enough to venture a part of the questions tumbling around in his head, he said "How are you feeling?"

She stuck her head around the screen. "Better than expected, actually. The museum was, well." She paused. "There's a thing I'd like to talk out with you, but perhaps not tonight." She retreated again, shrugging on another garment of some kind. A dressing gown, perhaps, there seemed to be plenty of fabric.

"But you enjoyed it?" He didn't know where to start asking her things. This wasn't an interrogation, after all. He knew how to do those, when called upon. He didn't want to demand she answer, but he knew he wanted to keep her talking.

Alysoun laughed, as if he'd said something hilarious. "Goodness. The professor they had speaking was awful. I need to write a firm note to the museum tomorrow about it.

But the chairs were comfortable, and I had an interesting conversation with one of the junior curators."

Richard was now entirely sure that he'd fallen into some obscure hole, and he was falling ever downward. He moved back, bumped into the bed, and did his best to perch on it, making it look like he'd meant to do that. She came out from behind the screen, drawing the dressing gown closed, tying the sash. She came to settle on the bed, more or less facing him.

There was a terribly awkward silence, that got longer and longer, until he realised it was his turn to say something. He was, he admitted, distracted by her being this close, about this intimacy he hadn't felt with her in ages. And by the continuing confusion about what she wanted.

A sensible man, who was competent and able to deal with new situations with aplomb, would ask. He was a trained officer in the Guard, for Arthur's sake. And yet, all that training fled him. His usual fallback - think what Captain Torham would do, and do the same - failed him utterly.

Finally, he said, almost stuttering. "I'm glad you've been feeling better. I was wondering if you might enjoy a trip to one of the spas. Before things get busy with the necessary winter entertaining."

She blinked at him, her eyes going wide for a moment, and then somehow, she withdrew. "Sending me away?"

"Oh, no, no, goodness, not that. But I know it's difficult for you, and you do so much, keeping the household going, I just thought." He swallowed, then offered, more weakly. "Captain Willoughby mentioned a spa her sister likes, and I just thought...." His voice trailed off.

"The same sister who has been looking for another post as a companion?" Alysoun's voice stayed even, firm, not rising in pitch. The officer in him was impressed, more than impressed. The man, the husband, the rest of him, was wincing.

"Um. Yes."

"I do not need a companion." Her voice stayed even, each word like the beat of a drum. "I do not need to go away to one of the fashionable spas. They will not tell me anything useful. Whatever remedies they have will be temporary. And honestly, likely both embarrassing and uncomfortable. I can get plenty of that without leaving home."

"But I just -" He stopped, and swallowed. "Is there anything you would like that I could help arrange?"

She looked him up and down, then her eyes shifted to the side. "Not that I can think of tonight."

The change in the mood of the room was definite, like a harsh light or a bucket of cold water. He deserved it, he knew. Standing, he said, quietly, "You were lovely tonight. I enjoyed it. I'd like to take you out again, much sooner than next anniversary, without interruptions."

That earned him a slight incline of her head. "You will have to see that no one knows where to find us then. Set yourself to the challenge." It was unyielding, and somehow, in the midst of that, he found tremendous respect for her.

"A suitable challenge." And then, daring, he said, "I feel a bit like some knight, sent off on a quest, my lady." Perhaps couching this in a more proper mode for courtly love might do something. Redeem him. It had worked in the romances of Roland and Arthur and Tristan he'd read as a boy. At least for a while.

Alysoun inclined her head, and then she considered, reaching into the dressing gown pocket, and drawing out an entirely fresh silk handkerchief, lace trimmed. "A proper favour, then." She tapped a fold of the cloth on his arm, she was close enough for that, and then stretched out her hand. "Find another time to take me out to supper, good sir knight."

He nodded, and stood, bowing. "My lady." He then ventured, "Sleep well. Should I send Wallis up again?"

"No, I'm fine. Thank you."

He couldn't ask why she was thanking him without risking hurting her again, so he just bowed once more, and retreated.

ELEVEN
8TH JULY, VERITAS

Alysoun felt like she had not only gotten out of the wrong side of the bed, but like she had gotten into the wrong side of the bed. Everything ached. There was a sharp pain in her shoulder she couldn't will away or even stretch out. Her head felt like cotton wool, all the worst parts of overindulgence without any of the pleasure of it.

She knew perfectly she had gotten out of bed on the same side as always, putting her right foot down first, as tradition dictated. Or superstition. By the time she managed to get her eyes to focus, Wallis was standing there with her dressing gown, the enveloping deep blue. "Cane, my lady?"

Alysoun grimaced, considered, then shifted her weight cautiously. "Yes, please." She begrudged the cane, but the way she felt she was risking a fall, and that wouldn't help anything. She hated having to be this unrelentingly sensible, always having to think ahead to what would fail her next. Not that thinking was easy at the moment. "Something comfortable today. I plan to settle in the library."

"Of course, my lady. The pale green tea gown?"

Alysoun nodded, waving her hand. "And my hair up simply. I've a headache already." It was tempting to consider one of the little potion bottles on the dressing table. But she wanted to be able to think today, if she could, and none of those little glass jars would help with that.

"Of course, my lady. Do you wish the baths first?"

Alysoun nodded. "I'll be half an hour or so." She suspected Richard was already long gone, peering out the window. She'd slept fitfully, but it was well into the morning. Glancing at the clock, she was sure he was away to Trellech again, it was half nine. "If you'd tell Mrs Glenwilliam to have a meal for - half ten, and something light for lunch around one, that would do."

"Yes, my lady. Shall I come down with you?"

Alysoun shook her head. "No, no." She didn't want anyone fussing over her, even Wallis, who usually was practical about it. Her previous lady's maid, dismissed in the first six months of her illness, was always bringing her things. Worse, she was always tutting over the heat or the cold or the height and angle of the pillows. Alysoun had found she couldn't bear it.

Newcomb was a fine lady's maid now for a woman a bit older who needed a bit of fussing and apparently thrived on it. Every time Newcomb's new mistress ran into Alysoun at a party, she went into frothy praise, wondering how Alysoun could bear to have let her go.

No matter. Wallis suited very well, and Alysoun tried not to be too difficult. She pulled the dressing gown more tightly around her. When she shifted the cane from right hand to left, she determined that the left was better today, and could then make her way slowly down the back stairs to the baths.

Wallis must have already come through, because there

was steam, not just the usual hot water in the tub. Alysoun sluiced herself off, then made her way carefully over to the great hot soaking tub, settling into it with a groan of pleasure mingled with aches.

She spent at least twenty minutes just sitting there, letting the hot water melt away some of the pain. Then she began doing some of the stretches she'd found that helped. It was infuriating that the healers she'd seen had no idea what to suggest. All they had been certain of was that her pain seemed to be related to curious and somewhat unpredictable tension in her muscles. That wasn't all of it, but it was the part they all admitted was happening.

A few minutes later, she heard Wallis from the entrance to the baths, her voice echoing against the stone. "My lady? Everything is laid out in the dressing room here."

They had built one down here, a year ago, constructing it out of a smaller room that might, once, have been something like a storage room. A more fantastical mind might think it a priest's hole, but that was foolishness, the family had never needed to hide such a thing. It did spare her going back upstairs to change after a bath. "Thank you, Wallis."

She rose in the bath, made her way carefully up the steps, using the sturdy railing added three generations ago, when the resident Lord became more frail, and much appreciated now. Then Wallis had a warm towel to wrap her in, and was leading the way to hold the door of the dressing room open.

It made for a small and rather ridiculous processional, but then she could sit on the comfortably padded chair, lean back, and relax. Wallis had even made sure the room was quite warm. That was easy, with them being so close to the hypocaust for the baths, and the profusion of warm air circulating. But it meant opening the vents and catches in good time for the room to heat up.

Wallis got her settled in the proper position, spreading out her hair to dry, combing the tangles out, letting the heat warm it. While it dried, she applied the necessary lotions. Even if no one other than the staff would see her, there were certain expectations, and she must look put together unless she spent the day in bed. That was depressing and tedious, so she tried to do it as little as possible. It worried the children, besides.

She opened her mouth, but Wallis had already anticipated that. "I thought that Nanny might bring the little ones down to join you for lunch, my lady, and a little treat for them, if that suits."

"Thank you, Wallis. You do think of everything." It earned her a smile, and Wallis went along with the other morning tasks. Wallis also had quite gentle hands, enough that the necessary fussing and pinning didn't hurt.

That left Alysoun alone with her thoughts. Last night, she had wanted Richard to stay, but she had found herself unable to say so. He'd been so proper about it, from the very beginning. Very clear that he found her attractive, but that he wouldn't presume, wouldn't press her. They had, she had thought, pleasant enough times in bed. He had certainly seemed delighted with her, and her responses.

But as soon as they were sure she was pregnant, he had kept to his own room. He came in a few times, late in pregnancy, to check on her, when he hadn't seen her all day. But after her illness began in earnest, he didn't even do that. They'd attempted time in bed together a few times after Charlotte, but something in it had pained her, visibly, in a way she couldn't describe to him, and he had withdrawn. He had seemed almost ashamed, but she had not been able to figure out exactly why, and she had no idea how to ask.

Part of her wanted another child, but her logic agreed with the Healers that it would be a dangerous thing. But like every woman with enough magic in her blood, she knew ways to keep from pregnancy and still have the pleasure of the bed. If her husband would share it, however briefly.

She had wondered if he had a mistress. She wouldn't blame him, of course. To begin with, blame was an entirely useless thing to put into the mix. It did no one much good, unless it helped identify something to be solved. And she had to admit, for all she'd fulfilled her marriage contract - and admirably, two lovely, intelligent, healthy children - she felt there was something missing.

She'd unstintingly gone to the social events he wanted her to attend. She'd built up her own circles among the wives of the Guard and the few men outside the Guard married to officers, though those weren't exactly friends. More like people to talk to at the necessary functions. There were the equally necessary philanthropic endeavours, though she could not help with those as much as she ought. She could at least blame being at Veritas for much of it.

It left her feeling hollow, though. Her parents had had a marriage much like hers, and they had been amiably but distantly fond. Appreciative of each other, without any understanding of the other's sphere beyond the places they met at a gala or a project. Her mother could be anxious and fussy, but she had shown Alysoun that it was entirely possible to have a life of her own interests as well as marriage.

Good thing too, since the marriage had been nearly mandatory, as the only way to resolve three different inheritance tangles. One set of properties and income now devolved on Gabriel, one on Charlotte, and one was held as a dower for Alysoun herself. All extremely old-fashioned, but her family had had its traditions for generations.

Which just brought her back to Richard. He wasn't a stupid man, so she could only assume he had some reason for not even responding to her invitation. Though now she thought about it, perhaps she hadn't been entirely clear. Or perhaps he needed something else, to encourage him?

She frowned, trying to remember how they had worked it when they were focusing on having the children. As far as she recalled, they had just both been clear what was needed, and when it would do the most good. They had gone about it with a good will, treating each other quite well in the process.

She still couldn't forget the sound he made when he was overwhelmed with pleasure, or the look in his eyes, however brief, afterwards. There had been something there of him putting a great burden down for a little while. It was the sort of expression that made her want him to have that over and over. The sort of expression that made her want to understand how she had that kind of power, and what it meant for him.

Instead, what they had was awkward conversations, distance, and a kind of amiable respect. It was much better than some of her social circle, but not at all satisfying to Alysoun. Not emotionally, not intellectually, and certainly not physically.

Then Wallis was putting things away, and it was time for her to go and have food. Then at least she could curl up on the long chaise in the library and lose herself in books for a bit.

TWELVE
13TH JULY, TRELLECH

It was the end of that week before Alysoun managed to make it back to Trellech, and specifically to the art museum. The intervening fortnight had been filled with a mix of fuzzy-headed awfulness, her body rebelling again, and the necessary rearrangement to the household for Richard's new role.

Dealing with Mrs Glenwilliam had taken a good deal of delicacy. She had to balance making sure Mrs Glenwilliam knew she was valued and respected, but they were offering her this position that would let her be closer to her family, and still able to provide the excellent service she'd provided for years.

It would be a slow transition, as the employment agency Alysoun preferred had several potential candidates for Veritas, but none of them were in a position to interview immediately. Two were on demanding short-term contracts, looking for something longer and steadier. One was abroad with his current employer, and would be returning in August. Two others were possible, but the agency had sounded uncertain if they'd want a household position, and were going to inquire.

The same agency was putting together a portfolio of possible candidates for a personal secretary for Richard, to handle correspondence. Richard hadn't had a chance to review those yet, she knew. He had been terribly busy with something since that tedious end to their anniversary evening. She didn't think he was deliberately avoiding her, just using the press of his work as a reason not to come to Kent, and to stay in Trellech.

Nothing could be done about that now, so she could set it aside, and return to Trellech again to address the necessary matters that could not be done at Veritas. There were visits from the dressmaker she preferred, to acquire a few dresses for events around Richard's investiture as magistrate, and several other occasions hovering in the future. It was none too early to think about winter gatherings, either, and there was the dress for the harvest rituals for her to make final decisions about.

Along with the shoes and accoutrements, and checking the family vault for jewellery to match colours to, that had taken the better part of two days. It was at least sorted for now, other than the future fittings, and those could more easily be done at Veritas, if needed. It was the initial planning that required the dressmaker's bolts of cloth and albums of lacework.

She hadn't seen Richard at all, even here, barring a few passing moments in the hallway, one of them on their way in or out. He looked a bit drawn, but she could not figure out how to ask. He did not often discuss his work with her, she had figured that much out, and he had not had time for even the most efficient supper out. Perhaps next week.

Now, she climbed the steps of the museum slowly, but

steadily. The summer had settled into something warmer, though the weather scryers were making rather dire predictions about heat and drought later in the month. The museum seemed quiet, without much hustle and bustle. Wallis trailed just behind her, handbag over her arm, hat on her head, and Alysoun stopped at the door. "I expect to be in the library, if you'd like some time on your own."

There was the kind of pause that made Alysoun sure someone had had a word with Wallis again about not leaving her alone. Whether that was Richard, or the healer who'd been out last week, she had no idea. "If you prefer, my lady."

"I do." Alysoun was firm. "You may come fetch me for tea, at four." She had had lunch at the town house, she could manage three hours or so on her own.

Wallis froze for a moment, but was entirely too aware of the necessary obedience here to argue. "Yes, my lady. I do have a few errands. Thread for those gloves."

Alysoun nodded. "You'd find my reading very boring, as well."

"Yes, my lady." That earned her a small smile. Wallis did not understand how Alysoun could have her nose in a book at all possible times. Alysoun kept failing to explain how it let her learn so much more than she'd ever see and do herself. She had a regimented predictable life, with the obligations and duties of her station, and bounded even more severely by the limitations of her body. Books were the most reliable escape, except when the pain or the foggy confusion were too much.

And with that, Wallis took herself back down the broad marble steps, and Alysoun went in. She had written to say she'd like to consult some items in the library earlier in the week. As soon as she appeared, one of the staff members came out and offered an escort. "Our librarian is most glad to help you, my lady. Please do let us know if you need anything else."

There were times the title was useful. And she was developing a reputation as a reliable patroness of the museum. Richard's mother preferred the musical arts, the opera and the chamber orchestra, but Alysoun found concerts often difficult to deal with these days, physically, as much as she missed them. At the museum she could sit when she needed to, stand and walk when she needed to, and no one would think much of it. Even the lectures usually were under an hour, or involved some walking around. In a performance, her standing could be seen as a great slight, even if they were in the family's traditional box.

The assistant led her along down a wood panelled hall, and stopped by double doors, with a neat label proclaiming that this was the art library. Then he held the door for her, finally leading her over to a small office off the main room. "Eunice, this is Lady Edgarton, who had the question about some of our materials. Lady Edgarton, Mistress Eunice Ogden, our chief librarian."

The chief librarian was well into her fifties, a rather sturdily built woman whose hair was salt and pepper, braided and pinned into a crown around her head. She wore the sort of sensible robes in muted colours that Alysoun expected of a senior member of the museum staff. There was a single brooch of rather nicely designed sterling silver with a wreath of enamelled harvest flowers.

Alysoun smiled, and inclined her head. "I do appreciate your taking time out of your day to help me. I do hope I won't be a bother."

Eunice and the assistant exchanged a look. They were deft enough at it Alysoun couldn't accurately read their intent, but she was sure they were wondering how difficult she'd be. The librarian nodded. "It's no bother at all. I've set out the books in the library, at our most comfortable desk, and the best light. Do, please, come this way? Thank you, William."

The assistant bowed, and Alysoun smiled at him. "Most helpful." She knew how this dance went and the necessary steps, particularly to put them at ease about her likelihood of being demanding. Then Eunice Ogden was leading her to a broad wooden table, with a comfortable looking padded chair and good light from tall windows, glazed in a pale opaque glass.

"Are the windows to prevent damage to the books?"

"They are, though they are not actually glass, for all they look it. They are made from thin sheets of marble. They do block light from harming the books, while allowing us to see. And of course, they are much less likely to shatter in a bad storm."

Alysoun turned, rather than crane her neck, and took a step closer to peer at the material, which indeed had the shifts of colour and veining she'd expect in stone. "How fascinating. And the glass I'm interested in?"

"You said you had read our exhibit catalogue, and the two other recommended works. I have copies for reference, but I thought these might better serve your questions. Here is what we have about Augustine Reynard, and here is a detailed overview of artists working at the same time as the bulk of his work. This one," she tapped a volume bound in a dusty purple. "Is rather more technical, but the senior curator for the exhibit assures me he would be delighted to speak with you if you have questions."

Alysoun nodded. "Not your area of expertise, then?" She said it with a smile.

Eunice shook her head. "The materials about the topic, yes, but glassmaking is even more technically complex than most colour work. I've picked up some, but alchemical design was never one of my strong points." She asked, after a moment, "You were at Schola, my lady?"

"Yes. And I did take alchemy, though I've not done much with it since leaving school." Not since they'd arranged her marriage to Richard. Alchemy did have risks in pregnancy, she'd not have taken the chance. And now that that was not a concern, she didn't trust herself not to spill something at the worst time. Then, she added, in case that was where Eunice had been angling, "Fox House, but I spent a lot of time with Mistress Hayes, in the Ritual lecture room."

Eunice inclined her head. "My daughter asked to be remembered to you. Iseult Ogden, she was, now Iseult Morgan, a year behind you."

"Oh, yes. Please do pass on my good wishes. And I would love to catch up, if she might be free for tea sometime. I had a conversation once with her, my last year, about anchoring ritual magics in an object, that turned out to be quite helpful for something at Veritas."

As Alysoun had hoped, Eunice beamed at that. "Oh, if it wouldn't be a bother." Alysoun shook her head, and reached for her small bag, drawing out a calling card. "A message at the townhouse or through the portal mail will get to us quite promptly. I am back and forth between Veritas and Trellech, but the staff at the house will know our expected return."

"Of course. You must be quite busy. We did hear the news, of course, about Lord Edgarton being among the next to take the magistrate's seal."

"Quite busy." Alysoun smiled. "But not too busy for a

good conversation." Then she gestured. "I'm sure I'll have some more questions, but perhaps if I start out on my own, and go from there?"

"Of course, of course."

Alysoun settled in, drawing out the small journal she'd brought for notes, feeling satisfied with the exchange. Now, if the research went as well, it would be a fine day.

THIRTEEN
THAT SAME DAY

The day had begun early and it had not improved. By lunchtime, Richard had the itch between his shoulder blades that made him sure something was going to happen. Master Trenton had said it was a useful touch to pay attention to, wherever it came from, but Richard distrusted things he couldn't lay out logically.

Instead, he'd gone down to the duelling field, hoping Captain Torham might have a few moments. When he got there, Torham was finishing up with a lecture on safety and sense to the apprentices, but he nodded at Richard. "Suit up, I'll just be a minute. You lot can stick around and see what proper duelling looks like."

Richard snorted, and ducked into the equipment room, finding his particular cupboard and pulling on the proper vest and gloves that would keep his shirt from being a flapping distraction. He pulled them on, and then went out. The floor of the salle was clear, the apprentices back in the protected viewing gallery. Torham had appointed one of them, a somewhat gangly young man, to do the officiating.

"Gorham rules, Richard?" Three touches, no charms

that would do lasting damage, making your opponent fall on their face thanks to a stunning spell spell was entirely permitted.

"Gorham, sir." Richard took up his place facing.

The apprentice swallowed, looking daunted. "Sirs. The proposal is a duel for the benefit of our training."

Torham laughed. "And ours, lad, and ours. Education all round." It made Richard grin, and the apprentice relaxed slightly. It was their chance to challenge each other. They knew each other well, from hours here and on the field outside, and Richard considered it part of his duty to bring something new to their duels now.

"Gorham rules, or five minutes." They'd get to three touches inside of two, Richard was sure. They were both excellent duellists, but that often meant things went very quickly indeed.

He nodded. "Agreed." He heard Torham echo it.

"Withdraw to your places, salute, and wait for my count." The apprentice was more sure now, this was the part that was the same every time. Richard turned, went precisely to the spot between two of the supporting pillars at the edges of the salle, and pivotted. Torham had done the same, and they faced each other, twenty feet apart.

Richard drew the wand from the holster that held it along his spine, and made a formal precise salute, first to the land, then to the sky, then across his heart. Torham did the same, and then he heard the count. "On my mark. Three, two, go."

The initial exchange was a flurry of charms. Richard set his own protections, and he could see Torham's more aggressive attempts bouncing off the shield charms. He hesitated, though, on his own attack, the uneasiness of his day making him uncertain how to go forward.

"You're overthinking, Richard. You can't stay behind your walls forever." It was, to be fair, something Torham said rather often. Richard took a step back, then bounced on his toes, feeling the magic in his blood shake out, like freeing a stone stuck in his boot. Then he advanced, a series of short sharp pulses of glowing golden light shooting out. Torham blocked them, of course, but not as easily as he might.

They went on like that for several exchanges. Richard's shielding slipped, as he had to lurch to one side, and he ended up with a single line of blood, like a scratch, along one arm. He got his own back, a charm that made the ground feel like a bog. They both managed a second touch, and then a third, almost simultaneously with each other.

"Yield!" Richard put the cry up first, but Torham was right behind him. They both lowered their wands. Both bent to one knee, pressing a hand into the wood of the salle floor, sending the extra energy from the duel into the walls and protections. By the time Richard stood again, Torham was standing and walking toward him, holding out his hand.

"An excellent duel, RIchard. You'll have to show me that bog cantrip, that's new, isn't it? And your stunning charms are much steadier, that cock of the wrist makes quite a difference. If I weren't me, that would have been quite effective."

Richard grinned right back, shaking Torham's hand. "Of course, sir. When you've a chance." Then he bowed. "I should get back to work."

"And I've got this lot to do something with. Right, all of you. Up for a bit of exercise."

He'd only been back in his office for twenty minutes when he heard the alarm bell go, the signal for all available to assemble. "What's the word, Simons?" Richard grabbed the few things from his office he might want - emergency healing kit, compass, paper and pencil. He glanced at his hand, then grabbed the tin of salve from his desk, rubbing a line of it down the scratch to start it healing.

"Something on the Severn, sir. All capable hands to block passage down river." The larger river, then, not the nearer Wye.

That meant something substantial was going on. "Any idea of the cause?"

"Theft or smuggling, sir. Care to be taken with cargo." Simons held out Richard's token, to be dropped into the duty bucket.

"Huh." Richard set off at a run, his footsteps echoing along with a dozen other people's as they poured through the halls. While he ran, he was thinking hard. Something on the river big enough to call them out in force meant someone would need to be on hand for illusions, for the non-magical folk. Possibly even memory alteration, though that was a delicate thing.

As he made it into the courtyard, he saw Franes and Beffort, the two top illusionists, arms crossed. Captain Arthur stood beside them, her foot tapping, ready to be released to go see to the mind-altering magics if required.

Captain Torham was in the centre, directing people into groupings as they came out. As soon as he spotted Richard, there was a "Richard, take a group to the Sharpness lock, see if you can catch them there. You four, with Captain Edgarton. Ride fast, there are horses waiting. If it's clear, come down river. The code is Hour of Mercury."

Richard nodded, saluting. "Orders received, Captain Torham. Hour of Mercury. To horse." The four assigned to him fell into formation, pair and pair, two men and two women. They quickly all settled into the same loping run drilled into them during training that covered ground with the least exertion. First to the portal, then to Lydney, to spare the horses the gallop all the way to the lock. Guard running through the streets of Trellech would worry people, but if this were a serious incident, there was no helping that. And the Guard did frequent enough training runs that it shouldn't be too alarming.

As he led the way to Portal Square, he got a glance at the four with him. All steady established men and women, experienced guards, no apprentices, older than Richard, but they seemed willing enough to follow his lead.

He got them up to the portals in a neat amount of time, through, and on the other side, the horses were waiting, including a long-legged bay for Richard. The mare turned out to have an easy trot, then a pleasant canter. The Guard with him picked up an easy formation behind him, heading straight for the Sharpness lock. There was no way to send a message downstream without someone taking it, so they were on their own and without more information.

Richard hailed the lock keeper's cottage, and got a grumpy "No one due."

"Captain Edgarton. Seal this lock until further notice." He summoned every bit of command voice. What he couldn't tell by looking was whether the man were magical or not, and that would affect what he did next.

"Why's that?" The man didn't seem to find a woman in uniform unusual, so that suggested he was at least enough in tune with his magic for that.

Richard nodded. "Orders from the Guard." He didn't elaborate. Captain Torham had drilled into him that you said as little as you could at this stage in an alarm.

"See your medallion?" Asking for that instead of a badge or card made it clear the man was magica. That was much simpler.

Richard tugged the chain out from under his uniform jacket, pressing the clips that kept his medallion attached. He held it out in his flat hand, leaning down from the horse. The man came over and peered at it.

It was the standard Guard medallion, the one he'd earned when he finished his apprenticeship, an inch in diameter. Stamped on it were the walls of Trellech, surrounded by five words: diligence, justice, prudence, temperance, and truth. In English, rather than the original Latin, so they could be read by anyone literate. "Captain Edgarton, based in Trellech." People had a right to know who was giving the order.

The lock keeper straightened, nodding. "Can I get a hand? Take half the time." One of the Guards, one of the women with a dark braid down her back, had vaulted off her horse and gone across to the other side.

That made the next steps easier, at least. "Someone will let you know, the code phrase is Hour of Mercury. If they don't tell you that, don't open anything." It wasn't a perfect system, but it worked well enough.

The old man muttered, but then moved off to twist the wheel that locked things. Another of his riders was getting down to charm it in place and hand over the proper token to the keeper for him to confirm to whoever came to open things up.

Richard reattached the medallion to the clips and slipped it under his uniform again and waited for the man to be done with the task. "No one has been by?"

"Not since first thing this morning, either direction. Been a quiet day on the river."

Richard nodded. "I would keep out of the way, until you see the Guard come to open things. Tricky business, I gather." Then he gestured, and his two riders remounted.

He switched into the Guard's Tongue, as was proper giving orders with an audience, the phrases flowing readily. "We ride downstream. You two, look to the far bank, anything of note. You two, to the right." He knew there would be others going further upstream, who would cover this far down.

They nodded, and he cued his mare into a loping canter along the river road. It was at least in good shape at the moment, no mud to be a danger.

They made it three miles, maybe four, at a steady canter, before they saw signs of anything afoot, exchanging names and specialities briefly as they rode. They'd made it past Brookend when the woman with the dark braid, Guard Martin, called out in the Tongue, "Ship downstream. And I see Franes."

"Full speed."

They set off at a proper gallop, a short enough distance the horses should be fine. When they got past the curve of the river, Richard could see a trow, one of the long flat cargo boats, pulled to one side. It had been forced there by a shallow spot in the river, or at least the appearance of one.

He suspected Franes, who was up on a hill looking down on the river, partially silhouetted in the changing light. There was fighting on the deck, all hand to hand. They all urged their horses on, coming to a stop just short of the boat and vaulting off to join the fray at Richard's order in the Tongue, "Go to."

The Guard there had been slowly gaining control, but an additional five allies turned the tide promptly. Richard used his wand to hobble two of the boat's crew. Instead of his hesitation in a duel, wanting to see what would happen, he felt everything flowing, snapping into place. He quickly picked out the man at the centre of the mess, well-dressed. The boat's owner, or perhaps the owner of the cargo, who was perhaps a boxer. He'd just landed a solid punch on one of the Guard.

Richard's stunning charm hit square on, and he fell like a toppled tree, most satisfying, and within another minute, the skirmish was over. Richard had always been particularly proud of his ability to take someone down without injury, how they collapsed the way he chose, onto a floor or some other safe space, and, in this case, not overboard.

The boat was in foul shape, already taking on water through a gash in the side, and the whole place smelled awful, like there was something rotting. Rather like slugs in a garden, Richard thought. There didn't seem to be much of note. His group was set to looking for any hidden compartments.

They found a few piles of spoiled and molding tobacco, some grain that smelled too much of ergot for anyone's comfort, and several things none of them wanted to touch except with a long stick. It suggested the boat had been pressed into service unexpectedly, somehow. The various hidden compartments were empty, though Richard kept glancing at their captives to see if their eyes flicked anywhere in particular, but as far as he could tell, there was nothing they were missing.

Searching the captives was also unrewarding. There were six of them, four who'd been managing the ship, the captain, and the man who seemed like an owner. That last one was wearing decently made magical cloth, with that particular shade of mauve that was in fashion two years ago. Someone fallen on harder times, perhaps.

He refused to give his name, and he had no identifying jewellery on him. No signet ring, no badge from Schola or any of the other Five Schools. Richard thought he looked slightly familiar, but most of the Great Families looked slightly familiar to him, that was no help. And he could be a by-blow, someone Richard had never met.

It took a good two hours to round everyone up and do a preliminary investigation of the ship, before turning it over to the senior Guard as they arrived. The one thing they sorted out, as new information came in, was that the boat had been going slowly, noticeably slowly, or else they might well have had it slip through their fingers.

In the end, Richard was left with their captives, waiting for wagons to come from Trellech and take them back for questioning under Silence oath. At least there was still plenty of light at this point in the summer, and they wouldn't be doing the last part of the trip in the dark.

All of their captives, down to the lowest member of the crew, had been keeping their mouths firmly shut, like there was some oath already in play. Richard found it curious, and he wanted to ask about it, but he didn't know any of the senior Guards well enough to ask them. And he didn't see Captain Torham.

It was only once they were bundled off, with his group assigned to guard them, but his presence not required, that the pace let up a bit. Finally, Richard could ask, "Does Captain Torham need help?"

The senior Guard, a Major Corwin, who Richard knew largely by reputation, turned, and said, "Oh, he's for the Healing Temple."

Richard couldn't restrain the unevenness in his voice. "Sir?"

"The report is confused. They managed to get a man out, on the other side of the river, and sent a package downstream. Hoping to get it to their contact, or some such, by another route. Torham intercepted them, and ended up cracking his shoulder. Possibly some ribs or a hip. They took him off to the Healing Temple a few hours ago." The senior Captain eyed him. "You still fresh enough to ride?"

"Sir." He wouldn't admit otherwise, but he'd had a fairly easy time of it, comparatively.

"Take my horse, she had a shorter run than yours. Ride down there, tell them to return to the Hall to make a formal report when they finish up with the immediate area. And then you can go check on Torham. You apprenticed with him, didn't you?" It wasn't entirely a question.

"I did, sir." Richard couldn't repress the worry now.

"He's less likely to take your head off for coming to the Temple then. Refused to have any of us. He was cursing fit to strip paint, so he'll likely mend." Major Corwin seemed quite glad to have Richard stick his head in that lion's den, but Richard was just as glad to take it on. He'd have gone by regardless.

The description did sound relatively reassuring, at least. Richard nodded. "Of course, sir. Tell the others to report in, go to the Healing Temple."

"The Healers will keep us informed, but you let us know if there's anything he wants seen to."

Richard was glad that someone senior in the Guard was keeping an ear out. "Of course, sir." He saluted, and made for the Major's horse. The sooner he got downstream, the sooner he could head for Trellech and the Healing Temple.

Richard cleared his throat outside the room he'd been shown to. They were very efficient here in the wing for acute injuries. The broad covered walkways around the interior courtyards were bustling with Healers and their assistants and the Healing Temple attendants going to and fro. He had been promptly brought to the room, with a "He expected someone would come by."

Richard hadn't been sure how to ask about the prognosis, but the fact Captain Torham had said he expected someone was promising. And he received no warning about visible injuries or anything to avoid mentioning. So he knocked, three times, the brisk pattern of raps his mentor preferred.

There was a pause, then "Richard?" It was followed immediately with "Come."

Captain Torham's command voice was still in fine form, then. Richard opened the door and offered a brisk nod. His mentor was propped up in bed. The visible injuries involved a left arm bound up flat against his chest, and another bandage around his forehead. Richard almost spoke before he realised there was someone else in the room, on the far side of the bed.

The other man seemed more or less Captain Torham's age, somewhere in his early fifties. But where Captain Torham was broad and sturdily built, a man's man, this man was far more slender. Where Torham had auburn hair streaked with grey, the other man was dark haired. He wore it much longer than men in the Guard would, braided in a neat queue down his back, well past his shoulders. Small round wire glasses were perched on his nose, as if Richard had interrupted him in the midst of reading. There was a book, in fact, on the side of the bed.

Torham nodded slightly. "Richard, Gilbert Oxley. Gil, this is the infamous Richard, Lord Edgarton." It had the sound of the conclusion of a longer conversation. Richard wasn't sure what to make of it. This man wasn't a Guard, he'd know him if he were.

The other man's eyebrows went up, and he looked Richard up and down. Richard was suddenly aware of how he must look. He'd stopped by the townhouse for a fresh change of clothes, for hygienic reasons, as he'd been on horseback or fighting all day. But he did not look put together; he just had on a clean daily uniform. Well-fitted, of course - his tailor didn't permit anything else - but without any of the more usual flourishes for a man of his rank.

"Magni's told me a great deal about you over the years, Captain." He was quite deliberately using the earned title, and Richard didn't know what to make of it. "He and I've been friends since - oh, what is it now, Mag?"

It wasn't the way anyone else Richard knew spoke to Captain Torham. Not just the nickname, though that was startling enough, but the ease of the speech. Richard could tell, immediately, that this was someone who knew his apprentice master well, and in ways Richard had no idea about. He glanced at Torham.

Captain Torham made a move as if to shrug, and then visibly winced, regretting it. It earned him a slight tsk from Gilbert. "Going on thirty years." Torham looked Richard up and down. "Sit, man, don't hover. Have you had anything to eat or drink since whatever you found?" There was no direct guidance there, but he was clearly fine with however this Oxley went about things.

Richard shook his head. Gilbert stood, with a little stretch. "I'll go see what I can round up."

"Oh, please don't put yourself to any trouble. I can get something at the Hall." Richard wasn't sure he wanted to entangle himself in obligation here.

Gilbert shook his head. "Do me good to stretch my leg a little." The wording was odd, for a moment, but then he picked up a cane tucked by his chair. There was the sway to his movement, as he took the first steps, that made Richard realise he'd lost at least a foot somehow, and was walking on a prosthetic.

"Thank you. Tea, that would be excellent."

Gilbert looked him up and down. "I am aiming for tea, sandwiches, and I hope a half-decent scone or two. Wish me luck." He was sharply amused by something and utterly confident in his success.

Richard wasn't even sure what to say to this, so he nodded and murmured a "Thank you," while the older man crossed the room, leaving his book on the bed.

He turned back to watch Captain Torham, who was looking after his friend with an entirely amused expression. "He knows at least half the staff here by first name, and two-thirds of the cooks."

"I, um, yes." Richard felt this conversation had gotten entirely turned around and it took him a minute to gather his thoughts. "First, sir, I am very glad to see you much yourself. May I inquire about the injuries?" It came out sounding prissy and overly proper.

It made Captain Torham suppress another laugh. "Use my forename, Richard, Magni. You're seeing me in bed, after all." Something had him right on the edge of laughter again. Richard began to suspect they'd provided some of the more broadly effective pain potions. "And I trust Gil a great deal, you may speak freely in front of him about anything other than oathed secrets."

He had to take a breath, and let it out, before saying carefully. "M... Magni." There, he'd done it once. It would get easier. "The injuries? Major Corwin asked that I report in to the Hall when I was through seeing you." That was easier than this strange new side of his apprentice master.

"The Healers will have sent along a report. Busted collar bone, something with the hip, a gash on the head. They were worried about other injuries, but seem to have decided I'm as tough as a rhinoceros."

"I am glad they are observant enough to spot that, sir. Magni." Something in the tone was carrying Richard along, and his dry teasing did make the older man smile. "So a good prognosis, then?"

"Here for a day or three, to make sure there's nothing internal, and so they can use the potions they don't let out of the place. A fortnight or two at home, convalescing."

Richard nodded, then offered, cautiously. "I don't know anything about your situation at home." Perhaps no name would be easier, for all he wanted to tack 'sir' onto it. "You would be welcome to stay at Veritas."

That earned him an amused huffing sound, and a "I

have a man, and I've been injured before. But that's a kind offer, Richard. Thank you." The praise was quite real and rather warm. "When I'm recuperating, perhaps I might come visit. Gil keeps asking me about the famous place."

Richard glanced over his shoulder, half-expecting Gilbert to have reappeared without warning. "May I ask why?"

"He's a scholar, no longer a fighter." There was a small wave of the right hand, the one that wasn't attached directly to the injury. Clearly he'd already learned that moving one shoulder affected the other. "The Sudan, with the Army. Early on, well before your time there. He was invalided back, and went into apprenticeship. He's quite an expert on what he calls transformative architecture, adapting spaces over time to take on new enchantments or protections."

"Oh, I can see why Veritas would be interesting." Richard considered. "I - I'd be glad to check with Alysoun, have you both...." His voice trailed off. "If he wouldn't mind?" He didn't need telling how bad it had been in the Sudan, he'd seen it himself, if rather later in that horrible lingering war.

That got him a very long, thoughtful look, as if Magni were trying to decide what to say next. "You're an open-hearted man, Richard." It had more weight to it than the earlier comment, before Magni took a breath, shifting modes smoothly. "What happened on the river, then?"

Richard was glad to settle into a much less baffling topic. "You sent us upstream, sir. We sealed the lock, headed downstream, found the trow caught up on the bank. There were Guard fighting, to capture those aboard, we joined in and made short work of it. Franes had a hand in the grounding, I suspect, but I didn't get a chance to ask him directly."

"How many on the trow?"

"Four men, the captain, and what we thought was the owner, or at least owner of the cargo. He wasn't saying anything."

"Looks better to do the oaths in full formal court," Magni agreed. "Especially when you catch them while fighting."

"Major Corwin took that part over, of course. He sent me down to where you'd gone in, to tell your people to head back when they were done with the investigation. They didn't fill me in, may I ask what you found?"

There was a pause, Magni's eyes shifting, checking to see if anyone was near. "I went in after a box, wrapped in waxed canvas. It's been safely delivered, but I'm curious what's inside it. They wanted, very much, to get it out and away. Quite firmly locked, magically and otherwise."

"Smuggling, then." Richard simply confirmed it. "I can ask, if they'll tell me."

"Pull rank. You never do." There was that amused lilt to his voice again, and Richard searched his expression to figure out what to do with it.

There were steps, then, right outside the door, and Gilbert came in, with the same sway, not bothering to knock. "They'll be along in a minute with something sustaining. And another potion and mug, Mag."

Magni grimaced. "No food for me yet?"

"Not until this dose has settled." It was firm, the way Alysoun would tell one of the children something.

Richard looked from one to the other, unsure what to say in the silence. It was Gilbert who answered, after he got himself settled in his chosen chair again. "Do you know much about the healer's arts?" His tone was entirely conversational, as if he and Magni were picking up a conversation and including Richard in it.

"No, sir. Not beyond the basics we get in the Guard." And what he'd gotten out of Alysoun's healers and midwives, but he suspected that didn't apply here.

"If there is a concern about unwanted bleeding or internal injury, there is a potion - quite fussy to make - that can be given, three doses, spaced apart. But it does badly with solid food. So Mag gets nutritious broth for the time being."

Richard nodded slowly, before venturing a more personal observation. "You seem to know a lot about it?"

Gilbert grinned broadly. "Self-preservation, originally. I wanted to learn more about what they were doing to me. I had rather a bad time with the leg." He said it in the understated way that made Richard certain the man had almost died, probably several times, and that the recovery had been long, painful, and unpredictable. "I've kept my hand in, since. And I see the healers here regularly, for the prosthesis and some other minor matters."

Richard nodded, and deliberately matched the tone. "Which explains how you can cadge sandwiches."

He was rewarded with a broad smile. "Just as sharp as you said, Mag."

They were so easy with each other, it began to catch at Richard's attention. He'd respected his mentor, nearly from the first minute they'd met. Magni Torham was an amiable man if you met his high standards. He was free with a laugh, generous with a compliment when it had been earned, and patient as the day was long when his pupils were doing their best. But he'd never seen the man properly at ease before. It wasn't just whatever pain potions he was on, there was something else.

"Richard offered to have me stay at Veritas. I turned him down, of course." Magni spoke companionably. "But he offered to have you round to sate your curiosity."

"And you, I hope." Gilbert was teasing again.

"Both of us, yes. I think you'd find Lady Edgarton a pleasant companion for conversation, too. Quite able to keep up with you." Richard blinked at that explanation. Magni had met Alysoun, of course, but he thought they hadn't had much opportunity to talk. "Mind, I've only had the pleasure of her company at formal events, the kind you hate."

Richard was saved from more complicated thoughts by the arrival of a temple attendant pushing a tea cart. She distributed sandwiches, tea, and multiple scones, with a little teasing comment to Gilbert, before making sure Magni drank his potion.

Gilbert then turned the conversation deliberately not to the architecture of Veritas, saying he'd save that for the promised visit, but asking instead about the landscape it sat in. That was an easy conversation for Richard, at least. He'd been riding the bounds since he was old enough to go along with his father. The topic kept them talking until the sandwiches were gone and Magni was visibly tiring. Richard excused himself, and went back to the Hall to make his report and see what further information had come in.

It kept nagging at Alysoun. Her research at the museum had taught her a bit more about the making of stained glass, and she had pages of notes on Augustine Reynard himself. Schola had taught her to take thorough notes, with the dates and other key information carefully written in the margin, and her particular symbols for notable points dotted the page. None of it was resolving into anything like an answer, though, about why the glass kept bothering her.

None of her investigation helped with any of her other duties, either. Richard had come home, tremendously late, two nights ago. He had told her briefly about a skirmish on the river, that his mentor was in the Healing Temple, and could she make arrangements for the right sort of basket. She had met Captain Torham a few times a year, but always at Guard festivities, places where conversation rarely strayed from the usual pleasantries.

It took her visiting three florists, two bookstores, and two cafes to figure out a basket appropriate to a Guard Captain in his early fifties, of unknown household needs. She had settled on high quality tea, a black with orange that she knew Captain Torham to like. She added a small potted plant that would encourage health and healing, and two books. One was a mystery she suspected he would enjoy, the other a newly published historical review of some of the Welsh border skirmishes.

That task done, she looked at the small notebook she carried to remind her of the things she meant to do. Sometimes, otherwise, they fell out of her head. The tasks for Richard's investiture were out of her hands and they were just waiting on final clothing fittings. There were a dozen other details she couldn't do anything about until at least next week. She didn't want to retreat to Veritas, yet.

She could, however, go see her mother at the family home, Harenden. It was one of her mother's weekly at-home days, and given the lovely weather, Alysoun rather suspected that if she went this afternoon, few other people would show up. There. That would do nicely. Alysoun rounded up Wallis, and went home to deposit the basket for Richard to take whenever he managed a visit to Captain Torham at home. She changed into a dress suitable for visiting, standing patiently while Wallis did up the buttons.

Once the carriage had dropped them by the portal, she went through, trusting Wallis would follow. The tiny shift in space brought her out into the green meadows of the family estate, in a grove of trees. She took a few deep breaths to steady herself. Alysoun hadn't brought the cane, it would only make her parents fuss exhaustingly. When she was ready, she made her way down the paved path, inhaling the scent of the flowers, and came along to the front entrance.

"Holt, good afternoon. Is Mama at home?" The butler stood ready to serve as always.

"Lady Alysoun, yes, she is on the back terrace, if you care to go through. May we fetch something to drink?"

"Oh, I'm sure she has lemonade out, that will be lovely. Thank you. Wallis, I'll let you know when I'm ready."

"Of course, my lady." Wallis bobbed once, more formal in company, and then nodded briskly at the other staff and turned to go around on the path to the servants' wing.

Alysoun made her way through the grand foyer, glancing up to see that the chandelier was glittering. She couldn't help noticing light at the moment, she found. Then she went through into the broad great hall, with the stained glass, and then out onto the terrace, where her mother was ensconced in a rather ornate piece of wicker furniture. "Alysoun, darling, I didn't expect to see you."

"Last minute decision, mama." She kissed her mother's cheek, then the other one, and smiled at the maid. "Oh, lemonade!"

"Sit, dear, sit. Isn't it beautiful out? I suspect that's why there are so few callers today. You are the first, and it's nearly three!"

"Well, I'm glad I caught you on your own, then." It was often quite hard to get time alone with her mother, in fact, and now Alysoun wasn't quite sure what to say.

"How are you, how are the children, and how is Richard?"

"Well, well, and very busy. That matter on the Severn, the one that made the papers but without any useful details."

"And I suppose you don't have any to share." Her mother did like to be the first with gossip.

"Nothing beyond what was in the paper. Captain Torham's supposed to go home from the Healing Temple in the next day or two. I spent the morning finding things for Richard to take along. He was rather worried, poor thing."

"Well, a man should have respect for his apprentice master. That's quite proper." Her mother nodded. "And the rest of it?"

"I have the final fitting for the investiture gown next week. Purple, of course." As was proper, as Richard's formal magistrate robes had purple fittings. "And Richard got a rather lovely garnet and amethyst set out of the vault for me, it brings out the light wonderfully." She could at least chatter to her mother about clothing easily, it was one of their best topics. This time was no exception and they went a good twenty minutes before her mother came up for breath.

That was largely because someone else had turned up, one of her mother's school friends. Alysoun nodded politely. "I'll let you catch up, I'll be back in a few minutes, Mama." Leaving them on the terrace, she wandered in to the lavatory, and then washed and dried her hands. She stopped in the great hall, distracted, looking up at the windows again. There was something there that caught her attention, but they weren't, outwardly, at least, anything like the windows that had been puzzling her in the museum.

The quality of the light, though, that was similar. The light here refracted - that was the word, her research had told her - differently. In some places, it had an almost dappled effect, like there were particles in the glass, smaller than dust, that blocked the light. In other places, there was an effect, a tiny prism.

Alysoun was still standing there, her arms crossed, when her mother came back through. "Melisande's walking in the garden. What are you doing, darling?"

"Remind me, would you? When are the windows here from?"

"Oh, there've been a few broken panes, I suppose. But they were made in the 12th century. Near Trellech, I think. Why?"

Alysoun waved a hand. "The light reminded me of one of the museum exhibits."

"You've been very taken with that, haven't you? How curious." That was her mother's slightly disapproving voice. Having interests, at least odd interests, was not generally considered appropriate in ladies of their station.

Alysoun shrugged. "It's a pleasant way to spend the afternoon. And I had a lovely chat with the head librarian. Her daughter was a year behind me at Schola. We're meeting for tea next week."

"A professional woman?"

"A scholar, a young daughter at home, I gather. I think it will be lovely to catch up."

Her mother nodded, uncertainly. "There's a book in the library, about the glass. Do you want to take it off with you? I'm sure we have a second copy."

"Oh, do you? Don't let me keep you, I can go look it up myself, if it's all about the glass."

Her mother nodded, and moved to kiss her cheek. "I expect Melisande will be in raptures over the statuary. She usually is. Do come again soon, darling, or we should find a time for me to come see the little ones."

"Of course, of course." With that, her mother kissed her other cheek, and then went trotting back off to the terrace, rearranging the hat on her head. Alysoun waited long enough to make sure she was properly gone, and then went along to the library.

Her father was out, at his club in Trellech or some such,

and the library had a rather disused feel to it. That wasn't a problem. She knew where the book lists were and how the idiosyncratic shelving system - designed four generations ago - worked.

It wasn't a fast process, but after twenty minutes or so, she found the shelf she wanted. It didn't even require one of the rolling ladders, just a small stepstool. She rearranged it, bringing it to the proper place, then climbed, carefully using the shelves to help her balance. There were several books on the glass in the house, but thumbing through, she found the one she wanted, and brushed the dust off with a handkerchief. And there was indeed a spare copy, so she didn't feel badly about taking this one.

Trying not to let the triumph show too much, she asked Holt to let Wallis know she was ready to go home. Five minutes later, they were back through the portal, and Alysoun looked forward to a quiet evening curled up on the chaise in her private sitting room with the book.

Getting to the museum at nine was rather earlier in the morning than Alysoun usually preferred to be moving. But she was here with a particular desire to examine the stained glass more closely, before the museum opened and other people might interfere.

"Lady Edgarton, good morning." Hebe Milton was waiting for her in the museum foyer. "I do hope I can be of help. I'm very sorry our senior curator isn't available this morning."

Alysoun smiled. That was better, honestly. "I'm sure you'll be able to be quite helpful. It's the details of setting up an exhibit I'm interested in, not the - what is it, the larger picture, is that what it's called?"

"Yes, my lady, or at least that is certainly the right idea. Would you prefer to come along to the exhibit? Or we've set aside one of our small meeting rooms if you'd like to discuss things with me somewhere more private."

"Exhibit first, and then the discussion, I expect. I do appreciate you arranging this, the chance to look at the works without bothering anyone else."

Hebe nodded slightly, and then turned, escorting Alysoun along the hallway, politely not commenting on the tap of the cane on the marble floor. At the entrance to the atrium, she nodded at the guard on the door who opened it for Alysoun. Once they were inside, Alysoun went straight to the Reynard pieces, and peered at them, looking once more at the shifts of the colours.

"May I ask, my lady, what you're curious about?"

Alysoun almost answered, the trained habit of keeping a conversation going, before she stopped herself, and said "In a moment." Miss Milton immediately took a step back, chastened, and Alysoun felt a moment of frustration. She was not an ogre. She was likely younger than Miss Milton, and not an expert in anything but her particular duties. But she wanted a look at the glass, so needs must.

She was able, now, to get quite close, moving slowly. Her body was being less rebellious than it might be, but she wanted to be cautious. Even if the glass was a fake, it was still lovely. On the front of the glass, the effect was less obvious, but she could also come around to what had been intended as the less visible part of the piece, and finally she saw what she was hoping to see.

It was not enough to look once, however. She drew out a small journal, making notes, carrying on from the notes she had already taken. Each piece, neatly labelled, with the information from the exhibition displays. When it was made, where it was made, what the explanatory plate said about it.

"Ah, right. There we are."

"My lady?" Miss Milton sounded quite nervous now.

"Before I say anything, I'd like you to look at this glass, here. And then at this one. The quality of the light through them, more than the colour." She indicated the two panes, supposedly made at the same time, in a studio not far from Trellech, in the river valley, far from any of the mines or quarries.

Miss Milton chewed her lip for a moment, but she came close, standing on tiptoe to peer at the glass from several angles. Then she drew out a small bound book of white paper from her pocket and held it up, letting the light shine through the window onto the book.

It took the curator several minutes, long enough that Alysoun could feel her hip start to cramp, sharp and painful, but this was important.

When Miss Milton turned back, she looked uncertain. "I see what you mean, my lady, but I'm afraid I don't understand."

Alysoun nodded. "I would gladly take you up on that offer of a private meeting room now. And perhaps some tea."

"Oh, yes, of course, my lady. This way."

Miss Milton led her back out of the atrium, and through a door labelled for staff only, into a much less ornate part of the building. Wood panelling lined the walls rather than sheets of carved marble and the floor was ordinary tile. The room itself had comfortable but entirely ordinary seats around a table for five or six to meet comfortably.

"Please, make yourself comfortable. I'll just be a moment to get someone to bring some tea."

Alysoun nodded, and settled down, bringing out the books she'd brought along, as well as her journal and notes. Miss Milton was gone for perhaps five minutes. She came back with a woman from the cafe and a tea cart, unloading a tray with a teapot and sugar and cream, along with some small scones.

"Thank you, Marie, for bringing things up." The older

woman nodded, and withdrew. It was only when the sound of the cart faded that Miss Milton said, "There's black tea with orange, or a green with roses, I wasn't sure of your preference, my lady. And a choice of scones."

"The green, thank you." Alysoun waited patiently through the little fuss with setting it to steep. "What did you think of the two pieces?"

"They are both supposed to have been made at about the same time, in the same place, by the same methods. I remember that." Miss Milton did settle down to the business at hand quite promptly, which Alysoun appreciated.

"And yet, the glass looks rather different."

"Yes." Miss Milton was very cautious now.

"I grew up at a house not too far from here, though closer to Stroud. We have half a dozen windows made in the 1100s, by a local glassmaker. Back before Trellech was a magical city."

Miss Milton nodded slowly, following but clearly unwilling to venture anything in specific yet.

"I had been trying to figure out where I had seen that quality of light before, and visiting my mother last week, I realised. The windows in the Great Hall have that same quality. A little - I believe the term is refracted? As if there are particles in the glass, for the light to bounce from. I am afraid I don't understand all the proper terminology."

"No, my lady, that part is quite right, as I understand it." Miss Milton then turned her attention to the idea. "I agree the quality is different, in some of the Reynard pieces. You, my lady, clearly have something specific in mind."

"I do. My parents had a book, which I borrowed." She slid the volume forward, so the other woman could take it and read it. "It talks about the manufactories that were here in Trellech under the deClares."

Miss Milton nodded. "I remember that - I grew up here, we were taught about how horrible it was. How bad for the magic, for the wildlife. Much better now."

"As may be." Alysoun agreed. She didn't care for the awful smogs she'd been in a few times visiting the areas of London where their sort of people, magical folks, went. "But it's rather like London, now. All sorts of things in the air, soot and dust and tiny little bits of metal..."

She hoped Miss Milton was bright enough to put the pieces together. There was another long pause, then the junior curator ventured, still cautious. "You're suggesting that some of these pieces weren't made where they say they were."

"Exactly. Which rather calls other things about either their provenance or the experts who examined them into question."

There was silence in the room. After a minute of it, Alysoun deliberately reached for her cup and a scone, breaking it apart delicately with her fingers, and enjoying the citrus that became much more prominent.

"My lady, I'm afraid this is not something I can resolve myself. And I am honestly not certain what you hope for here."

Alysoun nodded. She had, in thinking through this over the past week, thought it might come to this. Miss Milton was quite junior, there were powerful people involved. "My husband is a Captain in the Guard," she said. "I've learned from talking to him that one shouldn't rush an investigation."

That did not come out as reassuringly as she'd hoped, because Miss Milton flinched, just once.

"I didn't come here intending to tell the senior museum staff yet. I wanted to gather information, and you've been most helpful. I spotted this thing. More investigation is needed, someone to bring it forward at the proper time. I am willing enough to do that. And make it clear your only part was to allow me the kind of access you'd allow anyone who made our sort of donations to various programs."

Miss Milton was recovered enough to offer, "You have been rather less demanding than most of our significant patrons, my lady, actually."

"Exactly." Alysoun smiled at that. This was better. "May I ask a few more questions? If I ask something you'd rather not answer, just say so."

There was a small nod. "As you wish, my lady."

"I noticed that some of these pieces are on loan from an anonymous patron of the museum. Do you know who that is?"

Miss Milton shook her head. "The senior curators handled all of that, I was the one who drafted the descriptions from the notes they gave me." She considered, thinking back. "I think most of them came from one person, or a couple, though. There were mysterious meetings, but there weren't so many meetings as there would have been if it had been, oh, half a dozen anonymous patrons. Each person, each couple, that involves a whole string of discussions."

Alysoun nodded. "I sat in with the Dowager Lady Edgarton about the exhibit just after I was married, that had some of the family jewellery in it. I remember that was, oh, one to ask if she was willing, one to look at the pieces a first time. Another to agree to the contracts, then there was something that needed amending. Finally, actually someone taking them in hand, and of course bringing them back, after. Half a dozen meetings, at least."

"Exactly, my lady. I don't think the meetings were here,

I never saw anyone escorted in, and my office is quite close. I usually at least hear there are people. They ask us to tidy up a bit, too, especially notable patrons."

Alysoun nodded, and said. "Well. Let me think about how to raise the issue. Do you know of other possible experts besides those already involved in the exhibit?"

Miss Milton shook her head. "I might be able to find someone from abroad, but I would have to have Mistress Ogden in the library investigate who else is currently publishing. Should I ask her to do that?"

Alysoun considered. That couldn't cause too much trouble, if it were framed well. "If you would convey my compliments. I'm not able to come in again, my husband's upcoming investiture, but I would be interested if she could put together a, a bibliography, is that the word I want? Of people writing in the field more broadly. I read enough French and German as well as Latin, and I suppose there are some Americans or people elsewhere in the Empire doing things, as well. Perhaps you'd be willing to bring it along to our townhouse when it's ready, if you could be spared?"

Miss Milton bobbed her head. "That will do nicely, my lady." She then glanced at a clock on the wall, and said. "It's almost time for the museum to open. Did you want to go back to the atrium?"

"Oh, yes. I'll take another look, before it gets busy. You've been most helpful, and I will be letting your seniors know, without being too specific about how."

They left it at that. Alysoun spent a pleasant hour both examining the suspicious glass and enjoying the other pieces, before she felt she could retreat without attracting too much attention.

SEVENTEEN

THE SAME DAY, JUST OUTSIDE TRELLECH

Richard drew a breath, attempting to prepare himself. He hadn't been sure what to expect from Captain Torham's home. The idea he was here was still rather overwhelming, even if Captain Torham - Magni - had invited him, the last visit Richard made to the Healing Temple.

Whatever Richard had expected, it wasn't this, what looked like a renovated stone barn, about a mile from the walls of Trellech, nearest to the Guard district. It was square, and trim, the shutters painted a deep blue. There were broad wooden double doors at the front, much like there must have been when it was a barn, and a knocker.

He knocked. It was the only way forward.

The door was opened promptly, but not quite immediately, by a large blond man with a scar on his forehead. He bowed without saying anything, and gestured Richard in. The doors opened into a foyer about ten feet wide and twice that long, with French doors halfway down on each side and at the far end. Bookshelves to the ceilings covered every bit of wall not occupied by a door.

The doors on the right were closed and curtained. The doors on the left were propped open, held with little iron doorstops in the shape of a bear and a boar. The man who'd let him in gestured at the left set of doors, and Richard came over to them, standing on the threshold, saying, "Ca-Magni?"

Magni Torham was stretched out on a chaise, directly opposite the doors. He was sitting upright with pillows helping keep him from moving the bad arm too much, though it was still bound up. He looked better than he had, but somewhat faded. Two leather chairs were pulled up at a conversational angle, and Gil was in the right hand one, turning as Richard entered.

Magni nodded, "Richard, good afternoon. Grant, if you'd bring the tea?" The man - the servant - nodded; Richard just caught a hint of the gesture, before his mind caught up with his eyes. At the left end of the room, there were two desks, the same size and shape, on either side of the window.

One was set up like Captain Torham's desk in his office off the duelling salle, everything precisely in its place. The other had several piles of papers, set askew, flowing out to the bookshelf under the window which had several stacks of books at different angles.

Richard looked back at Magni, and then at Gil, and their expressions, and he went still, not at all sure what to say. He did not want to be insulting, but he didn't know what to do. The etiquette his parents had taught him did not cover this at all. And his usual go-to of doing what Captain Torham would do clearly wouldn't answer here.

Finally, he swallowed, and said. "Good afternoon, yes, of course. Magni. Gilbert." He held out the basket. "Should I put this somewhere?"

There was a slight approving nod from both of them, almost in unison, that was even more disconcerting than his realisations. "On my desk for the moment, unless there's something that will spoil." Magni's voice was even, but it had a note of a coming test in it. Richard had learned to spot that quickly, in the first weeks of his apprenticeship.

Richard nodded, and went to leave the basket on the tidy desk, where it wouldn't disturb anything. Turning back, he knew they were both watching him, and Magni gestured at the empty chair. "Sit, sit. Grant will bring the tea in a moment."

Richard sat, and there were about ten seconds of awkward silence. He took his courage in his hands, and said, carefully, "So am I one of the first you've had round from the Guard?"

There was a beat, then the two of them laughed, Magni's deeper bellow and Gilbert's tenor, before they both managed to get control of themselves. Gilbert patted his pockets and said, "My wallet's in the bedroom, Mag, I owe you."

Magni just looked delightfully smug. "You didn't know. Hadn't guessed." It wasn't a question.

"No, si- um. Magni. Not until I saw the desks. Or maybe the doorstops." Magni had been in Boar House at Schola, where Richard probably would have been if he hadn't been born an Edgarton. And more than a few who had a passion for warding and protection magics came from Bear. He then added, "I wondered, at the Healing Temple. Never having seen you so easy with someone. But I thought that might be the potions."

Magni chuckled, and then sobered. "You understand why we don't mention it. Why I don't invite people around."

"It's not - we're not bigots, like the non-magical. I know there are laws, but - ignored in our community, certainly." As he spoke, Richard felt that he'd misstepped somehow.

Magni just raised an eyebrow. Gilbert had kept quiet through this, but he shifted, moving to set a hand by Magni's shoulder, fingers barely brushing.

Richard thought through it, the test, and whether he'd manage to keep this man's respect. Whatever else, he wanted that, he realised with a rush. He wanted to walk out of this house, when he left, with this man thinking well of him. Both these men, it was clear Magni valued Gilbert's opinion. "Law doesn't dictate societal consequence, of course," he said, after a moment. It was the lesson he'd learned first from his father.

"You know that best of anyone I've trained." Magni's voice was quiet, a burr in it.

Richard pointed out, evenly. "You're a Captain, sir. You have no desire to move up, you've been clear about that."

"I don't, no. But if people knew, what would happen?"

Richard didn't care to think about it, but faced with the question, he would confront it. "Gossip." He spoke slowly, forcing himself to say things as he thought of them, rather than save them up and present them neatly. This was not a conversation for that kind of tidiness. It was the sort of duel where integrity required him not to hide his feelings or the order of his thoughts, no matter how much he'd prefer that.

"People would gossip about you. You'd be offered fewer apprentices. Certainly fewer young men, and that's at least two thirds of the Guard."

Magni nodded. "Your father, certainly, would not have signed an apprentice contract with me." His voice was resolutely neutral.

Richard immediately remembered things his father had

said over the years, and nodded. "You're right." He continued, more slowly. "Less time training the better duellists. Someone else would edge you out. Farrow or Holme or Macintosh."

Then he did some math. "You're past your twenty-year pension. You've no desire to stop what you're doing, but someone who wanted to could probably force a retirement. Many people like and respect you, but you're the one who taught me that that makes enemies as well. And what you do, you could set up your own salle, but you'd get plenty of the sort of rowdies, seeing duelling as a lark, rather than something, something vital."

There was probably more, but that seemed more than enough for the moment, and Richard didn't know how to begin to name the other things that might be there. Not right now in the moment. More overt threats. Even if Magni could out-duel almost everyone in the Guard, anyone could set up an ambush given enough time and opportunity.

It was only the arrival of the tea things, on a small rolling cart, that interrupted. Gilbert poured, handing a sturdy ceramic mug to Magni, in his good hand on the far side, then to Richard. "You take yours with cream, I know," he added, as he put it in.

Richard nodded. "You've talked about me, of course."

"Of course." Gilbert's voice was even and smooth, but there was a challenge there, just underneath the surface, like a waiting countercharm.

"You've been together a long time, then. You said before you've known each other thirty years." He considers. "Partners, is that the right word, somewhat less than that? After you had - your first experiences as adults." He was running all of the pieces together now, working the magic that happened when he managed to get out of his own way and trust his instincts. It worked far better than the patterns he'd been taught from the time he was a child.

Magni's voice cut in, smooth and even. "We met in Guard apprenticeship before Gil went off to the Army. Friends, then. Though we spotted each other, as people with, well, let us say compatible tastes."

"The Sudan wasn't kind to me. Bad injury, worse recovery, by the time they shipped me back, I barely knew my name or what century I was in. Could have been worse, I suppose. If I hadn't been injured I'd likely have been at Khartoum when the siege fell."

Richard could hear there was a deep fear there. He suddenly was utterly sure that when Gilbert's oaths to the Silence pressed on him, it was a loss of memory, of mind, that hit him. And knowing what happened at Khartoum could be no small fear either.

More lightly, Gilbert continued, "Himself turned up at the Healing Temple, after I'd been there a few months, almost entirely on my own. By the time they let me out, he'd arranged this place." His voice was even, but it had a hint of something more complex, even awed.

"I'd wondered what had happened, finally got someone to dig up the records. They'd been misfiled. And Gil - wasn't in contact with his family. Lots of us aren't, though it's hard to avoid, especially when you're living in Trellech." Magni picked up, just as evenly, though he glanced at Gil, with a startlingly warm smile. "We take care of our own."

"My people were - oh, Fourth Families, run to scholars and clerks the past few generations. They didn't approve of me going into the Army, and they approved even less of my lack of interest in making a decent match and settling down and producing grandbabies."

Richard had a sudden shiver, from realising that that

was his parents had insisted on, and what he'd done. Without any argument, or without even thinking about what he actually wanted. Though his family were Lords of the land, and there were obligations, considerations, that went far beyond his personal preferences.

Gilbert noticed, he seemed dangerously sharp that way, and added, "I do not object to children in a general way, so long as they do not come at my books and papers with sticky hands. But I have no desire for my own. I understand you have two?"

"A son and a daughter, yes. Six and four. I'm looking forward to teaching Gabriel to ride properly shortly, he's out on a leading rein already."

"I also understand you're nearly as good on a horse as you are in the duelling salle or on the field." Gilbert glanced to Magni. "You must have questions."

Richard suspected this was not what they expected, but it was the one that was nagging at him. "What was this place? And how is it - how is it arranged?"

Magni laughed, the deep rumbling laugh. "Old barn, renovated by someone who lost his legs at Waterloo. All flat, doors wide enough for a wheeled chair. Our personal space is the other side of the entrance hall."

Gil nodded. "I don't need a chair most of the time, but the stump never healed cleanly. So it's the chair a week or two a year, sometimes more, and I need someone around to help at those times. Grant served with me, helped escort me back, and we offered him a job on the strength of it. He doesn't talk much, so you're aware."

Before Richard could consider any of the implications, Magni went on. "The upstairs has the kitchen, Grant's rooms, and about half the space is books. We have rather a lot of books due to someone being unable to get rid of them."

"Oh, I see what Magni meant about you - my wife, she'll read anything. Not anything, I mean, she has taste." Richard felt his tongue had got tangled up. "She insisted I ask when you thought you'd be able to come round."

"Still?" Magni let the question hang there.

EIGHTEEN
THAT AFTERNOON

Richard nodded. "Still."

"Will you tell your wife?" Magni spoke evenly, his voice quiet, but there was that steel lurking right under it again.

"What would you prefer?" It certainly seemed like it should be their choice, not his.

Gilbert sat back at this, and the two older men had one of those wordless conversations in the space of a look and a raised eyebrow. It was Gilbert who spoke. "That is an excellent question. Tell us about your wife." They hadn't overtly discussed it, but Richard had the sense they - he was clear both of them were behind this - had something specific in mind.

Richard had no idea where to start. With most of their social circles, it would be the lineage, the lines of who begat who, if they didn't know that already. Or that she'd earned her right to be treated as a praiseworthy adult by having the appropriate children in the appropriate order. That wasn't what these men meant.

"Alysoun is five years younger. Fox House, but we

didn't overlap at school. We're an arranged match, but - fond enough." As he said it, though, it felt wrong, or at least wrong-footed. "She's from a good family, brought up to manage a large house and an estate."

"And what does arranged mean among your people?" Gil's voice had that edge to it again.

"Our parents consulted with others, and each of us was given a few people to consider, of suitable background. We found each other agreeable, though we only met a dozen times before the wedding, and in company. Father was ill, and of course, there were the expectations on all sides."

"Expectations." Magni's voice sounded dour. "And the estate?"

"Also an expectation, and quite demanding." Richard admitted. "But we have an excellent steward, and Alysoun handles the questions that come up brilliantly, when I'm not available."

He let out a long breath, and said, "Our children are healthy and thriving, but since Charlotte was born, she has had some health problems. Aches, pains, other symptoms the Healers can't solve. It is nothing contagious." That had been their first fear. "And nothing that seems to affect the children. It hasn't gotten shockingly worse, though she has a number of bad days. She stays at Veritas much of the time."

Gil nodded. "When one's body does not obey, being in a place you know well is rather easier."

He said it matter-of-factly, and Richard blinked at him, owlishly. "She doesn't like to talk about it."

"I have had some years more practice." Gil's voice was even, dryly amused. "I would be glad to talk to her about what I've learned, when we're there."

Richard considered that possibility, concentrating on it

so furiously he missed the next half sentence, only to hear a sharper, "Richard," from Magni.

"Pardon?"

"Your wife, man."

"I am not sure what else you want to know." Richard spread his hands slightly. "She reads. She organises things. She keeps the house running well."

"Do you share a bedroom? Talk about your day? Your cases? Her interests?"

"I... I bring her books she likes?" Richard offered it tentatively. "Um. No, we don't share a bedroom. Most people don't, in our..." He gathered himself, as much as he could. "And I'm not home much. Wherever home is. The townhouse, sometimes, Veritas sometimes. I - we talk every couple of days, I suppose. Leave notes. It, it is amiable."

The two older men exchanged looks and Gilbert flicked his fingers. "He's your apprentice, Mag. I'm presuming the same thing you are." He then leaned back in his chair, watching Richard with a discomforting attentiveness. Richard suddenly realized, with that little itch of intuition, that the man was enjoying having him there just to see how his theories played out. He wondered how often his foibles and insecurities had been the topic of their amused, easy conversation.

In the silence, Richard cleared his throat. "You've discussed me, of course. And Alysoun, as well."

Magni nodded. "But how I know her, and how you know her, I hope those are rather different things. We were curious what you would say about her, when pressed. Not just what, but how." A different kind of duelling, then, entirely.

Richard looked down at the floor for a moment. He knew he was being judged, and he found himself wanting.

It wasn't their judgement that bothered him, they were being kind, really. But he didn't know how to change any of it, any of the patterns that had been trained into him relentlessly, year after year.

Magni tapped his forefingers together, then steepled his hands, distracting Richard from his sudden selfconsciousness. "Is that the sort of relationship you would actually like to have, Richard? I have met your wife, though only in the sort of social situation where everyone was on reasonably good behaviour. She has always struck me as more intelligent than she permits herself to show, and moreover more curious than is generally encouraged in society."

Richard wanted to run, in that moment. No one, in all his life, had pinned him down about wanting things before. Including his wife. He did the things he was supposed to, he was good at them, he enjoyed succeeding at them. But there was Captain Torham, the person he most respected, more than his father, certainly more than his mother, more than his other relatives.

"No. But I - " He gestured, "I don't know what she wants. Would want. Besides the books." Then he flashed back to that evening, in her bedroom, where he hadn't been sure whether she was offering him something.

Magni kept watching him, and it made Richard shift in his chair. "Do you have a mistress?"

He could feel his eyes go wide, and a flush, neither of which he could do anything to stop. Looking away would just make it worse. "I'm barely home as it is," he pointed out. "No. No mistress. No desire to."

"And no men, either?"

Richard's jaw dropped open, but then he shook his head. "That's not for me." He managed it with a lighter tone, he didn't want to add insult to the difficulty of this conversation. "It's not that I don't want to, with Alysoun. Just, we haven't. I think it hurt her, the - the way her health is. The last time we tried."

"Which was?"

"Two months, three, after Charlotte was born." He blushed, more deeply, remembering that, how she'd flinched and pulled away, and he'd found himself completely unable to continue. He'd made his apologies to her, assuring her it was not her doing, and retreated with the few shreds of his dignity through the passage to his own rooms. The case that called him out next morning had been a relief, frankly.

"You might try talking to her. I know you posh sorts don't have the habit of it, but words really are quite useful." Gilbert's voice was back to that sharp edged barely repressed dry amusement. "More tea?"

Richard nodded. "Um. Yes." Then he grabbed his courage, and said, "How do I start?" They weren't mocking him. They'd spent time thinking about him, about his life. That was terrifying, on one hand, but it was also reassuring. He didn't think his mother had given his heart or his hopes more than a few moments thought. Nor his father.

"It is a little complicated to advise, not having met your wife. She reads? What does she read? What is she interested in at the moment? What is the last time you had a pleasant hour or two together? What does she value or respect? Is she the sort who is traditional because it is expected of her, or because the tradition suits her down to her bones?"

The questions rattled off like a dozen spells in a duel, and Richard had no idea how to parry them, except one by one. Gilbert finished pouring at the same time the flurry of questions ended, and handed the cup back over.

"Alysoun is - Magni is right." Richard could do this, lay

it out, the answers. "She is curious, about a great many things. She has gotten intrigued by something in the stained glass exhibit at the museum, there's a piece or two she keeps wanting to know more about. I could ask her more about that, I know she'd like it."

He looked up, got a mildly approving nod, and then carried on. "She likes things to run smoothly. At a party, or an event. She knows how to hold up a conversation, keep things pleasant, she's very good at that, even when people are being rather awful. They're not awful to her, usually. The title, the fact we've children, I'm attentive, that sort of thing."

"It makes it hard to find a chink in her warding." Gilbert's voice cut in, as if to especially highlight the point.

"You see it as warding, then?"

"Oh, I could give you a full three hour lecture on the ways that various aspects of noble etiquette have ties to warding methods, ancient and modern. Some of them more functional than others. But not right now." He paused, and added. "Mind, the interactions of the family are also part of my work, far more often than people realise. One of the reasons we've discussed you, besides the fact Mag is really quite fond of you."

Richard nodded. "I'd be interested. So would she, I suspect." He could answer that without touching on the rather more personal realisations. Then he carried on. "We went out for our anniversary. That was - we liked it, both of us. She invited me up to her room, after, and I didn't know what she wanted, or how to ask, and it got awkward." He felt like a schoolboy, now, laying it out for them. "But I should talk to her. I know that. She's... "

He thought back. "I think she knows how to use the traditions, like I know how to duel. But I don't think she's traditional by nature, the way some people are. She's impeccable about keeping the land obligations, but those actually matter, they're not just some fashion agreed on for show."

He looked up, and both men were nodding, in unison with each other. Then, with a sudden gentleness, Magni asked, "And what was it like in bed, before? Was she uncertain? Shy? Something else?"

The word came out of him before he could stop it. "Eager. When we - " He blushed and looked down and away, feeling a sudden gaping chasm between himself and these men, filled with their easy gentle affection for each other that never stopped showing.

Gilbert's voice cut away any ability Richard had to wall himself off. "Do you know why Mag took you on?"

It was probably the only question that could make Richard look up in that moment. Magni was watching him, entirely steady, and Gilbert leaned forward, his whole attention focused on Richard. It was terrifying. "No, I - no."

Gilbert nodded once, precisely. "He came home, on the day they were doing the interviews. They make him grumpy, usually. Too many people who think they know everything. Too many people who puff themselves up. Who want status and praise without earning it. Or worse, grasping for power and authority, though at least the Guard Oath rules the worst of those out."

Richard nodded, unable to look away from either of them. There was a slight smile from Magni now, who clearly had an idea where his partner was going.

"He came home. It was, oh, nine at night, he'd been there since dawn. I had a beer waiting for him, and everything ready to turn in. And I could tell it wasn't the usual run, not entirely. When we were settled for the night, I asked him how it went. He told me he'd found someone tangled up by what he should do. But he thought he could see how to free him - you - up, to do all the other things you could do, if you were given your head."

It was an odd way to think of himself. Richard couldn't help asking. "Defy convention?"

Magni answered. "Not that, precisely. You're right you've obligations, I respect that. But doing things the way that puts your best foot forward. Your best heart."

Richard peered at him. "Don't people usually do that?" It was the thing he'd found most compelling about the Guard Oath, about being in the Guard, that there were a set of standards there to live up to. Chivalry, in a word, living honourably, using his strength and magic for good, to protect those who couldn't do it themselves.

He'd never known how to put it into words, that desire, not beyond the oaths themselves. But there was always that sense of wanting to live the stories he'd grown up on. Of righting wrongs, fighting evil, even rescuing a damsel or two, if he were honest with himself.

The laugh - from both of them - went on for quite a while, but it wasn't mocking, more like a grand laugh at the foibles of the rest of the world. This time, instead of a chasm, something about it made Richard feel like he was included. When the laughter finally faded, Magni leaned forward a bit, ignoring the wince his collar bone caused. "Here's an example. That mysterious box."

Richard saw immediately where he was going. "I didn't want to put it in writing. Or anywhere people might overhear."

"That sounds promising." Gilbert had shifted now, hand resting lightly on Magni's shoulder, as if he couldn't resist the casual touch.

"I did pull rank. It took them five days to get the thing

open. Didn't respond to any of the usual charms, they had to get in one of the top Penelopes to counter-weave it."

"Mason or Witt?" Magni knew his preferences. And their own internal rankings.

"Witt. Major Corwin thought it might yield better to her precise and steady hand. She apparently found it quite formidable. You know she prides herself on a mind like a steel trap." Richard meant the latter partly for Gilbert, who nodded easily. They'd talked a lot about the Penelopes then, not just Richard.

"Some new technique, then. What was inside?"

Richard spread his hands. "We don't know. Whatever it was - just ash. They were going to see if they could pull an image from it." He added to Gilbert, in case Gilbert wasn't aware. "Doctrine of sympathies. There's a method to press an image of what the thing was on paper if you use the right cantrips and some of the ash, and so on."

"Huh." Magni frowned. "Something organic, then. And not something they wanted to have fall into someone's hands. Did they figure out how it was done?"

"A potion, in the box, they found the shattered glass. They think the courier set it off right before you got to him."

"Well, that's a fox in someone's henhouse." Magni shook his head. "Well. But you, that's not the way most people go at things. It's why we were willing to tell you."

Richard nodded, and gathered up the threads of where the conversation had wound. "I'd like to tell Alysoun about you both, before you visit. She'll keep it to herself, I'm sure. But it would -" He took a breath. "I want to be honest with her. But I also, there's the part of me, in the particular duel in question, it's a way of showing her something I care about. Care about doing right."

Magni nodded once. "Good man." It was the simple praise that did it.

Gilbert, on the other hand, grinned broadly. "Right, now, tell me all about what books you've brought home for her, and what she liked."

"Ah. There you are."

Alysoun had been curled up in the library, in the chaise she found most reliably comfortable, having a somewhat lazy afternoon. She had been dutiful that morning, going through details with the steward of repairs needed before the winter. They'd talked through the current crop predictions on the estate fields and all the other small things someone had to approve. In practice, she was very unlikely to countermand him. He knew his work, and he loved the land as deeply as Richard did. But there were proper dances to be followed.

She blinked up as Richard came in. "You were looking for me?" He never did that, generally. Run into her, yes, but he rarely sought her out. She had the impression he numbered leaving her to her own devices as one of his duties, though she had no idea why that might be.

He nodded. "I had a little more time free than I expected, so I came home."

"Are you feeling all right?" Alysoun pushed herself more upright, and peered at him, looking for the shine of fever in his eyes, or some other sign of illness. "You're not ill, are you?"

Richard blinked at her, then shook his head. "No, I feel fine. I just, I thought I'd like to see you."

She nodded, still a bit dubious, but moved her legs to let him sit on the end of the chaise comfortably. "I had a good meeting with Gordon this morning. Though I'm sure he'd feel better if you looked things over as well. The notes are on your desk."

Richard nodded. "I didn't come to talk about business. I'm sure you've got that well in hand, you're always very prompt, letting me know if you need me to do anything."

Alysoun nodded again, still not sure where this was going, or what he wanted. "I've not seen you since Tuesday. Is Captain Torham settled in at home? Does he need help with anything? I'm sure we could send one of the staff round."

There was a smile, for just a moment, that Alysoun couldn't read, before Richard said, "He has a man, everything seemed well in order. He was delighted with what you sent along, though. Complimented your choice of books, and asked me to tell you."

"Oh! I'm glad. It's, it helps to have a good book you can lose yourself in."

She looked up just in time to see an odd expression on Richard's face, before he said, entirely amiable, "What have you been up to beside the estate accounts? Reading?"

"Reading, mostly. Lunch with the children." She tilted her head. "Are you actually here for a bit? I do have a question. Maybe you can help." Alysoun fully expected him to beg off, but something in her wondered if this time might be different, if his peculiar behaviour might be a sign.

Richard nodded. "I was thinking I could use a quiet

night." Before she could say anything, he held up a hand. "Already let Mrs Glenwilliam know. How's that going, before we get into your question?"

It was not like him to be this interested in domestic affairs. She didn't think he meant she was doing it badly, but she didn't want to bore him, either. "She is quite taken with the idea now, especially if you let her make up packages of sandwiches for you when you eat on the go. You and whoever you take with you, I'm sure. We're still waiting on making a decision for here. I'm expecting to interview two people in the next fortnight, and ask at least one of them to make up a meal for me to try. You as well, if you'd like."

"Let me know when, and I'll see if I can get free, but let's not try and schedule around my diary, that always ends badly."

It made her smile again. It did. He did not live a steady scheduled life. "And the agency has five people to consider for your personal secretary, they said they'd send round the files tomorrow. Maybe this evening, they weren't sure, they were waiting on one last set of references."

"Grand. Thank you, for taking that on." His voice was earnestly pleased.

"We haven't hired anyone yet." Her voice was dry. "Save your thanks for when we've got lovely food, and all your files are sorted just how you like them."

She looked away for a moment, and when she looked back, he was watching her, rather fox-like. His head was tilted just a little to one side, in that curious way they had, not sure what the human was going to do. Then he nodded, and the moment broke, when he smiled his easy smile. "What was your question?"

Alysoun puffed out a breath, and said, "It's this stained glass exhibit." She expected to find him with that too-patient look people got when you went on about a thing you were interested in that they thought was foolish. She had had plenty of that from her parents, her governesses, and any number of housemates at school.

"The one you keep going back to." He didn't sound bored, he sounded like he'd been thinking about it too.

"Exactly. I told you, there's a piece that keeps bothering me."

He flicked his fingers, the little gesture he made when he was trying to remember something. "Something about the light. Why that one in particular? Or is it just the one?"

"The light, yes." She was delighted he remembered. "So, the piece is one of three made - or at least this is what the exhibit says - by Augustine Reynard. Made, reportedly, in the middle of last century. The glass is all supposed to come from a studio not that far from here, further up the Severn."

"But you're not sure?" Richard shifted a bit to better face her. "About one of them, or more than one?"

"At least one, probably not all three." she said, after a moment. "It's a little hard to tell. Not least because no one seem to know a lot about this Reynard. Which is odd, because making stained glass of that size is not usually a thing you do in a back room at home, yes? If it were stunning embroidery, or even dressmaking, that might be one person, on their own, very particular about materials. Or watercolours, or signet carving, some kinds of jewelry work."

Richard tilted his head to the other side, thinking. "You're right. Glass needs infrastructure. Some of it might be painting on, do I have that right? But there's firing it, and there's cutting the glass, and that needs space. And I'm thinking some sort of consistent temperature, you wouldn't want it to heat up or cool down too fast. Furnaces aren't exactly small things, or simple."

"Exactly. So, that part is curious, but I suppose not outside the realm of possibility. I mean, there are people doing their own thing. And I don't think any of the panels would require very large panes of glass, it could be pieced in."

"There must be something else, then." He shifted slightly, resting a hand on the seat, a few inches from her thigh. She found it rather distracting, trying to figure out what he was up to. Did he want a favour from her? Have something unpleasant to tell her? This was out of his usual pattern, and for all his schedule was impossible, he was a man of regular patterns.

"It's the glass itself. You remember the panels at Harenden." Her family home.

"I do, though I'm afraid I haven't been paying attention to the details much when I'm there." It had been rather busy at the wedding, really, and they'd only been back together for larger parties once they were married.

"I was visiting Mother, during her at-home day, and I - " Alysoun stopped. "There's a quality of the light through those windows, very similar to at least one of the Reynard windows. It's easiest to tell with the clear glass, and one of his is all coloured, and the other one has some other minor damage."

"What sort of quality?" He was curious, interested, as far as she could tell.

"The books talk about refraction. Particles in the glass that bounce the light. The windows at Harenden, they were made near Trellech, when it was much more industrial." Seeing the city now, it was odd to think it had been a centre of coal and iron work in the 13th century. "But Reynard's were supposed to be made in the 1850s, and there haven't been things making that kind of smoke and soot near Trellech in centuries."

Richard was quiet for an uncomfortably long time. Alysoun couldn't figure out if he were thinking, disapproving of her, or disapproving of the situation. When he spoke again, his voice had a new tone, puzzling it out. "So either the glass wasn't made where the records say it was, or it wasn't made when it was. Using older glass or something of the kind."

"I had mostly thought about a different place, not a different time, but you're right. I suppose it's possible they took older glass and reshaped it or something."

Richard tapped his fingers on the chaise. "What can I be of help with, then? You seem to have already figured out much of it."

"Well, I have a theory, but I don't know how to prove it. I don't even know where you'd start. And the museum obviously isn't going to put a lot of energy into it. They've called in a lot of favours putting this on, and I think they're relying on it to improve things. Bring in more patrons, all that."

She hadn't put that together until just now, either, but with the way the lecture had gone, it implied that. The way Miss Milton had been cautious. Alysoun didn't know about the inner workings of museums, but museums involved people and ambitions, and she had some sense of how those played out.

"What do you think would prove it, then?" She couldn't decide if Richard was just humouring her, or what, but at least he was listening.

"Is there someone in the Guard who could help? An analyst? I wouldn't need much of their time. I'm sure there are other people who could do the actual testing, but I don't even know what to look for, what to ask for."

Richard leaned back, with an expression on his face she had no idea how to read. "You know I've not wanted to impose. Use my status." She almost said something, but he held up his hand. "But if there is a problem here, a fake, or something, that could be a problem, a criminal problem, down the road." There was another of those long pauses before he nodded, as if deciding something. "Let me ask around, see if someone can give us twenty minutes."

"Us?"

"Oh, certainly. You'll need an escort, into the lairs of the Penelopes. Quite a lot of delicate magics at play." The Guard's term for those who unwove magics, she knew that much.

Alysoun nodded. "When can you ask? It's not urgent, exactly, only the exhibit isn't up forever."

"I'll ask around tomorrow, and see where we go from there."

She smiled, and then shifted to touch his hand. "Thank you. You might have time for a ride before dinner, if you don't dally. You haven't been out in a while."

Richard beamed at her. "Capital idea. Dinner, my lady." With that, he stood, and made a beeline to the staircase to his rooms.

TWENTY

18TH JULY, TRELLECH

"Good afternoon, my dear." Richard was waiting by the entrance to the Guard Hall, in uniform. Alysoun came up the broad steps, glancing around. She had been in here before, of course, but not often, and largely for ceremonial events.

He held his arm out to her, and when she took it, she smiled at him. "Richard."

"You look lovely, of course." She did, the dusty blue she favoured seeming cool and at ease despite the July heat - and heat it was. It was only the cooling embroideries that were keeping him from sweltering in the full uniform.

She inclined her head, her hat blocking a view of her face. "Who exactly are we going to see?"

"One of the Penelopes, Mason. She doesn't usually do this sort of thing, but she's one of the more creative thinkers, and when I asked her advice, she suggested she might have a look."

"I know the Penelopes are a - class of analysts, working on certain kinds of things." She had to know some of this, of course, but not the way he did. "But I'm not sure how that works."

"Unweaving magics, largely, in all the many applications that can have. Hence the name. All the things in an investigation that are about how items are connected, or linked, or how a magical device works. That sort of thing."

"But what does that mean, precisely? And are more of them women? I think every time I've heard you mention one, it's been a woman." Alysoun sounded decidedly curious about that, not accusatory.

"Well, I do prefer both Mason and Witt, and they're both women." He counted in his head, trying to formulate an estimate. "Of the top rank of Penelopes, I'd say better than two thirds are women, actually. There's something about creative thinking, some of them will argue for cyclical thinking. Mason herself argues it's not that women are better at it innately. Rather, society encourages a certain mode of thought for women, perhaps more inclined to this kind of puzzle solving. The easy puzzles respond to rote attempts or brute force. It's the complex ones that need a creative thinker."

They proceeded along the broad hallway, to the work-rooms in the courtyards at the back, people standing aside to let them pass. Once they got to a quieter stretch, Alysoun said, "People give you space, don't they?"

"The uniform. It does look impressive."

She snorted. "You look impressive in it, which is not the same thing." Then she considered. "And also that you're escorting a lady?"

"Escorting my wife? Oh, I'm quite sure many of them are envious." It came out more flirtatious than he'd expected, and she glanced at him quickly.

"Envious, is it now?" But now they were passing into the narrower halls, and the analyst spaces. He had to concentrate more on making sure she had an arm to lean on for the stairs, and that they moved around people in the hallways easily, and he didn't answer. The glances he was getting made him feel awkward. He wasn't entirely sure how to navigate having her here, in this space, having his separate selves collide like this.. But in a minute or two, they came to one of the larger offices for the Penelopes, and he knocked three times smartly on the door.

"Come." Mason's voice was pitched to carry, and Richard opened the door.

She was sitting behind her desk, her dark hair held in place, as far as he could tell, with a long slender wooden stirring stick, strands drooping untidily from it. She wore some of her uniform, at least. Her jacket was slung over a smaller table behind her, the sleeves of her shirtwaist were rolled up above her elbows exposing brown skin. He didn't want to know the state of her skirt. Mason gestured vaguely with two fingers, a ghost of a proper salute, but nodded at Alysoun. "Sir. And your wife?"

Alysoun glanced at him, and he made the introductions. "Penelope Elizabeth Mason. My wife, Alysoun. That's Lady Edgarton to you."

Mason grinned at him. "Sir. Of course, sir. It's a pleasure, Lady Edgarton." She was a good bit older than he was, but she had an impishness to her that made her often sound more like twenty-five than nearer forty. He suddenly wasn't entirely sure how Alysoun would take it. "You had a puzzle for me, sir?"

Richard nodded, glancing around, and escorting Alysoun to the one chair that wasn't covered in books or more dubious items. "Alysoun, perhaps you should explain, you know far more of it."

She settled down, and drew out a small fabric-bound book from her bag, before setting the bag down on the floor, her movements a little too precise. "What do you know about the situation?"

"There is stained glass of dubious provenance. You are trying to determine if there is a problem with it, or if it is just - oh, say a fluke of the artistic process."

Alysoun smiled suddenly, and relaxed. "And we are hoping that you might have suggestions about how to accomplish that. In a non-destructive way, naturally."

"Ah! No, you couldn't just scrape a bit off the glass, could you. There have been people doing that with oil paintings, taking a small amount from near the frame or some such. But that wouldn't do for glass. No, that's a tricky problem, isn't it." Mason fell silent, her eyes three-quarters closed, thinking.

Richard was quite familiar with her in this mode, and he just spread his hands when Alysoun looked at him. She smiled, and settled in with an amiable expression. He realised, watching her, it was the same expression she sometimes wore at social events. Pleasant, head tilted in a way that made her look attentive, not bored. But he had no idea what she was doing in her head.

When he was in that kind of situation, he made lists in his head. Depending on the moment, they might be all the things he needed to do or pass along, all while continuing to look attentive. And often one heard a useful comment or two, if one gave it a chance.

Finally, Mason said, "I don't know enough about the properties of making stained glass. In other cases, I might suggest finding materials that would have some sort of link.

Oh, if we had some of the artist's hair, or ashes from his workshop, or something. But I don't suppose there's any of that."

"In this case," Alysoun sounded very amused, "there's some doubt about whether he existed or at all. Which makes tracking down a hypothetical workshop a good fifty years later rather tricky."

"It could be worse, and, I don't know, in old Trellech or London before the Great Fire." Mason was cheerfully engaging in her habit of elaborate pessimism. "Not promising, though, no, my lady." She considered, and Richard caught her looking at Alysoun somewhat differently, as if Alysoun might have useful things to contribute beyond the summary. "My lady, would you lay out what you would like someone to solve, perhaps?"

Alysoun glanced over at Richard, and Richard gestured, open handed. "You have far more sense." He left it at that, since he meant both a sense of what was involved, and sense in general. She smiled, then shifted slightly in the chair.

"There are pieces purported to be by one Augustine Reynard, whom, despite not being that far in the past, no one seems to know much about. The curators for the exhibit have relied on, as far as I can tell, a particular academic, one Professor Arden. I did not like the way he lectured. Or the things he avoided discussing. I have not confronted him, but I have made a number of visits to the exhibit to see if I could figure out what bothered me about the items."

"And the artist was working around what time?" Mason's voice was crisp, entirely focused.

"Circa 1850. The three pieces in the exhibit all purportedly date from that decade. One has that refraction I mentioned. One there's something I can't pin down about the design. The third is … unremarkable, and could be a piece by someone else from the time."

"Ah, yes. If I were seeding a forgery, that is a plausible selection, isn't it? No two pieces with the same type of issue, and diverse enough to complicate any straightforward comparison."

Richard raised an eyebrow. "Have you given much thought to how you might produce a forgery, then?"

Mason grinned at him, unrepentant. "Only on my off-time, sir. It hasn't been relevant to a case I've worked on, but I knew it might come in handy."

"I was not," Richard said dryly, "aware that you actually spent time away from the Hall thinking about much else."

Alysoun shook her head. "You do something with pen and ink as a hobby, don't you? Calligraphy, perhaps, not artwork?"

Mason's eyes went quite wide, but she nodded. "Calligraphy, my lady. Sometimes a sideline, in invitations and cards and such, but often just for my pleasure." Then, much more cautious, she asked, "May I ask why you thought that?"

Alysoun gestured. "You like moving your hands, so I've seen your fingers. You've a dent on your writing hand that doesn't seem to match your pens here. Your desk seems more suited to someone tinkering or investigating an object than someone doing a lot of writing." She gestured at the lack of clear space. "Also, Richard has occasionally mentioned that the Penelopes he prefers are not so fond of writing reports as might be desirable."

Mason threw back her head and laughed, a rolling sound that echoed in the room, before she said, delighted, "My lady, are you sure you're not meant for the Guard?"

That was the highest praise from Mason he could think

of, and some part of Richard wanted to crow about it. There would be time for that later. For the moment, it meant Mason was thoroughly on their side, and that was no small thing. They might have gotten her usual level of skill at things she wasn't thinking much about otherwise, but this would be far better. Even if it meant she'd likely storm into his office at a most unexpected point in the day, slam her fist on his desk and rattle everything there, and then explain how she had been brilliant this time.

He put up with it because she was, of course.

Alysoun, though, was also showing her brains, and he found he liked it a great deal. He'd known she had some/ She certainly didn't confine her interests in reading to novels or light history, instead she read widely and deeply. It was then he realised both women were eyeing him with a very similar expression. "Yes?"

"You didn't answer, dear. Mason wanted to know if she had permission to make inquiries?"

"Not of the museum directly. I think we'll want to handle that delicately. But if you wish to investigate methods of making and testing stained glass."

"Sir." Mason sounded satisfied, that was good.

"I have an idea about the museum. Let me think about how to go forward there sensibly." Alysoun sounded thoughtful now, but she didn't expand on her idea.

Richard nodded, and decided that getting in the way of either plan would end badly for him, so he was left with a simple, "May I take you to tea, then, my dear?"

Alysoun found herself waiting for her husband. Again. He had come home at the last possible minute. He was rushing to change into formal robes for the dinner party they were attending this evening, as part of the coming magistrate investitures. She, of course, being much less tolerant of rushing around, was already dressed, and settled carefully in the chair in the library that wouldn't encourage the silk to wrinkle. The charms only did so much.

It left her time to think, at least. Even though the conversation with Penelope Mason had gone well, they had been foiled in making further progress. Richard had been interrupted while they were at tea by his aide, some complex issue that had come up, could he please come along.

Alysoun had waved him off, though she wished that didn't keep happening. Worse, for once, she hadn't particularly been in pain, and could have gone out to do things, but she couldn't settle on something to do. She and Richard had decided he should come with her to the museum, but she didn't want to go again by herself, in case it gave something away. She had never been fond of browsing in shops, even before her illness. Going back to Veritas wasn't an option since they had social commitments in Trellech all this week.

Finally, she heard Richard's shoes on the marble steps in the foyer, and then he came into the room. "Ah, my dear. Pardon. I see the carriage is ready. May I?" He extended his hand, and Alysoun took it, settling into the predictable dance of the social engagement. First into the carriage, and a short ride around the streets of Trellech to the larger home that was hosting them this evening. The carriage was unexceptional, at least. No one expected women to walk far in dress slippers.

The party itself had been much as she expected. It was a fairly sizable group. From any given angle, one could clearly see twenty or thirty people, and there were a number of rooms on the ground floor open to guests. She had lingered briefly by the buffet in the dining room. Her governess had always said one could get the measure of a party quickly by the food and drink served.

Bite-size foods, in moderately traditional modes, but well made, and a buffet in the long dining room. Some people drinking more than was entirely sensible. It was a wealthy household, quite possibly more so than her own husband's family, judging by the silver on display. That took some doing.

And the groups of people. Someone had pulled Richard away not long after they arrived, and she had moved from group of women to group of women. It wasn't too much bother to make pleasant commentary about the safe topics with the wives of magistrates. What was rather more tedious was the number of them teasing her about how busy her husband would be. The actual challenge, beyond the tedium, was not showing how uncomfortable that made her.

First, it rather presumed that he wasn't already extremely busy. She could count on both hands the number of quiet afternoons or evenings he'd had at home since the beginning of the year, and have fingers to spare. But worse, the comments tended to come with a teasing note. About how she'd have to make sure he had a grand time when he was home, so he'd turn up.

That was not a topic she was getting into with people, and certainly not women a decade or more older who were new to her. Alysoun had vastly more sense. She might wish for her husband to join her in bed occasionally. She did, in fact. But she was also largely resigned to the fact that their life would consist of him doing good and noble things for other people, and her visible support at intervals. She should perhaps take up a more involved cause of her own. Ideally one that could be largely managed from Veritas. She would have to think on that.

Alysoun felt the hand on her shoulder before she heard him, she was so caught up in her thoughts. Two fingers over-lapped onto her skin, and she could feel the warmth through the delicate lace. The rest of his hand followed the curve of her shoulder. He leaned in. "Do you need rescuing, my dear?" He was close enough his breath tickled her ear.

She turned her head, tilting it for a moment, and then smiled, and said, "You were thinking you should introduce me to Lady Addison, when she has a moment?"

"Ah, yes. Do pardon us, ladies, so many people to have a word with." He deftly cut her away from the pack of women, and she slipped her hand through his arm. He escorted her through into the foyer, where they could see other knots of people. "Did you actually want to talk to Lady Addison?"

"Eventually, but I could use a pause, thank you." She took a moment to catch her breath and organise her thoughts.

"Is anyone being unusually difficult?" Richard's voice had an intensity that made her look up to meet his eyes.

Alysoun shook her head. "Nothing I didn't expect. It was just..." She didn't even know how to begin to explain the dynamics. Or if he'd understand them if she did. She was clear that men had their methods of social duelling. He was as adept with the social necessities as on the duelling field, but the methods used by the women were different.

"You will let me know if you need me to make an excuse to escort you home. Some minor illness from the children, perhaps."

She smiled up at him. "I don't think that will be necessary."

It was then that one of the well-dressed women brushed by him, angling herself precisely to catch Richard's other shoulder slightly, rocking him onto the heel of his foot. Richard murmured "Do pardon." It seemed instinctive, but Alysoun caught something. She was wearing a shade of gold that was quite fashionable. It made for a rather dramatic contrast to pale skin and dark hair, in a way that felt too sharp on the eyes.

"Oh, you must be Lord Richard Edgarton." The emphasis firmly on his name. "Our new magistrate-to-be. I've just been hoping and hoping to meet you, I gather you're a duellist?"

Alysoun shifted, slightly, wondering what Richard

would do with this, and whether he'd noticed that she was coming on a bit strong. He shifted his arm a little. "Lord Edgarton, yes. My wife, Lady AlysounEdgarton. May I ask your name?"

"Oh, Hortensia Miller. My sister Madeline is married to Lord Delwyn's heir, Jupiter."

Richard inclined his head. "A pleasure." It was the sort of thing one had to say in such circumstances.

"Do you think I might come watch you duel, sometime? I do enjoy watching a man do things he's skilled at." There as a purring note to her voice that surely even Richard would notice.

Alysoun considered her options. It would not do to be nasty, there were many people here watching to see how she handled herself. She was trying to place one Hortensia Miller. She recalled one of the Millers being on the more dissolute end of things. Or at least, a well-off family followed by rumours that perhaps not all their income was honestly gained.

She'd not have expected the Delwyn heir to marry a Miller, now that she knew more about the dynamics than she had before her own wedding. The Millers were not the sort of family who would be invited to join the Albion Inheritance, though she could not quite bring to mind what they actually did. Manufacturing, perhaps, that had the right ring to it.

Then she settled on it. "Oh, I've found the most interesting times don't involve anyone having to prove anything, don't you? There's a comfort in being with someone who doesn't need to show off."

The look of gratitude Richard gave her was met with a rather infuriated one from Hortensia. Her reply was milder. "Oh, I suppose."

Richard obliged with a "Do you have any particular interests? We both enjoy a pleasant horseback ride when we're able to get out for a bit." He didn't continue the comment in a direction that might come across as more risque.

Alysoun appreciated the opening. "And I've been introducing him to some of the finer arts, beyond the basics he's picked up. So pleasant to share an exhibit or book with someone else just as interested."

Miss Miller looked even more put out, before she smoothed her expression into something more pleasant. "I was hoping, Lady Edgarton, that perhaps Lord Edgarton would escort me to the cloak room?"

Alysoun smiled pleasantly. "Oh, I'm so sorry, we've been hoping to catch Lady Addison, and I see she's free right now. We really mustn't keep her waiting." She nodded, the crisp precise nod she hoped came off the way she wanted. "Do have a good evening."

Richard, thankfully, took his cue. He echoed the nod, and then turned, leading her away. "You didn't care for her, at all, did you."

"Not one bit." This was neither the time nor the place to talk about how Miss Miller had been flirting and attempting to get Richard alone. She couldn't decide if Richard were ignoring it for her sake, or actually that unobservant. It seemed implausible that he was. He was a Captain in the Guard, and others had been clear to her that he had earned it. Perhaps he was simply incapable of reading a woman's interest. Any woman's, not just her more subtle attempts.

"You handled her very well, of course. Not giving her an opening." She glanced up at him, and the praise made her feel warm, suddenly. He squeezed her hand, and added, "A different kind of duelling, but I think you're quite deft."

She was trying to figure out what to say to that praise when Lady Addison beckoned them over. They were thrown into the necessary introductions and discussions of family and estate, so that she could get Alysoun's proper measure.

Richard wasn't sure what he thought about this party. Meant to welcome him and three of the other magistrates to be, it felt more restless than congenial. It wasn't just magistrates and their spouses here, of course, there were a good mix of people from the upper echelons of Trellech society as well. Several Majors in the Guard, half a dozen judges, and Richard certainly wasn't the only Lord of the land here, he counted at least a dozen. At least three from the Council, too, and people from their families.

Part of him had the sudden realisation that anyone with a particular grudge could do a great deal of damage to the judicial and legal hierarchy of Albion. And in quite a short time, if they managed to get close enough to one of these parties. There had been rising concerns about anarchism for some time. He thought he had better have a word with some of the senior Guard members here in the near future.

He had deposited Alysoun in a little nook with chairs, talking to one of the senior women who was very much holding court. A friend of Lady Addison's, Madam Belloir wasn't titled herself, but she had a long history of association with all the most notable people. There were quiet rumours of a most elite salon she hosted. If Alysoun made a favourable impression, well, that could be only to the good.

It took him a little longer to fetch drinks than he'd wanted. Alysoun didn't like to drink much at these gatherings, and he'd had to track down someone who could make sure she had something lighter. By the time he came back, Madam Belloir had picked up several other people. They included a man in peacock-green robes with trailing blond hair, leaning forward and talking animatedly to Alysoun.

Richard watched them carefully as he walked over. She was leaning forward too, smiling at him. He didn't recognise the man, but of course he didn't know everyone by sight, even people in their larger social circles. As he got closer, he heard the accent. No, someone French, or at least who had spent a lot of time there, from the sound of the vowels.

Alysoun looked up, and turned that same smile at him. "Richard, this is Monsieur Alain Brodeur. Monsieur Brodeur, my husband, Lord Richard Edgarton. Monsieur Brodeur is an embroidery specialist, here to visit with some of the Weaver's Guild, and Madam Belloir was kind enough to introduce us."

"Do call me Alain, please. Your lady wife is most well-read, I have been finding." The other man nodded at both Richard and Madam Belloir. "Many women know what they like in clothing, but not so many care to know what goes into the process. But you do not embroider yourself, madame?"

Richard wasn't sure about the apparent informality, and then remembered that in French, nearly all people, up to princesses, were monsieur or madame. He nodded, a bit more sharply than he meant to. He held out her drink, waiting until she had it securely in her hand before moving to stand behind her chair.

"I like the idea of embroidery. But I'm afraid I'm not nearly as deft with my fingers as I'd like to be, and it hasn't seemed to improve with practice. I do simple things, sometimes, but nothing like what I dream of. I do enjoy the history of the patterns, the symbols, how they change, though."

"Ah, that is a fine thing, madame. If we all made magic with our needles, who then would cook fine feasts, or make necessary potions for the healers, or whatever it is your husband does."

"I am a captain in the Guard, monsieur. I find people who have broken our laws or caused problems, and see justice is done." Richard returned the exquisite but pointed politeness.

"Ah ha! You are a man with a noble purpose, then. That is a fine thing, but it must keep you very busy, no? And such a lady as your wife, it must mean she becomes lonely." Alain's voice was easy, flowing, the kind of patter that made it clear he was not at all awkward at this rolling flirtatious talk.

Alysoun seemed to be soaking it up, too, her cheeks were glowing, her eyes brighter, and something in him clenched, hating feeling like this, like he didn't measure up. Again. "I keep busy. But you were saying about the fabrics, the newer dyes, the colours?"

"Ah, yes." There was a rolling discussion of different dyes, of new approaches to blending colours, and Richard let it flow along. There was more than a bit of flattery, each bit like another little cut to him. But Alysoun was pleased, and she didn't look so tired, and those were both good things.

Finally, Alain was drawn off by someone else, and Alysoun faded again. The party had begun to thin out, finally, and Richard offered, "We could make the rounds one more time, and then go home?"

"Would it be a terrible bother to go back to Veritas for a day or two?" She sounded uncertain.

"You don't need to be in town until the next party, do you? No, of course, we can go back. But tomorrow, perhaps, rather than have to move your things."

She deflated, momentarily, but then nodded. "Tomorrow morning, then. And your Captain Torham and his friend are coming."

That made Richard nod. The point at which he'd have to figure out what to tell her about that was rapidly approaching, looming, even. One thing at a time. "Come along, my dear. Let us go make the appropriate pleasantries."

That took them a good half hour, and by the time they were in the carriage, Alysoun was indeed a bit deflated. He helped her out on the other end. He intended only to walk her to the door. She turned, when he was about to bid her good night. "Come in for a few minutes? There's something about the party."

"Of course. Let me just go change into something easier, and be right back."

She made a slightly aggrieved noise, but nodded, and let Willis guide her on the bench. By the time Richard reappeared, under five minutes later, her hair was braided down to her waist, she had a peignoir on, and she was about to settle into bed. He had gotten out of the formal wear, and shrugged on a dressing gown. He tried to read her intentions, but she just patted the bed at her side. He sat. Of course he sat.

"Richard." Her voice was tentative. "Tonight. There were lots of new people."

He nodded, carefully. "There were." He wasn't sure where she was going with this, and he didn't want to try and predict. Was she going to apologise for flirting with the Frenchman? Mention something he hadn't seen among his colleagues to be?

Alysoun took a deep breath. "You remember the woman who bumped into you? Hortensia Miller."

He nodded cautiously.

"She was doing her best to proposition you. Without being quite so blunt about it, though she was rather inelegant."

Richard felt his mouth drop open. Of all the things that evening, that had not been one he had considered. "Why, why do you say that?"

"She made a direct line for you, knocked into you, and kept trying to find an opening." There was an amused tone in her voice now. "Did you really not realise?"

"I am not exactly used to women doing that to me." Richard tried to sound like he had some control, but then he coughed and had to swallow.

Alysoun reached out, and patted his hand. "I wondered. Well. That is what a woman throwing herself at you, really rather bluntly, looks like. For your future reference. Someone from the First Families would have had more decorum about it."

Richard nodded, then shifted his hand to take hers, or rather, let her palm rest on his. Holding was a bit more than he dared. She seemed in a somewhat fey mood. "Is that why you were flirting with the Frenchman?"

"Alain?" She considered. "He was flirting with me. Did it bother you?"

Part of him wanted to shout about it, loudly. But that was bad duelling. He stopped, took a breath, like Magni had taught him, over and over again, and thought about the conversation he'd been there for. And then back to the one with Hortensia Miller.

"She was pushing to find an opening. I thought she was testing you, the way the women were before, when I rescued you. But she was trying to..." He gestured with his free hand. "Make an opening, a doorway, with me."

Alysoun nodded. "That bit about wanting to watch you duel was a giveaway. Flatter a thing you're reasonably known for."

"I wish I weren't." It came out of Richard in a rush. "I'd be more use if people didn't know I could, or that I was as good as I am."

Alysoun considered, tilting her head to the side, and there was a long and increasingly uncomfortable silence. Finally, Richard looked away, feeling himself flush. A moment later, her hand closed around his. "Tell me about that, then."

"If people know I'm a good duellist, I'm not much use. They see me coming, and they don't do a thing that might require duelling. I suppose that's a certain amount of preventative good, but it's terribly dull. If people didn't know I was good at it, I could, I could do more subtle things." He didn't know how to explain his other fears about his position to her. His worry that he'd only been promoted because he'd become the local Lord, the same thing with the Magistrate's seal.

There was a different quality to the silence now. "Have you talked to Captain Torham about that?"

"He said that if I didn't want to be known as a duellist, I

should have apprenticed somewhere else. Because of course anyone he took on would be decent at it."

"He does have a point." She sounded amused again, and he risked a glance up. Alysoun was smiling at him, and her attention was fixed on him. Not with a hard focus, but a softer one, as if she were watching everything he did, down to a twitch of a foot.

He shrugged, a little jerk of his shoulder. "You must be tired. It's been a long day. I need to go into the Hall for some of the day, but I'll try to be back for tea with the children. And perhaps a ride?"

Alysoun opened her mouth, as if about to say something, then she nodded. "That sounds excellent, dear. Sleep well."

As he withdrew, he couldn't help but look over his shoulder once, as he closed the door to her room. She was settled in bed, a book loosely in her lap, looking up at the ceiling with an unreadable expression on her face. He flushed, again, realising that not only had he utterly missed Miss Miller's advances, but he had even less idea how to read his wife.

TWENTY-THREE
21ST JULY, VERITAS

The next day ebbed and flowed. Alysoun resigned herself to a necessary but unwanted nap in the middle of the afternoon, and she felt rather like her daughter Charlotte about it. She didn't mind curling up with a good book and taking it easy. Napping, however, always seemed like a waste of perfectly good time she could be doing something better with. Such as reading. Alternately, riding, spending time with her children, investigating curious and suspicious artworks, or even going to obligatory social events.

She was slow to get moving after the nap. She eventually worked around to having Willis help her into a tea gown, since no one outside the family would be here, and putting her hair up informally. She much preferred that, because pinned the right way, it didn't weigh her neck down and cause headaches.

By the time the children had their tea, Richard still hadn't shown up. At least not that she was aware of. Alysoun had to reconsider. Last night had been difficult. She had not expected him not to have noticed that Hortensia - what a name - had been flinging herself at him. It had been quite obvious, really. There were much more subtle ways to do it, and she had chosen none of those. On the one hand, she was rather pleased Richard had been quite that naive about it. If that's the word she wanted.

On the other hand, he had not responded the way she'd expected, given how he brought up Monsieur Brodeur. She'd thought, when he came back with the drinks, that he'd been almost jealous for a moment. Or at least, that's what she assumed. There had been an intensity to his attention to her that had felt good, even while it was unsettling, new, and different.

Did he think she'd seriously consider something with someone else? Oh, she'd fulfilled her marriage contract. So long as she had the right amount of discretion, plenty of people strayed. She knew it was more complicated for women without magic, but she could avoid pregnancy, at least in theory. She'd never tested the theory, of course, but plenty of women did. The charm she knew went back to the Romans. And there were certainly methods of enjoying someone's body, certainly someone's company, without that risk in the first place.

But doing so would require someone suitable, and a body that didn't hurt like hers did. Or at least someone being willing to patient when it did. The conversations of women at parties, when the men weren't around, covered the one topic, which she could have sorted out herself, and the other not at all.

Monsieur Alain had been flattering, certainly. And quite handsome, in his way, she supposed. Certainly he had been eye-catching, like the peacocks whose colours he favoured. Yet, she had kept finding her eye drawn to Richard, across the room, until he returned. He'd been dressed more somberly, in evening robes with the two awards, medals, he'd earned in the Guard. Understated, but steady.

It wasn't romantic, going for the steady option. On the other hand, she was not a maiden reading a romance now. She was a matron with two children, and steadiness was a sensible choice. And in this case, not unappealing. She'd almost asked him, directly, last night, and then the conversation had twisted away from her, and she couldn't figure out how to get it back.

Dwelling on it wouldn't improve it. She brushed her skirts out, and went up to the nursery. She could hear the children babbling, well before she got to the door, and she turned into the nursery to stop dead. Richard was settled in the comfortable reading chair facing the window, Gabriel on his left knee, Charlotte wriggling on his right, and his arms around them.

He was reading something to them, one of the old books, that they'd both grown up with, about all the magical creatures who lived in the woods. Well, the ones that made for good drawings and pleasant dreams, not nightmares.

She blinked, she hadn't expected that. Nanny occasionally mentioned when Richard had come up, but Alysoun had thought it was not terribly often. But here he was, and he seemed quite at ease. The children were delighted, both of them, leaning into him like flowers following the sun. It made her smile, watching them, how intent they all were, until he closed the book. It was only then that Charlotte caught sight of her as she wriggled on her father's knee, and then promptly dropped onto the floor to bounce over. "Mamamama!"

Alysoun smiled, but she didn't dare try and bend down, no matter how Charlotte reached up, she wasn't sure she'd make it back up. Richard had stood, Gabriel balanced on his hip, and said "Let your mama come have the chair, Charlotte, how's that?"

"Mama."

Alysoun reached down for her hand, which was slightly sticky. "Nanny, I believe we're both staying for tea."

"Everything is ready, my lady, when you are." There was a broad smile. Some nannies didn't approve of too much interaction with parents, but Alysoun had always felt that was unnatural. Also, one never really knew what the nanny was doing if you didn't check in. She'd always thought it dreadfully unfair that there were some things that were fine with Nanny but not with Mother, or the other way around. If she were a regular presence in the nursery, it would be far easier to match the two. And she much preferred being Mama, she felt, herself.

Alysoun settled in the chair for the moment, and Charlotte clambered up, using the footstool to help, awkward but adorable, and then settled in her lap. She got an arm securely around her daughter, then looked up at her husband. "You've been back for a bit?"

"You were napping when I came in, and I didn't want to wake you. And it gave us a chance to go have a walk and look at some birds, and have a story. No riding, but perhaps in the morning."

"Before your guests. Our guests." Who were coming early afternoon.

"We should talk about that a little more tonight, after supper, if that's all right."

"Quite all right. Especially if you've cleared the day."

Richard flushed and looked away. "It's - "

She smiled up at him. "Captain Torham's only been here a couple of times, and always with more people.

Showing off the house, that's different." She thought about asking about Captain Torham's friend, but she wasn't entirely sure where to start. Richard hadn't said much, beyond being clear about his interest in architectural warding. Alysoun had looked up several of his articles, and been able to follow the abstracts and summaries, but not necessarily the rest of it. She wondered if he was one of those owlish scholars so caught up in theory he forgot about anything else.

At any rate, she was here, and she could have a lovely long soak in the caldarium tomorrow. Then a visit that at least wouldn't involve the same dance of social pleasantries she had been doing far more frequently of late.

"Gabriel, can you tell Mama what we saw out in the garden?" That got a cheerful babble of more about birds and rabbits and a duck, and a falcon up high in the air. Gabriel was learning the birds and animals of the estate well, and Charlotte babbled along with him, rather less coherently, but interested and engaged. Once there had been plenty of that, they managed to disentangle the children. Everyone settled down at the table for tea, which involved small sandwiches, and scones, and a few other treats for all involved.

It was a quiet afternoon, but a rather pleasant one. Richard even managed to get Nanny to unbend enough to tell a few stories of her childhood and her previous postings. She talked about animals that lived near there, and a particularly amusing story about a stork who insisted on nesting in an interior courtyard who had to be carefully led out with its babies once they were hatched.

Finally, though, the children were winding down a bit, and Alysoun said, "We should see about our own evening. Thank you, Nanny."

"Of course, my lady. Come along, children, give your mother and father a kiss good night. It's nearly bath time."

Both the children managed this, and Alysoun kissed their hair. "Be good for Nanny now. We have people coming to visit tomorrow, but I'll stop in before lunch."

It took a little more work to disentangle themselves, and leave Nanny to the evening routine. When they were well out of sight, and nearly out of hearing range, Richard nodded. "Gabriel is getting quite curious about things."

"The birds, you mean?"

Richard nodded. "I liked telling him about the birds we saw, the animals. I'll have to brush up, though, he wanted to know all the proper names."

"The guide books we have in the library are a bit dated, I think. I'll see if I can find some new ones, with better illustrations. He might enjoy going through them with you some rainy day when you're home?"

"If you would, that sounds excellent. You're far better at sorting out what he'd like."

Alysoun considered, as he escorted her down the hall. "You do very well with him." She offered it quietly, a little uncertain how he'd take it.

"Better than Father did with me, I hope."

There was something in his tone that was beyond the usual wistfulness. She stopped, forcing him to pause as well. "Richard, you're a good man, and a fine father. You care about doing the thing right, which is a great deal more than many people. You don't just want the children trotted out for show, you go and see them, share your interests."

"Birds?" He offered it cautiously, like it didn't seem worthwhile.

She reached up to cup his cheek. "This estate. Which I know you love, and with good reason. It has history everywhere you look, besides all the things that live here. Plants and animals and fish and frogs and I don't even know what else."

"Fireflies."

She smiled up at him. "Fireflies. And there were mirabiles in the woods, didn't you say?"

"Quite rare, those. I've only seen them once. But perhaps again, sometime. We've had too many people going through the places I saw them, they don't like that."

"Come tell me about it over supper." He took the cue nicely, and it meant a meal listening to him talk about the nooks and crannies of the estate. She was still learning its secrets. Frankly, she wasn't even on secrets yet, it was more like working her way through the books on the less accessible shelves in plain sight.

TWENTY-FOUR
LATER THAT EVENING

Richard thought the supper conversation had gone quite well, really. It had been a pleasure to have time together without any likely interruptions. He enjoyed the time at the Guard Hall, his club, or parties. He forgot, though, how comfortable it felt to be here, at Veritas, with just the family.

Supper being over meant that he had to confront the conversation he still couldn't figure out how to have. Some part of him wanted to not bring it up, assume that either she would work it out from first principles, or that it just wouldn't come up. But that was a coward's way out, and more than that, he was quite sure that Magni would be judging him, by how this went.

Rightfully so. Richard didn't understand all the challenges Magni had. Or Gilbert, for that matter. But he could see there were some. He had been trusted with delicate and treasured knowledge, and he had made an offer of hospitality. The old laws, they had things to say about what someone in Richard's position did with that.

In the end, it came out awkwardly. "We should talk a

little about tomorrow. Perhaps once you're comfortably settled for the night?"

Alysoun looked at him, one of the thoughtful searching glances she had been giving him more frequently this past month. "As you like," she agreed. "You go, you go do whatever it is you do. I'll get Wallis to see to me. It won't be terribly long."

He retreated to the little reading nook in his bedroom, but he couldn't manage to settle into his book at all. In the end it was about fifteen minutes, before he heard the quiet knock on the door. "All set, my lord." Richard waited until the steps receded, then he went along the private passage to her bedroom, and knocked.

"Come in." She was settled in bed again, her hair in a looser braid. She wore a silky robe around her shoulders that looked really quite attractive, in a shade of soft blue-green that suited her almost as well as the dusty blue she often wore. He nodded, and waited for her to wave at the end of the bed. "You had more to talk about?"

He nodded, and now the moment was here, he still had no idea how to start. She was watching him, steadily, and that did not help.

Finally, carefully, he said, "I want to talk a little about Magni. Captain Torham. Will you listen, first?"

She tilted her head, the little curious gesture, but nodded. "You haven't called him that before."

"He's tried to get me to since the apprenticeship. I couldn't until - until he was hurt."

Alysoun nodded slowly. "That changed things for you. I can tell that much."

"It did. Both seeing him in the Healing Temple, and after." He took a breath. "He doesn't invite people around to his home often at all. But he decided he would invite me. Trust me."

"Surely he already trusted you?" Her voice was a bit incredulous. "You know he thinks well of you."

"That's not the same thing as trust." Richard pointed out. "He - there's no delicate way to say this. He prefers the company of men. Privately, not just the usual sort of club."

Alysoun's eyes went wide, and he could see her think through the implications. "This Gilbert Oxley, then. His... his, what is the right word?"

"Partner, I think. Or at least, that will do." Richard kept his voice steady. She wasn't giving him any sign of what she thought about it. Her voice had been even, at least, not outraged. There had been no shrieking or shrinking back in disgust. "Will there be a problem?"

She blinked at him several times. "We are having them over for the afternoon. A dinner party, that might be a challenge, doing the seating plans appropriately, and I suppose they're technically of somewhat different ranks, aren't they? It would be a trick to find a pair of women who suited evenly enough, and in personalities. But we're not having them for dinner, at least not yet. Do you expect there to be a problem?"

This was not at all the reaction he had expected. "You don't - many people think it's wrong." He still couldn't figure out what she actually thought.

"Many people do not know their classics, apparently." Her tone was rather dryly disapproving. "Honestly. There are all sorts of relationships under the sun, now, aren't there. Some of them are more approved than others, but we are at home, and our servants don't gossip about our guests. And I presume, if they've kept it private this long, they have perfectly good methods of continuing to do so." She then looked him up and down, and said, "You don't have a problem with it, do you?"

This was entirely not what Richard anticipated. "No! I mean. No, I don't. I rather liked Gilbert, actually. He has a very sharp mind."

"You do find that appealing, yes." She was roundly amused now, about something she wasn't apparently inclined to explain. "You said he'd been injured."

"In the Sudan, yes. Well before my time. He lost his leg. That sounds queer, doesn't it. He has a wooden one, at least I think it's wood, and he uses a cane. Quite easily, most of the time, but I gather sometimes it hurts him." He then sucked in a breath and said. "I mentioned you've had your own pains. Nothing specific, nothing, nothing delicate."

Alysoun went utterly still at this, and then she said, barely audible. "Why?"

"They asked about you. What you were like." He paused, then risked admitting what he'd realised. "They must have talked about me, about us, quite a lot. I am quite sure they wanted to see what I'd say, when they asked. How I'd put things."

Alysoun nodded, without saying anything. He worried that she'd be insulted, and went on. "And I said you had done brilliantly, all the things expected of you. The estate, seeing to the house, the children. But that it was challenging, your health. I was..." He swallowed. "I was trying to explain why you tended to stay here."

She nodded, very slightly, but he couldn't read her expression at all now. It was as if she had dropped behind a wall of frosted glass that let only the scantest information through. "And?"

"Gilbert said he'd be glad to talk to you, if you'd find it helpful. About managing when things are better one day, and worse another. I, I gather that's particularly frustrating."

Alysoun let out her breath, he could hear it, and then she nodded. "We haven't talked much about it. Not since the first round of Healers."

"No. I didn't want to press." Richard considered, then offered his hand, feeling awkward and ungainly. She looked down at it, as if she wasn't sure what to do with the gesture, then slowly set her palm against his. "You do so much, I know that, even if I don't see the details."

"You are rarely home, it's true." In another woman, he suspected that would be accusatory. Instead, it was even. As if that was the way the world was. The sun rose in the east and set in the rest. Rain fell downwards and plants grew upwards. Richard was never home.

"Today was..." He broke off, not sure how to finish it, other than a smile.

She leaned forward, searching his face. "Visiting them changed something for you, didn't it. That's why you've been home more the past week. Today, but when you came home early, too."

Richard nodded, a tiny movement of his head. "If I'm in the way, I could do something else."

Now she was tilting her head, contemplating him again. "Why would I want that?"

"You, you must have your own routines." She had the same tone Magni had had, when he was bringing Richard around to his own realisations. He paused, seeing how weak his comment was. He didn't know how to explain how he'd been told over and over that he was in the way, that men had their place, and it was their clubs, or their work if he insisted on that.

Alysoun waved a hand, broadly. "I enjoy your company.

It turns out." Before he could try and find words, she went on. "Do you think I don't like you, Richard?"

Put that bluntly, it was difficult to duck. He let out a breath, slowly, not wanting to answer and knowing he had to. "You are so focused on doing things right. Properly. But that means I don't know as much about how you feel as I might."

That made her smile, a slowly spreading amusement. "Our people, both sides, they did not encourage either of us to want things, or talk about wanting things, did they? I know my family didn't. All about duty, and expectations, and being a steward for the family down the generations."

"That, yes. Arthur, all the comments about the hundred year old oaks, and how it's a pity if one comes down in a storm. When that is, yes, the majestic old trees, but they have a cycle of living and dying, and we... " He ducked his chin. "Amber is lovely jewellery, but I don't want to live in it."

She laughed, and there was something open about it, daring him to be as vulnerable. She didn't get caught up inside her own head like he did, he realised. "Quite." She considered, her free hand plucking at the covers for a moment. "Well. Let us try talking, then. I enjoy your company, Richard. At home, here. With the children. When it is just us, alone. Out riding. I also enjoy going out with you, especially when we aren't interrupted twenty minutes in."

He almost apologised again, and she lifted her hand. "You do important work, and you're about to shoulder even more. Helping people who need it, and I don't want to take you away from that. But when you have time, when there are things you can bring home, I am delighted to have time with you. You are not interrupting or interfering. It isn't as if

I have much in my diary other than the occasional formal social event you'd already be at with me."

That last made him smile. "So the party..."

"You don't notice some things, Richard, darling." She was teasing him now. "But you are a fine and thoughtful escort."

"The Frenchman." He couldn't get that image out of his head. "I thought you'd like someone more like that."

"I like someone more like you. Monsieur Brodeur was a fine conversationalist, but he also knows how to read the conversation. He flirted, I was pleased to talk to him. He was frankly a pleasant change from some of the more catty conversation among the women. You missed it, but he said something I could have picked up, if I'd wanted more. I didn't, and he settled in to just being pleasant and, well, very French. But there's nothing wrong with that."

Richard fell quiet, and squeezed her hand. He couldn't quite manage to look at her, when he asked, "How do we go forward, then?"

"What changed things for you? Seeing them?" Alysoun's voice had an intensity to it now that made him look up, almost despite himself. She was watching him, barely blinking.

"The way they were. The house used to be a stone barn, Magni said. And their man let me in, showed me to the study, and Magni was on a chaise, recovering, I gather it's usually Gilbert's reading space. And there are two desks, on either side of the front window, one very tidy, and one chaos, papers and books in piles. It was so clear Gilbert wasn't just visiting."

That made her laugh. "More like your style of keeping a desk."

"Magni's complaints on that front do make a lot more

sense now, yes." Richard tried to keep things tidy. But it was a constant work in progress, and only going to get worse if he had a private secretary.

"How are they in private?"

"Magni said he thought Gilbert would get on well with you. He's, he's quick-witted. Sharp. Observant. Uncomfortably so, sometimes." Then he said, more carefully. "They care for each other, it's obvious. Even though I know what kind of hours Magni keeps."

"Ah, perhaps we can learn something from them." Her voice was quiet now, thoughtful.

He smiled. "I should let you get some rest, it's a busy afternoon tomorrow."

Alysoun looked up, and nodded. "Do this again, soon? Talking?" It was as if she wanted to say something else, but couldn't quite get there.

"Of course. Tomorrow, even. I'm sure we'll want to talk through the visit." He could tell, dimly, through a fog, that she wanted more, but he couldn't sort out what it was. He could only offer a future chance.

Her smile became broader. "Just so." Impulsively, he stood, bending to kiss her lips once, briefly, before he pulled away, and said, "Sleep well."

TWENTY-FIVE

22ND JULY, VERITAS

Given the new information, Alysoun had made arrangements for tea to be served in the library, with its large windows overlooking the gardens and the stained glass decoration along the top and sides. It was, she rather thought, likely to be a more comfortable room for the two men than one of the formal parlours. Certainly, the chairs were both comfortable and more varied.

Richard joined her, a few minutes before their guests were expected. The problem of this space was that they couldn't see them coming up the walk. The portal was at the front of the house, so it could be used by the village as well. They both settled, not particularly talking, until there was a knock on the door. "My lord, my lady. Your guests."

"Come in." Richard stood, and Alysoun joined him. The day was sunny, and she rather liked the effect of the light coming in behind them. It lit the two men as they entered. Captain Torham. It was the first time she'd seen him out of uniform, and he was wearing nearly the same sort of tweed country suit Richard wore, but in a darker brown. He looked like he was recovering fairly well, but his arm was still bound up in a sling.

The other man with him must be Gilbert Oxley, walking so the cane in his right hand didn't foul Captain Torham's feet. She considered him. Definitely a scholar, with the hair that long down his back. Richard had explained how long hair could be grabbed in a fight. Not that Oxley's hair was unduly long for many men, just in contrast to Richard and Torham. He was also somewhat informally dressed, considering, in a scholar's robe of deep green over his shirt and trousers.

Richard smiled. "Magni, Gilbert, do come in." He then turned. "Alysoun, this is Gilbert Oxley. Gilbert, my wife, Alysoun. And you remember Captain Magni Torham, of course."

"Captain Torham, Master Oxley." Alysoun was all smiles, coming forward to greet them. "Do sit down." She was clear he'd earned the title for his work, from what she'd read.

"Do please, call me Magni. And good afternoon, Richard. I see we picked an excellent day."

"And Gilbert, please, Lady Edgarton."

"If Richard is Richard to you, I am glad to be Alysoun." She caught Richard's raised eyebrow. Not the usual thing at all. Several things in this afternoon were not the usual sort of thing, and she thought it better to begin as they meant to go on. It earned her a startled look from Magni Torham, and a measuring one from Gilbert Oxley.

"Please do let me know if something would make either of you more comfortable. A different chair, a footstool." She gestured. "We thought a little time here, and then we could show you the house, and eventually move along eventually to tea here."

Gilbert leaned forward. "I'm quite curious about rather a lot of the house, I do hope you'll tell me if the questions are overly intrusive."

"Is that a thing that you find likely? Intrusive questions?"

"Well, there is the challenge that if you are talking to people about their home, and their wards, you are asking about quite intimate areas of their life. I've found the best wards reflect the dynamics of the current family. It's not the only reason one makes adjustments, of course, but it's one more neglected than it should be." He shrugged. "And then one does not talk much about it, because a good defense is at least one part not advertising your protections."

That made her laugh. "Oh, quite, yes." Then she considered, before she risked something she hadn't expected. "Are you expecting me to ask all sorts of prying questions in turn? I'm rather curious about how some things work for you, but Richard made your personal situation quite clear."

That earned her a wary look from both the men, but Gilbert replied, guarded but polite. "Curious, my lady?"

She snorted, and said, "How do you manage, with the hours Ca... Magni keeps? Worse than Richard's, I gather, and I didn't know that was possible without sleeping in the Guard Hall."

Gilbert threw his head back and laughed. "Oh, that, goodness. Well." He considered, looking from Magni to Richard back to Magni as if considering his answer. Magni looked a little helpless, honestly. "Honestly, he sleeps there sometimes, though less than he used to. We're old enough a cot's not at all appealing. We make the most of the time he's at home."

"Desks, I gather?"

There was a split-second silence, as if Gilbert was weighing the options in a duel, a glance at Magni, as if he were confirming it. "We aim for a balance between the study and the bedroom, as a general rule."

She did not dare to ask what men got up to in the bedroom. And truthfully, she had a perfectly reasonable education in the classics, including various art works from Greece and Rome that did not leave much to the imagination. She nodded slightly, and then eyed Richard. "We have been talking a little about spending more time together." She didn't specify where or how, but it did encourage Richard to reach out and take her hand, and she squeezed his.

"I told Gilbert that I was quite sure you would get along, Alysoun." Magni's voice was rolling with barely suppressed amusement. "And it is a pleasure to see you in a more relaxed setting."

Alysoun considered that. "We've been even busier than usual with the various events around the magistrate investitures. There's rather a lot on my end, not just Richard's."

"You're finding him a personal secretary, yes?"

"And a new cook, for here, and managing the clothing for the various events. But that must, surely, be rather tedious for you to hear about."

"Actually, no." Gilbert broke in. "Neither of us comes from a house like this, but it must have complexities. I know the architecture, of course, of the great houses, but that is not at all the same as knowing what it means to run one. I don't generally get much chance to ask about that."

Alysoun contemplated. "You were in the Army, yes? Did you learn much about the quartermaster's role?"

Both the guests looked blank for a moment, but then Gilbert nodded. "Not simply about having what is needed immediately available, but maintaining the supply chain," he said, suddenly.

"Exactly. For the investiture, I need certain kinds of dresses, and of course, my dressmaker has only so many slots she can spend on me. It isn't in her best interests to have me as her only client, or only a few clients. And I do not need that many new dresses, as a rule."

"But more than - oh, replacements."

"Quite. There are social standards to be maintained. One may wear the same dress multiple times. But not to a dinner party with the same guests, nor to a large event where the dress is part of the thing. There must be some adjustment, some variation, something that makes it look different, at a minimum. And for significant events, rather more than that."

"So for the investiture, where you will be out in front of many people..." Gilbert's voice trailed off.

"That needs a particular sort of dress. And for the magistrate's oath, it needs to be a particular shade of purple, to match Richard's robes." She glanced over, and Richard apparently hadn't quite put that together. "We are not hosting yet, but Richard has made it clear we will be doing so several times a year. So it would be sensible to make arrangements for a cook who could manage that kind of party comfortably now. Our current cook, Mrs Glen-william, is a dear, but getting on a bit, and more comfortable with smaller gatherings. And we haven't been hosting extensively, not since Charlotte was born."

"You have a townhouse in Trellech, I understand?"

"Yes, and she has family there, so it will be a good move all round. But we don't entertain there, as a rule, beyond a very small gathering. Another couple, maybe two. The space is laid out a tad awkwardly."

Richard glanced at her again. "My mother still has the larger family townhouse. It's Georgian, I admit I find it stifling." Not so much the space, Alysoun thought, but his mother in general, not that she had figured out how to explain that to him. Alysoun certainly found her stifling and oppressive, but she knew bringing it up could scarcely go well.

That made Gilbert tilt his head. "But you like it here." He was stating something, as if it were obvious to him.

Richard nodded. "I think we both prefer it here. There are baths, going back to the Roman villa, which are grand after a long day. The grounds, you'll get a chance to see some of that in a few minutes, and the house itself. It has character. Mother's townhouse is much like the houses on either side, or the other side of the street."

Gilbert tilted his head, then he nodded, as if he'd sorted out something in his head that pleased him.

Alysoun raised an eyebrow, and said, risking a further informality, "Care to spell it out for the rest of us who aren't as quick?" It made Gilbert laugh, and Magni chuckle, while Richard blinked at her for a moment, before peering at Gilbert.

"I have heard quite a lot about your husband's duelling skills. And seen him, once or twice, though I don't think he was aware of it at the time." From the way Richard's chin went up, Alysoun suspected not. "But Magni and I have talked about him a great deal over the years. There are some who prefer predictability, even lines, symmetry. They make very showy duellists in controlled situations."

"Which is not, I gather, the same thing as being good." Alysoun nodded. "That would require more adaptability, elaboration."

"Do you know much about duelling?"

Richard almost said something, but Alysoun reached out her fingers to brush his wrist, and said, "We are sitting in our library. That set of shelves have the classic duelling manuals, of course, as you'd expect. And those are historical treatises on various secondary charms, enchantments, cantrips, and jinxes. I've read, oh, four fifths of them, now. Some of them are untranslated, and in languages I don't read. Those shelves there are the more modern ones, the last century or so."

She waited a beat, and added. "I'm sure I don't understand all of them fully. It being a set of magics that are very much about a physical ability I didn't have in my better days, even if I'd been permitted to try my hand at it. And reading about it is not the same as seeing it happen. But I feel confident I have read enough to follow the conversation."

The look on her husband's face was far beyond his ability to hide. She was delighted to see it was a mix of fascination, interest, and utter startlement.

TWENTY-SIX
THAT AFTERNOON

Richard had that moment he often had at the beginning of a duel. He could feel everything come swooping into his awareness all at once, as if time had paused or at least stuttered.

He caught Magni's expression, and then Gilbert's, but what he fixed on, almost immediately, was Alysoun. She was watching him, with that regal patience that was so much a marker of their shared house at school, and that frankly she did much better than he did.

The other men were clearly letting him reply. Or rather, if he did not reply, he would be unlikely to hear the end of it for some years to come. He trusted to that moment that served him so well in duelling, where things made sense and flowed, naturally. It did not fail him now, either.

"You were quite right last night that we'll have a lot to talk about. Have you had a chance at the new Walsingham edition I brought home last week?"

She threw her head back, and laughed, pure and clean, and she said, "Not yet. I was saving it for a treat. But I have questions about the Dashingwood you got last month - there are several places where his theories make no sense at all."

Magni leaned forward and said, laughing, "Oh, that's because Dashingwood is an idiot. When I'm back in fighting form, we should arrange a demonstration, Richard, of how flawed."

Richard was rather grateful for Magni's smoothness there. Grateful both for turning the conversation, and in giving him a way to settle into this new and startling intimacy he hadn't expected with his wife, ever. He nodded. "My lady, I would be delighted to carry your favour in that duel."

She beamed at him, patted his hand. "For that, I might even stretch to doing some embroidery."

Gilbert picked up on that immediately. "Not one of your skills?"

"Oh, I'm perfectly competent. I just don't enjoy it much. It does well to keep the hands busy during a social call when the conversation is dull, or at a hunting party when the men are off doing whatever men do. I make very slow progress." Then she tilted her head, with that attentive smile. "You were about to say something about my husband's duelling skill before I ambushed him."

Gilbert laughed, and settled himself, relaxing. "You understand that Mag comes home talking about things. Which is excellent, I don't get out much. Over the years, we have developed a shorthand for discussing his duellists."

Alysoun inclined her head to Magni. "I understand they all come through the duelling field and salle, and you are master of them both."

"A tenuous sort of master, there are others yapping at my heels, but yes." He leaned back, clearly content to let

Gilbert lead this set of the dance they were doing, whatever it was.

Indeed, Gilbert picked up smoothly. "There are quite a few duellists - Dashingwood among them - who favour a mannerly, orderly sort of duelling. An exchange of castings, within fixed limits. Much like fencer's duels, if you've read about those."

Alysoun nodded slowly. "That seems impractical to me." Her voice was careful. "Given the presumed purpose."

"It depends what that purpose is. If one wishes to improve one's health, to hone one's ability with magics, to build habits, then an orderly sort of duelling might well serve." Gilbert spoke easily.

"But if one is in the Guard, and called upon to use one's skills regularly, well, I do not expect those the Guard is seeking are so mannerly and well-behaved. Or they would not be sought in the first place." Alysoun was piecing through that.

Richard murmured. "We've talked about the Oath, a bit. In apprenticeship, one of the things they drill into us is that any idiot can use brute force, if they have the ability. But it takes skill and training to take someone who is fighting you or fleeing with the least harm possible. And it takes resolve to defer to people who do have those skills, if you don't."

Magni chuckled. "And your husband is better skilled than many. On that boat, Richard, how was the fighting before you got there?"

Richard saw the point immediately. "Hand to hand, and I think they'd been at it a bit, in a stalemate. I'm quite good with a stunning charm and it turned the tide." Magni beamed at him.

Gilbert picked up smoothly. "Which is why Mag - and I - prefer your husband's mode. It being much like our own."

"One of the things I try to get through their sometimes thick heads is that sometimes we get things wrong. Stun someone, no harm done, except a bit of fuss. But if you hurt someone, and they were innocent? That's against the Oath, and if your goodness and virtue didn't stop you, the penalties there should make you wish you'd never tried."

Gilbert murmured, "The trick, of course, is that the other side doesn't have the same limits. So one must protect against worse than you might do, and often from very creative thinkers and duellers."

There was a long pause, long enough Richard almost ventured something.

Then, speaking quickly, as if she didn't want to lose her courage, he heard Alysoun's voice. "Clearly, you have adapted to circumstance."

Richard looked up, sharply, not sure if Alysoun had given offence. Instead, there was a slow smile across Magni's face, and Gilbert was grinning. "It is a choice, just as each duel is a choice," he said. Then his tone changed, as if he'd decided on something. "Your husband mentioned you do not have a clear cause. That must be horribly frustrating. At least I have the comfort of knowing exactly how I got myself into this mess."

Alysoun nodded. "I hadn't thought to put it like that, but yes. Wondering if I could have done something different. I would rather like to discuss with you, at some point, what kinds of things you find help. Or not. But perhaps not right this moment. I need to work up to it."

Richard shifted his hand now, to cover hers, before he said, "We actually had a question, something Alysoun has been doing, when not reading duelling treatises." He caught the flash of her smile out of the corner of his eye. He was watching Magni and Gilbert more directly. "If, Magni, you are permitted to engage your brain in a bit of a puzzle, while your body is not allowed on duty."

As he hoped, Magni grinned. "Oh, if it's just talking through a situation, I think I am up for that. So long as we don't neglect the house."

Richard shook his head. "Alysoun discovered an intriguing irregularity with a piece of stained glass on exhibit." He sketched out the facts as they knew them so far. There was the mysterious artist, the glass that didn't match its supposed provenance. Alysoun explained her meetings and research.

By the time they were finished, Gilbert was leaning one hand on his chin. His eyes half-closed in the manner of someone who was listening so hard he couldn't keep his gaze focused. "You both have this sense that there's something off." His voice was clear.

"I haven't seen the glass myself yet, that's for next week, but I trust Alysoun's eye here."

"Then the first question is why the museum didn't catch it. This is an exceedingly high profile exhibit, I saw it myself, but I was focused on the older pieces, honestly, some of them are wonders."

Alysoun nodded slightly. "I keep wondering that. My attention was particularly drawn by that lecture. And there were only, what, forty or fifty people there. Not a bad number for one of those talks, but most of them are society ladies, having a pleasant afternoon out between other events."

"Not terribly inclined to notice small details of the glass, no. And you said the lecture didn't talk much about the glass making itself, or draw attention to the details of colour." Richard remembered that much. "Nor notice much about the quality of the light, which is what you noticed. And those do all seem rather relevant, for glass.

"Professor Arden went on about whether it was a singular artist or a studio, not nearly so much about the process of the glass. He did get some details of the glass elsewhere in the exhibit wrong, but they were the kind of confusion most people would overlook between two similar pieces." Alysoun was thinking this through, too. "It was curious, the absences."

"And most people would assume an esteemed professor in the field merely misspoke, or that they must have gotten it wrong." Gilbert leaned back, and raised an eyebrow at Magni, another of their silent conversations.

Magni cleared his throat, and Richard instinctively shifted to stabilise himself, the little tells he'd learned through the years. "Criminals often think themselves much cleverer than they are. And certainly much more clever than the people they are trying to fool. It is an arcane art form, poorly understood by most people, for all the results are more available to the public than many. The museum staff are certainly much more comfortable with paintings or ceramics or even mastery medallions. The advantage of an exhibit that has not been attempted before is that almost no one knows what to expect."

That resolved the nagging feeling Richard had had throughout this, ever since Alysoun first brought it up. "That, sir." It came out instinctively. "Magni, also the question of who benefits." A key question drilled into every Guard who took on investigations, just as much as fighting stances or first aid skills.

"The professor. And perhaps whoever donated the pieces, if they can then arrange a sale to the museum or a gallery. You said they were on loan from an anonymous patron."

Alysoun nodded. "I'm afraid my contact wasn't able to find out who, or even guess at who it was. Which does suggest it might be someone who has pieces in the exhibit under their name."

"Why do you say that?" Gilbert was leaning forward again.

"I sat in on several of the meetings with Richard's mother, the Dowager Lady Edgarton, when she lent some jewellery to the museum for that exhibit a few years ago." Alysoun gestured broadly. "There were a whole series of meetings, very precisely done, like, oh, pearls on a string. Each one placed in proper sequence, a half dozen or so in all. One might miss a single meeting, but my contact struck me as quite observant, if still junior in her field, and I do not think she would miss that many. Especially if they took place outside the museum, with the staff needing to go somewhere."

"That does imply that rather than meeting with someone different, instead, the piece came from people who were already in meetings with the museum." Gilbert let out a puff of breath. "Well, that's a puzzle. Do you have a list of who? Perhaps we might spot something you haven't."

Alysoun stood, then she paused for a moment, and sat, carefully. "Richard, if you'd not mind? The catalogue is on the table by the windows, with my other notes."

He caught the wince as she settled. "Of course, my dear." he said. He stood, and got three or four steps toward the windows, before he heard Gilbert say, "So dreadfully tedious, isn't it," in a tone of complete understanding. By the time he got to the table where her materials were spread out, and looked back, Alysoun was smiling again, and Magni was asking her something more quietly.

He brought the catalogue back, and said, "Could we send this off with them, do you think? I don't want to lose the light."

She looked up, and nodded. "Perhaps talk through the history here for a few minutes, and then we can do the tour?" She added, as if something Gilbert had said encouraged her in it, "My leg rather complained. Give me a minute, and I should be quite able to manage."

He noticed that she avoided saying she'd be fine, but he understood well enough why. "Well, then." he said, handing the book over to Gilbert. "The original villa was Roman, as I mentioned." It was easy to settle into the history, telling it in more detail than he was normally encouraged to.

Alysoun thought the visit had gone splendidly. It was well into twilight by the time their guests left after not only tea, but an informal supper. The conversation had been surprisingly wide-ranging. She would have thought that Magni had focused interests, rather like Richard's. He was not so knowledgeable about the arts or music as Gilbert, or about Gilbert's areas of research, but he chimed in on a variety of topics.

Gilbert, now, he was delightful to talk to. He was sharp-witted, but unlike some people she knew, he didn't use his wit to make people feel stupid. Instead, he'd offer a comment that supported something she said, and then showed a way to expand it, or do something more with it. She wondered, now, what it would have been like if he'd stayed in the Guard, and what Richard would be like now if he'd known both of them for longer.

No matter. She could make sure they had regular invitations, and she certainly wanted to keep talking to Gilbert. Richard had seemed quite pleased, as well, at some of the discussion about the household warding, and the way the architecture of the house anchored it. There had been suggestions, things that might be encouraged with certain horticultural plantings, or adding a hint of colour to a window. That would give them a pleasant challenge to sort out, if not an urgent one.

Richard had escorted her upstairs after the two guests left. She had changed into a peignoir and robe, settling in bed with her daybook open, so she could write a few notes. As she had hoped, there was a knock about fifteen minutes after they'd parted. "May I?" He came fully into the room, rather than just sticking his head around the door.

"I was hoping you would." She set the book aside and smiled at him, then shifted her braided hair over her shoulder so it wouldn't tug quite so much at the back of her head.

He gestured at the bed. "May I?" He kept checking, each step. It could have been irritating, but she found it rather charming, not least because it meant she could keep telling him he was wanted and welcome. Perhaps he needed that coaxing and reassurance.

"Of course." He settled on the bed, close enough to reach for her hand, and then he offered his. She settled hers into it, and waited to see where he would start.

"I'm glad you liked them." As beginnings went, that was promising.

"I do. And I can see why you do."

He tilted his head, watching her. "I had no idea you'd read the duelling books."

There it was. Alysoun considered how to say what she wanted without hurting him unnecessarily. "I wanted to know what interested you. About what you are good at. And Magni has been quite clear, you are an exceptional duellist."

"You know I have no idea what you're interested in. Beyond the things we've talked about. And most of that quite recent." He flushed and looked away. "I feel like I've failed in a quest."

"Richard." She said it clearly enough to bring his eyes up, to get him to focus on her again. "You have been quite busy with important work. I know you don't like to talk about most of your Guard business."

"Magni does. With Gilbert." It came out of Richard's mouth like he hadn't meant to say it. She was revelling in the fact he was not keeping himself under such rigid control as he had been. That they might finally be moving beyond formalities, after seven years of marriage.

"Gilbert was in the Guard. I certainly wasn't." Alysoun kept her voice even, avoiding any hint she might be scolding.

He squeezed her hand. "But you see things I don't. That conversation about the wards, whether adding holly or roses might be better. The risks of the poison plants, I know they're traditional for the use, but with the children." He added, considering. "Or the horses."

"The children are more likely to be free-ranging, but you're quite right." It amused her how he'd put that. "You don't mind?"

"Merlin, no. I just." Richard looked down and away again, finding a spot on the floor by her bed very interesting. "I haven't paid nearly enough attention to you."

This was true. However, rubbing it in at this stage wouldn't do any good. It wasn't that Alysoun hadn't been frustrated, even hurt by it. She was human, after all, and as capable of being petty about her emotions as anyone else. But she'd had time to get over it. Largely. Especially if he could be induced to do something different now.

"Well, then. That gives us somewhere to start talking, doesn't it?"

He looked up and nodded, just the once. "I'd like that." She beamed, that was one of the clearer expressions of personal desire she'd gotten out of him in years.

Then, of course, he was blinking at her and not suggesting a topic, so she supposed she'd have to start somewhere. "Let me... actually, Gilbert said something that had me thinking."

"He said a number of things." There was good humour there, at least. "On which topic?"

"The challenge with the glass is that it seems, at least on the surface, to be reasonable enough, as what it claims to be. But people make copies of paintings all the time, forgeries. Not all the time, but regularly enough. There are stories going back to the Romans, with statues, and oh, dozens of stories from the Renaissance."

"But those, you have details like brush strokes, or the wood or the stone."

"Exactly. What if we could find a way to link the glass to something that wasn't the right thing?"

He frowned. "Tell me more about that." She could tell he was non-committal, and she wondered whether she should risk whatever fragile new beginning they had on this. But she couldn't get it out of her head, and he wanted to know what she was interested in. Which, right now, was the glass.

"I was thinking about what Gilbert said, about the various theories of magic. How some of them are not as broadly useful as people thought, but that doesn't mean they don't have purposes. Uses. Specifically, the doctrine of sympathies."

Richard raised an eyebrow. He didn't say anything, but

he leaned forward a little, and shifted his hand to squeeze hers once. She took that as encouragement.

"We have on one hand, a piece of glass, of suspect provenance," she said. "We could take other pieces of glass, of known provenance. I don't know, one of the mediaeval pieces, one Renaissance, one of about the same period as Reynard, one entirely modern. And then we could see how strong the resonance was."

"Glass is complex, though. The colour, the pigments, that would alter things."

"Perhaps multiple dishes, with the likely pigments? And then see if something doesn't respond?"

"What are you thinking for it to respond to that shouldn't be there?"

Alysoun shrugged, slightly. "I was thinking someone could go get a bit of soot from London, and that might do well enough. Something from, oh, above street level, so you don't get all the street dirt in. A third floor roof or something of the kind."

"Pigeons might be a problem." Richard said it so deadpan for a moment that she blinked at him, feeling rather like a fish out of water, and then he grinned broadly. She beamed back at him. They both started laughing, until she got a stitch in her side, and had to clamp her hand there to give herself a little more support. He immediately calmed. "Can I help?"

She smiled at him again, ducking her head. "Kind." Then, tentatively. "Could I lean against you? The pressure helps a bit."

It wasn't what he was expecting, something in him seemed uncertain, but he nodded. "May I?" He gestured at her other side, where he might relocate.

Alysoun shifted a bit to allow him to come around the

other side of the bed, and settle in beside her, then offering an arm around her shoulders.

"Is this all right?" It took a little thought for her to rearrange herself into something that was comfortable, but she entirely liked him being right there. She could feel his shoulder, warm against her, sturdy, somehow.

"Excellent. So, the doctrine of sympathies." She gathered her thoughts as best she could. Her breathing was settling out. "There is the problem of pigeons, yes. But I think we could narrow down things. If the glass was made where the provenance says, there shouldn't be lots of industrial soot in it."

"No. And if you worked from the soot, then it should resonate without the glass. Without having to destroy the glass, or get scrapings." He had to stop and think. "I can't tell if that's the doctrine of sympathies or the law of contagion. But I see the way you're going at it."

"Exactly. Take the things that shouldn't be in the glass, and resonate for them, along with things that are in the glass, to prove the point."

There was a silence, as Richard worked through it. She knew he could be quick witted when he needed to be, but given a choice, he did like to examine things from every angle. "How do we go about arranging that, then?"

"That is the tricky part, since we'd need access to the piece in question. And possibly well away from the other items. I don't even know how you'd set up the rituals for it."

"That is something Mason can arrange. That kind of isolating ritual circle or square or whatever geometric shape you might want. We might need to rearrange things in the space a bit, but I shouldn't think we'd need to remove the window from display. Mason's very good at what she does."

"Which is why you like working with her." Alysoun was amused. "I have noticed you appreciate competence."

Richard snorted. "More like, in this case, I paid attention to Magni. He drilled into me - along with a great many other things - that how you treat the Penelopes goes a long way in your own work. And your reputation. That it was well worth my time to cultivate the best of the staff, for when I needed a favour. Besides being a decent thing to do."

"And you are a decent person, Richard." She felt he might not know that, but he was.

He said, after a long moment. "I'm not sure I know what decent is. In the overall context. That may be part of the trouble." His voice sounded distant, all at once, like he was peering at himself with an oddly angled magnifying glass.

Richard felt utterly at sea. Or at least as if he'd been dropped into a bit of Albion's landscape that was entirely unknown. He felt forced to navigate by the most blunt mechanisms, the movement of the sun, that water flows down to the sea eventually, and that the wind is more likely to be blowing from the south-west. But he had seen how Alysoun had lit up, relaxed, enjoyed today's conversations in a way that she didn't seem to enjoy the obligatory social events. He'd only seen her like that, reliably, with a few of her closer friends.

Now she was turning to peer at him, and he almost wanted to squirm under her attention, like Gabriel did when he thought he'd done something naughty. It wouldn't help at all.

"You really don't think you're decent, do you?" She sounded startled, and he risked meeting her eyes.

"I do what I am expected to. I don't know that that should be anything special." He had never been able to articulate this, though admittedly, the few times he'd tried, people had made it clear the whole concept made them uncomfortable.

"That is part of what makes you decent, Richard. You do the right thing without expecting praise for it. But that doesn't mean you're not doing the right thing."

He gestured with his free hand. "By a quirk of birth, I have power, position, influence. Oh, the idea of the divine right of kingship is long since ignored, but why was I born to be Lord of the land and not, say, a tenant? A footman, a stable hand. Don't I have an obligation to do the thing properly, not skimping?"

She nodded slightly, and that encouraged him to add, "I shouldn't get praised for doing the thing I should be doing. That's like praising Gabriel and Charlotte for breathing or walking and growing."

Alysoun considered, running her thumb along his skin as she thought. The intimacy, the way she did that instinctively, made him shiver and want more. "Is that why you went into the Guard?"

No one had ever actually asked him that, though he rather thought Magni had guessed correctly. Plenty of people had tried to talk him out of it, of course. "The Guard oath, it's a framework for what is good and virtuous." He frowned, fumbling for words again. "Being Lord Edgarton, that is about doing the right things for the land. It's about what flows through me. The magistrate's oath, that's about a specific set of actions, a particular role. But the Guard, that's about who I am, what I value, what I've chosen."

She tilted her head, considering him again. "There are people in the Guard who aren't like that about it."

Richard knew that, too, though he'd never really made sense of that, how someone could split themselves into pieces. "True. I know it. I might be idealistic, but I'm not ignoring that. But it's better than the Lords. Or the Magistrates. The Guard Oath, you can't be awful off duty, not the worst ways, the ones that hurt people."

Then, he had a sudden realisation. Because he'd hurt her, and his oath hadn't caught at him. "I know I hurt you, leaving you alone, not asking about things, all sorts of ways."

Alysoun's voice was very gentle. "You did, but that's a different sort of hurt than those who ignore their duties, or are nasty because they can be, or who drink and abuse their wives and children. You do, perhaps, spend a tad more time at work than your family would prefer, but given that you are doing good in the world, it's hard to argue with. And if that is the greatest flaw you have, well, we can manage that."

"You'd like me to be home more?" That was the first thing that struck him. And then a "Do you know people who - wives, I mean, who are abused?"

"Yes, darling, I would enjoy it if you were home more often. I like you, I am interested in spending time with you. Talking." She swallowed, before adding, "Wives, yes. But don't push me to tell you who. There's not much the law will do, until a certain point, and they risk being hurt much more if their husbands find out. Not Guard, any of them, you're right that the oath helps there. Or at least that someone who'd do that wouldn't take the oath."

He didn't much like that, but he understood and nodded. "If I can be a help, I hope you will tell me immediately. I'm not used to people being interested, not like you say you are." He felt her hand twine a bit more in his, and then she moved to kiss his cheek, once, before leaning a bit more against his shoulder. It felt like a hound settling on the hearth in her proper place. It was strange, queer, but also comfortable. He could almost feel her weighing whether to say something.

"You don't have many close friends, do you?"

It was not what he had expected, but after a moment, he shook his head. "Not like you and Isabella or Emmeline. A lot of pleasant acquaintances, I suppose. There are plenty of people I get on well with."

Alysoun nodded, and squeezed his hand. "And it's been like that for a while, then?"

He nodded, thinking back. She made him want to take his time, to look at things again, and he found himself leaning into that more and more. "Forever, really. I suppose I never really got close to anyone at the tutoring house. Those were the same people in Fox House, at school, and then I went into the Guard and most of them didn't."

"Gilbert had a few things to say to me, when you took Magni off to look at the maze."

"He rather looked like he might." Then Richard added, quickly, "I hope that was all right? I suppose it wasn't proper."

"We were on the back terrace of our own home, with you largely within line of sight." Alysoun pointed out. "Also, Gilbert made it quite clear he has no objection to social interactions with women, though he's a tad out of practice. And he has no eyes for anyone other than Magni when it comes to more private matters."

"Did he tell you that?" Richard couldn't quite keep the startlement out of his voice. It made Alysoun lift her head, peer at him, grin, and then kiss his cheek again.

"We have gathered that we are the partners more inclined to actually talk about things. Apparently Magni's as terse as you are. Not that there's not some reason. Gilbert started out checking with me how I felt about how much, or rather how little, you tell me about Guard matters."

Richard felt both aggrieved and a bit on edge, and

soothed, at the same time. He was amazed that she saw him, seemed to understand him that clearly. And yet, it made the way he'd failed to measure up to his heroic and noble dreams all the more obvious.

He took a breath to settle himself. "To come back to the original topic, now you bring it up, no close friends, other than a few in the Guard. Magni. Having them over felt very different, but - good. He talked to me while we were in the maze."

"About anything in particular?" Dash it, of course she picked up on that right away.

"Let me work around to that."

"Training over low fences." She was smiling now, easily, and he liked her being pleased.

He had to smile at the equestrian metaphor. "May I ask what else you and Gilbert talked about?"

"The tapestries - he's working on a theory about some of the older worked tapestries being integrally tied into the protections of the house. He says it's hard to get evidence, and of course ours were redone fifty years ago and I'm sure no one was really thinking about it."

Richard nodded. "I can see how that might be an area of interest."

"And he talked a little bit about the health issues. About being able to do a thing one day, and not the next. Or hour to hour."

"I got the impression his leg bothers him more than he admits to."

"He was very frank with me, because he said my experience is different. But that I was in the best position to figure out what he could tell me that was helpful." She shifted to run her thumb against Richard's hand. "But he understands what it's like to - feel betrayed."

Richard took a deep breath, and swallowed. "Is that what you feel?" He kept his voice low and even.

She shrugged, he could feel her shoulder move, the one that wasn't leaning on him. "Sometimes. Enough." Her voice had gotten small, and very vulnerable now.

He drew in a breath. "I think if it were me, I'd be angry for a very long time."

That made her stop and look at him, blinking at short distance. "You're almost never angry. I don't think I've ever heard you lose your temper."

"That, my dear, is because you do not do things that tempt me that way. I have a few times. Fighting, when people were being foolish. Stupidly, dangerously foolish. In the Sudan, at Omdurman, it was - why I was glad to be recalled." He had the sudden realisation that there was something else there, what it had been like to be shoulder to shoulder with people not bound by that kind of oath, just by their commitment to fight when told.

He had his eyes open enough that he could see her consider that, and then not ask him something further. Instead, she said, "I wake up angry, sometimes. That I'm hurting, that it doesn't get better, even if I do all the things I should do."

Richard considered. "It would be simpler if it did. Magni's collar bone. He does the things he is supposed to, and he will heal, and it is all rather predictable, isn't it?"

Her voice got rather quieter. "I try to do the right things, but they keep changing. Sometimes heat is good, sometimes cold is, sometimes moving is, sometimes moving is absolutely wrong. It is, it is unsettling."

Richard nodded slowly. "Like your body can't even bother to tell you what would help. A particular kind of betrayal. Very personal."

"Is impersonal betrayal better?" There was a sharpness to her tone now.

"I think it might be easier to heal from." Richard waved a hand. "And it might be over and done. What you're talking about keeps happening. You don't get a break, harried from all sides, at unpredictable intervals."

"Not the position an experienced duellist would prefer, then." Her voice had turned more amused and dry now.

"Decidedly not. Unfortunately, sometimes we don't get to choose our ground."

He heard her inhale, then there was a very deliberate pause. Just as he was considering saying something, she reached for his other hand. "What can we choose, then? You and I?"

TWENTY-NINE
THAT EVENING

Alysoun wasn't at all sure how to begin with this, this new kind of conversation with him. But now that he was here, and they were talking, she was not at all inclined to give him too much chance to back away. If they made a try of it, and it didn't work, well, at least then she'd know.

Richard blinked at her, then squeezed her hands, each of them, very carefully, like he wasn't sure what would hurt her. Which was fair, given that they'd just been talking about how unpredictable it was. Being cross with him for being overcautious would be several steps back from what she wanted. He was thinking, visibly, and she took a breath and gave him space to do it in, not rushing him.

Finally, softly, he spoke. "Could we, would you dim the lights? I may not be brave enough to do this with them on."

She smiled, and shifted just enough to kiss his cheek. "There's something more private, talking in the dark. Safer. Did you do that at school?" She extracted one of her hands to touch the panel at the end of her headboard that would bring the charm lights down into darkness. She took his hand again before they went entirely out. It left them with the crack under the door to the hallway and the light of the waxing moon through the windows.

Once the charms went fully dark, he took a breath and let it out, measured and deliberate. She held her tongue, just waiting, feeling something fragile there.

When he spoke, his voice was quiet, nearly a whisper, but it had an edge to it. "No one told me how to do this right. Be a husband, a father." He couldn't find the words for it, not yet, but he rather suspected it was worse than that, that everything he had been told had been wrong.

Alysoun waited, but when it became clear he wasn't going to continue, she squeezed his hands once and offered, as gently as she could. "I suspect I had more formal education on being a wife and mother." She considered. "When you did your Guard apprenticeship, it was - structured, wasn't it? Learning things in a specific order."

He nodded, and then added, "Yes. Not orderly, exactly, but disciplined. Coordinated. Planned, at least until we went to the apprentice masters. And of course, Magni was very clear on what he expected."

"And with the marriage, it was different. You were in the Sudan, and then you came back. We went from probably getting married sometime, to getting married in three months, all higgledy-piggledy, and barely any time to talk to each other."

"Like that. And I was still settling into the Guard here again, and Father was ill, and I had a lot to learn about the estate, quite quickly."

She thought she began to see where some of this had begun to fracture. "Are you worried you treated me badly?"

There was a silence long enough to strain her comfort, so she was nearly on the edge of speaking when he said, "Yes. That

I was rough. Demanding. That I put too many expectations on you." Then he swallowed, and said, "Mother made it clear men are a bother, they impose, that a sensible woman didn't want any of that. I know I hurt you, a lot, after Charlotte, too."

There it was, out in the open at least. Alysoun considered which piece of this to go at first, like unpicking fine silk embroidery, each strand delicate and likely to snap. "I knew what marrying you would mean. Managing the estate, making the proper offerings and rites, having your children. That's the part I was trained for."

"Your own apprenticeship." He was trying that on for size - good.

"With my mother and aunts and the women they introduced me to, yes."

"It seems like rather a waste. You were brilliant in school, I gathered that. Some of the ritual magics, some of the charms. Why shouldn't you have had a chance to go on and do more of that?"

She shrugged, a little twitch of her shoulder. "All sorts of reasons. But I could go back to some of it if I wanted. Especially as the children get older."

"Did you want it? This?" His voice had gotten very quiet. She was so clear that how she handled this, how she answered him, would set the course for the rest of their lives together. Whether it was distant and civil, or something strange and new and, she hoped, much better.

"It feels odd to say it, but I wanted you. Meeting you, the first time. You looked so secure, solid, in your Guard uniform. And you were pleasant, and you didn't try to sneak a kiss and slobber, and you didn't treat me like I had no brains in my head. I hoped we would have a good life together. I thought we could." She squeezed his hand. "It seems a weak foundation for building a life, but you were notably better than the other options."

She could feel Richard consider that, the stillness that he had when his mind was working faster than his body. Then, in the dark next to her, he said, "The other options were that awful?"

Alysoun shrugged slightly. "You have turned out, actually, to exceed 'notably better'." She hesitated. "You asked about women being abused. One of the women I know about married one of them. And the marriage charms are wrapped tightly - it's going to be complicated to unweave them."

He went still against her, startlingly so, before he spoke. "Talk to Mason. She hasn't ever said, but I'm fairly sure she's done that kind of thing before. Consulted, at least, referred to someone who could do the charmwork to the necessary standard if she couldn't. Tell her I told you to ask."

It was not at all what Alysoun expected. In that moment, she knew both that she had made a superb choice, and that she hadn't known how good until right now. Not many men, presented with that information, would have immediately done the same.

She shifted, enough to kiss his cheek, then she ventured to rearrange herself awkwardly, enough to meet his mouth, lips against lips. He hadn't expected it, and he didn't press to continue the kiss, but let her guide it. When she pulled away, she could see his eyes gleam for a moment in the dim light. "My lady?"

"I am most glad I chose you." Alysoun wanted that to be as clear as she could make it.

"It really was your choice? Not just the best of a bad

lot? I rather feel like I let you in for benign neglect, at the least."

It was a fair accusation, by some standards, but given the situation, it was utterly unfair. She took a breath, let it out, and said. "Let's talk that out, then."

He nodded, and then shifted, extending his arm against the headboard so she could lean against him more thoroughly. She took advantage immediately, rearranging her hip before it could cramp up more painfully. Then, finally, she continued. "I knew I'd have to marry. There are the family properties. And you know Mother, I couldn't marry just anyone. Someone proper. But I liked what I knew of you. People had talked about you at school, that you'd been kind, not snobbish or prickly. Willing to help."

Richard grunted. "Not much to build a marriage on."

"Hush, let me talk. And I don't like that the Guard keeps you away so much, and Nimue, I worry about you sometimes. But I like very much that you have a thing you are so good at, that you care about, that improves things. That you chose those oaths."

He was quiet as if he was thinking through things, and had nearly forgotten she was there. After the silence had gone on for at least a minute, she shifted, and that reminded him to speak. "That matters to you?"

"Plenty of men of our class who consider that hunting, fishing, and sex are the only necessary things in life. Also good food and wine."

"Nothing against any of those." And then he went still again, as if he had confessed to something he had rather not.

This was so delicate. "I'm quite sure you don't have a mistress. I can't see where you'd have time." She kept her voice light. "I'm clear you really are at the Guard Hall, or out on circuit, when you're not here. I suppose you could duck away for an hour or two, while riding, but... I'd feel rather sorry for her if you were. So I'm fairly sure you aren't."

There was another long silence. "That's not the sort of thing I expected you to say."

"You are, as you demonstrated when we were working on producing Gabriel and Charlotte, a man of quite pleasing appetites."

His voice was a whisper, when he said, "Pleasing?" He was absolutely incredulous, as if she had said that the sun were blue or the winter warm.

She shifted, so she could peer at him in the faint light. "Quite pleasing. I enjoyed our time."

"But then you - I hurt you, didn't I?" He kept coming back to that, and she decided it was time to take it in hand.

"Oh, Richard." She tried to keep her voice even. "A lot of things hurt. If I stopped doing anything that might hurt, I wouldn't ever do anything. I wouldn't hug our children, or go or a ride, or get in the bath - even if the bath helps, too - or enjoy the garden or go to the museum. And I would like to think that the pleasure of being in bed with you again might be worth a certain amount of discomfort I might well have had anyway."

"Oh." He took in a deep breath. "I hadn't expected to ever..." His voice trailed off, then there was something different when he spoke again, something she suspected was rather like him preparing himself for a duel. "Not tonight, then, but let us see how that plays out."

She beamed, not caring he couldn't see it, she was sure he'd hear it properly. "Do join me some night, then. Soon."

Richard woke with a start the next morning, the instinctive jerk of trained reflexes that had noticed despite his sleep that someone was moving in the room. He was half-upright before he realised it was a housemaid he barely recognised, coming in with a fresh pitcher of water. She yelped, put the pitcher down, managing not to break it, and scurried out.

Alysoun shifted lazily in her sleep, then blinked. She had turned on her side, facing away from him. He was still above the covers, not beneath them, but he must have fallen asleep here. Both of them had. They had been up talking late into the dark, and then, well, he supposed he must have fallen asleep first.

He coughed, quietly. "Alysoun?" She blinked, shifting and wincing, then peered at him, before rubbing her face.

"Morning. Wait. Um."

"I fell asleep. Possibly also startled the housemaid? She brought water in."

That made Alysoun snort, and then wince again, before she stretched carefully and levered herself upright on her other arm. Richard watched, not sure what to make of this particular intimacy.

"Mmmm." Then she stretched again, and blinked up at him. "Did you get enough sleep?"

Richard considered. "I was quite rude, falling asleep on you like that. But I think I did, yes. Should I let you get on with the morning?"

Alysoun considered, cocking her head, watching him. "They'll be gossiping, downstairs. Mabel is a fine young woman, but that kind of thing always gets passed along."

"The housemaid? Wait, do they... I suppose they must." One way forward was to learn to think about what she noticed, and it had become quite clear she thought about the household in an entirely different way than he did.

"We are central to the household, dear. Of course they are attentive to what we do, not just because of their jobs, but because it makes a difference in their day. In their security."

He got distracted for a moment thinking about the networks of conversation he had largely, no, entirely, ignored. "What would be easiest for you, then?"

Alysoun eyed him speculatively. "I usually have a tray up here, you know. But let me ring and ask for breakfast downstairs."

He snorted. "Give them more to talk about?"

She nodded. "I find I am not inclined to let you go off yet. Unless you need to be somewhere?"

Richard glanced at the clock he could see from the bed. "I need to be at the Guard Hall, hmm. Leave here in forty-five minutes."

"I will be prompt, then." She reached out and touched the panel that would summon Wallis, who promptly rapped on the door. Alysoun called out, "Come."

The expression on her face was delightful, if immediately repressed. She bobbed, and said, "My lady?"

"Richard and I will be breakfasting downstairs. Let them know to set places for both of us, please, and then help me into a tea gown. Promptly, if you can, he needs to leave for the Guard Hall on time."

Richard stood, bending over to kiss her cheek. "I'll dress, my lady." It felt queer and awkward to be in the midst of this. Even when they'd been newly married, he'd often slipped out of her bed first thing in the morning, leaving her to her more leisurely day. Given their conversation, he rather suspected that had been one of the first ways he'd hurt her.

He couldn't change the past. He didn't even entirely know, not rationally, why he'd done that, other than having been told over and over that men were oppressing by their mere presence. By his mother, of course. Now, he began to wonder what would have been different if he'd asked what Alysoun preferred.

Twenty minutes later, they were both downstairs, with plates set out before them. Eggs, bacon, and toast for him, broth and toast for her. He tilted his head, and she said, "I'm not very hungry first thing in the morning. The strawberry jam is excellent this year, though." He was in his uniform, but in shirtsleeves and waistcoat at the moment, since it was a rather warm morning.

"From the village?"

"This pot, yes. We ran out of Cook's last jar a few weeks ago, and she's working on making the new batch. More this year, mind."

There was a slightly awkward silence, before Richard realised it was his turn to say something. "I'll make sure everyone is aware not to disturb me for the gala at the Museum." That was at the end of the week. "I might need to work rather late the next few days to manage it, if that's not a problem."

"Depending on what's on your desk when you get in?"

"Exactly." Then he asked, quietly, hoping she'd say yes, "Would you be willing to come up to town early?"

She looked up, her eyes dancing. She was sitting at the end of the table, and he had taken the seat beside her. "Oh, I was planning on it. For tonight, we could at least have a nightcap, even if you can't get free for supper."

He felt, more than heard, a little shuffle of the footman at the door to the breakfast room, and he leaned in. "Giving them more to gossip about, my dear?"

"I am merely being practical. So you know, my dress for the gala is already packed, and we were planning on coming up around two on Wednesday, and missing the worst of the portal wait." That would give her plenty of time to recover.

"In that case, I will see what I can do about the nightcap." He considered. "Tell the children I love them, and I'll come see them tomorrow?"

"If you're sure you can manage that."

Richard took a breath, wanting to defend himself, but he knew as well as she did that if something came up with the Guard, he'd be there. "Tell them I miss them and I'll do my best."

Alysoun nodded. "That will do well. They do miss you."

He tried not to feel guilty about that, and a moment later she broke the tension, enough, by saying, "Do have a good day. And a quiet one, I hope."

Richard smiled at that, and stood. "A kiss, before I go?" He sounded like a school boy now, but there was something in him bursting to ask. Hoping it wasn't asking too much.

Alysoun smiled, and stood, leaning on the arm of the chair for a moment, then turned to hold out a hand to him. He slipped his fingers into it, and then his hand carefully against her hip, taking his time with the kiss. She encouraged it, leaning into him a little, her hand coming up to rest on his shoulder for balance. She was not short for a woman, and it wasn't too much of a stretch for her. They didn't linger, but it was a newly potent intimacy, different than last night, but adding to what he'd felt then.

"Be safe," she said. "Oh, and if I wanted to ask Mason to help, when could I catch her?"

"Until five, unless she has a case that calls her out, in the office." He did some mental calculations about the calendar. "Or eight to eleven most mornings. If you're up for coming in with me on Thursday, I could walk you there."

"Let me see how I feel, then." Alysoun smiled at him again, and then nudged him with her hand. "Go on. You'll be late."

Alysoun took the glass that Richard held out to her, carefully. She had been working hard all night to camouflage how difficult she was finding the evening. The tingling in her hands and her right foot had not progressed to numbness today, at least. But neither were a help on an evening that was meant to be about standing around looking elegant and engaging. She'd been quiet all night because her brain felt like cotton batting, and she could not remember names for the life of her.

She had thought she was masking it well enough. At these sorts of events, you could often pick up the name, and then the trick was just remembering it for the length of the conversation. Sometimes the name fell right back out of her head like into a deep well. Fortunately, she could often manage without the name if she had to, after the initial introductions.

Now Richard was looking at her, and leaning in, with a "We could make our excuses." Just enough she could hear it. She wondered, for a moment, what it looked like to him, compared to what she felt like. She took a breath, and brushed out her skirts. Alysoun rather liked the overlay skirt that reminded one of bird feathers, though in a somewhat more muted range than a peacock, with copper highlights.

Not nearly as showy as Madeline Delwyn, over there, who was about her age, wife to the heir to the current lord. She had taken the theme of 'creatures' rather more elaborately than Alysoun had, and was wearing a rather brightly coloured dress of almost garish yellows and oranges, with suggestions of tiger stripes. It drew the eye, but Alysoun was not at all sure she liked the implied effect.

She was talking now to Hortensia Miller, her sister, who was being proud and haughty and rather conspicuously not looking at Richard and Alysoun. She had favoured something more Amazonian in dress. Alysoun felt that Hortensia must not be aware of the lore there, given the number of rather fervent commentaries about how they were a women-only society. That would not suit Hortensia at all, Alysoun suspected.

Alysoun sipped her drink, considering their options. "Not for at least half an hour, my dear," she said, finally. "Must make the right sort of show."

"Would you prefer to sit?"

She shook her head minutely. "I'd rather sit, but it would look wrong. I don't think I can manage a gavotte at the moment, but a waltz?"

Richard inclined his head. She had, she realised, handed him a duellist's problem, and that made her feel that they might in fact emerge on the other side. "The limitations, my lady?"

"My balance, at the moment. And my memory, but that isn't a problem with a waltz."

"Then I shall be a steady arm." He said it evenly. "And

we should have a waltz in two songs, if I remember the order correctly. Shall we take our time drinking..."

Focusing on one's spouse at these things was not entirely the done thing, but she did not want him to wander off, or let someone else monopolise her. She looked around, trying to find something to talk about, so that they wouldn't be interrupted. "Do you see Lord and Lady Delwyn?"

"I was more intrigued by the son and his wife. Jupiter and..." He had forgotten her name.

"Madeline. Sister to Hortensia Miller, who was rather blatant at the gathering for the new magistrates."

Richard wrinkled his nose, for just a moment. "Oh, yes. Is that dress quite the thing?" He sounded entirely dubious, and she shifted to kiss his cheek.

"Not the sort of thing I'd wear, no. But if you want a discourse on women's fashion, that must wait for some other time." She caught a movement out of the corner of her eye. "Captain, um. Does something with locks? Coming up behind you." He would, at least, be a suitable distraction until the waltz.

Richard waited a moment or two, then turned naturally, before smiling. "Captain Oxhampton. You remember my wife, of course. Alysoun, Captain Oxhampton, who heads the Rivers division." Bless him, he'd made sense out of that mish-mash she'd mumbled.

"Lady Edgarton." He made a sharp little bow, being one of those older men who were somewhat fussy about manners. His wife was a rather disconcertingly proper dowager-in-waiting, but she was thankfully engaged in conversation with several of her relatives on the other side of the room. "Pardon, I wanted a word, Edgarton, if you've a moment."

Alysoun considered, weighing whether to excuse

herself to the powder room. "Please don't mind me, I know Richard's work sometimes intrudes." She took a step or two back, inclining her head amiably, and let the two men settle into quiet conversation. Several ladies passed by, behind her, and she nodded at them, polite and cordial, without actually saying anything worth remembering. Her eyes kept sliding back to the Delwyns.

It wasn't just Madeline who was dressed a tad garishily, but also Lady Delwyn. It was harder to tell with the men. Fashions changed more slowly, and men tended to be more resistant to the momentary whims of couture. In clothing, at least, they were certainly faddish about any number of other things. But both Lady Delwyn and her daughter-in-law were wearing what were obviously new frocks, but of less than the highest quality fabric. It had the sheen of cheaper materials to it, and a dye that was less vibrant than those around them.

There were charms to enhance the designs, but they were not as well executed as Alysoun would have expected from that sort of family. If it had been just the younger generation, she might have suspected a generational rift or a difference in style. But a closer look at Lord Delwyn suggested the cuffs of his formal robes had had a bit of wear and not been replaced.

She had to remind herself not to let what she was thinking show. And so she turned, and smiled, and made a passing comment about the choices for one of the flower displays, and then a compliment about a young woman's dress. She was looking a tad nervous, and Alysoun knew that feeling very well. She didn't recognise the girl, so Alysoun suspected she was in her first season.

Then she glanced back, and Captain Whatshisname was visibly finishing up. It had taken them through one dance, and most of the next, and Richard was holding out his hand to her. She slipped her arm into his. His colleague nodded and withdrew.

"About events on the...?" The word failed her, and she let her voice trail off.

"That mysterious box, yes. More to the point, the people involved. All known along the river, no one with a particular reputation for smuggling."

Alysoun pursed her lips. "Does that mean they don't do it, or does it just mean no one's caught them at it before?"

Richard couldn't repress a laugh, it made other people near them turn to look. "Probably the second, if you put it that way." He considered, then added, "I'd like to talk it through with you, Not tonight, you'll want your rest. Perhaps tomorrow."

She inclined her head, but before she could say anything, the dance came to an end. Richard took her glass from her, and placed it on the tray of a passing waiter along with his own. "A dance, my lady? Make a proper show of it?"

Alysoun nodded, and then he was drawing her out on the dance floor. She was not a talented dancer, but she was practised, or at least, she had been before her body became so unpredictable. And the waltz, at least, was a dance where her role was to follow his lead.

He bowed to her, she curtsied, and then he settled his hand at her waist, presented his other for her own, and she settled her hand on his shoulder. It made her feel more stable and secure, the way she could feel the muscles of his shoulders shift. And then the music was going, and he was moving, and she could just focus on getting her feet to go in the right places. He was keeping his steps small. Some men liked to stride about, forgetting that she was managing weighty skirts, even if they were better than what her mother complained about wearing in her youth.

He swung her gently, once they got into the rhythm of it, nothing terribly showy, but enough. She felt the shifts of his shoulder, the angle of his chest, and just trusted that it would be all right. One of the turns made her dizzy, and she closed her eyes.

"Let me know if you need me to stop, my lady." She nodded, unable to say anything directly. He just kept things up smoothly, moving them around the floor in a measured way, always giving her enough warning of where he was going and what she needed to do. Her mind flittered away to all the stories about the waltz being terribly scandalous when it was introduced.

Right here and now, pressed against him, she could certainly feel that. He was right there, undeniably, his body lined up with hers. She had to trust his movement, to match them with hers, even more so with him guiding everything like this.

Finally, the music came to the final bars, and he came to a stop, near a quiet corner of the dance floor. Alysoun opened her eyes, and realised he must have planned that. They were near the cloakroom. He bowed, and said, "May I escort you home?"

All of a sudden, she thought that was a wonderful idea. Better to leave now than fade and shatter into pieces where other people could see. She nodded. "Please." Just the one word.

He swung into action, with all the efficient movement she imagined as part of a duel. He got one of the staff to fetch her shawl, another to fetch a carriage. Richard himself went and made his goodbyes to a few people, coming back promptly to offer his arm. "My lady."

Gratefully, she let him lead her out to the carriage. On the other end, he walked her up to her rooms in the town house, and waited while she changed. Once she sent Willis away, he settled in to read to her in a quiet voice from one of the duelling treatises she had been rereading, with a promise to demonstrate the movements at some point. Of course, she was asleep in minutes.

"Sir?"

Richard looked up from his desk, which had the various proper piles sorted out. He was ploughing through the necessary paperwork.

"Mason. Come in?" He hadn't been expecting her, she rarely came up to see him. But he supposed she might have come up with something urgent enough a message wouldn't do.

"Sir." She closed the door behind her. "Simons said you have half an hour?"

"If Simons says so, I do," he agreed. "Have a seat. Did a problem come up?"

She nodded. "First, your wife had asked about help with a particular concern, and I'm glad to help, sir, so long as it's not a difficulty."

"I'd not have recommended you if it was."

"It's a delicate thing, sir. Not that I'd work on it during my hours here, of course, but it - there are reagents, sir, and I didn't know who, there's no budget line."

"Let me know what's needed, and I'll cover it."

When he looked up, Mason was eyeing him dubiously. "You are supposed to set a limit, sir."

"Usual department limits without permissions, then." He waved a hand. "I do trust you, Mason, that's why I sent my wife to you." He thought the whole thing was entirely self-explanatory, but apparently not. "And if it's more than that, let me know."

"Thank you, sir." She settled down in his visitor's chair, finally.

He looked her up and down, and said, "More than one reason to come out of your lair, then?"

That got him the flashing smile. "More than one reason to do anything worth doing, sir."

"Which case?" Richard leaned back in his chair, stretching a bit. He'd been in the office for two hours already. He'd left Alysoun in bed in the townhouse. She'd slept restlessly, as far as he could tell. When he looked in on her in the morning, the blankets had been tangled around her legs, and she was sprawled across the bed. Rather than linger in hopes she'd wake up, he had instead gone out for a long walk around the townhouses of his peers. It was very quiet, with only the early dog walkers and others out for one reason or another.

"Both the current ones, sir. The river and the glass. I did get the official notice for the glass, I appreciate that, sir. Marked confidential, of course."

"Captain Torham suggested I put it through that way." Richard agreed. Which had been brilliant of Magni. There was certainly enough there to support a further investigation, but asking the Penelopes to do their work without a requisition order was asking for long term trouble.

"Is he taking an interest in the glass case, then?" Mason

settled herself more comfortably, shifting into her preferred mode for investigative gossip.

Richard laughed. "He has, rather. He visited Veritas, and Alysoun talked to him about it. She is rather certain. Is she right, do you think?"

"The tests won't be ready for a few more days, we have to collect more samples before we can test them appropriately. It wouldn't do to have polluted samples. But I'm making good progress. And yes, I do think there's something in it. I went and had a look at the piece myself, and the rest of the exhibit."

Richard tilted his head. "Did you. I didn't expect that."

"Well, I wanted to be able to suggest how to do the sampling, whether we'd need to move it to a corner or something. I think it would be better to move the piece next to it over, three feet, five feet, depending on the radius of the circle of control. And that seems easy enough to move, it is a small pedestal."

Richard nodded. "I know the one you mean." He gestured, sketching out the shape of the larger, questionable piece. "What did you think?"

"Lady Edgarton has an excellent eye, to spot that without anything else to give it away." Mason considered. "It doesn't seem like the sort of thing that would normally draw your attention, sir. If you don't mind my saying so."

"It is a tad more subtle than a duel on a river boat, yes." Richard grinned at her, and she grinned back. "My wife does have a good eye, though. We were at the museum gala last night, and I'm sure she was paying attention to things there, but we haven't had a chance to talk about it privately yet."

Mason nodded, and chewed on her lip. "There's something about this I don't like, sir. If it's rich and powerful people doing something, hiding something. What do they want to get out of it?"

"Do you know much about the fine arts, Mason? Other than the paints and such?"

Mason shrugged. "The paints are the interesting part. One of these days I'd love the chance to analyse something with mummia, there's a whole class of enchantments you can use on - well, things that are made from people. And there isn't much scope for them in the rest of the work."

Richard said, amused, "If such a case comes to my attention, I will make sure you're assigned to it. I can see it would be an interesting analytical challenge."

"It needn't be mummia, directly. There are sometimes cases about mummies being identified, or misidentified, or ..." She offered, in the nature of a consolation prize. "Some of them might be useful in missing person cases, or perhaps concerns about false identity. But I'd want to do a lot of tests. May I start that as a project, sir?"

Richard tapped his fingers on the desk, considering what else he knew was in the works. "Write up a proposal. No more than three hours a week, but you can clump the time if it works for your other projects."

"Sir!" Mason lit up, like he'd just given her a grand present. "Usual investigatory research budget limits?"

"Just so. But let me know if you have promising results. I'll tell Simons, he'll sort the paperwork." He then gestured broadly. "We were talking about the museum."

"Sir, of course. I don't know all that much about fine arts. Is there a reason it's relevant?"

"An item has been validated and been on display, very much in public, made a fuss of. It would be very easy to sell it for rather a lot more. That's part of the angle Alysoun thinks is in play."

"Would stained glass go for an awful lot?"

"Many pieces are institutionally owned, by churches or palaces, or they're in homes entailed to particular families. Removing them is complex, and rather dangerous to the finished piece. You can just take a reasonably large painting off the wall, and crate it up. Books and jewellery are even easier."

She flicked her fingers, almost dismissively. "But they're also very easy to forge. I mean, I can forge an incunabulum in a few months, and something from the 18th century in a few weeks."

It was the 'can' that caught his attention. "Can, Mason?"

She grinned. "Can't untangle some things without knowing how they're made. I make forgery copies as presents for friends. Properly labelled. Journals belonging to mistresses of kings, or for that matter, queens. The sort of herbal that makes sense for about ten pages and then gets increasingly more bizarre." She flicked her fingers. "Some friends and I have a habit of coming up with things and swapping them. It keeps our hands in."

"Things I never knew, Mason. Right, next time I need a forgery investigated, I'll make sure you're brought in. But you're right about the stained glass, that that's a different sort of challenge, in equipment. What would you need, do you know?"

"Space to make the glass, which means a furnace and space to shape it, with some climate controls. Access to materials for colour and other aspects, such as frosting. Space to assemble it. We're not looking at something that could be done at a personal workbench, in a regular flat, sir."

"Who has that kind of space? Resources?"

"Space - oh, any of the manor houses, certainly. A decent sized outbuilding. With a furnace, a stone tithe barn or stable or something of the kind, by preference not thatched, but slate shingled. But someone in need might trust the thatch wouldn't go up. And if it were recently cut, it would still be somewhat damp anyway."

Richard nodded. "So, outside of Trellech, do you think? Or any city?"

Mason cocked her head. "I don't know. A large warehouse might do. I think it might be noticeable here, in Trellech - furnaces of a good size make noise, you notice the fuel going in, the heat coming out. I haven't heard gossip, but you might ask the patrols down in the warehouse district."

Richard made a note in the bound book he kept for such things. "I will ask around. But some other city, possibly?"

"Possibly. The more anonymous, the better. But they would have to transport it here, or rather wherever it came from, and then here."

"And stained glass is delicate that way. I quite agree. Getting something here from London, even with the portals, that would be a trick." He shook his head. "Is there a way to tell if something has come through a portal, relatively recently? Though I suppose it might have come from the home it was supposed to be from."

He looked up, and he caught the most amazing series of expressions crossing Mason's face. First amusement, then an impish delight, then it smoothed into professional neutrality. She said, primly, "We have our secrets, sir. Would you like me to investigate in that direction? I'd need access to the museum exhibit."

"Could it be done when we do our other investigations? As a first step?"

She thought deeply. "It's possible they might take steps that would blur the results. It would be better if I could stop by. It takes only a damp cloth on the item, sir."

"And that will identify the portal transits."

"Secrets, sir." Then she thawed, and added, "How many transits, and approximately how long ago. Days or weeks - the traces fade after about six months, due to the way the portals are aligned."

Richard nodded. "Talk to the junior curator that Alysoun's been talking to." He pulled out her information and wrote it on a small card, passing it over. "Miss Milton. She is there in the mornings, and I gather the senior curators turn up a bit later, so I might try for first thing in the day."

Mason nodded, and seemed about to say something, when there was a knock on the door.

"Come."

Simons stuck his head around the door and said, "Your next appointment, sir, a bit early. Should I have him wait?"

Richard glanced at Mason, but she shook her head minutely. "Thank you, Simons. Penelope Mason was just on her way out."

THIRTY-THREE
THAT EVENING

"Alysoun?"

She heard Richard's voice before she heard anything else, not his knock, not his footstep. She was curled up in bed, having failed to get comfortable half a dozen times since she woke up. Alysoun had not made it out of bed, in fact, other than the necessary visits to the lavatory.

"Here." Her voice cracked as she said it. She focused on pushing herself upright, and tugging the sea green silk bed jacket she wore into slightly better fit. A moment later, the door opened, and Richard came in.

She hadn't realised it had gotten that late, it must be well past tea time. Richard looked at her, then shrugged off his uniform jacket, laying it over one of the chairs in the little sitting area, and came over to sit on the bed.

"Not doing well?"

Alysoun wasn't sure, in the moment, what to do with that. Her mind was a little less cotton wool than yesterday, but the aches were worse. The two together more or less left her unable to do much of anything, at any speed. In the end she shook her head. "Not one of the better days."

"May I?" He gestured at the side of the bed. "Only if it won't hurt you more."

She considered. It probably would hurt - everything hurt today - but the idea of him joining her was novel. And he didn't seem put off by her admitting that it was a bad day. She offered a smile, as best she could manage. "Please."

"The party last night, that was difficult for you, then?"

She shrugged, slightly, just one shoulder. "The parties are tricky. So many people, the noise, the hard floors, the uncomfortable shoes."

"The fussy dresses?"

"The fussy dresses. Managing the food. Looking like nothing's wrong, that's the hardest part."

"That's one I've learned too, for different reasons. If someone in the Guard looks worried about something, everyone gets nervous. So if we're talking together, it has to be all smiles and laughs and like we're sharing jokes or amusing tidbits."

"Even if you're talking to someone like - pardon, lost his name again. Last night, the rivers."

"That was entirely serious, yes, and no, we couldn't look it."

Alysoun considered. "I'm afraid I'm rather letting you down on this investigation."

Richard snorted, and reached out to take her hand. "May I?" She shifted, putting her hand into his. He curled his fingers under hers, supporting. "Mason came to see me today. She's almost ready to test the glass, but she needs to talk to your junior curator, to get quick access for something." He hesitated for a moment. "Also, apparently, should you ever need a spot of forgery done, she can definitely do that."

"You hadn't known that?" Alysoun blinked. She'd rather assumed, admittedly without much evidence, that Mason's interest in calligraphy was at least partially driven by a desire to understand the forger's art. "Should she be able to do that?"

"She pointed out, not unreasonably, that you couldn't investigate a thing you didn't know about. It did make me think, though. May I talk to you about that river smuggling?"

Alysoun was not entirely following the train of thought here, but she thought, perhaps, it might not be her fault. "Did you just change the subject?"

Richard had the good grace to blush. "Yes, pardon. I've been thinking about half a dozen things. It was something Mason said, about needing to know a thing so you could investigate it. I am not likely to go out and gain all sorts of knowledge of the river, but I started wondering what happened before the river. Where the thing came from."

Alysoun nodded. "And what it was that was worth destroying, rather than letting you guess what it was or where it came from. Since we can presume it was something precious."

"So I started wondering what it could be, and that's something I'd like your help with. Didn't you say you were rather good at silly party games when you were growing up?"

"It's an important social skill in some circles." Alysoun considered. "You mean like Twenty Questions, is it bigger than a breadbox?"

"Exactly like that. In this case, smaller than a breadbox, because the case was smaller than a breadbox." He gestured with his free hand. "But was it one thing in the box, or multiple things?"

Alysoun closed her eyes. "What kinds of things do people smuggle?"

"Expensive small things. Spices. Ingredients for potions or magical reagents. Metals that have been magically enhanced or enchanted. Some kinds of - oh, bird feathers. Clippings taken from a particular kind of wild cat at midnight on the third day after the first new moon after the spring equinox. Or whatever the appropriate timing is."

The last one made her giggle, then it turned into a laugh as he added, "That is not one of my better academic subjects. It does sometimes come in handy, if you wanted something to brush up on besides duelling manuals."

"I will add it to my reading list," she offered, mock-solemn. "So. Some of those wouldn't burn to ash."

"Not without a great deal of powerful magic, and we can probably rule that out. Not that many people know how to do that kind of thing, and the people with that kind of ability don't generally need to smuggle to get what they want."

Alysoun frowned at that, poking at the fuzziness in her head. "Explain that?"

"Well. Someone with that kind of power either has the kind of power that would lead to a good solid job, well-rewarded. Or they would be... smuggling is, I gather, rather a lot of work and risk, for an unsure thing. Someone who had so much power could get money in other ways."

Alysoun tried to track down something tickling the edges of her memory and mind. She chewed on her lip, one of the habits her mother had almost broken her of. The silence stretched out, and out.

"Alysoun?"

She startled, jerking instinctively, and then regretted it when it caused a sharp ache. "Pardon. Trying to - words aren't working so well right now."

Richard cocked his head. "Does it help to have me talk?"

She shook her head slightly. "Give me a minute."

Richard nodded and settled a bit more comfortably in the bed. Alysoun spent the next several minutes running that thought down and getting a sense of it. Finally, slowly, she said, "What if the smuggling wasn't about money?"

"What do you mean? I'm not sure I'm following."

She looked up, hating this moment, sure he was laughing at her, sure she hadn't made sense, that the fuzziness in her head was on full display. Richard was watching her, earnestly, with a patient stillness she couldn't figure out how to describe, even in her own head. She took a breath, and tried again. "Smuggling might be about money. But couldn't it also be about - " She fumbled for the word again. "People." She wiggled her hand, as if it would help her grasp the word. It did something, because then she managed, "Connecting people. Trading favours."

"That, oh, that's an idea." Richard sounded like he hadn't thought of it, which made her tilt her head.

"You're not just being nice?"

He laughed, his head going back. "Goodness, no. I mean, I don't want to be unpleasant to you. That's not kind, and it's not sensible, either. But you're not the sort of woman, I have been learning, who wants to be patted on the head and praised if it's not true. Honestly, I hadn't looked at it like that."

"I suppose it's hard to tell, from what we know, which one it is. Or it could be both. Some about the connections, some about money."

"Very few things are as simple as novel plots, true." Richard seemed to be thinking through something else.

"Copper for your thoughts?"

"Oh, just thinking where something would have come from, to have that river make sense. And why they wouldn't have taken it through the portal."

"We're back to the 'smaller than a bread box', aren't we?" That amused her, and he grinned at her. "What kinds of things can't go through portals?"

"It damages some of the reagents. That's why some of them are expensive, in fact, because the transportation is so difficult. The portal energies mess with it, something like that. Mason could probably explain the details."

Alysoun grunted softly. The thought of going anywhere seemed overwhelming at the moment. "So. If you make a list of the things that might be worth smuggling. And then a list of those things you'd have to take overland. Or over river, is that even a word? And compare them."

"That might give us an idea what kinds of things are being traded. Which would be a way to figure out who might be trading. You're brilliant!" Richard leaned over and kissed her cheek.

She blinked, not feeling very brilliant at all, but if it was helpful, she couldn't really argue. "What do we do next?"

"I will talk to Mason, and find a time to investigate the glass, and also to get her working on a list of possible items. Chances are quite good she's already got a working list, or knows where to find one, I don't think that part will be terribly difficult."

"And me?"

"I would be delighted, my dear, if I might join you for tea. Up here? I can go see about a tray."

Alysoun blinked, but nodded. "I'd like that."

"And perhaps bring the children down after, and we could read a story or two? So you don't have to get up."

She was not at all sure what to do with this but agree. He seemed to find no shame in being stuck in bed, even though she knew he'd barely ever been ill in his life. The way he was taking it in stride now, it was baffling. But fascinating. She didn't want to turn away from the tiny ember of rekindled hope.

Richard felt rather like they were getting away with something nearly illegal. He had made arrangements with the senior staff at the Museum for access first thing in the morning, along with the assistance of Hebe Milton, the junior curator. They had gathered at eight in the morning, despite the fact it was very early for Alysoun to be up and about. Two hours should give them plenty of time to do the testing Mason had in mind, and to put everything back.

He wasn't at all sure what to make of Miss Milton. Some people became effusive in the presence of one of the Guard, especially an officer. Some became shy and extremely retiring. Both often suggested they were hiding something. Miss Milton seemed almost distracted, as if shepherding them into the exhibit were a minor detail in her day. She'd acquired one of the staff responsible for moving things, and he was waiting behind her when she let them in.

"Come along this way, please." Miss Milton's voice was crisp.

Richard offered his arm to Alysoun, and took one of the bags of equipment in the other. Mason had two more, one in each hand. They made a small procession down the marble hallway, which felt endless to Richard. There was the little tapping clack of Alysoun's shoes, and the softer sound of his and Mason's. No one spoke, not until Miss Milton unlocked the atrium doors.

"Now, to be clear, we have permission to move one piece - that one - to provide a clear circle. The other tests do not require touching any piece, other than the cotton swabs. Do I have that right?"

Mason set down her bags about fifteen feet from the piece they had questions about. "Exactly so, Miss Milton. I'll need to construct a circle of control, here, but I'm using temporary items, charged stones and a powder mix that can be completely swept up when we are done. It will avoid other magical influences or materia influences getting in the way."

"Just you in the circle?" Miss Milton's voice was brisk.

"If I could have your help, Captain Edgarton. And Lady Edgarton, if you could keep a record? You're welcome to do so as well, Miss Milton, if you like."

That made the curator let out a small harumph. "How long will it be?"

"Twenty minutes for the circle, once we move that piece. Twenty to forty to do the testing, depending on how it goes and how much I can narrow things down. Twenty minutes or so to clean up."

"Let's get to it, then. Where do you want this one moved?" Miss Milton moved to stand beside the piece they weren't interested in.

"Anywhere you like, so long as it's at least ten feet away. I'll be doing the circle roughly here." Mason paused, then walked a circle. She arranged it so she got enough space for people to move comfortably around the questionable stained glass from all angles, without fear of interference. "Over there should be fine."

There was a bit of a fuss while the second piece was moved, and it took rather longer than Richard expected. Alysoun had found one of the exhibit benches and was sitting down, and he came over to settle by her. "Are you all right?"

"Achy, still. Sitting's good. I should be able to do notes from here, unless you want me in the circle?"

"Mason?" He pitched his voice to carry, and Mason turned, and came over promptly.

"Sir?" She glanced over her shoulder to watch the movements, then angled her body so she could talk to them both and watch at the same time.

"Should Alysoun be in the circle with us, or can she sit here, outside it?"

That got one of Mason's patent expressions, that mix of contemplation and calculation. "I was planning on using Rehudit's Circle of Control. It doesn't normally create a visual distortion field, but we're in an unusual circumstance with the metal and glass of the atrium, and the light, and we're working with a narrow visual range. And Lady Edgarton, you're the one who spotted the visual difference in the first place. I would prefer, if it's possible, that you be in the circle."

Richard nodded. "Can we move a bench for you, then? Should we?"

Alysoun considered, half-closing her eyes, and taking inventory, he suspected. "If there's a bench, I'd rather."

Richard nodded, and stood. "Moment, dear, let me see what we can arrange." He walked around the space, and found a smaller wooden chair, designed for the docent or guard, and then came to Miss Milton. "May we move the chair here to the circle, for my wife?"

Miss Milton blinked at him, and said, her voice frustrated, "If you must." He began to suspect she was feeling like she was in over her head, not sure what she'd agreed to, but the best way out was to press on.

"I'll see to it." He went to the chair and laid his hands on it, intending to call up one of the cantrips Magni had drilled into him,before he stopped. "Mason, doing magic in here would be a problem, yes?"

Mason nodded. "It would muddy the results."

"Right. Can you help me move this chair, then?" She came over promptly. The chair wasn't heavy, but it didn't fold and it was something of an awkward shape, two curved arms and a broad seat. He let Mason guide him to a suitable spot.

She then nodded briskly. "Lady Edgarton, if you could? And I'll set the circle around you."

Richard came over, offering his arm to Alysoun and escorting her to the chair, then standing behind her, hands resting on the back of the chair. She leaned her head back against his chest and peered up at him. "You ready?"

"I am. You take notes, and tell us what you spot, and I will do the same. Ready when you are, Mason."

Mason nodded. "Stay where you are, please, and please keep quiet. This will take a few minutes." She then moved to draw out one of the kit boxes from the bag she had brought. Then she set the other two cases in the middle of the circle, just in front of where Alysoun was sitting, between the chair and the stained glass. Last, Mason took out a large stick of soft chalk, then began drawing on the floor, and Richard watched her build up the signs and symbols of the circle of control.

He knew the theory. He could even cast one if necessary. But Mason's circles were rather more solid than his. It created a space that magically delineated what was inside the circle as being separate from - and unaffected by - what was outside the circle. Quite useful for a number of complex magical activities. She was using Rehudit's version, he assumed, because it was one of the simpler to set up outside of a dedicated magical workroom. It had been designed in the early 19th century to be portable, one of the side effects of the imperial progress of Britain across the map. It could be drawn in chalk, sand, or coal dust, or any material that allowed one to make the symbols.

He closed his eyes. He'd seen it once done in a mix of blood and water, in the Sudan, and that once was plenty. Alysoun caught something in his shift of mood, and reached up a hand to touch his chest. He curled his fingers around it and smiled at her, squeezing her fingers lightly.

Mason worked her way around the circle, marking the directions, what his instructors had called the ritual geometry of the constructed space. Magni had been more direct about it. Richard remembered him saying it was a salle, with a door and with windows. It let in certain things, and kept out other things, so you could focus on the duel without the sun getting in your eyes. He kept his feet planted, breathing evenly, the way he did before a practice duel, when he had time to plan.

Finally, Mason finished the last of the chalk markings. She made another pass with some powder, then poured more through a funnel onto the points of the compass she had drawn, each one turning a different colour with the addition of a particular reagent. The little circles glowed, almost the same way the light glowed through the stained glass - now he was standing in a room of coloured glass. Finally, she made one more pass, murmuring words under her breath, until a cascade of light, like a curtain, rose from the floor to the ceiling, completely encasing them. He knew from his own training that it would encompass the area right below their feet, an inch or two, and up to the ceiling, in the same way.

Mason turned back to him, and bowed, formally. "Sir. Now I'll begin the tests, if you're ready."

"Do continue."

She nodded. "Miss Milton, this is the part where I'll be touching the glass briefly." Without him noticing, she'd pulled on cotton gloves. She took a corked testing tube out of her pocket, then another. She opened the first one and took out two cotton swabs. Going to the glass, she carefully brushed it once with a clean swab. Then she murmured the cantrip to dampen a cloth over the other, and ran it over the surface of the glass. Nothing changed that he could see, but she seemed satisfied as she tucked it into the second vial.

The testing involved laying out a series of metal testing containers, rather like salve or lotion tins. Possibly they once had been. Mason set them out in a specific order, based on labelling with wax pencil on the lid. There were a series of alchemical symbols and shorthand he could only begin to guess at. Richard took the notebook and pencil out of his pocket, and prepared to make notes.

They worked through. He numbered each one with the numbers she called out to him from her own list. Each time, she spoke a word to trigger the charms that would resonate, and then gave him a number. He could only assume they were a measurement of some kind. Some of the materials she looked at through a piece of coloured glass, some through a lens mounted on a cap she set on her head. Finally, after she worked her way through three cases of the sample materials, she closed the last tin. "That's the last of them, sir. I'll need to do the analysis now."

She was tight lipped, the sort of expression that made it clear to him, at least, that she'd turned something up. What, however, he was not going to get out of her until she was good and ready.

Taking down the circle of control was fussy, and by the time they were done, he could tell that Alysoun was done in. "Let me see my wife home, Mason, and I'll catch up with you later today."

Mason just nodded and tucked her various items up into the bags they had come in. Finally, she swept up the chalk and powder from the circle, and poured it neatly using a handbroom into a glass container for proper disposal. "Sir."

"It's very kind of you to escort me until Richard can join us." Alysoun slipped her hand through Magni's good arm. They were in one of the covered walkways around the eastern interior courtyard of the Guard Hall.

Richard had been whisked off to preparations elsewhere in the building Special guests were tucked away in the anteroom to her right and in this courtyard. They were waiting until it was time for them to be seated in the Great Hall itself for the investiture. All very fussy, and there were dozens of coordinated junior Guards around guiding people this way and that.

"A pleasure, Alysoun." His voice was rumbly, and he leaned down. "And since I'm on my own at these things, I much prefer squiring you around to making small talk with people who are largely strangers."

"That must be frustrating. Though honestly, Richard gets pulled away for work. I hope things are going well at home?" She didn't want to ask directly after Gil, given how many people might overhear, but she did want to let him know she cared.

"Oh, quite, thank you for asking." Magni was beaming now. He lowered his voice. "We thought we might have you and Richard over sometime, once his schedule settles down, if you'd like."

"That would be lovely, absolutely." No matter how achy she was that day, that wasn't an invitation she wanted to turn down. And she did like talking to Gil. "When do you go back to work properly?" She smiled at someone who was passing by. "And it's a mutual pleasure, honestly, having you as escort. We shall save each other from the tedious social pleasantries."

"Monday week. Since I've an active post, they want a week beyond the full healing, just to make sure. But the arm's fine, now."

"Hmmm." Alysoun considered, looking at him. "You're still favouring it."

"Damnation." Then he grinned. "Pardon."

"Oh, I forgive you. Now, can you point out the people you know that I don't? The Guard I won't have met other places."

That kept them occupied for a good twenty minutes. At the end of it, Magni asked, "May I excuse myself for a few minutes? Will you be all right on your own?"

Alysoun nodded. "Oh, quite fine, we're out of the press of people here. And there's a good fifteen minutes before they'll be rounding us up to be seated."

Magni bowed slightly and made his way through the crowd. Alysoun, for her part, didn't want to move from where she was, tucked into an alcove out of the way. She wondered what Richard was up to. He had told her the rituals involved formal washing, incense, all sorts of things. Nothing too unfamiliar - they used similar methods before some of the planting and harvest rites - but they did take time.

Richard was not precisely body-shy. He had spent too much time playing bohort and pavo, changing with a lot of other young people, and time in the Guard changing rooms. But she had learned early that he didn't much like people fussing at him while he dressed or undressed. He barely tolerated his valet then, most of the time.

She shifted her dress, with the deep purple pooling at her feet, feeling rather obvious. The clothing requirements for this were rather ridiculous, she felt, but the Ministry did like their pomp and circumstance. She was still thinking about what Richard had passed on from Mason's tests when he'd gotten home yesterday. He'd even gone so far as to bring a copy of the report home for her to read. She suspected that was not entirely the usual protocol, but it had been very helpful.

There had been quite a lot more soot in the glass than anything made in Trellech in the last five hundred years should have. More to the point, there was a mineral called asbestos there. Mason had highlighted that that was common in and around London, but not much used in Trellech, and certainly not in a small village forge.

It was used for insulation, apparently, which explained why it wasn't common in the magical community, which had other options. Half a dozen other materials also pointed to the glass being made relatively recently, and near London or at least a major non-magical city. Nothing absolutely conclusive, but it was point piled upon point, and if they could find some way to link all their evidence, it would confirm things nicely.

None of which got them much closer to an answer, but it

was at least enough to make her feel she was not on a false trail. Richard had been so supportive, surprisingly engaged. Of course, she wanted this mystery answered, but she hated the idea of having dug in for an answer to something that turned out to be innocent. She was sure Richard would be reasonable about it, but this collaboration with him, this talking with him, about anything that mattered, was so new and fragile. If the investigation that had allowed that seed to sprout had come to naught, the whole thing might have gone to pieces.

She was lost in her thoughts when she heard people near her. She caught half a sentence from the hallway near her, just around a corner, so she couldn't see who was talking.

"....telling you, it's a pity we couldn't get the..." The last word was muffled.

"Daffyd's looking for more." That was no help, half of Wales was named Daffyd, it seemed.

"And the museum?"

"The exhibit's over soon. I'm glad. I didn't like that cousin of your wife's, blasted Arden, drawing attention to that piece, not one bit."

Someone shushed the speaker, even more audibly. After a few seconds, the voices picked up a different conversation, something about someone's dress, and how it didn't suit the occasion at all, before the sound faded. Alysoun stayed where she was, out of the line of sight of the door, waiting for Magni to come back.

When he reappeared, there were a good five minutes before they were likely to be ushered in to sit. "Might we make a loop of the courtyard, with a pause on the far side?" She smiled prettily at the Guardswoman who was keeping an eye out, with a "Just want to stretch my legs a little before the ceremony."

Magni immediately got the hint, and settled into an easy pace, pausing on the far side of the courtyard. "We don't have long."

"I heard something. Did you see any of the people - two or three of them talked - by the door when you came back?"

"There was no one there by the time I got to the door, but I saw a few people nearby." He considered. "I don't know all their names, but tell me if you spot them in the crowd? And do we expect Richard's family, afterwards?"

"His mother, a few of his cousins and aunts. And my mother and father, probably. There's a reception, I'm sure they'll be there."

"And no one to be with you?"

"I prefer solitary splendour." She then had to smile. "I'm not terribly... his mother isn't as awful as she could be if she wanted to put her mind to it, but she isn't very nice sometimes, very set on her own things being her own way. We manage at holidays, but I'm sure Richard's glad she would rather be in her townhouse here in Trellech rather than Veritas."

"Oh, he's told me a few stories. She didn't want him in the Guard, but I think you knew that."

Alysoun considered. "I'd picked it up, but I don't think anyone ever told me directly."

"Far too dangerous and bringing one into conversation with lower class criminals. She was somewhat mollified when he showed such a gift for duelling, which has a certain nobility to it."

Alysoun laughed. "Well, that's a fair way to put her priorities, yes. Anyway, they're in the regular seats somewhere. And you can escort me as one of the senior Guard, and his apprentice master, and it's all completely appropriate. Also much appreciated."

Magni chuckled. "To be honest, I wasn't entirely sure what to make of his marriage to you. He didn't talk about it. He was out of his apprenticeship by then, at least formally, but he came in to practise one day. Just after he'd gotten back from the Sudan. Just right out with it, 'I'm getting married,' and I couldn't for the life of me figure out what he thought about it."

"He was the best of the choices they gave me. And I gather the other way around, for him. At least one of the other women his parents approved of has turned into a rather dreadful bore. And spendthrift. Our estates are doing decently, but they don't run to, oh, gilt all over everything. Also." She sniffed slightly, because she was sure Gil had expressed opinions at length about this sort of thing, "Also, that's just tacky."

That made him roar with laughter, and at about that point, there was a gesture from the Guardswoman at the door for them to come and line up. Alysoun beamed up at him. "Keep your eyes open, and I will too. See if I spot them." They made their way back through the assembled crowd, up toward the front of the line. The honoured guests divided into three main groups: those associated with those about to be invested as magistrates, the existing magistrates, and senior members of the judiciary and the Guard, as representatives of law and justice in Albion.

Richard closed his eyes briefly, trying to find a place of balance. Something in this whole elaborate programme had him deeply unsettled. It had deep threads of ritual magic, he kept brushing against them, but no one was had explained what was going on. It was sloppy magical work, and Richard did not approve.

He'd asked. More than once, after they'd invited him, he'd asked what to expect, what the ritual was like. No one had been very informative. There hadn't been many people he felt he could ask, because asking felt terribly vulnerable. Finally, trusting in Alysoun's sense of the Dowager Lady Witham, he'd gone to her. He had made it through a properly formal tea with her, and then asked as politely as he could what he should expect. She was a magistrate, and she knew more about the Guard than many of them. He had certainly not wanted to discuss concerns with the few others of the Guard who were also magistrates.

She had been the most helpful of the lot, in the end, but it was not very direct. And of course, she hadn't had experience with the Guard Oath. He could hear her now, telling him that it was a mystery, in the religious sense. She insisted it was better not to fight that, but to accept the weight of the cloak of justice on his shoulders, and do it with an open heart. That the people who did had an easier time with it. She'd ended up looking him up and down, and added, "I don't approve of them making magistrates so young, but I suspect you'll do." It had been the greatest praise he'd ever heard from her.

Now, he had been sent off to wash in the Guard bathing rooms, then washed again in a tub of water scented with herbs. Someone chanted something in Latin over his head, and he could only make out about one word in three, because the others were aimed away from him, in a room that echoed oddly. This part, at least, was familiar, if not the full vigil he'd done for the Guard. Then he'd been encouraged to dry off. His valet appeared to help him put on the underrobes.

He remained lost in thought until someone appeared at his elbow, an older man whose name he didn't know. "Lord Edgarton, this way, please." He was led into a long, narrow room, where each of the new magistrates had their own little dais. With a gesture, the man indicated he should stand there, and three separate people swarmed around him, bearing the second layer of sombre black robes with their narrow lines of purple trim. The full Magistrate's robes would be part of the investiture itself. They were there to brush his hair, see to his coat and all the fittings, making sure everything was ready to go.

Finally, the fussing was over, and they were gotten into a line, ready to go out into the Great Hall. He could hear the hum of the crowd, now, hundreds of people, all talking quietly, but so many. He hoped Alysoun was doing all right, and that Magni was helping her manage the crowds.

What seemed like hours later, the presiding judges and magistrates went out, and then each of them followed, with an appropriately weighty introduction. "Lord Richard Edgarton, Kent" was his. It felt odd to have it be so bare, but the presentation here did not include the rank or honours he'd earned. As happened every time someone focused on his title, Richard felt that edge of discomfort.

There was nothing for it right now than to look out at the sea of people, many of the women in decidedly ridiculous hats. He nodded and offered the polite, formal smile he'd been trained in for so long. He took his place in the row of the others, barely glancing side to side.

A few names later, everyone was on stage, and there was an expectant silence. Above them, in the tower, bells began to ring, the great bells that were used only for certain formal rituals, the deep sound of metal reverberating and filling the space. It was not the more common change ringing, but a series of patterns outlining thirds and fifths and octaves, setting out the geometry and alignment of the world in sound, as thoroughly as the hall below did in space.

When the invocation pattern finally died away, everyone was completely quiet for the space of three breaths. The chief magistrate stepped forward into the spot where the sound-amplifying charms were focused. "Be welcome in the halls of justice, all of good heart." The traditional welcome, with the weight of centuries of ritual behind it. He began the formal invocations, and Richard began to smell the incense filtering through the hall, from the censers at each direction, the way they mingled. As always, he couldn't quite identify the individual scents. There was the sharp bite of something herbal, and something deeper and earthy, as if it were forming a base for the whole.

The invocations rolled on as well. It was a diverse land, and so the invocations of justice had multiple forms. There were the deities there, but also the call to the archetypal Justice, beyond human comprehension. There were the calls to tradition, the gestures at roots and the works of man, exhortations to the magistrates to be open to the touch of justice in their work.

That was a part no one had really explained to him, what that meant. He knew, with an absolute logic, born of the evidence of his own life, that being invested as a magistrate did not make someone a good man. Or a good woman, for that matter, though he suspected that the women had to have fewer obvious flaws to be presented as candidates than the men. He knew magistrates who in their private lives were drunkards, or quarrelsome over the smallest and least important things. There were those who ignored their wives, or worse. His father had been a magistrate, and his father had certainly not been a perfect man.

To decline would admit there was something wrong with him, something flawed. More flawed than all the others. He didn't think that was the case. He was human and had good points and bad, but was on the whole honourable and committed to justice.

Last time he'd stood here, it was to take the Guard oath, and that had been entirely different. There had been the bathing, but then there was a vigil, like the knights of old. He'd been tended and watched over with the others of his cohort in silence, supported by their apprentice masters and colleagues through the dark of the night. That had soothed him, that they had demanded so much of him before taking the oath.

Here, now, the fussing to prepare to be a magistrate had been largely social, the parties and gatherings, barring a few brief hours of training and review, mostly about the logistical dance of the ceremony itself. His conversation with Dowager Lady Witham had been the most informative, and he had sought that out entirely on his own. It made him feel unanchored, like he was being asked to take on something he had no way to really agree to.

The chief magistrate pounded his staff on the stage three times, the sound reverberating, almost as much as the bells had. Richard could feel it under his feet, and it jarred him out of his thoughts. Now, they would be called forward, individually, to make their oaths. They went in an order based on some arcane formula Richard did not understand, but which meant he would be one of the last.

That left him to listen and watch, as each person stepped forward into a circle illuminated by charm lights above and the windows of the great hall. Each made their oaths, repeating the words with the chief magistrate's hands on their shoulders. Each bowed, and straightened, and had the formal robes settled upon them.

Try though he might, Richard couldn't read any of them well enough. He had no idea if they'd had some transcendent ritual experience, or if they were just waiting for the ceremony to be over so they could get on to the celebration.

Finally, it was his turn to step forward, next to last in the list. He settled into the at-ease position, back straight, feeling the weight sink down into his heels, like Magni had taught him, drilled into him. The chief magistrate stood there, repeating the words of the oath. "State your name."

"I am Richard, Lord Edgarton."

From there, he barely needed the prompting. "I swear that I will well and truly serve the heart of Albion as magistrate in all her places. Let justice roam in all the lands of Albion, in all the places touched by sun and moon and stars within our borders. My hand to the Pact, keeping it and upholding it, my shoulder to the work. In my service to the office of magistrate, I swear I will well and truly serve Justice in all her faces, and that I will do right to all manner of people, after the laws and customs of the Realm, without fear or favour, affection or ill will. Let justice cloak me."

He could feel something building, as he said the words, and as he managed the last phrase, it took him with a physical shudder he only barely repressed. He could feel someone behind him, lifting the robes of office onto his shoulders, the rich purple and deep black, and the chain of office on top of it. It was not cold, but it had a sharpness to it, like the edge of a knife, for just an instant. Then it settled into a weight like earth, or the roots of an ancient yew. Possibly this was what dragon bones felt like.

It took him a moment, entirely too long, to realise that he had to move, to step back to his place, for the last of the investitures. He turned to make a proper bow one more time to the great statue of Justice. Just as he turned, he saw a flash of light over the heads of two or three people, clearly together, a third of the way back, on the left side of the seating facing the stage. He couldn't make sense of it, but he did his best to fix that glimpse into his memory as firmly as he could.

The last oath went smoothly, and then there were a few final words, social pleasantries. So pleased to welcome these men and women to the work of justice, fine people all, come join us for the celebration that has been set out. Then, finally, they were escorted off the stage, and he could see about finding Alysoun, before anything else. He suddenly wanted her comforting touch on his arm, to settle him and remind him what to focus on.

Alysoun wasn't certain what to expect. She thought she knew Richard well enough now to realise that some part of the investiture, some part of his oath, had hit him hard. She hadn't been able to look away, but when Richard had returned to his place on the stage, she glanced at Magni. He gave her a small nod, which meant he'd spotted it too, and she wasn't imagining whatever it was.

Once the spectators were dismissed to make their way to the celebration, the most honoured guests were escorted back into the anteroom they'd been in earlier. Alysoun was rather glad Magni would be easy to spot, and indeed, Richard made his way right over to them, as soon as the crowd permitted. He took a breath, the heavy robes shifting around him. "Can - the courtyard?" He gestured, more than anything.

"Of course." Magni shifted, letting Alysoun take Richard's arm, and they managed to find a corner on the opposite side of the courtyard.

"I will have to go and greet people in a few minutes." Richard sounded tired, more than anything.

"Are you all right? You - there was a moment," Alysoun's voice trailed off, she wasn't sure how to finish that sentence.

"It is a ritual experience of its own. Behold, a mystery." There was a queer echo in his tone, one Alysoun couldn't make sense of.

"More than just that, wasn't there?"

Richard looked up, a little sharp jerk of his head. "There were three people. Two in their fifties or so. Mauve dress, for the woman, and the two men in something - grey, something like that. Not black, not bright. Too far for me to have a good look at their faces."

"Did you see something?" Magni's voice was suddenly edged.

"A flash, nothing more. But I want, very much, to know who they are. The woman was blonde, dyed, possibly, it had a flatness to the colour. One man was going grey, the other had darker hair. Pale complexions, except for the younger man, who looked like he spent some time in the sun."

Magni nodded. "You two go along. I'll mingle."

Richard nodded. "Drink with us, at home, after? If Gil can shake loose, he's welcome." He kept his voice quiet, but the sentence seemed to Alysoun to be sufficiently ambiguous.

Magni tilted his head. "The townhouse? I'll send a messenger round."

Richard nodded. One of the Guardswomen came over and bowed slightly. "Captain Edgarton, your mother was hoping for a word, and then there is a receiving line forming."

"Come along, dear." Alysoun tucked her arm through

Richard's. "Best to keep things moving."

She did not like getting trapped with his mother at all. It had been fine when she was first pregnant, and when Gabriel was born. But since Charlotte, since her illness, it had gotten much more complicated.

Her mother-in-law had a small horde of people, three or four dozen, who orbited the same set of charitable events, social gatherings, and various musical evenings. All women, mostly widows but some women who clearly had entirely separate lives from their husbands now. Alysoun wouldn't commit to the various fussy meetings. She didn't have the stamina for long concerts, and she found at least half the social gatherings not only boring but often ignorant.

It had left her rather at sea with his mother. Fortunately, she had gathered Richard and his mother preferred a largely amiable distance, except when the social setting called for all the ritualised gestures of fondness. At any rate, she would not get in the way. She was quite clear the Dowager Lady Edgarton would be terribly difficult to deal with if they didn't make the appropriate noises.

Richard blinked at her, but steered them over toward where the Guardswoman had pointed. His mother had claimed one of the carved wooden chairs, rather by right of rule, and was holding court among a number of her particular circle. "There, Richard, oh, look at you, don't you look as handsome as your dear father did, those robes suit beautifully, such a sense of presence."

Richard nodded. "Mother. Ladies." Then, to the smattering of men, escorting one or the other, he added, "Gentlemen."

Alysoun smiled and nodded pleasantly. "Good afternoon. A splendid ceremony, I thought."

Richard's mother began speaking over her, as if Alysoun

weren't there, with no acknowledgement. "Now, Richard, the Belightlys are here, you really must have word with them. And Agnes Morrel, you know that she always wants to see you."

"Mother, I'm afraid I've some obligations, first. I just stopped by to speak briefly. Perhaps as things quiet down."

Alysoun settled her arm. "I see that nice Guardswoman over there, I think she's hoping you'll form up, dear? Oh, and spouses, too, it looks like."

"Oh, in that case, we mustn't keep people waiting." Richard bowed slightly. "Do enjoy the celebration, please."

Only once they pulled away, did he speak again, "Pardon, Alysoun, about Mother."

"She isn't likely to change at this late date." It came out more edged than Alysoun meant, especially at what should be a celebration.

Richard stopped dead in the middle of the room, and turned to her. For a moment, it was clear there was nothing in the room for him but her. Quietly enough that she had to strain to hear it, but with a fierceness underneath it, he said, "I'll be making it clear there will be no more of that from her." He had all the strength of a man about to undertake a quest.

It was not what Alysoun had expected at all. She took a breath and let it out. "Later. We've other people to talk to."

He nodded, a small determined nod. "We, together, do." Then he settled her hand in the crook of his elbow again, and led her off, beaming. His official robes billowed as he walked, and she thought the overall effect likely rather splendid. The other new magistrates were largely rather older, and Richard's broad shoulders and overall fitness - not to mention his dark hair - were drawing a bit of attention.

One of the Guards quickly gestured them into line,

then spoke to the new magistrates near him. "Please do let us know if you need something to drink, as people come through. It may take a little bit."

Richard considered for about a second, and then leaned over. "Would you like a chair, my dear?"

It startled her. Not just that he thought about the fact that one might be helpful, but that he was leaving it up to her. She smiled at him. "Let me ask if one can be ready."

"Allow me." He lifted his head, crooked a finger, and one of the Guardswomen came over, promptly, with the slight bow she'd noticed many of the junior Guards using reflexively with him.

"Guard Oldham, yes? Assigned to the Rivers?"

"Yes, thank you, sir. May I be of help?"

"Could you have a chair ready, somewhere nearby, in case my lady wife needs it? We don't want to have to fuss."

The Guardswoman looked her up and down, and nodded. "Of course, sir, my lady. If you decide you need one, I'll be right over there, paying attention."

"Excellent, thank you. And if there were something refreshing to drink. Lemonade, perhaps?"

She bowed once more, after saying, "Of course, sir." She made a beeline for a back corner of the room, and Alysoun lost track of her.

"You know her?"

"Oh, yes. Solidly competent, though her skills put her in a difficult place. She's more often limited to this kind of thing, social events which need a Guard presence, or routine work on the river or with the portals. She's as solid in hand-to-hand fighting as most of the men, but women need to be that much better to get the good positions, even those where physical prowess isn't what's needed. Not fair at all." He kept his voice low, in a way that made Alysoun

sure that some of the people around would disagree with
that.

"Is that why you make a point of giving people chances?
Like Mason?" Alysoun had gathered, from their few conversations, that Mason's people were recent arrivals from somewhere in the Empire, though she'd not spelled out where
her brown skin and dark hair came from.

"When I can. I can't always do that much, though."

Before she could ask more about it, there was a little stir,
and the receiving line began. They settled quickly into a
rhythm. Someone would congratulate Richard, he would
present her as his wife, if they weren't acquainted already.
The person would often make some sort of comment about
an issue that Richard might want to take an interest in.
Richard would smile and say he had a lot to learn about the
current concerns, and he'd take it under consideration.

After the twelfth time that happened, she asked, "Are
you actually remembering those things?"

"Oh, yes. Right of access, building of walls, whether a
ha-ha needs better signage, the problems of poaching in
Swineshead Wood. Theft of sheep, more right of access, an
inheritance question. A sudden and unexpected death - that
should be referred to the healers, first, I know that much."
He counted mentally for a moment. "A fine being appealed,
a bull that repeatedly gets loose, watering of beer in the pub,
and a bit of minor burglary."

Alysoun blinked again, entirely impressed, and then her
eyes got drawn to a point across the room. "What did you
say the people you got the glimpse of looked like?"

"Mauve dress, blonde hair, two men in dull colours, one
older and grey, one dark haired."

"Those, there? That's the Delywns. Lord and Lady
Delwyn, and the eldest son. And someone I don't know."

Richard got settled on the sofa in the townhouse library. Alysoun was beside him, and Magni and Gil across from them. He was immensely glad they'd arranged this, because now that he had information, he wasn't at all sure what to do with it. After all, a sudden flash, even if it might come from Justice Herself, wasn't exactly easy to verify.

"Sir - um. Magni." He cleared his throat. "Gil." He then stopped, not sure where to begin this.

"I told Gil you'd had an experience during the investiture. He, of course, has read about it." Magni sounded amused, rather than worried, and that tone did a lot to make Richard feel better about the whole thing.

Gil nodded, leaning back slightly in his chair, and stretching out his bad leg. "There's a solid history - I can dig up the book we have about it, and send it along, it was upstairs." Richard nodded.

"At any rate, that kind of thing has been accepted as sufficient evidence for further investigation in the past, but it depends a great deal on the dynamics. To investigate Lord and Lady Delwyn...." Gil glanced around. "What do you know about them?"

Alysoun was the one who answered, shifting to lean a little against Richard's shoulder. "They were principal patrons for the stained glass exhibit. Three, four of the pieces come from their estate. But that was something that caught my attention, first. Professor Arden didn't focus on those pieces the way I would have expected. Usually at these kinds of lectures, there's a lot of fluff about the patrons, the particular ones. Especially if they're there.'"

"And there wasn't?"

"No. And they didn't seem particularly upset. Most people would be, I think."

Magni nodded. "Suggestive, but not sufficient."

Alysoun opened her mouth to speak, and Richard glanced at her. "Go ahead." She seemed to be hesitating.

"It's a bit like your flash of insight, dear, but not - I don't have the same reason."

"Still. You notice things. You always have, as long as I've known you."

She took a breath. "At the museum gala, I noticed their dresses. The women, I mean, it's harder to tell about men, sometimes." She looked at Magni and Gil. "How much of it do I need to explain?"

Richard snorted. "Start with the basics, please, my dear. I'm sure I need them."

"I noticed because it seemed out of character. It would have seemed more so if it hadn't been a costume party. Everyone sort of expects a masked ball, or something with costumes, some of them won't be top quality. People remake things in their closets, or tack on a few feathers or sparkles or whatever."

Gil coughed. "Alysoun, I am not usually invited to that sort of party. How far do the costumes go?"

"Oh, that depends. At the gala, it was fairly modest. The theme was 'creatures'. That is the sort of theme people pick when they want to give people lots of scope. Not have anyone be too fussy about their costumes, but give people space if they want to do something really artistic. Much easier to put something together for than, say, a particular time period, or even historical figures in general. Once you get out of the Greeks and Romans, the clothing was rather specific, and it's hard to do convincingly without rather a lot of attention to detail."

"And not giving that attention is a social faux pas?" Magni was trying to figure out how this worked, from the way he asked.

"Exactly." Alysoun beamed at him. "I mean, everyone has parties they care about more than others. But showing up with only a gesture at the theme, it's sort of an insult to the hostess and host. Political duels have been made out of much less."

"Is that why we don't host costumed events?" Richard had known she'd not been fond of the idea, the couple of times he'd suggested it over the years.

Alysoun nodded. "It makes who cares about your idea exceedingly obvious, and to everyone. I don't know, in twenty years, we might well have more than enough status to be sure that anyone who didn't meet the standard would get tutted over, not us. But I don't want to risk it until we're sure it'd come out in our favour."

"Social duelling again. Talk me through it, next time there's a suitable party, then, so I can learn the details." Richard knew there was more there she wasn't saying right now.

She leaned over and kissed his cheek. "Of course." When he returned his attention to the two men across from them, Magni's eyes had crinkled up, and Gil had shifted to hold his hand lightly. They approved, then, of how he and Alysoun were sorting themselves out. That was a great relief.

"Richard." The considering tone in Magni's voice brought his head up. "How did that feel to you, then?" He gestured. "Sorting that out with Alysoun."

Another of those times when Magni called his attention to something. Richard couldn't resent it, he knew how many times it had made him better. Happier. "Easy, sir." Then he grimaced at the formality, and Magni chuckled, gesturing for him to go on. "Doing it together. Trusting in her skills, knowing I'll have a better view of things later."

"And not dithering." Magni was definitely amused now.

"And not dithering," Richard agreed. "You have a reason for bringing it up?"

"I'm curious what our next duel will be like, honestly. You seem more solidly yourself now. And you know as well as I do that may change some things."

Richard nodded slowly. "Sir." This time, it was deliberate deference to Magni's experience, not just as duellist, but as teacher and mentor. "I'll look forward to that. For the moment..." He nodded at Alysoun. "You were talking about the costume party."

Alysoun picked up easily. "So I noticed the Delwyns. And their heir's wife, Madeline Delwyn."

"It was her sister who'd been - difficult, before?"

"Hortensia Miller. Who was rather avoiding the theme." She added to Magni and Gil, "She was dressed as an Amazon, which is not really on par, even if they were reputed to be excellent horsewomen. Madeline Delwyn was wearing a rather brightly striped costume suggesting a tiger, but it was not of particularly good fabric. Or design. Normally, I'd have expected them to be setting the mode, not - barely living up to it. A year ago, they would have been."

Gil got there first. "Which suggests some limitation on funds or resources, or whatever it takes to put a costume together. And something relatively recent."

Alysoun nodded. "And then, today..." She turned to Richard.

"Today, the three people I got that flash of, during the investiture, we're quite sure they were Lord and Lady Delwyn, and their heir, Jupiter."

Magni shook his head. "I half remember hearing something. You know how people talk when changing. They didn't throw their usual summer party this year, and no one could figure out why. No comment about it, just they didn't schedule it."

Richard tapped his fingers on his leg. "Today, what was it you said, after, Alysoun?"

"They looked a little faded. I don't know, there's something, there's a crispness, with formal clothes that are maintained properly. And Lord and Lady Delwyn, they didn't have that. Her dress might have been remade, too, from a few years ago, and the silhouettes have changed rather a lot."

"What were they like, their behaviour?"

"A bit reserved, I thought. But I'm not close to anyone in that family. Lord and Lady Delwyn are around my mother's age, but not her set. I'm not sure why Mother didn't approve, though. And my father was a generation older. Jupiter didn't overlap me in school and his younger brother is just finishing, I think. And I think they're both Boar

House. Which might be why Mother disapproved, if they took after their father that way." He paused, and added. "The daughter was schooled at home, I'm fairly sure."

"Charging at things, you mean." Gil was thinking, but that bit of analysis was simple, apparently. "Recklessness, perhaps."

Magni leaned back, though Richard noticed he didn't move his hand. "Let us posit, then, that there is some sort of financial difficulty in the family. Remaking clothing, not throwing a large party that would be expensive, that sort of thing. Seeing as we don't have access to their financial accounts. What are you working on, Richard, where they might be relevant?"

Richard considered. "The two big cases right now are that mysterious smuggling case, and the stained glass."

It was Gil who spoke up. "Are we sure those aren't possibly related?"

Magni turned, peering at Gil, then he looked at Richard, evenly. "Gil has a point here."

"I hadn't thought about it that way, mostly because we don't know much about where whatever was in that box came from."

Alysoun had gone entirely pensive and quiet, and when he realised it, Richard asked, "Dear?"

She waved a hand, "Could you, the same thing we did with the stained glass, samples of where it was from, do something with that?"

Gil said, promptly. "See if you could isolate where it came from, to figure out who was involved? But that would be rather tricky, wouldn't it? If it's ashes. Though I suppose ashes would have the same inherent identity, magically, as the whole object, if you approached it the right way. The Berebellum variation on the identification, maybe, that is about inherent fundamental nature, rather than physical state."

Magni snorted. "Well. Can we put Gil and your Mason in the same room, Richard? Not at the museum, and not the Guard, that's too complicated."

Richard waved a hand, gesturing at the room. "You're welcome to use this room, or any other of the public rooms here. There's a small workroom on this floor, if Mason wants it for testing, I'll have the staff clean it properly."

Gil looked up, and it was so obvious gears were whirring in his head, now that Richard had gotten to know him. "Can I leave a list of what I'll need? When do you think she'll be free?"

"Let me send someone round with a note." Richard extracted himself from beside Alysoun. "Anyone need more to drink?"

At the end of the evening, she had suddenly felt faded, like all the colour had washed out of the world. She hated those moments. Pain, she could stubborn her way through. Fatigue, she could sit down. The cotton wool head, she could make notes and rely on the little tricks she'd learned over the past few years.

But the moment where everything was just done, there was no more, those were hard to plan for, and harder to hide. Richard had spotted it before the other two men. While he was trying to figure out how to ask, Gil had said, "We should let you get about your evening. If you could call a carriage, that would be easiest on our end."

Yet again, Alysoun appreciated how he was so matter of fact about it. Magni by himself would likely have walked. Richard almost certainly would have. It was under two miles, a half hour walk for his usual pace. But of course, that wouldn't do for Gil. She had gracefully taken the excuse to head upstairs, collecting amiable farewells from Magni and Gil.

Twenty minutes later, there was the soft knock on her

door. She had had enough time to have Wallis help her undress, slip into a nightdress and robe, and tuck her into bed. She hadn't wanted to pick up a book - too much bother in her current state. She had been staring at the wall, vaguely wondering how the odd shape of the room had come to be. Much less spacious than Veritas, though honestly that could be said of most homes. The knock startled her out of her thoughts.

"Come in?"

Richard peered round the door, and then came in, closing it behind him, wearing his own robe, belted around his waist. She had a brief flickering moment of appreciation for his shoulders, for his steadiness, before he came and gestured at the bed. "May I join you? To talk."

Some small part of her hoped, for just an instant, that it might be more than talking. But she knew she was in no fit state for something delicate, as any further exploration might be. She nodded, and then shifted to make it easier for him to pull back the covers. This bed was overly large for the room, perhaps, but a comfortable size for two people. He caught her eyeing the edge, and asked, amused, "Is there something about the bed?"

"I was thinking about the odd shape of the room, and the bed in proportion. Do you know what - was this your mother's suite, or?"

"Oh, goodness, no. Mother's never liked this townhouse, that's why she kept the bigger one, the more elaborate one, after Father died." Where she reigned, dowager lady supreme, with people coming and going at her whim.

Alysoun weighed whether to say something she'd never said to Richard before, a new kind of intimacy. "I don't understand your mother at all, really."

Something in that, or perhaps in how she said it, made

Richard throw back his head and laugh. It was long, and easy, and something in the laugh wrapped around her, drawing her close. Then his arm was around her, and he was moving, so he could kiss her, in a rush of headlong delight that took her breath away.

When he finally pulled back, his eyes were dancing, and he gave her space to catch her breath, then blink at him.

"You don't have aspirations of being like Mother? Thank the lares. I didn't think you did, but that seems awfully uncomfortable to live with. More, I mean."

It made her grin, it made her set aside the caution she'd held on to. "You - your mother, I know you don't see her often."

"I have never seen her often." Richard's voice was softer now, but with the edge like a fencing foil, nominally blunted but still a viable weapon if he needed. "Not when I was a child. Not when I was on school holidays, not as a grown man. Once every few weeks, usually. Less now. Do tell me if she's difficult to you. I am quite content to let her have the larger townhouse, and parade around Trellech, but I'll not have her bothering you with her assumptions and expectations."

Alysoun gathered her wits, what she had of them. "That's why you're so insistent about going up to the nursery. You're there more than I realised, aren't you?"

That made him suddenly smile. "What makes you say that?"

"I came up, oh, three weeks ago and you had Gabriel and Charlotte on your lap, reading stories. And it was - it was a common thing. Not daily, you're busy with work, with other things. But regularly."

He nodded. "I try not to disrupt their schedule, it does

them no good, but sometimes I'm there in the morning, before I go to work. They both tend to wake early."

She laughed. "They get that from you, not from me, I'm sure. Even before…" She gestured vaguely at her body with her hand. "I was never an early riser unless I had to be."

It got her another kiss, as well. "Nothing wrong with taking your time. And you have rather more fussing with your clothing than I do. Or they do. Did I mention how much I liked your dress today?"

Alysoun tutted. "Not my best colour, but we did have to suit." She shook her head. "How do you feel about it? Now that you've said the words, the oath? We got so caught up in the new information I didn't even think to ask."

Richard considered, and rearranged while he was thinking, encouraging her to lean on him a bit, settling an arm around her waist for support and more contact. She found it soothing, comforting. It took him a minute to begin to speak again. She just rested there, letting her eyes half close, so she could focus on what he was going to say better.

"It feels like a cloak. I asked the Dowager Lady Witham, did you know?"

"You didn't tell me!" She was delighted, clearly, perhaps especially because he had found the Dowager intimidating from the beginning. "What did she say?"

"That it would go much better if I were open to the experience. That it was like putting a cloak on, accepting it. Not fighting it. And she was right. Of course." His voice went wry at the end. "I'll have to tell her so, it will please her. But perhaps you might come with me for that?"

"I would like that very much." She was feeling her way into asking the next piece. "And do you feel different now?"

Again, he took his time before answering. Then, softly, he said, "I think so. I feel less nervous about doing it, the actual judicial rites, now. It's like having a pitcher of water, and knowing how to pour it into a basin. Or becoming the basin. It's odd, I remember the Ritual classes at school talking about it, but I never felt anything there. I never have much, except occasionally at the household shrine, that was like that. I have when duelling. The rituals of the salle. Getting fitted up with the gear, saluting, and then afterwards, being a good sport, and then helping repair any damage."

Alysoun leaned back a little more, feeling him shift to hold her more securely. "And the rest of it can be managed by a good private secretary."

"Likely, yes. The record keeping and the diary and the making sure I'm home from the Guard in good time. Is there progress on someone?"

"They can set up interviews starting next week. Or whenever you like, though I gather at least one of the ones you liked has another potential position."

"Him first, then. And - there was a woman, yes? Would you rather a woman, or rather not a woman?"

That made her consider. Some would not want their husband in close quarters with another woman, on a regular basis. Especially not in their home, and with their marriage in a fragile sort of place. Not that she worried he'd divorce her, but there were other ways to be far more isolated than she had been.

But she did not, in principle, have that concern, and she said as much. "Not in principle. Though it would depend on the woman. As it would on the man. If we're providing room and board, as well as the work space."

"That did seem to be the best option, given the need to have someone around when I'm available."

"Right, I'll send a note to the agency tomorrow, when I get a chance, and we can see about the specific people."

"You'd like to sit in, then? Or be part of it? Schedule it so it makes sense, then, and you're right, we should do it at Veritas, so they can see the house."

"The rooms are all ready - that little suite in the east wing, quite private, and we're not terribly likely to host a large house party, or at least not often. And the office by the library is all ready."

"The sitting room and bedroom, and near enough a private bath, unless we're full up. Really excellent, my dear."

Alysoun smiled. "Would you just, just talk to me, until I fall asleep? Stories, or what you tell the children, maybe?"

"Do you want me to stay?"

She went entirely still for a moment, then nodded. "If you'd get enough sleep."

"I'd much rather be with you."

FORTY

9TH AUGUST, THE TOWNHOUSE

It was ten in the morning, and they'd been in the townhouse workroom for an hour and a half. The heat was beginning to seep in, despite the cool marble of the room. "Lemonade, or something else cold, anyone? Sandwiches?"

"Both, sir, if it's not a bother." That was Mason, who had sunk down onto the little wooden stool they kept for the work room. Sweat was trickling down her temple and making the loose strands of hair on her neck droop.

"Can you leave that, for the moment?"

Mason considered, as if weighing half a dozen factors, then nodded. "So long as no one bothers it."

"Right, then. All of you, into the library, it's far more pleasant in there. I'll lock the door, see about refreshments, and see if Alysoun's about." Richard stood, escorting Mason, Magni, and Gil, waiting for them to go through the hall into the library on the other side, with the long space drawing air from the cooler garden at the back. It was helped quite a bit by a particular enchantment to keep the air moving. Once they were settled, he went off to lock and ward the workroom door, ring for the maid and request food. That done, he could finally go upstairs to check on Alysoun.

She was curled up on the sofa in her bedroom. It was rather oddly shaped, now that he looked at it, with no particular view. He knocked on the edge of the door. "Alysoun? The others are downstairs. We found something interesting, but I thought you might want to come join us for the discussion."

Alysoun blinked up at him. "Are you sure? I feel particularly slow-witted today."

"In that case, you might ask just the question we need." He added, "I'd like you there. If you're up to it."

That won him a smile, if a little shy. "Well. Can't disappoint you then."

He grinned back at her, feeling giddy as a schoolboy, then he held out his hand. "They're bringing up some sandwiches and lemonade with plenty of ice."

"Oh, good. The lemonade in particular." Alysoun settled her hand in his. "Shouldn't keep them waiting."

Richard looked down at her, and then, impulsively, leaned down to kiss her, trusting that she would welcome it, no longer uncertain that she did. It felt wonderful, not just the way she moved to encourage him, but knowing that she would, that she wanted this too. He felt her hand at his waist, that added touch. He pulled away first, reluctantly, as she said, "We should go down. Even if..."

He let his thumb brush her fingers for a moment. "We have time later, don't we." It wasn't a question, but she smiled and nodded.

Leading her down toward the stairs, he said, "Please do ask whatever comes to mind. I think we're all so used to the way things are normally done we may miss things." The comment appeared to take her by surprise, but she nodded. She focused her attention on the stairs, while he did his best to be helpful and not awkwardly in her way.

"If you insist. If you're sure it will be helpful." She got down to the landing, and then looked at him. "I don't want to cause problems."

"Alysoun." He turned, to face her. "This is our home. If there is a problem, it is not with you."

She leaned against the wall, closing her eyes in concentration. "No pedestals, Richard, please. I can be wrong, I will be wrong, I will make mistakes."

"So will I." He could see her point. "But this is our home. I want you to feel you do not - always need to be on your guard here, against, against..." He stopped, trying to decide how to say this.

"I know you worry your body will betray you, your mind fail you, that you will say something poorly. These are our friends down there. Well, and Mason, who is in a class of her own, but who has been very clear she thinks you are observant and clever. To be precise, she told me earlier that it was a pity you hadn't had to work, you'd have made a superb Penelope. That is her highest form of praise. I don't rank, apparently."

That, at least, made Alysoun look at him and smile. She moved to kiss him once, gently, on the lips. "Well. We should give her more chances to see you being observant, then. Come along." She slipped her hand into his, and he took his cue, leading her back downstairs.

The others had settled into the library, and he was pleased to see they were all relaxed. Mason hadn't been sure what to make of dealing with both Magni and Gil, certainly not at the same time. She'd had very little to do with Captain Torham and the salle. None of the Penelopes did, beyond the basics of how to get out of the way quickly if a case they were on turned dangerous.

"Lady Edgarton." Mason caught sight of them first. "Sir. We were trying to figure out the pattern of the results."

"What did you find? Richard said it was best discussed together." Alysoun's voice sounded solid, determined, not as uncertain as she'd been for a moment on the stairs. Richard led her to settle on the remaining sofa, then sat beside her.

"I can show you in the workroom. We have samples of a number of different plants, and I was able to do testing that convinces us that it was one of the orchid family. We think but can't determine for certain - it was plants from the genus *Epipogium.*" Mason waited, as if that should mean something.

Richard said, "I am not a botanist, Mason."

It, or something in his tone, made Gil snort. "It's a very small genus, and the plant we think it is - again, hard to tell - is a ghost orchid."

Richard almost let it pass. "Explain why, at least the outline?"

"There are thousands of types of orchids, so Mason narrowed it down by trying common types. The trick is that we don't have a comparison sample for ghost orchids, because they're exceedingly rare. They need a wet winter, and a hot dry summer."

"We certainly have the second." Richard gestured at the windows. "But the first?"

"It was fairly dry, most of the winter, but there are some places it was wet. It might just be a valley that trapped moisture for some reason. It's possible it could be done deliberately, with magic, by someone who had one plant, and hoped to get more."

"How do you know it's a ghost orchid?" Alysoun felt they had skipped over this part, Richard could tell.

Mason waved a hand. "I do have samples for most of the other ones that grow here, and it wasn't those, and it was related to the ones I tested in the right ways. It's a process of elimination. There's a series of branching checklists. I'm not certain, but it seems as likely as anything."

"What do they do, then, that's so particularly important?"

"Magically, they have substantial healing properties, if properly prepared. But the plant has to be fresh, preserved in a keep-fresh charm, and not transported by magic or anything else that would risk bruising or upsetting it. They grow on trees, on fungi, not roots. You can, if you're careful, often remove them from the trees and keep them whole and fresh for a bit." Mason reeled it off as if reading from a book, and Richard was sure it was only lightly paraphrased.

"Do you think they were using it themselves or selling it on?" Alysoun was chewing on something, Richard had begun to recognise that expression properly.

It was Gil who said, thinking through it. "Why would they be bringing it down the river if they were going to process it themselves? They weren't stopping in Trellech, they were going somewhere else with it."

"The boat got caught north of Trellech."

"They were going ahead, not pulling over to dock at the path." Magni pointed this out, evenly. "We caught them a little downstream of that, though I suppose they might have been running at that point and just trying to get ahead of us."

"So where were they taking it, then? Around the coast to London? Across the Channel?" Alysoun was being like a terrier with it.

"Either. I don't know that we'll find out until we've untangled the rest of it."

"Which is not easy to do, if we don't know where it was going, who it was going to, or anything else."

Magni shook his head. "Do we have any other evidence? What kinds of resources would they need to do something with it? We're not talking a transatlantic voyage, are we?"

Mason counted, silently, on her fingers. "Probably not. I don't think it would stay alive and fresh long enough. Better to process it and move that, but that would mean - London might do, or Paris. Paris has a lot of perfume distillers, they would have the physical equipment for some of it."

"What - what was involved in getting the orchid in the first place?"

Mason considered. "Sir, the book here." She gestured at the book she'd brought from the workroom. "It says they're quite rare, and bloom unpredictably, mostly in very small numbers, but sometimes in larger patches, if the conditions are just right, twenty or thirty plants. Usually between June and August. The box doesn't sound large enough for twenty, maybe five or ten at most."

"But it means someone would have had to chance upon it, be able to identify it, and have the connections to make use of it. Which suggests it's not your average farmer."

Alysoun kept trying to get her thoughts straight. "Let us work the other direction," she said, finally. "Though it's rather needle in the haystack. Who would be in a position to hear about that kind of thing, rare orchids, growing unpredictably?"

Richard nodded. "Thinking through the summer. Is there any chance the earthquake did something?"

"The one in June?" Magni was following, at least. "End of June."

Alysoun considered, there was something nagging at her. "Richard, when you came home from that, you mentioned something had felt odd. But I don't remember why."

Richard, by the expression on his face, didn't remember either, but he said, "Do you remember anything else about it?"

She tapped her fingers again on the table. "It was something about... I hate this." She let that spill out before she could manage to stop it. "Give me a minute." Alysoun pushed herself upright. Sometimes playing the aches against the cotton wool got her somewhere. Sometimes it didn't, of course. It would be entirely manageable if things worked reliably minute to minute.

Richard half pushed himself out of his chair before she waved at him. "Work on some other piece of it, while I think."

"It is not such a large community as all that," Richard said, after a moment. "If there are people resorting to unusual methods, unsubtle methods, you would think it would be at least a little bit obvious."

Gil nodded. "And for smuggling down the river, with that kind of crew, it would need to be someone with some kind of influence. Especially if it were going to a skilled herbalist or alchemist. They aren't as thick on the ground as all that, and all but a handful went to Schola. A more limited set to choose from."

"They were taking it past Trellech, we think. Let's start with that as a supposition. They might have been running when you caught them, but it would have been safer to bring it overland to Trellech, if they were only going that far."

Magni nodded. "It seems a reasonable place to start. Do we have an idea of the options?"

Richard stood then, while Alysoun slowly made a circuit of the open end of the library, getting glimpses as he went and rummaged for one of the big atlases. "Here. Map of the south coastline. I don't have my working notes here, but I think I remember enough, or between us, we probably do." He then went to pull a few of the side tables together to have somewhere everyone could see the book.

Next time Alysoun went by the large desk at the end of the library, she gathered up a box of the little pins, and several large sheets of paper. She dropped them on top of

Richard's book. "You are perfectly capable of making copies. Do that and put the pins in."

She could hear Mason chortle with delight as she turned to make another circuit. She could not pin that thought down. It was something not about the orchids, if they were right, but something about the museum. Alysoun let the drone of the charms to make a copy of the map onto clean paper fade out of her awareness. They moved on to a discussion of what to pin the map to, before Magni went to grab the blotter from the desk, passing her gracefully as she made another turn around the library.

Alysoun changed direction, to help her hip stop complaining, and also in case it shook something different loose. All that lore about going sunwise or widdershins, she had always thought there might be something in it. It did not immediately help, but the shift meant she caught a comment from Richard. "Right, so what level of skill is needed, here?"

Mason was frowning. "Sir, do you have a copy of the *Liber de arte destillandi?*"

Richard nodded. "Every library, yes." He turned, walking over to a set of shelves and ran his fingers along the bound volumes. He pulled off a volume bound in the deep red of the other alchemy books in the collection. "Here."

Gil was watching. "I'm now wondering how you sort your library, of course." Irrepressible.

Alysoun offered, "Publication date, or topic and then date. Depending."

Gil raised an eyebrow. "Looking at the influences between books more broadly than purely by topic. Huh." He then forcibly turned his attention back to the discussion. Alysoun shrugged slightly, and kept walking, though she could feel her body complaining more loudly about it.

Mason looked up from where she'd thumbed through the book to a particular passage she was obviously familiar with. "I'm fairly certain it would require a Master Alchemist or Herbalist, sir. Or nearly so."

"That means we could check the guild lists, but let's see who we can mark out now." The rest of them settled into low voiced commentary, agreeing where to place pins, making a list. That was Gil, she suspected, from the questions he was asking about the spelling of some of the names.

It took them a good few minutes. Alysoun had decided this was not getting her anywhere when she turned back to come find her seat, before she did something undignified like fall over. Somehow, turning again, looking up at the windows, the light coming in from them, finally sparked the idea she'd been chasing.

"What do we know about the Delwyns?"

"You'd said their dresses were cheaper fabric than you'd expect, at the gala." Richard, bless him, had remembered what she'd said. "And there was the flash of them at the investiture. Do we think the two things are linked?"

"They could be, couldn't they?" Alysoun settled down next to Richard, taking a moment to catch her breath. "The signs seem to suggest."

"Lead us through what you're thinking, if you would." Magni was leaning forward. "You know the players better than I do."

Alysoun glanced at her husband, who replied, "I'll fill in."

She took a breath. "Lord and Lady Delwyn are in their fifties. Three children, son and daughter both a little older than Richard and I, but not by terribly much. And then a younger son, not long out of school. I don't think the daughter is likely directly involved. Willis told me she is expecting, and spending her time at her husband's country home, in Scotland."

They could all hear Gil's pen, scratching away, quickly. Alysoun waited a moment, before continuing. "The heir, Jupiter, was at the investiture, but without his wife. His wife has a sister who did her best to make a pass at Richard at one of the events." She waited a beat, then added, beatifically, "He didn't notice, mind you."

That got a roar of laughter from Magni and something that might almost be called a giggle from Mason, both of them drowning out Gil's chuckle. Richard, for his part, looked resigned. "I did apologise."

She leaned to kiss his cheek. "I found it very sweet. At any rate, they have been striking me as a rather tarnished gilt. So, why would they be put forward as the patrons of an unusual exhibit at the museum?"

Magni settled into his chair. "Not a thing I've needed to know, but are there costs involved in putting on a show like that?"

"Usually, that is part of the patronage, but I suppose it's possible they instead offered several pieces of glass." Alysoun flicked her fingers. "The exhibit guide is at Veritas. Blast."

Mason offered, "Someone could go get another from the museum?"

Richard stood. "I'll get one of the staff to go, and be quick about it." He shifted away from Alysoun, and went to ring the bell and wait for one of the staff to appear at the door.

Alysoun nodded. "That will do for confirmation and whatever evidence you need for the Guard." She wanted to press on, now. She could feel things quivering under her fingertips. "I know that at least three of the pieces were theirs, of about thirty, total. A tenth. And if my theory is right, at least one of the anonymous pieces, and I suspect more than three others." She named them off, but the others were all unremarkable, the kind of thing a long-standing family might have access to.

Gil was thinking along the same lines. "I suppose one of the things about stained glass is that it's not like other art, you would need to have access to the space where it was installed to know it belonged to the family. If the pieces came from private family spaces..." He frowned. "I don't know much about their holdings, do you?"

"There's no reason to assume the pieces came from within the magical community. They might have asked tenant farmers or churches or some such. It's an old family, they have land in several parts of the country."

"Including near London." Richard pointed out. "For making the glass. Possibly also this distillation."

It was then that it finally hit Alysoun. "Richard, the earthquake. Where were you riding? On the map?"

Richard stood, peering at the map, then he put his finger down, and then put a pin in it, this one with a copper head, unlike any of the others. "Here. It was a little farmholding. I remember now, why I mentioned it. It looked better off than it ought. Newer furniture, not patched up, or all different ages. An influx of ready money, enough they weren't stashing it all away for a rainy day. Well, that valley, an extra rainy day."

"So, damp." Alysoun was amused now. "That valley."

"It might trap the rain clouds a bit."

Mason offered, "If they wanted damp, there's some magical workings that could do it. Keeping it local, the size of a house. Not your house, sir, but an ordinary house and garden. Keeping that damp wouldn't be that hard, especially if anyone involved had a touch of weather witching."

Alysoun nodded, then pushed herself to stand again, and picked up a pin with a deep red head. "Why I ask." she says. "The Delwyns have a home here." She pushed it into the map, an easy ride from the copper one. "Nothing big, a hunting cottage."

Then she paused, and said. "And if it was them I overheard at the investiture, they mentioned getting something from Wales. If Professor Arden is cousin to the Miller sisters, well..."

Eventually, even the best discussion with the most intelligent people must wind to an end. Mason had to return to other tasks, as did Magni, and Gil excused himself. That left Richard to return to where Alysoun was still sitting in the parlour.

"You look..." He looked her up and down. "You look like a woman who would rather be home. Let's get you back to Veritas."

She blinked up at him. "But don't you have things here?"

"Mason and Magni are putting the ones in motion that need scheduling. I am off until tomorrow, remember, officially?"

She let out a sigh, as if all the breath were escaping, and then she nodded. "I'd like that. I'd like a proper soak, at least."

That gave him an idea, but he simply said, "Let me tell Wallis and so on. Do you need anything from upstairs?" The benefit of having two houses was having two sets of most things. "Your book?"

Alysoun gave him a glowing smile. "My book," she agreed. "The two on the side table, too, please, and whatever Wallis thinks she needs to bring."

"I will be giving her fifteen minutes. You settle there, and drink the lemonade and in a bit we'll be back in the country."

It was not quite as simple as that. A carriage had to be summoned, and his man had gone ahead to pay the surcharge to get them through the line at the portal faster. Though they were lucky enough that two other people in line had been going to the Veritas portal, and that always made things easier. On the other end, he had to make sure Alysoun got clear without tripping. He liked how she trusted him to lean on, but at the same time, he worried at how much she seemed to need him there.

"Bath?"

"Bath, yes." He left her to Wallis's attention, with a promise that he would be back in a few minutes. He went to consult with the housekeeper about the evening meal, and how he hoped they would not be disturbed thereafter. By the time he got back to the bath, he was grinning. Alysoun was amiable, not quite drowsy, but certainly not inclined to talk. A long soak seemed to do her good, and when they parted to dress again for supper, she looked rather more together.

They talked about the children over supper, and about some of the letters she'd gotten about the investiture, delivered to Veritas that morning. Mostly people currying favour, but a note from the Dowager Lady Witham.

"Marietta wrote." Richard had to mentally substitute her formal name. "She would like to have us to supper, next week if we can arrange it. She implies she is rather interested in whether you took her advice for the investiture, and if so she says..." Alysoun peered at the letter. "She would very much enjoy discussing the experience with someone sensibly observant."

"You'd enjoy it, so we shall. I'll check the duty roster and let you know but I don't think I have any evening obligations next week. And I think I perhaps find her a tad less intimidating than I used to. Only a tad, though."

Alysoun laughed, and her entire face lit up with it. It made Richard far more certain about what he'd like to do next. Standing, once they finished with the meal, he held out his hand. "If I may escort you upstairs? Do let Wallis know I'll be seeing to your undressing."

That made Alysoun giggle and blush, looking much more like she had when they married for a moment. He'd been such a stiff little lordling then, so unsure of what to do. He'd wanted to treat her well, and he hadn't had the first idea how to go about it. But thanks to something - the gods, the fates, sheer good fortune - he seemed to have been gifted a second chance, and the sense not to waste it.

By the time they got upstairs, she was teasing him, watching his reactions. "You haven't looked at me quite like this, well... " Then she shifted, kissing his cheek. "You have something in mind. You're laying out a duel in your head."

"Duels depend on the response of your," he kissed her on the nose, "opponent. But I think that is perhaps a trifle antagonistic for our desires this evening."

She was laughing when she drew him into her room. "You said something about not needing Wallis? Do you actually know how to undo things?"

He drew himself up, puffing up with mock pride. "I am a Captain in the Guard, a properly invested magistrate, and Lord of the land. I am quite certain I can figure it out."

Naturally, two minutes later, he had to admit defeat. "I

am rather stumped, my dear. If you simply could be cut out of the thing, I would know what to do, but I am not certain how one unlaces it. Not without causing an awful lot of bother."

She turned over her shoulder and snorted. "You are starting at the wrong side. You did manage the dress well enough, I'll give you that."

Richard came around to the front, and blinked. "The front?"

She gestured to a long line of fastenings down the front. "See these. This is the busk, I don't quite have the strength tonight to pull them, the angle. Keep this in place, pull this part here, until the hooks unlatch." She let out her breath, and Richard could feel a bit of the give there. He gave it a tug, then a stronger one. The whole set of little metal tabs pulled apart, and the corset came loose in his hands.

Alysoun blinked up at him, and then stretched, settling her arms around his shoulders, leaning into him. "Mmm." She then kissed his cheek. "Never seen a corset like that before?"

"Not that close up. And before yours, well. Mother. I was tiny. It was a very...."

Alysoun laughed, suddenly. "Goodness. Your mother would be traditional about her corsets, yes. The older ones were horrific, Mother says, if they were tight-laced."

"We are not talking about my mother right now. Or your mother. And especially not their corsets. Here. Where does this go?" He pulled her closer, then nuzzled at her forehead. "Tell me if something hurts. Anything. Or if you want more of something I'm doing."

Her hand moved to his back, then down to his hip. "Too many clothes. Far too many layers." Then, distracted. "Corset wherever. Both hands, please."

"Lady." He chuckled, and then shifted enough to get hands to begin to undo the numerous fastenings, first the shirt and then the trousers. "At your service." Then he paused, not quite sure how to venture what he was thinking.

Her hand came up, cupping his cheek. "You're afraid of hurting me. Hurt happens. I want some pleasure with it. You aim yourself at that."

Richard went still for a moment, at the fierceness in her voice. "You're sure." It came out hesitant, and he didn't want to question her choices. Then he swallowed. "Of course you are. You'll tell me, if you need ..."

"If something will bring me more pleasure, I will tell you." Her voice was clear, sharp, like the edge of a blade.

Of course he wasn't going to argue. He had more sense. He finished pulling his clothing off, and asked, "Charm?"

There was a tiny sigh. "Another child would not be a good idea, no." The healers had been very clear with him, and he assumed with her as well. Part of him wished he could ease that wistfulness. It was something to talk about in the morning, in the coming days. Not now.

Now was for other things, and he rubbed his cheek against her hand. "Come to bed, my lady." Then, a moment later, he shifted, moving to pick her up. She laughed, her arms going around him, as he carried her ten steps to the bed, then spread her out on it. "There should be flowers, strewn across the bed. Music."

"Are you a romantic, then?" Alysoun was stretched out, and somewhere in the process she'd loosened the clips in her hair, so it spread out in dark waves against the cream coloured sheets. It made for a striking contrast, and he settled on the bed to run a finger against her cheek.

"In my heart of hearts, yes." He admitted it, finally,

without feeling too shy for words. "What would you like best, my lady?"

"You." Just the single word, but she was grinning at him.

"Besides that." The fact they were teasing, that felt wonderful, the way it was supporting something he hadn't thought that he'd have. That they were in this together.

She laughed. "I don't know what I like best, we will just have to explore. Together." She then tugged at his hand. "Now, please." It was an order, but so pleasantly given, he laughed, then moved to settle himself between her legs, where he could kiss her first, holding himself up on one arm.

It brought them close together, feeling her breasts against his chest, the warmth and softness of her. Now, finally, in the charm light, he could see the faint tracework of the changes of her body, the way her shape had softened and shifted. He let his hand drift to her hip, thumb rubbing over the skin for a moment.

Alysoun blinked up at him. "You're thinking of something?"

He nodded. "I'm thinking that what I like about art is that it has history. Like us. Time - deepens things." He bent to kiss her on the lips, taking his time, before he pulled back. "I am very glad we are doing this together. Now. Much better."

"More doing, please. Talking in the morning."

It took him more time than he liked to figure out what she liked best, but the exploration was largely delightful. Once, he shifted in a way that made her expression immediately flicker with pain. She didn't say anything, but she didn't have to since he moved immediately. Richard went back to something she'd liked better, steady movements of his hands. It was not quite a massage, but a sureness that she leaned into, much like a horse being groomed. A few minutes of that, and she let out a sigh, contented, her legs opening.

He took it as the offering it was, and moved, watching her face, the entire time. When he slid into her finally, her hips rolled against him as he filled her. Her head went back, and she let out a long needy sigh, like what she'd hoped for and wanted was finally hers.

It awed him, enough that he held himself there, as deep inside her as he could be, just looking down at her face. His hands were braced on either side of her. She blinked up at him, then, before she could urge him on, he began to move. Slowly, at first, so he could watch her reactions, the little gasps and moans of pleasure. So he could feel how her body arched beneath him when she gave herself over to the movements.

Finally, he could not focus on her face, only on the mounting pleasure, the need they were both feeling. She was following along with him, as easily as she did on horseback, given the chance. He dropped one hand between them, fumbling for a moment before finding a way to touch her that made her cry out, decidedly in pleasure. They held each other there, at the edge of a cliff, before he rolled his thumb one more time, and sent her shattering into ecstasy. That brought him off too, with four last deep thrusts and a deep groan.

There was nothing in the world but her, and the smile on her face as he managed to collapse to one side, an arm across and around her.

Richard couldn't decide if he found this month's meeting terribly tedious or terribly fascinating. The monthly meeting at the Ministry to discuss matters of significance to the community could be both, sometimes in alternate sentences. This month was fairly minimal, with three members of the Council, a representative each from the Guard, the Ministry, and the Guilds, and whatever others cared to show up. Today, that meant a small crowd, thirty people or so, though it had been a fairly energetic discussion.

Richard was here today as the representative of the Guard, seated at a table on the main dais at the front. He glanced up at the gallery, where Alysoun was seated. She was paying close attention, and looked contented enough. He was glad she was here.

Much of today's discussion had been about new potential approaches to the keep-away enchantments on houses and villages like Veritas that were near spaces that got periodic waves of non-magical folk. They'd already had a few close encounters, and with the hops picking season approaching. Richard and Alysoun both hoped for a better way to avoid people wandering into the local village when they shouldn't.

He felt antsy, however, because he had been told that there would be some further news about his cases, soon, and he hadn't heard anything before coming down to the meeting hall. On the other hand, people knew where he was. As the meeting finally decided that those near harvest workers were permitted to take additional precautions, he breathed a sigh of relief. They were almost through the agenda, and he could take Alysoun for lunch if he weren't needed elsewhere immediately.

Just as they got into the end of meeting pleasantries, there was a commotion at the double doors leading to the hall. Someone forced his way through, into the middle of the hall, the empty space that normally held whoever was presenting to the gathering. The light was behind him, so it wasn't until he got up within fifteen feet of the front that Richard could see it was Lord Delwyn, his hair disheveled. Two of the Guard had followed after him, but were standing at the doors looking uncertain how to proceed.

"Lord Edgarton, you have done me a great wrong. I seek satisfaction by magic." His voice was too loud in the space, and it had an edge to it.

Richard's head went up sharply. That was the traditional challenge to a duel. He knew, instantly, that he must reply appropriately, keeping all the myriad layers of commitment and oath and expected behaviour aligned. He inclined his head to Lord Delwyn, but spoke first to the others on the dais. "Council members, do I have your permission to address Lord Delwyn in an alternate capacity?"

All three nodded, and the senior member of the Council, Magister FitzAlan, gestured. "We declare the meeting ended." Brief, but effective.

Richard turned back to face Lord Delwyn. He caught someone signalling from the back of the room, using the hand signs the Guard used at distance. Warrant. Issued. That would do it, then. "In what way have I wronged you, Lord Delwyn?" He kept his voice even, not daring to look up to the gallery and Alysoun.

"You have caused me and my family great distress."

"How have I done so, Lord Delwyn?" There were the traditional exchanges. Richard would keep to them.

"A warrant has been issued for my arrest, that of my wife, my heir, and his wife. You are named as the investigator, and I claim you have callously and without cause brought dishonour and shame to my family. I demand satisfaction, lord to lord, magician to magician, man to man."

Richard held himself still and erect. On one hand, it was a ridiculous charge. He had brought the evidence to his superior officers for review, but he had had no notice of their decision, unless it was waiting for him on his desk. On the other hand, he suspected he saw where Lord Delwyn was going with this. He might be wishing to sacrifice himself. If he duelled and was killed, it might spare their names, save whatever property they still had. Possibly. It would depend on the complex calculations of the courts, on how much property was recompense for the taking of a life.

Worse, the challenge was explicitly to Richard as Lord. He knew the old laws as well as he suspected Lord Delwyn did. He could, technically, decline, but he didn't like to think of what it would do to the land ties if he did. Or rather, he didn't want to risk it. He was still too new to the Lordship, still under a decade, still setting his own patterns with that magic. "I presented the evidence I found to the

Guard, Lord Delwyn. None of us acts alone, except in the most urgent of need."

"Still. I take issue with your action. Will you meet with me?"

Richard didn't dare to look around, to show any concern, but he could feel the tension in the room. He was not, by his oath as a Guard, permitted to challenge someone to a duel, he knew that. He and Magni had gone through the specifics several times. But he could answer the challenge, if presented.

It would be up to him to avoid breaking his oath, to avoid a killing blow, or an injury that might become fatal. And it would become his duty to see to the care and support of widows and orphans produced, and the healing of his opponent if he survived. Which was one very good reason why the Guard generally avoided such challenges if they could.

But he was not only one of the Guard, and he could feel the newer cloak of the magistrate's oath tug on him. If he had been challenged for a personal offence, that would be one thing, but this was a challenge for doing his duty, by magic and the law.

"Will first touch satisfy your challenge?" Richard could at least turn it into a battle of charms and protections, using something that would not hurt.

"It will not. To the death." Lord Delwyn's voice was firm, Richard had to grant him that.

Richard closed his eyes for just a moment, a long blink, before he inclined his head. "And you will not yield to some other form of justice?" He would try every avenue he could.

"No other form will serve." The man was resolute. Desperate - Richard could hear a hint of it now in his voice - but stubborn.

"I will meet you in the Guard Salle, at four, with magic as the weapon. Guards, if you would escort Lord Delwyn to a room where he may prepare, in keeping with custom and law. Lord Delwyn, I will send my second along to make arrangements, if you would summon yours."

Lord Delwyn himself said nothing, just nodded once. There was a "Captain, yes, Captain." from the end of the hall, and two of the Guards came up to step beside Lord Delwyn. They would make sure he did not leave, but that he had food and drink and a comfortable space to prepare in, as he chose. Here, at least, the customs were clear, since he was also under arrest.

It was only after they led Lord Delwyn away that Richard could look around. Alysoun had disappeared from the gallery, and he wondered how much of it she had seen, if she had already left, how he would explain it to her. He turned to make his bow to the Council and the other representatives.

Magister FitzAlan nodded once to him. "I will make my own report, to confirm you gave every opportunity to withdraw." Richard did not know the man terribly well, as many of the Council kept to their own circles, but he had found him easy to work with, fair if sometimes terrifyingly precise.

"Thank you, sir. Most appreciated." Then he caught Magister FitzAlan's eyes sliding past him, and he turned. Alysoun was there, escorted by Simons, as if she had appeared from nowhere.

"My pardon, all." He then turned, and strode down the steps at the side of the dais, coming around to take Alysoun's hand. "You heard, then?"

Alysoun squeezed his hand. "All of it, yes." She paused. "I would like a minute alone, but I know you must prepare."

Richard nodded, swallowing a breath and a torrent of

things he wanted to say to her. "Simons, would you go tell Captain Torham I have agreed to meet a challenge, and beg use of the salle at four. Please tell him I will come to call in his office presently, if he could clear his schedule for the afternoon." He added the phrase in the Guard's Tongue that made it clear he was asking for a significant assistance.

"Your second, sir?" Simons offered a small bow, all formality.

"I very much hope so, yes, but I would like to ask him myself."

"Of course, sir." If Simons had wondered if he'd be asked, he showed no sign of it. "There is a side room here, if you would like, Lady Edgarton. And I will see about arranging some sandwiches, sir, as well, for your discussion with Captain Torham. And, um." There was a pause. "Clear your own calendar."

Richard nodded. "Thank you, yes. Is the warrant on my desk, do you know?"

"I was down here, sir, in case you needed anything, but I gather they were issued just as the meeting started. Lord Delwyn was already in the building and coming into the meeting hall before the Guards at the door realised. He may have had an earlier warning. I'll go collect that and bring it and any other relevant material once I've spoken to Captain Torham."

"Thank you, Simons, a great help." He gave the little nod of dismissal, and Simons went off, at a steady ground-covering trot, after the briefest of polite murmurs. Richard took Alysoun's arm and guided her to the small withdrawing room at the side of the dais. The charm lights were on, and he closed the door behind them.

"Pardon, I..." "Richard, I..."

They both spoke over each other, and Richard had to smile. "Please, Alysoun."

"What do you want of me?"

He blinked. He hadn't even thought of that. Other than being worried she had seen too much of the challenge, but clearly she had. He reached for both her hands, then gave that up and drew her into his arms, as securely as he could. "I cannot promise to be safe, but I promise to take as much care as I can."

"You know why he challenged you?"

Richard nodded. "I think he hopes I will kill him, and it will spare his family. The old blood-debts."

Alysoun shivered. "That's brutal." Then she clearly considered. "We'd be responsible for them, wouldn't we? Ugh."

He agreed with her, though that 'we' made him glow, despite the circumstances. "I will be doing my best to see we aren't. If we are going to take on widows and orphans, I would prefer those with better sense. And less criminality."

It made her snort, and pull back enough to look him in the eye. "I want to watch. No, don't tell me no. I will watch. Whatever happens." There was her own steel in her voice.

"I have not the wits or magic to stop you. But will you rest, for now? Here or at home? Come to the salle at half-three, I will make sure Simons can escort you."

She let out a breath, as if she had been gearing up for her own fight. "Oh. Oh. Good." Then, more daring, she added, "I thought you'd refuse."

"I - " He stopped, tried again. "I don't know what I think about it, what I would rather, so I must let you choose."

Alysoun nodded, then pulled back further, rummaging, reaching into her pocket, and withdrawing a handkerchief. "Not what I planned, but Richard, love, will you bear my favour, where all may see it and know that you fight with honour?"

He almost spoke, but she held up her hand. "You are many things, Richard, but I give this to you not as my husband and chosen lord, not as Lord Edgarton, but as Captain Edgarton, who lives and breathes his oaths, and who will see justice done, as fairly and kindly as he can. And, I hope, with more than sufficient skill."

Richard went entirely still as she pressed the linen into his hand. He drew it up to his mouth to kiss it, and it smelled like her, the light floral water perfume she preferred, nothing overpowering.

He kissed it, reverently, with his whole being, and then carefully hung it over his belt, adding a charm to keep it in place with the flat of his hand, before he pulled her against him again, kissing her far more energetically. She responded, arching against him, both of them forgetting where they were, or what the rest of the afternoon would hold, for just a minute, before he finally pulled back.

"You find the places I didn't know I had, my lady." He couldn't quite look at her, as if that might break the spell he felt he was under. "I will do you honour." Then he swallowed. He had so much to do, and not much time to arrange it. Richard met her eyes, at last.

She nodded, as clear and strong as he could hope to ask for. "I'll be back at half-three." It was a command and a certainty.

It was approaching four, and Alysoun was exceedingly worried. Simons had met her, and escorted her to a seat in the viewing gallery, nervously explaining the protections that would keep the observers safe from any danger. The room was perhaps forty yards long, and twenty wide, a surprisingly large space to put a few people in.

Simons repeated himself twice before she had murmured, as gently as she could, that she would sit here, and perhaps he could help somewhere else. Just then, one of the other Guard had beckoned to him, and he had gone that way. It gave her time to look around, and realise the crowd was perhaps two-thirds Guard uniforms. The rest were in ordinary clothes, and she could see none of the immediate Delwyn family. She could not help but wonder if they had any notion of what he had planned.

She could see Richard, dimly, in the archway that led to the offices, gesturing while in conversation with someone. Magni, she presumed, or one of the other officers who were milling about. She was leaning forward, trying to get a better glimpse, when she heard the voice behind her, and then someone coming to settle on the bench.

"They're almost ready. If we need an excuse, may I say I've been interested in your tapestries, and you've been kind enough to indulge me over the past few weeks?" It was Gilbert, his voice low and even. "Mag sent a carriage for me as soon as he heard. I've been back there with them. Richard thought you'd prefer someone who could explain the details you haven't read about."

Alysoun let out a sigh of relief. "Oh, yes, please. There's a difference between books and realities." The viewing space ran along the length of the salle, and most people were toward the centre, or the far end. "And," she admitted, "the company."

"Richard will be duelling from here, as the Guard. It's the worse angle for the sun. Most of them..." Gilbert nodded at the crowd, though he nodded at her comment. "Will be looking to see the details of the fight. Would you prefer to be further down?"

"I'd prefer to be closer to Richard, if that's not a problem."

"Of course not. Now, they'll come out, there will be one more attempt to find agreement without a duel, and the neutral party will announce the terms they've agreed to. There are healers, here and there." One in each corner. "No skimping." He paused. "Delwyn's second is that Professor Arden. Little ferret of a man, isn't he?"

Alysoun blinked, considering the implications of that. "Is that permitted? He's surely not able to fight."

Gilbert shook his head. "It makes it rather clear the goal is for Delwyn to be fatally hurt or killed." He paused. "That might still happen. It does not take much skill to use brute force. It takes a great deal more ability to use enough to end a duel without hurting someone. Richard and Mags have been talking through approaches non-stop since before I joined them. I think Richard stands a good chance of ending the duel without permanent harm to his opponent, but that's a desperate man, fighting for his family."

Alysoun inhaled, about to say something, when she saw movement from the office, and a stir by the hallway that led to the salle itself. Richard came out, wearing a proper duelling uniform. He looked heroic, in tightfitting breeches and jacket of the deep Guard blue and the white belt, from which hung her favour. His wand was in the sheath on his left hip, where other men might have worn a sword. Magni followed him, his hands clasped in front of him, to indicate that he was not using his magic. They took up a place half way down the salle.

Lord Delwyn and Professor Arden came out, taking up their place on the other side, putting them about twenty feet apart. Lord Delwyn wore what must be an old outfit, since she could see the lacing had been let out on the sides. It had once been deep black, she thought, but now had that muted brown-black of faded dyes. Professor Arden seemed entirely out of his element, his hands fluttering in the long sleeves of his academic gown.

Finally, the last man strode out, entirely confident and in control. This was the neutral party, who would ensure all was done according to law. She was startled to realise it was Council Member FitzAlan. Many of the Council were accomplished duellists in their own right.

"Good people." His voice had been magically amplified; it rang out sharp and clear. "I am Council Member FitzA-lan, asked to see that this duel observes all proper forms. I know both Lord Delwyn, the challenger, and Lord Edgarton, as I know all the lords of the land, but I have no particular ties to either man or their family. I am here to see if they cannot be reconciled. Lord Delwyn, you know that duelling is permitted only when no other satisfaction can be found. Is there no other way to resolve your claim?"

Lord Delwyn shook his head. "I claim the right to combat." His voice did not project half so well, but the salle was so quiet she could hear easily.

Magister FitzAlan inclined his head. "And Lord Edgarton, will you answer the challenge?"

"In service to my oaths and my honour, I will answer." Richard's voice was louder.

"The duel is with whatever magic each man can summon, and to death or utter incapacitation." Magister FitzAlan sounded both regretful and something else. "Gentlemen, prepare yourselves."

The parties withdrew to their ends of the salle, and Richard pivoted, looking up at the gallery. He met her eyes, then lifted the favour, kissed it once more, and tucked it back into his belt, before saluting her. There was nothing in the moment for Alysoun but that, as if she had been frozen in place. Finally, after what felt like hours, she blew him a kiss, and he bowed and turned to face his opponent. Magni backed up to the corner nearest them, into a nook in the wall.

"There are protections, all along here, and they were checked thoroughly this afternoon." Gilbert's voice began again, reassuring. "They'll salute and go to."

"Are you ready, my lords?" Magister FitzAlan's voice was loud again, quieting the room.

"I am." It came as an echo, though Richard's voice was much stronger. FitzAlan moved to stand in the arch that led to the offices, and then said, "On my count. Three, two, one, go to."

Richard's wand was already coming up, a pattern moving back and forth. "Protection, a shielding charm. Richard generally starts that way." Gilbert's voice was quiet in her ear, but clear.

Lord Delwyn was doing something else, that sent out widely spaced sparks of light, and Alysoun recognised that herself. "Roget's second charm. A weak opening, yes?"

"Yes." Gilbert shifted beside her, and then there was another charm from Richard, another flash of light, a steady stream of it that bounced off the first shield. "The challenge for Richard is attacking and subduing without doing significant damage."

The further exchanges, the next half dozen, went like that, with Alysoun identifying many of them - her reading stood her in good stead. Lord Delwyn tried conventional opening after conventional opening, all cast visibly, but without much strength. Richard advanced, slowly, as if he were penning a wayward sheep into a corner, moving his shielding to press Delwyn back.

"He's avoiding how the light shines in the eyes, from further back. Besides getting closer for some of the subdual charms." There was a note in Gilbert's voice, an edge of excitement. Alysoun couldn't completely muffle her distress, but muffled her slight squawk of discomfort, not taking her eyes off her husband. Next to her, Gilbert snorted. "It's not Richard at his finest, he's poorly matched. But it is a beautifully executed show of control and patience. Not the flash some admire, but far more difficult to do. If he continues like this, he will solidify his reputation beautifully."

She had not thought about that set of implications at all, what seeing this might do for the people Richard worked with. The entire room was watching, a murmur here or there at a particular enchantment, but largely entranced.

Something shifted, then. She sensed it before she saw Richard's posture shift. Lord Delwyn's wand moved, quickly, and Gilbert inhaled sharply. "That's a sacrifice move. Tying his magic into what comes next, all of it."

Before he could say anything more, there was a huge burst of brilliant red-orange flame, surging out from Delwyn's hands, like a tidal wave. It roared toward Richard, directly, and Alysoun could not look away. The light flared up around him, hiding him from sight, and she found herself grabbing for Gilbert's hand, unable to breathe.

Nothing changed for one heartbeat, two, three, fast as her heart was pounding, but then, as quickly as it had flooded out, that light receded, leaving Richard standing there, his hands in front of him, turned upwards, to cup a glowing ball of fire and magic hovering just above his skin, like a miniature sun.

The entire crowd gasped, almost as one, and Gilbert breathed out. "Oh, Minerva's blessing. He did it. It requires being absolutely sure of yourself, your capability. Your capacity. Magni was sure he could now, but I've never seen anyone do it properly." Richard was advancing now, that fire hovering. Lord Delwyn looked afraid now, properly afraid, and he reached for something in his boot, a boot knife, lifting it as if to throw it.

A line of glowing fire struck out, stretching Lord Delwyn's arm out from his body and coiling around it until he dropped the knife. Immediately after, a wave of power, dense and translucent like water, pushed him back and back, into the far wall of the salle, with such great force that dust fell from the rafters. The magic coiled, forming a net until Lord Delwyn could not move. If he tried to speak, no one heard anything.

There was a moment of complete silence, before Richard took the radiance in his hands, and spoke to it quietly, bending his head to it like he bent his head to talk to Gabriel and Charlotte, like nothing mattered in the world in that moment except that. It was intimate, daring, and the most potent thing she had ever seen in her life. Then, like he was sending a horse out into the paddock, the fire in his hands spun and twisted, dancing up into the roof of the salle and cascading down, in sheets of light like a waterfall, before it faded away.

Gilbert said something under his breath that Alysoun thought must have been an extended bit of swearing, before he gathered himself. "He did it, bless him, he did it. That's reinforced the wardings here, all the protections. Powerfully so."

Alysoun finally found herself able to breathe again. "It's done?"

Richard had turned now, bowing low to Magister FitzAlan. Magni came out of his protected area, coming across to bow as well, and they had a brief conference there, in the centre of the salle, completely ignoring the rest of the room.

"Do you want to go down? May I escort you? Or would you rather go somewhere private?"

Alysoun took a breath. "Go down, please."

"This way." Gilbert clearly knew the salle well. He showed her a staircase that went down the far side, out through where Magni had stood, and then she was on the smooth packed dirt of the floor. She wasn't sure for a moment if this were the right thing, but then Richard turned, at Magni's nod, and he was beaming, coming toward her.

When he reached her, part way, he kissed her, fiercely. She could feel the hum of his magic through his skin, still buzzing through him. Spinning her around, he settled his arm around her waist, protective and possessive, and brought her back to the little knot of people, including her as if he'd done it all along.

FORTY-FIVE
THAT EVENING, VERITAS

It had taken Richard some time to arrange various formalities and make the necessary noises at the long queue of admirers waiting for him. It was not until well after seven that they had gone through the portal, back to Veritas, and could be alone.

Richard could still feel the magic bubbling through him. He'd not loosed that much magic in a very long time, and he felt like it had inflated him, made him bigger, brighter, like everything was simply more. He had not been able to bear to let Alysoun go, other than briefly, when his superior officers spoke with him.

Now, he murmured, "Come join me in the bath?" She seemed not to want to leave him either, because she didn't wait to summon Wallis. Instead, she just asked for a meal to be prepared, something filling and substantial that could be eaten when they were ready. Once they reached the baths, he silently moved to help her undress, then found her fingers reaching to undo the buttons of his shirt and breeches.

It wasn't until they were both settled in the hot water that he spoke. "You - are you all right, my lady?"

There was a long pause, as if she were thinking through the implications of the question. "Physically, better than I might. I took one of the potions, after my nap." She used them sparingly, because she would pay for it tomorrow and for days after, but they granted her less pain and more energy for half a day.

He lifted her hand to his lips. "It meant a great deal for me to know you were there. To remind me, what matters. You. The children. My oaths."

"Not always in that order, as it should be." She was decidedly amused, turning her wrist to slip her fingers into his, twining them. "Watching you fight was, it was complicated. But I am most glad I did." Alysoun glanced up, they were close enough he could see her eyes. "Gilbert was a great help."

"I'm glad Magni thought to send for him. He gave me a few ideas." Richard let out a long breath. "Including - I wouldn't have dared - the last."

Alysoun's voice was very careful now, like she was picking her way along a narrow path. "Will you tell me about it?"

He nodded, before he had words. "It's usually called Merlin's Certainty, these days. You may not have read about it, it is not often used. It requires a tremendous amount of power in play, both the caster's and in the space. Being near a portal, being somewhere prepared for it, like some siege castles."

"But not the Hall?" Alysoun shifted to lean against him, and he slipped his arm around her waist to make it easier.

"A different flavour to the magic. Our magic goes into the Hall, we can't draw it out, not like that."

"Is that - no, let me take this in order. So it needed him doing that, Gil said it was a sacrifice move."

"It did. And if we hadn't resolved things, quickly, it would likely have killed him inside a minute or two. Last strike, some call it. It often stops the heart shortly after."

Alysoun shivered. "I think that makes it worse. Knowing he wanted to die. However he could do it."

"He didn't. And he won't, he's in the Healer's care until his trial. And it wouldn't do him any good, now. If he died in the duel, there are protections for his family. If he dies by his own action or inaction, that's different."

"Inaction. Refusing to... refusing to eat?" Alysoun sounded distressed. Richard nodded, and tugged her a little closer. She hesitated, then asked "May I, your lap? Closer?"

"Of course. Anything you like, especially today." He wasn't sure what had brought them both here, beyond tremendous good fortune, but he could not deny her anything, certainly not something he wanted so much himself. She rearranged herself, settling into his lap, which made him suddenly aware of how close she was, how intimate this was, how much he wanted her. Once her head was settled on his shoulder, her weight against him, he wasn't sure what to say next.

"Better." Alysoun sounded very contented. "Watching you, I was scared. Even though you were, the protective charms. Sometime, later, can you walk me through them? The reasons you chose them?"

"Certainly. Demonstrating them, even. A number of them you might find handy, if you're willing to learn them. Useful for keeping children from something you can't get to in time, for example."

"Huh." She snorted at the implications. "But that, the - the fire." Of course she'd circle back to that.

"That was a tremendous amount of energy. You have to be very certain what is you, and what is not you, to manage it."

"And you were." It wasn't a question. They both knew he must have sorted that out. "That's new?" Her voice was softer now.

"That's new." Richard agreed, matching her, and letting his hand come down to cup her hip now, pulling her more securely against him. "The conversations with you, with Magni and Gilbert. About what I care about. What I don't."

Alysoun paused, the way she did before she suggested something that would be more of a challenge to him. "Are you in trouble, do you think? Gilbert said you'd have made quite an impression on the Guard."

"And that's not always the best thing. I had to show my hand, my strength, such as it is. But a lot of people assume if you're strong in one way, you're good at everything, and I'm certainly not."

He held up his free hand before she could argue. "I am good at many things, my lady, but I am not good at everything. I am, I am sure, horrible at embroidery. Managing a household. Any number of minor bureaucratic necessities, from which Simons saves me on the regular. I do well leading some Guards, but not well with others. I can't begin to follow some of the rituals and maths calculations Mason uses. Any number of other things."

It made her giggle, as he'd hoped it would, and then she leaned up to kiss his cheek. "Fair."

"As to being in trouble, there will be an investigation. There always is when a Guard duels, even if it is as well witnessed as this one was. They will check the investigation, and the start of that is, admittedly, a bit unconventional, seeing as how half of it started with you."

"Will that be a problem?" Her voice was very small now.

"No, love, it won't." Richard kissed her hair. "I've made the proper reports since I thought you had something, and so has Mason, everything that's needed. And they reviewed everything before issuing the warrant. The only question, I think, will be whether I could have avoided the duel."

"Oh." She'd gone thoughtful again, another one of those anticipatory silences. "What ... what do you think?"

"I think I am very glad that Magister FitzAlan was there, and a witness, and the other two from the Council. They're not truly neutral, of course, no one is, but he was right that he has no particular ties to us, or to the Delwyns. I think I'll be on leave a week or so, and they'll make their decision." He let out a long breath. "I, I am one of the Guard. The oath doesn't stop, even if they send me away. But if they did, if they removed me from duty, well. I'd find something else to do, that matters. Somehow. And spend more time here."

She hesitated, for a moment, then shifted to kiss him, slow and steady, insistent. When she pulled back, she said, her voice as clear as anything, "I would love for you to be home more, but not for that reason. So we're clear."

"Clear." He was so glad they saw eye to eye about this. "But perhaps I might get Gabriel properly started on his riding lessons, not just the leading rein."

Alysoun laughed. "That is permitted, yes. And he'll be delighted. And the rest of it?"

"That Professor Arden you have disapproved of all along was rather more entangled than we'd realised. I'm curious what that turns up. Even more curious, that Delwyn chose him, not anyone else, as his second. It makes you wonder how desperate he was."

"As if he didn't have any other choice. A series of sacrifices. Mmm. Do we, you don't know why it was so desperate?"

Richard shook his head. "I only looked at the warrant proper, not the documentation. And now, I'll have to wait." That bothered him, and more than a little, not to know, but he would just have to be patient. "What matters is that it is in the proper hands."

"A system for that, not just trusting to any one person's goodness, or insight.'

Richard nodded. "And that's all to the good. Drawing that closer, you and Magni, even Gilbert and Mason, that's been a thing I didn't know I needed."

She let her hand wander up his chest, considering something. "Watching you was - I hadn't seen your strength, before, not properly. Your kindness, your gentleness, your intelligence, your fondness. But not your power."

She let her hand wander down, then, and Richard had a sudden urgent certainty of what she had in mind. "My power." He couldn't keep the pleasure out of his voice, or the purr. "Is that what we're calling it?"

Alysoun laughed, warm and delighted. "Yes. And at the moment I don't hurt, and won't until tomorrow, and I know you're...." Her voice trailed off has her hand reached to tease him deliberately. "Ready."

"For you, always. Shall we, here? We never have in the bath, and you do like it so."

There was a moment of shocked delight on her face, then she was twisting to kiss him, as he moved to guide her to straddle his lap. This would be new to both of them, and he loved it.

FORTY-SIX
22ND AUGUST, VERITAS

Alysoun frowned as the messenger from the Guard left. He had brought two parchment scrolls, formally done up with green ribbon and darker green sealing wax. That was something formal from the government, green always was. The seal itself had the walls of Trellech overlaid with the scales of Justice, so that meant the Guard. The larger question, of why the Guard would be sending a formal message to her, not just to Richard, was worrisome.

"When is Richard expected?"

Francis Connover, his new secretary, coughed. He was still settling in, and not yet certain of his role, when the day's events took a new turn. He was an acquaintance Gil had recommended, in his later forties. He hadn't had the flashy background of some of the other candidates, but Alysoun had liked him at once, the way he asked interesting questions about what Richard needed and wanted in a secretary. "He was checking on the warding on the village, Lady Alysoun. He expected to be back around now, when I took the messages after lunch."

"Well. I'll wait, then." It was almost as if the Guard messenger had timed it to miss Richard. She had to respect the skill in that, even if it were currently frustrating.

It was not a long wait, thankfully. Alysoun could see Richard coming up the drive from the village road, walking quickly, eager to be home.

"I'll see about a drink for him." Connover nodded. He'd spent the afternoon at the long table in the library, sorting Richard's earlier correspondence. There was rather a backlog to file, but he was making good headway with it. Alysoun stood, grimaced at the unexpected ache in her right knee, and went to the decanters. She poured a brandy for Richard, and then collected the letter opener from the desk as Connover retreated to his personal office.

She had time to settle down and confirm the seal was legitimate, pressing her thumb against it, and feeling the answering buzz of magic from the seal. Then she slit it open, but didn't open the letter. That would wait for Richard.

He came straight in, not pausing to change or wash up, but instead of going right for the scroll, murmuring, "I saw the messenger at the portal." Before he opened it, he came over and kissed her cheek. They had both been making a deliberate effort, these last weeks, to welcome and part from each other with something joyful, something fond, rather than taking anything for granted. "Dearest. Before we get to the obvious, how was your day?"

She laughed. "A good ride in the morning, before it got hot, a long bath, lunch with the children, and then I've been reading. You'll like the current notes, I think. You?"

"Certain the warding is solid, and the keep-away charms will hold well through harvest." He stretched and shrugged out of the tweed jacket, looking a little damp around the edges. It was still phenomenally hot out for August, weeks of sweltering heat that surely must break soon. She waved a hand at the brandy. "Drink. There's chilled lemonade, if you prefer that."

"Reading first."

She held out the letter opener, hilt first, and he took it. "You haven't read yours?"

"I was waiting for you."

Richard nodded, and when he began to unroll his, she did the same to hers, reading through carefully, then blinking up at him. He'd just finished reading as well, and their eyes met as he laughed. "Well, not in too much trouble, then. What does yours say?"

She passed it over to him. "A request to be present on Friday morning. You as well?"

"The results of the investigation, and they made it clear there's some pleasant news as well. I'm assuming you feel up to a trip to town?"

"The townhouse is awful in this weather, can we go up Friday in the morning?"

"Of course. I can arrange a carriage, if you like. And you have something suitable to wear, I'm hoping?" There was an edge of nervous amusement.

"Not long after we married, Marietta recommended I keep a dress or two in my wardrobe suitable for such last-minute events. She is an immensely practical woman, and right, so of course I have something that will do."

"Right. Well. We will turn up, properly garbed, at the correct time, and see what they have to say."

A day and a half later, Alysoun took Richard's hand and let him help her out of the carriage. She rather liked the appropriately sedate summer-weight dress, of a dusty blue that went well with the deeper indigo of Richard's uniform.

He, for his part, looked particularly smart, with all the formal touches perfectly done.

She could feel Richard's slight surprise when they were met at the entrance by one of the senior aides. She recognised the woman slightly, in her later fifties, silver strands twining through her bun with the dark brown.

"Lady Edgarton. Captain Edgarton." It came with a sharp little bow, and Richard shifted to return a brief salute. "Welcome. I am Guardswoman Bright, and it is my pleasure to see to your needs during your visit. Before I take you to the Appointments Room, may I see to your comfort in any way? There are refreshments waiting."

The Appointments Room, Alysoun knew, was where they often did more formal announcements that did not require the size of the formal great hall or the courts. Richard glanced at her, and she shook her head. She did not need the powder room, or anything else of that kind. Guardswoman Bright nodded and led them both along the central corridor, then turned right, and along a perpendicular hallway, to a room Alysoun hadn't been in before. Richard leaned to say in her ear, "This is the more formal one, also the one that is on the ground floor."

When they got to the great double doors, Guardswoman Bright knocked loudly three times. The doors swung open, and they were escorted inside, with Guardswoman Bright leading them up to the dais at the front of the room. Alysoun noticed that she had paced things for Alysoun's comfort, not her own. As soon as the two of them were in place, the older woman strode briskly off to the far corner, taking up a place by the door.

It was only when she got a good look at the three senior officials waiting that she was sure there was no problem. Marietta Witham was smiling broadly, her silver hair pinned up in a loose bun, seated to one side of the Chief Guard.

On his other side was another woman. Alysoun recognised her as the person in charge of crimes involving families and inheritances, a highly specialised and arcane line of law and magic. Captain Orland, that was her name. Antimony Orland. There were a handful of people seated in the benches along the side, including Magister FitzAlan and two other of the Council members. She wasn't sure what to make of that.

Alysoun inclined her head, remembering the etiquette lessons her mother had drilled into her, and the way they'd changed when Richard had inherited. And the way things were complicated, now, when he was a Guard, but also Lord. At any rate, it meant she didn't bow, in the normal way of things, to anyone bar the Council in some settings, but she should be polite.

"Good morning, and thank you for attending us. By the circle and the compass, by magic and justice, we are gathered." He finished the formal opening, and added, more personably, "Would you prefer a chair, Lady Edgarton?"

Alysoun shook her head, "Thank you, but I am fine for the moment."

The Chief Guard nodded. "Lady Edgarton, Captain Edgarton, we wished to formally commend you both on the thoughtful attention to detail that brought this particular problem to light. Rather literally, in this case, as I gather it was an infelicity in glass that first made you wonder, Lady Edgarton."

Alysoun smiled, relaxing just slightly at his even, slightly amused tone. "It was, sir."

"You know, of course, that we have issued warrants for the arrest of Lord and Lady Delwyn, Jupiter, their heir, and his wife Madeline. In the ensuing investigation, we have also charged three others: Curator Bromell, from the museum, Professor Arden, and Madeline Delwyn's sister, Hortensia Miller, with aiding and abetting in multiple crimes. The charges variously include destruction of endangered magical plants, intended fraud of great magnitude, breach of trust, smuggling, subversion of justice, and manipulation of those in their power. Along with various minor charges. They have been questioned in private, and their punishments will be announced in court on Monday. Before we did that, we wished to discuss various relevant matters with you."

Richard inclined his head, and he shifted a little, his arm settling more securely under Alysoun's.

"The Delwyns found themselves desperately in need of funds, a gambling problem, we gather. They became aware of exceedingly rare plants found near their lands outside Cardiff. Those ghost orchids were picked, processed, and were sent across land, and down the river, toward London, when you, Captain Edgarton, and others, captured the boat. The orchids were destroyed, but through the excellent work of several of the Penelopes, the original plants were identified."

Richard nodded slightly at that.

"At the same time, they were mounting an effort - through the collaboration of Professor Arden, and one of the senior curators at the museum - to create false artworks. They intended to highlight them in a formal exhibit, and then sell them privately. The indications we have at the moment suggest they wished to sell the pieces in the non-magical community. Professor Arden has a sufficient reputation in both sets of art-loving society to have made that feasible. If you had not spotted the disparities, and been able to demonstrate it, Lady Edgarton, it would have gone entirely unnoticed. Certainly, I do not think we would have succeeded in confirming the origin of the orchids."

"May I ask where the glass was actually made?" Alysoun could not restrain herself, even though she knew she should.

The Chief Guard smiled, as if he had anticipated her curiosity. "Just north of London, as you suspected." He waved a hand. "We are most pleased that one of our newest Magistrates is so thorough and detailed in his work. And we, singly and together, are most pleased to let you know, Captain Edgarton, that we welcome and look forward to your return to duty on Monday morning."

Beside her, Richard let out his breath, and saluted. "Sir, it is my pleasure and honour, as always."

The Chief Guard nodded, returning the salute properly, before he made it clear he had more to say. "But we have also heard from many sources that you, Lady Edgarton, played a substantial role. We wished, therefore, to acknowledge you."

Marietta Witham stood, then, and one of the Guards on duty came forward with two small velvet-covered boxes. Standing before Alysoun, she smiled, and said, "You do not wear a uniform, but I expect you will accumulate more of these, in time. They may be hung like charms on a necklace or brooch." She reached to touch a necklace Alysoun had seen her wear before. It had more than a dozen small stones suspended from tiny rings in the chain itself, in a rainbow of colours that Alysoun was certain now had specific meanings.

Marietta took a small charm on a tiny clasp, with a clear stone. She deftly clipped it to the simple chain Alysoun currently wore, the locket with Gabriel and Charlotte's photographs. "Not so showy as some, but we did think the stone for clear sight entirely appropriate here, due to the glasswork. I'm sure Richard can explain the associations to you for the ones he wears."

Then she turned and took the second box from the waiting Guard, and moved to pin a formal award pin on Richard's jacket. This one had a strip of deep green. "For the orchids, the plants," Marietta added, largely for Alysoun's benefit.

When she stepped back, Alysoun took advantage of the fact that they were explaining things to her. "May I ask what happens next?"

"On Monday, the court will require that Delwyn abdicate his title, responsibilities, and lands, in favour of his younger son, who is entirely innocent and unaware of the various plots and crimes, confirmed under Silence oath. Delwyn senior and the others will receive appropriate punishment, and never be able to claim status or power over others, and have their magic bound except for the most routine personal needs."

Alysoun thought about that. "He's quite young, isn't he? Barely twenty."

Marietta said smoothly, "We were rather hoping you and Richard would take him under your wings. Set a good example. He is betrothed, but the wedding is not yet scheduled. He is apprenticed currently to a horse breeder. He has a knack for the more agricultural charms, and we feel the estates that will remain in his care might flourish again with some guidance."

Alysoun glanced at Richard. As politely and clearly as she could, she replied, "We would be glad to take it under consideration, once we learn more about him and his circumstances."

It made Marietta laugh and say "See? I said as much. That, Alysoun, you would not agree or disagree right away, but see how it fit into those things you are already committed to. There, Galahad. We've done the formalities. May I take them off for luncheon now?"

The Chief Guard had the sort of expression that people get when their older aunt has sliced through half a dozen social proprieties. He nodded. "In a moment."

"Captain Edgarton, we value your work as much as your wife's, even though your service in this regard was already promised to us. You are showing the judgement, discretion, and wide-ranging thought we seek in our officers. We will be speaking in the next months about additional duties and responsibilities now that you have proven yourself thoroughly capable."

Richard bowed slightly. "Thank you, Keeper of the Table." The most formal of titles, then.

And with that, the Chief Guard stood. "Good day, everyone. And do enjoy Marietta's plans. It's usually best to go along with them."

Marietta immediately came back down from the dais. "I have reservations at Summer's End, one of their private rooms." That was one of Alysoun's favourites.

EPILOGUE
20TH SEPTEMBER, VERITAS

It had been a delightful day, and an even better evening.

Alysoun had spent the afternoon with Marietta, talking in detail about the upcoming social season, and which events would be more interesting, or present particular intellectual challenges. It had been delightful, and Marietta's sharp observations about whom to court and whom to spend less attention on had been extremely helpful.

She had come home to consult with Connover about the upcoming week's schedule, so that she could invite Magni and Gil for supper. Gil thought this idea of regular suppers was a grand plan, since it got both Richard and Magni out of the Guard Hall on time at least occasionally. And in confidence, he'd told her it helped on other nights as well. She, for her part, was entirely looking forward to discussing a new book she'd read with Gil. She was sure it was two-thirds nonsense, but the other third had some promising ideas.

Richard had, delightfully, turned up in plenty of time to

bathe and change. Alysoun had made arrangements with Nanny, so when he came downstairs, he found Alysoun and both children in the smaller dining room, the one they preferred for family meals. The children were playing with small illusion-charm bubbles, chasing them in the sunset light.

"Everyone having a good time, then? Good evening, love." Gabriel turned away from the bubbles first, charging at his father, and flinging his arms around his knees. Charlotte took a moment to pop one of the bubbles before she bounced her way over, just as insistent. Richard bent to swing her up into his arms, balancing her on the other hip, before he said, "A good afternoon, then?"

"Pleasant and productive, the best kind. And I feel much better now the weather's settled down, so I took advantage of doing a little more shopping. There are books in the library for you." That was a rare treat, to have enough energy she could do something like that, and she intended to take full advantage.

"There's a new restaurant, I have reservations for Saturday, though I can cancel, if you'd prefer not."

Alysoun considered. "No, Saturday should be lovely. Which one?"

"The Breton place, they only opened a few weeks ago. One of the other Captains highly recommended it." He must have gone to some lengths to get the reservation then, especially on a Saturday night. It would be good for them to be seen, but she'd also heard some excellent reviews of the food, especially the variety of crepes.

She smiled, and then they were swept into the business of making sure both children were in chairs, and eating their food rather than smearing it on the furniture. To be fair, both of them did very well, and the erring food was generally due to accident rather than carelessness. They had started doing this at least once a week, and it had turned into a joyful time for them, and a wonderful reward for the children. If they had misbehaved, the dinner was up in the nursery. Eating downstairs had turned out to be quite an incentive.

Alysoun rather suspected Richard had more to talk about, but she didn't press him during the meal, keeping to stories of the day and discussion of Gabriel's riding lesson. He had progressed to a bouncing trot on a remarkably tolerant small pony, with a groom running alongside.

It was only after Nanny had taken the children up to bed that Richard gestured. "Shall we?" She had moved into his rooms, both here and in Trellech, when the weather turned. She kept her old bed in case she had a particularly bad night and didn't want even Richard to accidentally touch her, but she hated using it. Waking up with him, that was worth a few aches from ending up in some less than ideal position. Much of the time, anyway.

Once they were settled in bed, he dimmed the lights, and said, "I had an interesting conversation today."

"Oh?"

"Major Monkton called me in. He handles a variety of more delicate investigations. He's approaching retirement, mandatory retirement, and he said he'd heard good reports about me, and would I be interested in taking on a case. Not much duelling, he said, but I'd have plenty of chances to use my wits, and I should consult with anyone qualified. I am starting with you."

She blinked. "You are?"

"That little charm you've earned." Richard grinned. "Did I not explain that part?"

Alysoun pushed up on one elbow. "No, you didn't. And

neither did the book. Or Marietta. Who sends her affection."

Richard snorted at the last, and obligingly answered the question she'd asked. "It qualifies you as a consultant, in terms of what you may be told at the discretion of the officer in charge."

She considered that for a moment. "A consultant. Any other rights and privileges?"

"You may come meet me at my office without an escort, if you like. And I could arrange for you to get access to the Guard library, to work on specific projects. If you come up with one."

Alysoun nodded. "This conversation. What was it about?"

Richard laughed. "There are some concerns about adulteration of various foodstuffs, but our efforts so far have not been terribly helpful in tracking the problem to the source. Part of it involves items that are being sold as something they're not, which is far from ideal, but not necessarily dangerous. However, in some cases, the adulteration involves things that can be dangerous, and that's the priority."

Alysoun tilted her head. "What kind of foods?"

"Baked goods, in a pattern that suggests someone who supplies flour or some other common ingredient commercially. Some generally available teas, nothing fancy, builder's tea sorts of things. Some dairy, but the patterns there are less easy to sort out."

"And the adulterant, whatever's being put in?" Alysoun wasn't sure if that was the right word.

"Whitening agents, which have included arsenic more than once. Or at least we think it's more than one batch. Various preservative agents, which make me think the foods are starting somewhere outside the magical community, or at least on the edges of it."

"Because most of the magical sources would use preservation charms, not alchemical agents." She thought about that. "Do you have someone who knows about this I can talk to? An expert in what the variations are?"

She could feel his amusement, and then he leaned in to kiss her nose. "I was hoping you'd see about finding one. Mason would be glad to see you to talk about what we've found so far at your convenience. You should use Mason's skills and ask for whatever other resources would be useful, but this is a problem that has not been yielding to our usual methods. Which is where you come in."

"Oh, well, that's all right then. Mason and I can sort out what the questions are. What's your role in it, then?"

"Collecting evidence, at the moment, which does involve a certain amount of direct, well, enforcement. People who are doing dangerous things are not actually terribly fond of the Guard poking their nose in."

"Even your quite attractive and well-mannered nose," Alysoun agreed. "Dangerous?"

There was a long enough pause she could figure it out for herself. "I'm being sensible. And I was permitted to pick my own people for this. They're all observant and not hot-headed, which is what I was most worried about."

"And you're duelling regularly with Magni?" Which would keep anyone sharp.

"Magni, and that group he's put together, yes. I don't take unnecessary risks, you know that. I have every reason not to."

"Just the necessary ones, to keep people safe. I did have some idea what your priorities were when I married you."

There was a longer silence. Just when Alysoun was

about to say something, Richard spoke again, his voice a little cautious. "Things are so much better now. For me. And I hope very much for you."

She smiled, then shifted, to pull him down to the bed. "Exceedingly better. Come here, let me show you just one of the ways."

~

If you enjoyed *Pastiche* and would like to read more of this series, please sign up for my mailing list to get all the latest news and fun extras. Your reviews (on whatever review site you use) are much appreciated, too!

You can read more about Richard and Alysoun later in their lives (the 1920s) in *Wards of the Roses* and *On The Bias*, where they appear in supporting roles.

Read on for more historical details about this book.

AUTHOR NOTES

Thank you so much for reading *Pastiche*. I hope you've enjoyed this dip into the Edwardian era with me, and a chance to see how Richard and Alysoun began their lives together.

My thanks (as always) to Kiya Nicoll, my inestimable friend and editor. And I owe a lot to my early readers, including Erin and Anne Libby (along with half a dozen others) for making this book much better through their comments and suggestions .

I should start with the most complicated piece of this book: The Guard. I wrote this book in the winter of 2019. I started editing it in May of 2020, a week or so before the massive protests (rightful protests) around police brutality and the death of George Floyd and far too many others. The news from Minneapolis hit me particularly hard: I lived there for over a decade, at the edge of one of the neighbourhoods most affected.

I knew, long before I started this book, that The Guard worked differently than police in the United States or modern Britain (which has a rather different police history). Those protests and the real injustices they brought up, however, made me certain I needed to explain not only how it was different, but why.

In short, it's a lot easier with magic.

As explained in the book, the Guard take an oath that binds them specifically in how and when they use magic in pursuit of their duties. Much like the oaths each person in the magical community takes at the age of twelve to protect magic, these oaths are self-enforcing. Someone who abuses their power or position for self-benefit won't be doing so for terribly long.

They are also anchored rather firmly in Arthuriana. Richard's love of chivalry has a comfortable home here, the idea of protecting those who need help and protection is at the core of what the Guard should be doing.

And yet, those oaths are also quite limiting. As Richard notes, the oaths he takes as Lord are very specific about a particular set of duties. The oaths a magistrate takes are about performing a specific set of rather complex magical actions, and do not particularly limit the magistrate's activities outside of the formal court settings. It's a tentative balance, helped by magic, but magic doesn't solve everything.

On the other hand, Albion desperately needs its Guard. A community spread out over a substantial distance but with access to nearly instant transportation (through the portals) needs a unified way to respond to everything from a natural disaster to a fleeing criminal to a missing child. Or for that matter, notice-me-not wards failing or a dangerous magical creature too close to people. Individual village

Guards report back to the Guard Hall in Trellech, who then send out suitable help.

And on the Trellech side, as you see by some of Richard's comments, while there are some specialists, many of the Guard take on whatever cases come up, since they also handle a number of fairly routine magical checks and safety concerns.

On to the rest of the book.

First, the title. A **pastiche**, if you're not familiar with the word, is a creative work in the style of someone else. I chose it for the title here, both because of the art forgery and because of the way that Richard and Alysoun are trying to form their lives in a way that does not actually suit them.

Wedding customs in Albion vary, but the First Families trace their origins back to Rome, and they have over the. Years built up their own customs over the historical Roman scaffolding. Many of the details here - the flowers and palla, particularly - are Roman. Others, like the burning flame on the cup, are taken from traditional omens, with a magical flare.

Veritas itself does date back to the Romans, at least in the basic outline, as you can see by the **baths**. To be honest, this is here partly because I've always wanted a Roman bathing setup all my own, but also because it fit particularly well with Alysoun's needs. The ability to go from a cool bath to a hot one, to steam, has always seemed the height of luxury to me. With magic, a hypocaust system is an eminently efficient method of heating a manor house, too.

The **earthquake** in chapter 3 actually happened (and as Richard says, there were no casualties.) It was centred on Swansea in Wales. The **heatwave** that summer is also entirely historical.

I never directly explain what Alysoun's chronic illness, largely because it wasn't named in the non-magical literature until later in 1906. Then, they'd have called it fibrositis, and now we call it **fibromyalgia**. Alysoun's insistence on wanting to have a good life despite the pain, and her deep fondness for immersion in a hot bath both come from one of my dear friends who has fibro. One of the things that's particularly frustrating about it is the variation without being able to sort out why one feels better some days and much worse on others.

The variations of **stained glass** are much as they are discussed in the book itself: it is an art form that has had a rich history for a surprisingly long time. The trick they use to track it down is a variant on the doctrine of sympathies, one of my favourite magical theories, partly because it allows some truly ridiculous applications. (Look up the powder of sympathy and the use of a dog and a knife to figure out longitude in the 1600s...)

The **library windows** in the museum being made of translucent sheets of stone are like the walls of the Beinecke Library, the special collections library at Yale University. I've come across occasional other references to the technique, but it was a natural application here.

Both Gil and Richard served in the horrible war and fighting in the **Sudan** (also known as the Mahdist War), though about ten years apart. Gil was injured in 1884, but he was spared the seige of Khartoum. Richard served briefly, including at the battle of Omdurman in 1898. The fighting was bloody, brutal, and horribly managed imperialism. Both of them have very complex thoughts about the army that you'll see a bit more of in the future.

Ghost orchids are an exceedingly rare species of orchid that grow on trees, rather than in the soil. They require very specific growing conditions, but do in fact sometimes appear in a fairly sizeable number. Only a few samples exist in museums, though.

Duelling is of course a classic activity through the centuries, and Albion is no different. Many people duel for style or show, but Richard and Magni take it seriously, as a deadly martial art. You may imagine my references to various authors and styles to be quite similar to historical fencing manuals.

Finally, the **Penelopes** are the forensic experts of the Guard, the people you go to when you need some arcane magic unwoven, or a new technique to investigate a particular crime. They're named for Penelope from Homer's *Odyssey*, unweaving her work every day.

~

As I said earlier, if you'd like to see more of Richard and Alysoun later in their lives, you can find them in *Wards of the Roses* where Richard is overseeing the investigation of a mysterious reappearing manor house and Alysoun appears briefly at the end. They both have a role in the costume party and later events at the end of *On The Bias*.

Oh, and you'll be getting a book featuring their son, Gabriel, in the forthcoming *The Fossil Door*. Gabe is a delight and entirely their child, in all the best possible ways. You'll also get a lot more about the Penelopes, and more about Mason.

Sign up for my mailing list if you want to be the first to know when it's available.

* 9 7 8 1 7 3 5 5 4 7 4 0 4 *